we were here

MATT DE LA PEÑA

we
were
here

Delacorte Press

Copyright © 2009 by Matt de la Peña

Photographs © 2009 Nick Haas

All rights reserved. Published in the United States by Delacorte Press, an imprint of Random House Children's Books, a division of Random House, Inc., New York. Delacorte Press is a registered trademark and the colophon is a trademark of Random House, Inc.

Grateful acknowledgment is made to Carnegie-Mellon University Press for permission to reprint an excerpt from "From a Berkeley Notebook" by Denis Johnson, from *The Incognito Lounge*, copyright © 2007 by Denis Johnson.

Visit us on the Web! www.randomhouse.com/teens

Educators and librarians, for a variety of teaching tools, visit us at www.randomhouse.com/teachers

Library of Congress Cataloging-in-Publication Data

Peña, Matt de la.
We were here / Matt de la Peña. – 1st ed.
p. cm.
Summary: Haunted by the event that sentences him to time in a group home, Miguel breaks out with two unlikely companions and together they begin their journey down the California coast hoping to get to Mexico and a new life.
ISBN 978-0-385-73667-1 (hardcover) – ISBN 978-0-385-90622-7 (Gibraltar lib. bdg.) – ISBN 978-0-375-89383-4 (e-book) [1. Juvenile delinquents–Fiction. 2. Runaways–Fiction. 3. Friendship–Fiction. 4. Guilt–Fiction. 5. Brothers–Fiction. 6. Group homes–Fiction. 7. California–Fiction.] I. Title.
PZ7.P3725We 2009
[Fic]–dc22
2008044568

The text of this book is set in 11.5-point Garamond.

Book design by Angela Carlino

Printed in the United States of America

10 9 8 7 6 5 4 3 2

First Edition

To Spencer Figueroa

(My bad about all those times I dunked over you when we were kids.)

we were here

One changes so much
from moment to moment
that when one hugs
oneself against the chill
air at the inception of spring, at night,
knees drawn to chin,
he finds himself in the arms
of a total stranger,
the arms of one he might move
away from on the dark playground.

—Denis Johnson, "From a Berkeley Notebook"

May 13

Here's the thing: I was probably gonna write a book when I got older anyways. About what it's like growing up on the levee in Stockton, where every other person you meet has missing teeth or is leaning against a liquor store wall begging for change to buy beer. Or maybe it'd be about my dad dying in the stupid war and how at the funeral they gave my mom some cheap medal and a folded flag and shot a bunch of rifles at the clouds. Or maybe the book would just be something about me and my brother, Diego. How we hang mostly by ourselves, pulling corroded-looking fish out of the murky levee water and throwing them back. How sometimes when Moms falls asleep in front of the TV we'll sneak out of the apartment and walk around the neighborhood, looking into other people's windows, watching them sleep.

That's the weirdest thing, by the way. That every person you come across lays down in a bed, under the covers, and closes their eyes at night. Cops, teachers, parents, hot girls, pro ballers, everybody. For some reason it makes people seem so much less real when I look at them.

Anyways, at first I was worried standing there next to the hunchback old man they gave me for a lawyer, both of us waiting for the judge to make his verdict. I thought maybe they'd put me away for a grip of years because of what I did. But then I thought real hard about it. I squinted my eyes and concentrated with my whole mind. That's something you don't know about me. I can sometimes make stuff happen just by thinking about it. I try not to do it too much because my head mostly gets stuck on bad stuff, but this time something good actually happened: the judge only gave me a year in a group home. Said I had to write in a journal so some counselor could try to figure out how I think. Dude didn't know I was probably gonna write a book anyways. Or that it's hard as hell bein' at home these days, after what happened. So when he gave out my sentence it was almost like he didn't give me a sentence at all.

I told my moms the same thing when we were walking out of the courtroom together. I said, "Yo, Ma, this isn't so bad, right? I thought those people would lock me up and throw away the key."

She didn't say anything back, though. Didn't look at me either. Matter of fact, she didn't look at me all the way up till the day she had to drive me to Juvenile Hall, drop me off at the gate, where two big beefy white guards were waiting to escort me into the building. And even then she just barely glanced at me for a split second. And we didn't hug or anything. Her face seemed plain, like it would on any other day. I tried to look at her real good as we stood there. I knew I wasn't gonna see her for a while. Her skin was so much whiter than mine and her eyes were big and blue. And she was wearing the fake diamond earrings she always wears that sparkle when the sun hits 'em at a certain angle. Her blond hair all pulled back in a ponytail.

For some reason it hit me hard right then—as one of the guards took me by the arm and started leading me away—how mad pretty my mom is. For real, man, it's like someone's picture you'd see in one of them magazines laying around the dentist's office. Or on a TV show. And she's actually my moms.

I looked over my shoulder as they walked me through the gate, but she still wasn't looking at me. It's okay, though. I understood why.

It's 'cause of what I did.

June 1

I'll put it to you like this: I'm about ten times smarter than everyone in Juvi. For real. These guys are a bunch of straight-up dummies, man. Take this big black kid they put me in a cell with, Rondell. He can't even read. I know 'cause three nights ago he stepped to me when I was writing in my journal. He said: "Yo, Mexico, wha'chu writin' 'bout in there?"

"Whatever I *wanna* write about," I said without looking up. "How 'bout *them* apples, homey?"

He paused. "What you just said?"

I shook my head, told him: "And Mexico's a pretty stupid thing to call me, by the way, considering I've never even *been* to Mexico."

His ass stood there a quick sec, thinking about what I'd just said to him—or at least trying. Then he bum-rushed me. Shoved me right off my chair and onto the ground, pressed his giant grass-stained shoe down on my neck. He said: "Don't you never talk like that to Rondell again. You hear? Nobody talk to Rondell like that."

I tried to nod, but he had my neck pinned, so I couldn't really move my head. Couldn't make a sound either. Or breathe too good.

He swiped my journal off the table and stared at the page I was writing, his kick weighing down on my neck. And I'm not gonna lie, man, I got a little spooked. Rondell's a freak for a sixteen-year-old: six foot something with huge-ass arms and legs and a face that already looks like he's a grown man. And I'd just written some pretty bad stuff about him in my journal. Called him a retarded ape who smelled like when a rat dies in the wall of your apartment. But at the same time I almost *wanted* Rondell to push down harder with his shoe. Almost *wanted* him to crush my neck, break my windpipe, end my stupid-ass journal right then and there. I started imagining the shoe pushing all the way through, rubber hitting cement. Them telling my moms what happened as she stood with the phone cupped to her ear in the kitchen, crying but at the same time looking sort of relieved, too.

After a couple minutes like that—Rondell staring at the page I'd been writing and me pinned to the nasty cement floor of our cell—he tossed the journal back on the table and took his foot off my neck.

And that's how I knew he couldn't read. Dude was staring right at the sentences I'd just written about him, right? And he didn't do nothin'. Just hopped up on his bunk, linked his fingers behind his head and stared at the paint-chipped ceiling.

What Rondell Thinks About:

There was a long silence in our cell as I got up off the floor and sat back in the chair, tried to stretch out my neck and jaw. Then Rondell said: "Hey, Mexico."

I rolled my eyes. Like we were gonna be boys after he just tried to kill my ass.

"Yo. Mexico."

People are straight-up ignorant, man.

He leaned over to look at me. "Mexico! I'm talkin' to you, man!"

"What!" I shouted back. "Go on, man. Talk. Damn."

"Yo, you think God could really see the stuff you do down here? Even when you locked up like me and you is?"

"I think he sees about as much as Santa Claus," I said, opening my journal back up, ripping out my last entry and crumpling it in a ball.

He laid back down, stared at the ceiling again. " 'Cause I been thinkin' about that lately. If he could see me even when

I'm in here. Behind bars. I been thinkin' he maybe don't like what he see too much."

I looked up at Rondell's bunk, stared at his big black leg hanging off the bed. I looked at my brown arm and then back at his leg. It was probably the blackest damn thing I'd ever seen in my life—and more than half my school back in Stockton is either black kids or Mexicans like me. You ever wonder why some people get so much darker than others? It's about people's genes, I know. And how all the continents were once connected or whatever. But how'd it start? Who was the first person to come out looking all different from everybody else? Sometimes I trip on little shit like that.

"Wha'chu think, Mexico?"

He couldn't see me, but I shrugged anyway, told him: "I don't think any of us know *what* he can see, Rondell. You ever think maybe that's the point?"

And that was it, we didn't say another word to each other for the next two days. And on the third day, early in the morning, a guard came for me. He slid open our cell door holding a clipboard, looking down at it, and said: "Miguel Castañeda? Grab your stuff and come with me, kid. You're being transferred."

"To where?" I said.

"Group home in San Jose. Let's go."

Rondell didn't look down at me while I was gathering up all my stuff. Even though I was being all loud on purpose. Even though I could tell he was awake.

June 2

I'll tell you this: my brother Diego's a trip, man. He's probably the quickest kid you could ever meet when it comes to making up a lie. I'm not playing, yo, he could do it right there on the spot. Fool anybody, anytime. Anyplace.

Take the morning Principal Cody caught me and him fighting in the hall three months before I got locked up— Diego was in eleventh grade, I was in tenth. The bell had just rung and we were still going at it pretty good, like we always did: pushing and wrestling and landing an occasional fist to each other's neck or rib cage (we never hit each other in the face, though; that was Diego's one rule). He was pissed at me because I forgot to bring our money for the school field trip to see the Stockton Ports play baseball. Left it sitting right there on the kitchen table next to our empty cereal bowls. Or maybe that was the time he found out I rode his dirt bike up and down the levee in the rain without asking, got mad mud all over his spokes and tires and the bottom part of his frame. I don't remember exactly why we were fighting that day, but right in the middle of it Principal Cody blew his whistle and said, "What the hell's going on here!"

Me and Diego separated quick, turned to Principal Cody, straightening out our plain white T-shirts.

I was scared as hell 'cause Moms had just told me and Diego that if we got one more detention she was gonna ship us down to Gramps's place in Fresno, where they pick strawberries and raisins and figs all day under a sun so damn hot it looks blurry. Me and Diego did it for one week last summer and we pretty much almost died, man. I'm not even playing. And all Gramps did was laugh the whole time. He told us in Spanish that we were tired 'cause we weren't real Mexicans like everyone else who was out there picking in his group. We were Americans. Told us we might be dark on the outside, but inside we were white like a couple blond boys from Hollywood. And then he laughed some more and so did all his buddies.

Like pretty much every time my gramps says something, I only understood half the words, but as soon as the old man went back to the picking, Diego filled in the blanks.

Diego's Play:

Anyways, there was Principal Cody scowling at us, right? Freckled-ass arms folded, stupid whistle hanging from a red string around his neck. But Diego's mad quick, like I told you. He reached into his backpack and pulled out a copy of *West Side Story*, some play his English teacher was about to put on in front of the whole school.

"My little brother's helping me rehearse, sir," he said. "Mrs. Nichols thinks I could maybe play that guy Action, the one that starts all the fights. She says bein' in a play would maybe be a good outlet. My moms thinks so, too."

Principal Cody looked at me.

I nodded—even though I didn't know what the hell Diego was talking about.

He looked at my bro again. "Well, I didn't know you had an interest in the theater, son."

"It started with this one right here, sir," Diego said, flipping through the playbook.

"Well, that doesn't surprise me at all. *West Side Story*'s a classic."

"I don't even mind the singing and dancing parts."

Principal Cody unfolded his arms and took the playbook from Diego. He flipped through the pages himself and said: "My wife and I caught a production of this musical in New York City back in '74. Right after we were married." A big smile came on his face.

"You been all the way to New York?" Diego said.

Principal Cody laughed a little under his breath, said: "Many times."

"That's awesome, sir."

I kept looking back and forth between them, thinking how crazy it was that me and my bro were this close to a principal and we weren't even in trouble. Dude was actually *smiling*. The only other times I'd been this close to one is when I got my ass sent to his office 'cause of something I did in class or if I got caught stealing from the campus store or whatever. And trust me, on those times there wasn't no smiling involved.

Principal Cody stared at one of the pages for a minute, then he looked up and said: "I was actually thinking about getting my wife the DVD as a gift. It's our twenty-eighth anniversary in, let's see"—he used his fingers to count—"thirteen days."

Diego nodded, so I nodded too.

"Congratulations, sir," Diego said. And then after a short pause he said: "Anyway, sir, Mrs. Nichols told me I needed to get someone to rehearse with since tryouts are comin' up soon. So I got my brother here, right, Miguel?"

I nodded.

Principal Cody handed the playbook back to Diego and smiled at me. He said: "Well, I wish you kids all the best." He checked his watch, then turned back to Diego and clapped his hands together. "Okay, let's hurry on to class now, gentlemen. You're already ten minutes late. You can get back to the Jets and the Sharks at break, all right?"

"Yes, sir," Diego said.

"Yes, sir," I said.

Diego packed his playbook in his backpack and we both smiled and nodded and then walked past the cafeteria toward the classroom buildings. Diego looked back after we rounded the corner, and when he saw we were out of Principal Cody's line of vision he whacked me on the back of my head one last time. But we were both sort of laughing when he did it. We weren't serious anymore.

"Who's the Jets and the Sharks?" I said.

"Don't worry about it," he told me, pulling a pack of gum from his jeans pocket.

"You aren't really trying out for that play, are you?" I said.

"Wha'chu think, Guelly?" Diego said, chewing his gum and wadding up his wrapper. He flipped me a piece too.

I caught it, unwrapped it and popped it in my mouth.

"I ain't even read that shit, boy," Diego said, and then he slipped right into his classroom without saying bye. Like he always did.

I walked down a few more buildings cracking up about my bro, until I got to my own classroom. I peeked around the door, and when I saw my teacher writing out an equation on the chalkboard, I ducked in without her seeing me and grabbed a desk in the last row.

Later that night I snuck the playbook out of Diego's bag and read the whole thing to see who the Jets and Sharks were. And what the character Action was like. When I was finished I couldn't believe what a perfect lie Diego came up with. Right there on the spot too.

But that's just an example of my bro. I swear to God, man, he thinks up lies faster than anybody you could ever meet. Trust me.

June 3

Yo, this group home's full of punks and posers and loud-mouths and skeleton-ass baseheads. Nothing but ugly, stupid-looking gangster-wannabes. I guarantee there's not a person in the place who could spell his own damn name without a cheat sheet. And you should peep the weak-ass decorations they got in this place. Corny paintings and posters on every wall: a sailboat leaving some fake island, two polar bears fondling on each other in the snow, a giant rainbow waterfall coming off a cliff in Hawaii or some shit. There's this big blown-up photo of Martin Luther King, Jr., on a stage pointing out at a crowd of black people back in the day and a bunch of goofy inspirational sayings like: "Life is 5% what happens to you and 95% how you deal with it."

Yo, deal with *this,* I said in my head, and when I saw nobody was watching I spit a fat loogie on the cheap plastic frame.

On every single door there's a typed-up sheet of rules so nobody forgets they're in a group home, forgets their ass is locked up, put away, bad kids. On the dry-erase board in the kitchen there's a list of all the chores we gotta do every day—"Miguel" written in over the name that's been crossed out, "Marquee."

I guess it's only the damn names that change.

A Serious Question for Whatever Counselor's Reading This:

Yo, you really think a punk-ass place like this could make a kid *better*? How's that make any sense, man?

Lemme ask you something: If you send a normal kid to a group home with a bunch of dummies for nine months what's more likely to happen? The normal kid ignores all the shady shit around him and gets his life straight, or he just turns into a damn dummy his own self?

For real, think about it.

June 3—more

This ancient-looking black dude named Lester drove me here in a house minivan. Didn't stop yapping the whole time either. He told me how they got seven houses total and each one has six residents and a minivan. The residents are all between fourteen and eighteen years old and are placed here to "rehabilitate." I damn near pissed myself when he said that word, by the way, 'cause he could hardly pronounce it. He's like Jamaican or whatever, so it came out sounding like "rehubby-litate."

"Something the matter?" he said, turning to look at me.

I just shook my head at him, though, and kept laughing. And after a while he went on.

He told me about the history of the place, how it was founded and who by and what for and a bunch of other random stuff too, but after a while, man, I just tuned his Jamaican ass out. Instead I counted how many cars passed us on the freeway, thinking back on how me and Diego used to flip people off from the back of our old man's truck when we passed 'em. How we'd make bets about which people would flip us back. You'd be surprised how many people just take shit like that, by the way. Or act like they don't see you. For real, most people ain't got no kinda balls, man. It's sad.

When we got to the place, Lester handed my file and my bag of group-home clothes to the counselor, this surfer-looking white guy named Jaden.

Jaden:

Blond floppy hair, blue eyes and perfect white teeth when he smiled at me. He looked pretty damn out of place, considering all the black and Mexican ex-Juvi kids he was supposed to be watching. He and Lester talked in the office for a sec with the door closed and then Lester came back out, told me good luck, waved to the rest of the residents sitting around the couch watching TV and took off out the front door.

Jaden came up to me and patted me on the back. "What's up, bro? Welcome to the Lighthouse. Ha ha! That's what everybody calls it, bro. Because all the other houses on this street are old and brown and gray and ours is bright yellow like a lighthouse. Ha ha! Anyway, bro, you wanna meet the guys now or in the morning?"

I didn't say anything back.

He peeked in at the rest of the residents, then turned back to me: "Tell you what, let's do it tomorrow. We'll start fresh and all that good stuff. Ha ha!"

He waved for me to follow him into one of the three rooms, where he set down my stuff. "Go 'head and use that dresser, bro," he said, pointing to the one closest to the window. "And this is your bed right here with the light blue blanket. You're rooming with Jackson. He's from Oakland. Little bit of a drug habit that keeps setting him back, but we really like the guy overall."

I sat on my new bed and stared at the scuffed-up headboard. There were like twenty different sets of initials carved into the wood. This how many other people slept in this bed? I thought. And what was I supposed to do, carve in my initials too? Another set of stupid-ass letters on a stupid headboard in a stupid group home surrounded by stupid people?

Really? That's what's up?

And right then something clicked in my head. I realized how alone I was. Just another random kid in their system. A half-Mexican ghost from Stockton who messed up his family. I'd spend this year with a bunch of other ghosts from other nowhere places until they said I could leave, and then

I'd have to go haunt some other spot. And I was trying to think if I could ever go back home. Maybe when my moms dropped me off she was dropping my ass off for good. My whole family would probably turn their backs on me. And I'd have to roll solo like this forever.

Anyways, staring at all those initials, the shit hit me hard. I didn't have nobody that cared about me anymore.

Not even my own self.

And right then I had to put my hands on my middle. And lean over. I didn't know what was going on, but I had mad cramps in my stomach. And my head was spinning. Jaden stopped talking for a sec, asked me if I was okay, but I just sat there. I tried to be as still as possible so I wouldn't be sick or nothin'. And eventually he started talking again.

He moved toward the door, peeked outside and then leaned against the doorframe. "Les tells me you're cool beans, bro. That's sweet. We need some chill factor in this place. Sometimes the guys get a little— You know, they get worked up about stuff. But it's not a bad house overall. We're like any other group home: we got some positive energy flow and we got some static. While I'm here during the day, before the night watch comes in, it's my job to build on the positive flow and limit the static. You see what I'm saying, bro? It's Miguel, right?"

I didn't say anything back.

He opened my file, then closed it and said: "Listen, let's go sit in my office for a sec."

I cringed when I stood up because my stomach was killing me and I didn't know why. Probably the rubbery-ass micro-waved cheeseburger they gave me earlier in the day, my last meal at Juvi. I thought about ducking into the bathroom real quick, but I didn't. I followed Jaden into his office.

He sat down at his desk, leaned back in his chair and pointed for me to sit on an empty stool. "Les also tells me you're from Stockton." He sat up straight. "Bro, that's where I went to college. Small world, right? Elements of energy flowing together into one body of water. Six degrees of separation. Hey, what's up with that little Italian spot, Guido's?"

I didn't say anything back.

"That was my hang, bro. Ha ha! Me and my boys used to go there on Sundays to watch football and eat calzones and drink pitchers of cheap beer. Talk to honeys. Those were some of the best days of my life, Miguel."

He looked down at my folder, said: "Hey, you ever think about going to college, bro? It's pretty awesome. And I see you got really good grades. Three point four, bro. That's amazing, actually. I think that's the highest GPA I've ever seen in a resident file."

I didn't say anything back.

I watched Jaden flip through the next few pages of my file, nodding his head. "Anyway, Stockton," he said, smiling. "I got memories for days."

I figured his eyes would get all big when he got to the part about what I did, but they didn't. He just nodded some more and then closed up the file and put it in a drawer with the others, next to a shiny lockbox—the kind people use to store money.

"Bro, I've been at the Lighthouse for going on four months," he said, turning back to me. "I try to run it on the chill side, you know? That's my motto. You guys handle your biz, do your chores, stay out of trouble, et cetera, everything's cool. But check it out, bro. It's a serious adjustment, living with five other guys. Dealing with the social pressures of a group-home environment. Don't be afraid to lean on me at first. I was a psych major, bro. I got a handle on this kind of thing. You feel me?"

"I gotta pee," I said, pushing off the stool.

Jaden smiled and stood up. "Out this door, hang a right, third door on your left."

I turned to leave.

"Door doesn't lock," Jaden called after me as I hurried my ass down the hall. "Just so you know. None of the doors here lock, bro. Except the office—"

I shut the bathroom door behind me and rushed the toilet, wrapped my arms around the cold porcelain and heaved. But nothing came out. All the blood in my body went to my head, the back of my eyes, and I dry-heaved again. My face was burning. I heaved again and again, but nothing came up. I didn't know what the hell was happening to me. Or if I was sick or what. I spit in the toilet and stood up, looked at my bloodshot eyes in the mirror, and I couldn't believe it. There were tears running down my stupid-ass face, man. I was crying like a bitch.

I pictured Diego behind me pointing and laughing. Telling me I was mad soft.

I slapped myself in the face so I'd stop. Slapped myself a second time, harder. "Look at your bitch ass," I said to my reflection. "Punk bitch." I punched my stomach for cramping up on me like that. Elbowed myself in the ribs. The tears weren't coming out anymore, but I slapped my face again anyway. I wasn't gonna let myself turn into no punk. Punched my right temple and grabbed my hair and pulled as hard as I could. Then I spit in the toilet again and sat on the edge of the tub, rocking back and forth. I didn't know what was wrong with me. And I didn't know where to go or what to think.

There was a knock on the door, and I turned around and shouted, "Yo, somebody's in here!"

Then I stared at the floor where the tile was all cracked and worn out and listened for the sound of somebody's shoes walking away.

June 4

Took me less than one day to get in a damn fight.

Right before breakfast, Jaden brought me into the TV room and introduced me to all the posers sitting around on the couches watching a rap video. Three black kids, Jackson, Reggie and Demarcus; a shaved-head Chinese kid with these nasty-looking scars on his cheeks, Mong; another Mexican kid, Rene; and a fat white boy named Tommy. Only Tommy looked up when Jaden told 'em: "I'd like you guys to say what's up to our new resident, Miguel."

I laughed at the rest of their sorry asses and said under my breath: "Bitches."

Right after I said it, though, the Chinese kid, Mong, stood up and said: "What'd you just say?"

"Bitches!" I shouted in his face.

And he spit on me.

I couldn't believe it, yo. The guy straight up hawked a loogie right in front of Jaden and *spit* at me. It landed on the bottom of my damn pants, dripped down onto my shoe. I flipped like a mother and charged his skinny ass with my fists clenched. I threw a wild overhead right at one of his cheek scars, but he caught my fist in his bare hand and squeezed so hard I thought he was gonna break all my stupid fingers. But I didn't even care. I kneed his ass in the side and went to throw a left, but before I could connect Jaden wrapped me in a bear hug and pulled me back.

Jackson and Rene stepped between us and pulled my hand out of Mong's grip, and then they both stood there swiveling their heads back and forth between us.

"Let him go," Mong said in this calm-ass voice. He had an ugly brown tooth hanging from a string around his neck. A smile even came over his scarred-up face, and he said it again: "Let him go."

I been in mad fights before—with Diego and random kids in school or at the park—but I'd never seen somebody smile right in the middle of one. Shit pissed me off even more, man. But at the same time it was kind of confusing, too.

"Lemme go!" I yelled. "I'll kill this bitch!"

"Breathe easy!" Jaden shouted, still bear-hugging me. "Both of you, just breathe easy. It's not worth it."

The fat white kid, Tommy, leaned in near my ear and said: "I'd back off, man. Trust me." But I didn't even look at the guy.

"Let him go," Mong said again, still smiling. He wouldn't take his eyes off me or even blink. He just stared at me with this crazy-looking smile on his face. He wasn't big or anything. I'm like five eleven and he had to be at least two inches shorter. And he was even skinnier than me. But you could tell by looking in his eyes that he really wanted to throw down. He wasn't faking.

Diego taught me about that after my first real fight in junior high school. He said you could tell if somebody really wants to get down or not just by looking in their eyes. If their heart isn't in it all you gotta do is look mad crazy and hit 'em once in the face and it'll be game over. Which is exactly what happened with me and that first kid. I barely grazed his chin and he acted like he just got shot and collapsed to the damn ground crying. Almost every fight I been in since has gone the same way—except the few times Diego's whupped me. But this Mong dude had a different look in his eyes. He was for real about it.

"Let him go," he said again, nodding his head.

"Lemme go," I said.

The Asian kids in my school back in Stockton barely even talked. They just sat there at the front of the class and took notes and got As on all the math tests. They packed together at the two far tables in the cafeteria at lunch. But this Mong dude wasn't like that. He was a different kind of Asian kid.

Jackson told me: "Miguel, man, squash it. Mong don't play."

"I don't give a shit," I said. "I ain't lettin' no Chinese fuck spit on me. I'm gonna kill—"

Then dude spit at me *again*! Right in the face. Before I could even get my damn sentence out. And he started laughing.

I straight up lost it, yo. Wrestled out of Jaden's grip and charged Mong. Pushed him and then threw the hardest right I could. But he ducked it and shoved me into the wall. And then he spit on me again. This time in my hair.

I growled and went for Mong again, ready to rip his damn eyes out, but Jaden tackled me. And Jackson and Tommy pulled Mong over to the couch and sat him down and stood in front of him so he couldn't go anywhere.

Jaden turned and shouted: "Reggie, go get the cordless! Now!"

Reggie took off into the kitchen.

I was so out-of-my-mind pissed I damn near punched Jaden, just to punch somebody. But I didn't. I gritted my teeth together instead, breathed through my mouth super loud as I wiped Mong's spit off my face and out of my hair.

And I rattled off every curse word I knew and threatened to kill the guy like a hundred times.

Reggie came back with the phone and handed it to Jaden.

"Here's the situation," Jaden said, holding the phone out. "Mong: all you did was spit so far. That's it. You're gonna get written up, but it's not a major. If you hurt Miguel—I'm serious, Mong, if you harm him in any way, even if he throws the first punch—they're not gonna send you back to Juvi this time. We talked about this."

Jaden turned to me.

"Miguel: Today's your first full day, bro. Ask any one of these guys, you play by the rules, do your time, you'll most likely get out early and move on with your life. You start right off getting in trouble like this, though, and they'll just extend your sentence. Make it so you're part of the system all the way until you're eighteen. Trust me, bro, that's no way to live out your high school years. Take a deep breath, bros, and really think about it. How do you want this to go? It's a choice. It's in your hands. Right now. This very second."

Mong leaned back on the couch, still smiling. He touched the stupid tooth around his neck and then turned his attention toward the TV, focused on another rap video that had started. I stopped trying to fight past Jaden and calmed down, dropped my arms, unclenched my fists. I looked at Jaden for a sec and he didn't even look spooked. Which sort of surprised me. All the other residents started talking again and moving around the front room sneaking glances at me and Mong.

Jaden pulled me to the side and asked me a couple questions about my "head space" or whatever, but I didn't have any answers for him. I couldn't concentrate. I stared at Mong, who was staring at the rap video, smiling. He looked crazy just sitting there smiling, eyes all calm, shaved head. I'd never seen a Chinese kid look so crazy. Shit, I'd never seen *any* kid look that crazy. It kind of weirded me out a little, to be straight. I started thinking maybe this is what a person looks like when they're a damn psycho.

And then I did that thing I can do with my mind. I stared at the rug and concentrated about Mong, wishing something bad would happen to him. Something worse than bad. Something that would make it so he could never spit on nobody ever again. And I actually felt what I was thinking bouncing back and forth in my chest. I looked up at Mong and it shot out of my body.

Eventually everybody cleared the room and took showers and got dressed and ate breakfast, and after breakfast we did our chores. I cleaned the bathroom sink and the mirror and mopped the floor and scrubbed the toilet—the one I'd just been hanging all on last night—and then Jaden called us back into the kitchen to start preparing lunch. On my way I peeked in the living room and there was Mong, still sitting there watching TV with the same dopey-ass smile on his scarred-up face. He didn't even look at me as I passed by. Like he was in some kind of weird trance or something. I don't think he was really even watching TV.

He was the only resident who didn't eat lunch or do any chores.

A few hours later Lester came by. He walked in without knocking and waved at Jaden. Then he nodded for Mong to follow him and they both walked outside and climbed into Lester's house van.

Me and Tommy took a break from cleaning up the game room to watch them shut their doors. I nodded toward the

24

van, said: "He takin' him 'cause of what happened this morning?"

Tommy shook his head. "Nah, man, Les picks Mong up every other day at this time. Brings him back a couple hours later."

"For what?" I said.

"Nobody knows."

I shrugged, and we both watched Lester's van pull away from the curb and drive off. I tried to think where he'd be taking Mong. Like a special psychologist or a probation officer. But I don't really know that much about how group homes work yet, so I just put it out of my head. And me and Tommy both went back to doing our chores.

June 5

Today at lunch Tommy and the only other Mexican kid, Rene, walked over to where I was sitting, on a cinder block in the far corner of the yard. They sat down on the blocks on either side of me and at first they didn't say anything more than "Hey."

I didn't say hey back, though. I'd already decided about that. How it's probably better in a group home to just roll solo and do your time and don't mess with nobody. So the fact that they even came over by me in the first place kind of pissed me off.

It was quiet for a minute as we ate. All three of us had paper plates with microwaved corn dogs and big piles of ketchup and mustard. Tommy lifted a corn dog to his mouth, took a huge-ass bite and chewed. He was wearing short sleeves, the same generic white T-shirt we all had to wear, and I stared at his fat-ass arm as he looked at the ground.

Sometimes I can't even look at fat when it jiggles, man. Straight up. I know it's wrong to think that way, and some people can't help it 'cause of their thyroid glands or whatever, but I'm sayin'. Jiggling fat makes me kind of sick. I don't even know why. Shit's even worse when the dude whose fat it is, like Tommy, is sitting there chewing on a damn corn dog with his mouth all open.

I turned to look at Rene, who was waving at a fly buzzing in his face. There were a grip of flies in the backyard, by the way. At a certain point you just had to give up trying to wave their asses away.

I finished my first rubbery dog, tossed the stick back on my plate and picked up the second. Dipped it half in ketchup, half in mustard, and took a bite.

"Me and Rene thought we'd better tell you somethin'," Tommy finally said. "Right, Rene?"

Rene nodded. He swatted at another fly, then kicked at it.

I didn't say a word back, thinking maybe they'd get the hint, but they just kept on talking.

"Mong's touched, man," Tommy said, tapping his right temple with his pointer finger. "Me and Rene been here longer than anybody, and trust me, man, that dude's sick in his head."

"Don't seem like nothin' when you look at 'im," Rene said. "But *vato* never lost no fights here. He's out his mind, that's why."

I lowered my food and looked right in Rene's eyes, said: "Yo, dawg. I got an idea."

"What's up?"

"Why don't you go tell this to somebody who gives a shit."

They both looked at me, stunned. Then they looked at each other.

26

"Oh, it's like that?" Tommy said. Then he paused for a long time, trying to think up what he was gonna say next.

"You that much of a badass?" Rene said.

I shrugged. "Nobody's callin' anybody a badass. I'm just sayin'."

"You know what?" Tommy said. "I didn't even wanna come over here. Rene *made* me 'cause you're both Mexican."

"We was just tryin' to tell your dumb ass," Rene said.

I shrugged and looked at the ground. I felt kind of bad for popping off like that, but at the same time, man, it's not like I asked people to come over and tell me how messed-up some Chinese kid is.

Rene swatted at another fly and shook his head. He took a deep breath and said: "Look, I'm just sayin', all right? That boy don't got no morals. And you and him had a beef. Like Tommy said, I look out for my people. It's how my uncles raised me."

"Watch it, that's all he's telling you," Tommy added.

Rene nodded. "That *vato* will just do any single thing that comes in his head."

I took another bite of corn dog and stared at the patch of dead grass under my feet, chewing. Flies all in my face, ketchup soaking through my bullshit paper plate and getting on my pants. The more I thought about the situation, the more depressed I got. Not just for me, but for the two dudes sitting next to me too. The three of us eating on cement blocks, waving away flies that supposedly puke on you every time they land, wearing the exact same clothes and stupid white shoes. I'm not saying we didn't deserve to be there. It's just weird to think we still had to act like we were alive like anybody else. We still had to eat and sleep and walk and talk. For some reason I started picturing us all on some video people could watch on YouTube. Like there was a hidden camera

27

on us at all times, 24/7, and people could watch us eat our corn dogs and fight and talk shit and spit on each other. I pictured three normal kids sitting around one of their fancy computers eating popcorn, pointing at us and laughing, like we were monkeys in a damn zoo or some shit. Ah, look at the group-home kids! And when they got bored they could just go outside and ride their skateboards or bikes or go to the mall. But we'd have to stay right here, under the cameras, for when somebody else wanted to watch us.

That's one thing I hate about myself, by the way. When I start thinking about something like that I can't get it out of my head. No matter how hard I try. I just keep stressing on it, nonstop.

"Anyways." Tommy was still yapping. "Mong's probably the craziest kid I've ever seen. Including all the ones I met in Juvi. You know those scars on his face? I heard somebody speared him with a sword, man. Back in China—"

"Nah, man," Rene interrupted, dipping his second corn dog in mustard. "I heard *vato* fell off a fishing boat and the propeller sliced his ass up. Shit happened in the water, Tom." Rene took a big bite, chewed for a few seconds and then swallowed.

Tommy set down his plate and wiped his fat mouth with a ketchup-stained napkin. "Point is he's off, man. First time he got booted from here wasn't even 'cause he hurt somebody," Tommy said. "We used to have this old Indian counselor in here, right? About four people before Jaden."

"They always change, by the way," Rene said, giving Tommy a fist pound. "Nobody can be around kids like us too long, man. They just quit. That's something you'll figure out. We already got bets on Jaden."

"Anyways, the old Indian counselor was always telling

Mong not to sit on the kitchen table or else it was gonna break. But Mong never listened to him. Then one day the table *did* break. It cracked down the middle with Mong on it, right in front of the Indian guy. He went off to the office to get his book, wrote out a restitution paper and handed it to Mong. They argued a little while and then the counselor yelled for Mong to go in his room and said he had to stay in there the rest of the day. But Mong didn't go anywhere. He hopped right up on the kitchen counter and dropped his drawers. And you wouldn't believe what he did. He took a shit, man. I swear to God. I put that on my aunt Mary and her new baby. He pulled down his pants, squatted and took a shit on the counter. Right there in front of everybody."

I set my plate in the dirt and looked at Tommy's fat face. Dude thought he was gonna scare me. Come on, man. I turned and looked at Rene. He was one of those little skinny Mexicans you see out on a soccer field during recess, running all around after the ball, never getting tired. I shook my head, spit on the ground by my feet.

Tommy nudged Rene, said: "Second time was when he snapped that kid Jimmy's arm right in half, man. You remember that. Sickest thing I've ever seen."

Rene got a disgusted look on his face and nodded.

"My stomach gets all messed up just thinking about it," Tommy said. "He was only like fifteen years old at the time, a hundred twenty pounds or something. He and Jimmy were playin' cards, right? And after Jimmy loses six straight hands he comes right out and accuses Mong of cheating. At first Mong said he wasn't and seemed like he was just trying to laugh it off. And to be honest, I don't even think he *was* cheating. But when Jimmy stood up and said it for a second time—'You's a cheater, Mong!'—Mong threw the table over, grabbed Jimmy's arm, hopped in the air and snapped the poor kid's arm over his knee. Clear in two, man. Like it was nothin'. All the resies in the house were freaking out."

I just stared right back at Tommy with a straight face. Dude thought he was scaring somebody. Shit.

Rene kicked at another fly, said: "Jimmy made a scream like I ain't never heard in my life. We all had to cover our ears. And the bone was stickin' straight out of his arm."

"And Mong just stood over him sayin' the same thing over and over: 'I didn't cheat! I didn't cheat!' "

"Les came to get him with the cops that time."

"Took him away in handcuffs," Tommy said, shaking his head. "We all said it was an accident, just happened during their fight. Even Jimmy said that."

"Don't nobody rat on each other in here, man. That's another thing you'll learn."

I rolled my eyes again and spit next to my shoes but they just kept on talking.

"They took him back to Juvi for nine months that time. And nobody ever found out how it really happened. Point is, though, how many people do you know that are capable of something like that?"

"Weird thing is, he's smart as hell, too," Rene said. "If you get him talking, I mean. Probably the smartest kid I ever met."

"Yeah," Tommy said, "but if they knew how he was really like he wouldn't even be here. They'd put him in solitary confinement. Or they'd try him as an adult."

I looked back and forth between these two busters, shaking my head, making like I was barely listening anymore even though I was.

Tommy ran his hand through his hair and said: "Demarcus

heard Les tellin' someone on the phone he doesn't think Mong'll see eighteen. It's 'cause he so crazy."

"That's what I'm thinkin'," Rene said, swatting another fly.

I picked up my plate and folded it in half, corn-dog sticks inside, ketchup squeezing out of the far end. "Lemme ask you guys somethin'," I finally said, switching the plate from one hand to the other.

"What's up?" Tommy said.

I stood up, looked at Rene again and then back at Tommy. "What makes you think I wanna hear about some Chinese kid takin' a shit on the kitchen counter?" I shook my head and started walking away, said over my shoulder: "You ask me, that's some straight-up gay talk, man."

"It's called lookin' out, dumb-ass," Rene said.

"Screw it," Tommy added. "You're on your own then, man. I don't care what happens to you now. It's game over for you, dude. Peace."

Peace, I thought, laughing to myself. I slid open the sliding glass door and went back into the kitchen. Peace. I tossed my plate in the trash and walked through the hall to my bedroom and plopped down on my bed.

Peace.

What the hell's that word even mean, man? There's no such thing. It's bad enough when I'm awake. Living in this bullshit group home in San Jose listening to all these dummies try and tell stories about people taking shits. But then when I close my eyes to go to sleep it's even *worse*. I go back to what happened. Every single night. It's the only dream I dream. I see his face, man, just inches above mine. In the kitchen back in Stockton. My head hitting the counter. His eyes all big and looking right at me. Looking *through* me.

Then looking away. In the kitchen. Middle of the day. His eyes—on me, and then not.

Nah, man, there ain't no such thing as peace no more.

That shit's dead and buried.

And my dumb ass with it.

June 7

Middle of the night and I'm dead asleep. Out cold and on my stomach, mouth open. Drool all on my pillow. And then suddenly I wake up. Not because I hear something, but 'cause I *feel* something. A ghost hovering over me in the room. At first I have no idea where I am—could be in me and Diego's room back in Stockton, or stretched out on the grass by the levee, or in my bottom bunk at Juvi—but then it comes to me.

The Lighthouse.

I roll over quick and open my eyes and there's Mong. It's not a dream. He's really standing over my bed with his arms crossed. Smiling. Chinese Mong. The brown tooth around his neck. Big ugly scars on both cheeks. Shaved head.

I freeze. Don't say a word, or move none. My body completely paralyzed. Limp. Only my lungs tell me I'm still alive—my breaths coming quicker and quicker. I can't help what's happening with my lungs. In my head I try to concentrate on all the different parts of my body in case he's already done something to me with a knife. And now he's just watching to see me squirm in pain. But there's nothing wrong.

I try to imagine I'm just dreaming. But I know it's not true. I'm awake. And Mong's really standing over my bed with his arms crossed. Smiling. Thinking the bad things he could do to me.

And I'm not gonna lie, I sort of panic inside. I can't catch my breath. Like I'm hyperventilating. Or drowning. And I don't know what I should do 'cause I keep thinking about the story Tommy said where Mong broke that kid's arm right in half. I can hear the crack in my head, can hear it echo through the room. The big white bone sticking out of the skin. I can hear the kid's screams, so loud everybody has to cover their ears.

I close my eyes again. Pretend to fall back asleep, like I don't care. Try to make my breaths all long and drawn-out and my face muscles limp. I do this for a long-ass time, pretending it'll all just go away, and at one point I almost think I *am* back asleep. But really I'm just trying to think what I should do. Like, do I jump up at him swinging? Yell something out? Call Jackson for help?

Then this weird thought comes in my head.

Maybe I actually *don't* care what happens. I'm being straight up. If Mong does something to me maybe it doesn't even matter none. 'Cause I remember how I ain't even a real person no more. Just a ghost. Same as Mong. Both of us just two beings floating around in the world but not really living no more. Empty snail shells who don't mean nothin' to nobody. Including our own selves. And if you ain't nothin' more than a ghost nobody could really hurt you, right? Even if they hurt you real bad. Like breaking your arm in half.

I open my eyes again and stare up at Mong. He's in the same spot, standing over me with his arms folded. Still smiling. And I say in a calm voice: "I don't care what you do, man."

He stays standing there with his arms crossed, but his smile slowly fades off his face.

I say it again, even quieter this time: "Go on and do it, Mong. I don't even care. It doesn't matter."

Mong stands there a couple seconds longer and then he turns and walks out of my room. Just like that.

And I watch him go.

Looking Back at It Now:

Here's the weird thing: at first I thought I was just telling Mong that for something to say. Like maybe it made me sound tough. And really it was just an act.

But when I closed my eyes and rolled over and felt my breathing was already back to normal again, I realized something about myself. I really meant what I said. I didn't care what happened one way or the other. After what happened back in Stockton it's like I'm already dead. What I told Mong was the straight-up truth. I wish it wasn't, but it was. And what makes me sad as hell is that back when I was a kid I cared so much, man. About every little thing. My mom and pop, Diego, the levee. Just being alive. And breathing. Following my big bro around. But things are different now.

Everything's changed. Forever.

June 10

There's this thing I gotta say about my brother Diego, man. It cracks me up just thinking about it. Dude's got more girls than there is hours in a day. Trust me. Every time you turn around he's got three or four hanging off his arm or following him around during lunch. And I'm not talking about no ugly chicks either. The finest ones in school, man. Don't matter what kind: he's got white girls, black girls, Mexican girls, Asian girls, whatever you could think up.

When I first got to high school I spent a lot of time trying to figure the shit out. For one thing, Diego's a good-lookin' dude, all right? I'm not even gonna lie. He's a little lighter-skinned and taller with bluer eyes than I got. He's thin but with mad cuts and a smooth face. Another thing is that he talks in this super chill voice. One of his girls, Jamile, told me when Diego talks to women it's like he's singing some love jam in their ear—even when he's just mentioning about something normal, like getting Mexican food at the spot or some random movie that just came out.

But it's more than just Diego's voice, I think. It's also how he always knows exactly what to say.

Like imagine some heina's acting all mad 'cause Diego forgot it was her birthday or he didn't call her all weekend even though he swore to God he would. I've seen it a million times. The girl's got her arms crossed in the parking lot after school. She's frownin', all pissed and refusing to look at him. Leaning against her friend's souped-up Civic and tapping her sandal on the asphalt.

You'd probably think my bro was done, right? Well, you don't know Diego. He'll just smile calm, lean in on her all chill and whisper something smooth in her ear. I'll be standing off to the side watching ol' girl just melt like a Popsicle, man. She'll uncross her arms. Start to smile a little. Maybe play-punch Diego in the shoulder.

That's when I know it's all over, by the way. Whenever a girl play-punches Diego it's a wrap.

Soon they'll be laughing and hugging on each other, and just before she hops in her girl's Civic she'll say: "So you promise you're gonna meet me at Maria's later, right? Don't play me this time, Diego." And Diego'll hold his hands out all innocent-like and say: "Course I'm gonna meet you there. You my girl, ain't you?" And her face will beam and she'll blow Diego a kiss before slamming shut her door and her and her girl drive off, waving.

Diego, man.

But this is the part that gets me. He'll walk over all chill right after, right? Won't even mention what he just did. He'll talk about ball instead, or he'll ask me what I think about Moms only sleepin' on the living room couch these days, or he'll see if I wanna go fishing in the levee later. The dude won't even mention how in less than a minute's time he just got the finest white girl in Stockton to go from crossing her arms and frowning to blowing him dumb-ass kisses.

Diego, man.

My big bro.

When I was a kid I used to try and think how he did it, you know? What'd he say? How'd he say it? I used to copy his clothes style and how he did his hair. But after a while I stopped, man. I realized that's just how it is for Diego. He's mad smooth like that. Like he can see in a girl's head and know exactly what she's thinking without barely even trying. Girls just come to him. And the less he puts in, the more he gets out. It's the exact opposite of how you'd think, right? But I'm telling you.

Nah, when it comes to girls, my brother's lounging on the inside. He's getting fanned down by the finest girls you could ever imagine. While the rest of us are sitting around outside, in the hot Stockton sun, sweatin' our balls off.

I swear, man. Sometimes when I'm doing chores and thinking about my brother I just sit there and crack up.

June 21

I know I haven't written in here for a grip, but there's a reason for that. Nothing's really happened. And nothing's really happened because I've been chillin' solo. I don't mess with anybody or even make any eye contact. It's just easier this way. I wake up, do my chores, eat by myself on one of the cinder blocks outside, do more chores, go to my counseling appointment with this manly-looking lady named Jenny (ol' girl gots a handlebar mustache, I swear to God), eat alone again, read whatever book I'm reading and go to sleep. That's pretty much it. Once the school year starts again I'll go to class. But it's summer, so we got mad downtime. Each house only gets two outings per week, and most times it's something lame like going to the park down the road, where everybody just stands around on the handball court. The rest of the time we're at the Lighthouse doing chores or eating or having free time.

I know the judge said for me to write in here four times a week, but what's dude want me to do, man, make shit up? Even the whole thing with Mong has chilled out since the night I caught him standing over me.

My roommate, Jackson, got booted a couple days back 'cause they found meth taped underneath his sock drawer—second time in two weeks he got caught. The first time they found it in his shoe. They do that here, by the way. A counselor from another house comes around every few days and goes through all your stuff to make sure you don't have nothin' illegal. Since Jackson left I've had my own room, which is crazy mellow.

Ways to Escape Your Mind in a Group Home:

At first I'd come in here and just lay on my bed staring up at the ceiling, thinking. But I realized when I do that I usually start thinking about something I don't really wanna think about, like my moms or Diego, so I decided to start reading books. Back in Stockton I read a few for school. I even read some on my own, though I never let my bro catch me. I'd always sneak the shit—in the bathroom, or under the covers, or I'd hide it inside a sports magazine. Trust me, where we're from it ain't cool to read no book unless some teacher's making you.

Anyways, the first one I pulled off the shelf was called *The Color Purple*. It's about this ignorant black woman who gets the shit kicked out of her by her husband and writes all these letters to God. At first I couldn't get into it because of how she talked—she's mad stupid. But after a while it got kind of interesting. She had a hard-ass life, man. Now I keep trying to get back in my room so I can find out what's gonna happen.

I know that shit sounds mad nerdy, right? Me wanting to rush back to my room so I could read. But there ain't nothing else to do in a group home, man. I ain't trying to watch no TV 'cause that's where everybody else is. And like I said, where everybody else is, is where I don't wanna be. So I might as well read a damn book, you know?

Later On:

Demarcus and Reggie made fun of my ass for reading in the backyard. They said only a bike thief like me would read books in a group home. That's what some of the guys call me now, by the way. The bike thief. Everybody in this place likes to brag about what got them thrown in here. The bigger the crime they claim, the more cred they got in the system. Tommy tells people he robbed a bank for fifty G back in Walnut Creek. Rene says he beat down some history teacher so bad he put dude in a coma. Reggie and Demarcus both say they're in here for attempted murder and other gang-type shit. Jackson, before he got kicked out, said he got caught selling coke and weed to business dudes up in San Francisco— which I'm pretty sure is true. (Anybody who tries to smoke dead leaves in the damn backyard, you know what I'm say-in'?) And everybody thinks it's all funny to say I'm in here 'cause I stole a bike.

"Yo, Miguel. What they catch you doin', dawg? Swipin' somebody's ten-speed?"

"Dude clipped a chain lock and rode off on some little girl's banana seat, handlebar tassels all blowin' in the wind."

"Yo, it probably had a little basket in the front so he had a place to put his panties."

"Ha ha! Pink with sparkles, yo."

"What, the bike or the panties?"

"Both!"

Ha! Ha! Ha! Ha! Ha! Ha! Ha! Ha! Ha! Ha!

"Look, there he go, dawg. Runnin' back to his room to go finger-bang hisself."

"The bike thief."

Trust me, man, pretty much every dude in here swears they're some kind of comedian.

Most times I don't say anything back, though. Know why? 'Cause on the DL sometimes I pretend it's true myself. I stole a bike. Somebody's ten-speed. I clipped a chain and the cops came along and caught me red-handed. That's all I did.

I'm a bike thief.

Okay.

Anyways, when Demarcus and Reggie laughed at me for read-ing a book in the backyard I flipped both their asses off and closed my book up. I moved past them toward the house and said: "Yo, at least I know how to read."

"Ain't gotta read to pull no trigger, homey," Demarcus said, faking like he was firing a gun at me.

"Man," I said, turning back around, "that's such an ineffi-cient use of space."

"Wha'chu mean?" Demarcus said.

"Yo, you got the biggest-ass head in the house, right? And there ain't nothin' in it but damn carbon dioxide."

As I slid open the door and ducked back inside I could hear Reggie telling his boy: "Oh, shit, D. Miguel just took his little taquito out his pants and pissed all over you. Oh, damn!"

But I don't read my book outside anymore. It's not worth the hassle. And I can just as easily sneak back in my room, where there's peace and quiet.

June 24

The Color Purple is pretty much the saddest book you could ever read, man. When I got done with the last couple pages I couldn't believe how sad it was. But at the same time I liked it a whole lot. It's probably my favorite book ever. It's mad crazy how just writing letters makes the woman feel better about herself. And the last one's to everybody, not just God, which is pretty cool. And also symbolic.

Now I'm reading this book called *Their Eyes Were Watching God*. I'm not gonna lie, I had to read the first page over and over again to know what the hell the writer was even saying, 'cause she doesn't use regular English in her book. She uses black talk like I used to hear at my school back in Stockton. Ebonics. Like Demarcus and Reggie. Only a back-in-the-day version. It's actually pretty cool how she does it. Once you catch the rhythm, I mean.

By the way, I decided what I like about reading books. When I'm following what a character does in a book I don't have to think about my own life. Where I am. Why I'm here. My moms and my brother and my old man. I can just think about the character's life and try and figure out what's gonna happen. Plus when you're in a group home you pretty much can't go anywhere, right? But when you read books you almost feel like you're out there in the world. Like you're going on this adventure right with the main character. At least, that's the way I do it.

It's actually not that bad.

Even if it *is* mad nerdy.

So here's what I decided I'm gonna do. I'm gonna try and read every single book they got on the bookshelf in the game room. Jaden told me that's what Malcolm X did when he was in prison. He just learned as much as he could, starting with all the words in the dictionary, 'cause he couldn't go anywhere anyway so why not take advantage of his time.

Anyways, that's what I decided today after lunch. I'm gonna read every single book they got in the place. Even if it's something that doesn't seem like I'd like it that much. And by the time I'm done reading all the books my year will probably be up, and they'll let my ass out, and when I walk through them front doors I won't just be a free man. I'll also be smart as goddamn hell.

See what I'm sayin'?

June 28

They made me call home today.

The first two Sundays I was here, Jenny (the house counselor) and Jaden said I didn't have to do it because I was new and still adjusting to a different environment. But today they made me. Jaden even had me go first. They both sat with me and explained how Sundays are phone-call days. Everybody has to call somebody. If you don't have parents you have to call your grandparents or your foster parents or some relative or family friend.

I'm not gonna lie, I felt pretty weird thinking about calling my house back in Stockton. I didn't know what I was gonna say or if my moms would even wanna talk to me. Actually, I was pretty sure she didn't. But Jaden and Jenny were staring at me, so I dialed the number and sat there listening to it ring, wishing I could just hang up. My hand actually started shaking, and when Jenny saw it she patted my shoulder. Which was nice except I don't really like it when people touch me. I always hold my breath until they stop.

And then I heard the machine pick up, and Diego's voice came on telling people to leave a message. And I swear to God, man. I almost lost it. My head got all dizzy and I felt like I was gonna faint or some shit. I hadn't heard Diego's voice in forever. My big bro, man. "Peoples, we're not home right now. Leave a message at the . . ." My moms laughing in the background and then the beep sounding. Those stupid, simple words, man. That beep. It made me almost wanna cry 'cause I miss 'em so much. Peoples, we're not home right now. Leave a message at the . . . I tensed up all my muscles and kept everything super still and looked at the same spot on the wall, trying to make out what shape it was: a tiny person diving off a cliff, a boomerang, a cocoon.

I handed the phone back to Jaden, told 'im: "Nobody's home."

Jaden and Jenny looked at each other and nodded and then let me leave the office, saying we'd try again next week.

But just hearing my bro's voice on the answering machine, man. Thinking about my moms sitting there listening to it 'cause she probably just didn't want to talk to nobody. Tears going down her face. Or even worse, if there wasn't no tears left. Picturing her sitting there at the kitchen table with both hands around her mug of tea, listening to the answering machine message. It got me thinking. Since everything that happened, me and her haven't said more than ten words to each other. Ten words in four months. That's gotta be some kind of record for a mom and her son. Especially when you consider we used to talk all the time.

Instead of going straight back to my room to read I went in the backyard, sat on one of the cinder blocks so I could think about everything. The rest of the guys were inside waiting to make their calls or playing cards or watching rap videos on BET. So I had some space outside for once.

Man, I started to feel really bad about myself and where I was in life and how maybe I was gonna end up being a total failure or something, like one of those guys who has nowhere else to go so they just lay around the park all day. Acting all crazy and talking to themselves and digging through the nasty-ass trash. I've always known Diego's her favorite—which never really bothers me since he's older and he's pretty much every-damn-body's favorite. And besides, my moms used to still like talking to me about school or stuff that was happening in the news or how our days went and all that. Especially after my old man died. Whenever Diego was out with his friends on a week-end night she'd come into our bedroom with her CD player, and we'd sit on the end of my bed listening to music.

She'd tell me who was singing. This is Bob Dylan, Miguel. This is Simon and Garfunkel. This is Crosby, Stills and Nash. Al Green. Marvin Gaye. Nina Simone. Cat Stevens. She'd tell me to pay special attention to the words, because according to her, good lyrics were what made a song. And then we'd just sit there. On my bed. Listening to music. Paying attention to the lyrics. Hanging out, almost like if we were friends and not just a mom and her son.

I stayed outside on my cinder block for a long-ass time after my call home. Thinking about that shit. Swatting damn flies. And then I decided something. Maybe it's nobody's fault how we don't talk no more. Me and my moms. Maybe it's just the situation and it won't go on forever. I still care about her as much as back when we used to listen to music. Who says people have to talk all the time to care about each other?

So from now on I'm gonna do something to make it even easier on her. Next Sunday, when Jenny and Jaden bring me in the office to call home, I'm gonna dial a fake number. And I'm gonna pretend we're talking back and forth like a normal call would go. Like we're catching up about our weeks. But the whole time I'll just be listening to dead air in my ear. That way Jaden won't have to write me up, and my mom won't have to talk to me when I know she probably doesn't really want to, and I'll know I'm making it easy on everybody, including myself.

Kind of mad smart, right?

That's another thing about me you should know. Sometimes I can be good as hell at figuring out stuff when it seems like there's no possible way.

Here's the thing: at some point I hope my moms will wanna listen to music again. Even if it's not in our old apartment, but out somewhere, like a coffee shop. I know it won't ever be like it was before, but just anything would be cool with me. 'Cause I really do like her a lot, man. And deep down she might even still like me too. She just can't show it 'cause of what I did and 'cause she's the mom. If you think about it, she's been through about ten times more than most people. And she still means well. She really does.

Anyways, long as they got me stuck in here and I gotta

make calls home I'm gonna dial a fake number. Every Sunday. I'm just gonna pretend like we're on the phone together, talking about what everybody else talks about when they call home. And that way everybody'll be happy.

July 1

Sometimes when I wake up in the middle of the night I still wonder if I'll open my eyes and find Mong's crazy ass standing over me again. This time with a machete or a rifle. A damn Chinese throwing star. But it never happens.

During the day we don't say a word or even look at each other. He just does his thing, and I do mine. Even when we gotta do a chore together we just get it over with and then don't bother with each other. Like yesterday. I swept the kitchen floor, made a pile, and Mong set down the dustpan. He pushed the pile in and emptied it in the trash. Then he took the broom from me, put the stuff away, and we went our separate ways.

I'm not gonna lie, the whole time I was waiting for his crazy ass to make a move on me. And I was planning what I'd do back with the broom or my knee. But nothing ever happened. Dude was all business.

Or take the house meeting this morning, when Jaden told us about the new system that's gonna start in a month. How the rules are gonna be a little tighter and most people's sentences will now go the full length (instead of how they usually get cut mad short because they need space and don't have enough funding). Jaden told us he'd know the exact details in a couple weeks when some deal went through. We all rolled our eyes and complained 'cause that's the one thing everybody had to look forward to, getting out early for good behavior. Everybody started getting all loud—except Mong. He was just sitting there across from me, all calm like he didn't even care.

"But I have some good news too, bros," Jaden broke in. "Our house was picked to go on a special day trip to Alcatraz next Saturday. They're even funding a nice little dinner for us in a three-star restaurant in SF. We're gonna be doing some fine dining, bros. Cloth napkins and the whole thing."

A couple guys nodded their heads in approval, but most of us didn't seem blown away. Especially after we just heard the news about our sentences.

Point is, if you sat there and watched how me and Mong were around each other, you'd think nothin' ever happened. No spit, no haymakers, no standing over the bed. You'd think we were just two regular group-home kids living out our sentences. Which is weird if you think about it. Where I'm from people don't just forget about the scraps they have until somebody wins and somebody loses (unless it's with family like me and Diego). But maybe that's how it is in a group home. I don't even know yet.

Mong:

What I've learned the past couple weeks is that Mong stays as much to himself as I do. He eats solo. Never really talks to anybody except Lester—which I've only seen two or three times. Some days he even just stays in the living room after wake-up call. All day. Even when it's time to eat. He just sits there, staring at the TV. Not even moving his position or flipping through the channels. And Jaden doesn't say anything to him either. Just leaves him alone. And so does everybody else. Nobody even asks any questions. Lately, I've been trying to figure out why it's so different for Mong. What, are people scared? Is it 'cause they think he's psycho and they don't wanna set dude off? Even the counselors? 'Cause that seems pretty messed-up, right? You shouldn't get no special treatment just because you're a psycho.

Lester still picks him up every other day too. He'll let himself in, wave to all us residents and Jaden, and then Mong will get up without a word and walk out the door with Les. At first I thought maybe they were going to an unusual psychologist. One specializing in the emotionally disturbed or something. But now I'm not so sure. For one thing, if you go to a psychologist, aren't you supposed to come back feeling better about yourself? 'Cause when Mong comes back he usually seems even more depressed or pissed off than when he left. Like this one time when he totally snapped on Reggie.

Jaden was in his office with Tommy when Lester dropped Mong off. And when Reggie asked him a simple question, if he was still gonna help out with dinner or not, Mong just totally flipped. He threw down his bag and leaped at Reggie, got him in some crazy sleeper hold and pulled him to the kitchen floor. And he kept saying the same thing over and over: "I could kill you! I could just kill you right now! Do you even understand that?"

We all just stood there watching. It was so weird seeing some skinny-ass Chinese kid on top of this big muscular black kid. But Reggie didn't even fight back at all. He just stayed quiet and laid there, stared straight ahead. Even when Mong finally let him go and stood up, grabbed his bag. All Reggie did was slowly reach for his own neck where Mong was choking him, and then he stood up carefully and went back to cooking dinner. He never even *looked* at Mong. The rest of us went back to what we were doing too.

I gotta say, man, there's something freakish about Mong.

I can't put my finger on it, but I been watching him lately. And it's more than just the fights he gets in or the nasty scars on his cheeks. There's something else. Like how depressed he seems and the way he keeps to himself even worse than me. And people walk on eggshells when he's around. Tommy just looks at the ground. Reggie and Demarcus don't have any jokes. Even Jaden acts different.

July 3

Tonight Jaden came up to me when I was washing the dishes and asked if I could join him in his office for a few minutes. I shrugged, dried my hands on the dish towel and followed him, thinking if maybe I was in trouble and what for. I was pretty sure I hadn't done anything.

Jaden keyed open the door, set down a bag and told me to have a seat. I watched him then key open the desk drawer, put a fat envelope into the petty-cash tin and close and lock it back up. He put the keys back on his side belt loop, where he always has them.

Watching him, though, I thought how easy it would be to swipe all that cash late one night and bury it out back until my time was up. Then I could buy whatever the hell I wanted when I was free. Like new hoop shoes from Foot Locker or some low-tops to roll in. That's another thing about me, by the way. I love getting new kicks. I take care of 'em too. Take a wet rag to the leather and wash the laces so they always seem like I just got 'em. And I always keep 'em in the box when I'm not rockin' 'em.

Anyways, I was already at the damn mall in my head when Jaden spoke up. "You've been here a full month now, bro," he said, leaning back in his chair, linking his fingers behind his head. "Did you know that?"

I shook my head and said I didn't, even though obviously I did 'cause of my journal.

"Well, you're a veteran now, Miguel. And I just wanted to bring you in here and get your status on things, know what I'm saying?"

I shrugged and looked at that spot on the wall again, the boomerang or cocoon or whatever. Now I had a feeling how this was gonna go down. I wasn't in trouble or nothin', dude just wanted to know how I *feel.* If me and Diego were watching this scene in some movie we'd be laughing for days at how mad gay it was. But I kept a straight face in front of Jaden.

He sat up, said: "Let's get it all out on the table, bro. You give me your honest take, and I'll give you mine, cool?"

I rubbed the back of my head and took a deep breath.

He kept quiet for a sec and then he set his hand on the desk and said: "You haven't really been mixing much with the rest of the fellas. Not that I've seen, anyway. Look, you don't have to befriend anybody for life in here, bro. But it makes it easier if you have someone to goof off with a little, maybe make fun of your counselor behind his back." He winked and reached out to smack my knee, smiling. "Right, bro?"

I shrugged.

"Any idea why you're isolating yourself?"

I had about a thousand ideas why I was isolating myself, mostly to do with how retarded everybody here was and how all they wanted to do was talk about peoples' shits or spit on you or hide meth in their damn shoes, but I didn't tell him any of that. Just shrugged again.

Jaden pulled my file out of a drawer and opened it up. He

ran his finger over a couple lines and said: "Jenny says you're still refusing to talk in therapy." He looked up at me. "Any idea why that is, bro?"

Something happened inside me as I watched him sitting there looking in my file. I sort of snapped. I don't even know why. I clenched up my fists and stared right back at him, not saying shit.

"Miguel?"

I was close enough that I could reach out and punch dude right in his pretty-boy face. Toss him out of his chair. Step on his neck like what happened to me in Juvi. It was a crazy feeling, too, 'cause I don't even really hate the guy that much. I just felt pissed off.

"Jenny's one of the top counselors in the entire system. Look, the only way to move past what happened back home—"

"What the fuck do you do here?" I interrupted.

His eyes got mad wide and he tilted his head a little, said: "Excuse me?"

"You bring people in here and talk and talk and talk. You open up their stupid-ass files and act like it has all the answers about 'em, and then you talk some more. But you don't know me, man. You don't know the first thing about who I am or where I come from."

Jaden leaned forward a little, nodding slow. He looked me in the eye a few seconds and then said: "You know what, Miguel? I think you're right."

"I *know* I'm right," I snapped back, waving his ass off.

"I *don't* know the first thing about you. I really don't." He closed my folder and put it on the desk. "I'd argue that nobody really knows anybody. Not even members of their own family. But I can promise you this, okay? I really wanna help, Miguel. Whatever that means. I wanna help."

50

I looked at him and then leaned back and crossed my arms. I started calming down, which pissed me off even more. I hated that something some damn counselor could say would make me calm down when I didn't even feel like it. I looked at the cocoon on the wall again and shook my head.

Jaden looked at where I was looking and then put his eyes back on me. "And I'm going to continue trying to help, Miguel. Every single day. And if you ever wanna come in here and talk about anything—seriously, anything. The books you're reading, basketball, girls, whatever. You come get me and we'll talk, okay?"

"Can I be dismissed?" I said.

Jaden looked at my file on his desk. Then he nodded and said: "Absolutely, bro. And I wanna thank you for talking with me tonight."

I got up and went toward the door, but he called out: "Miguel!"

I stopped, turned around. But I didn't really look at him.

"It's a huge burden is all I'm saying. What happened with you back home. I know you're a tough kid, Miguel. And you're smart, too. Even so, it's hard to carry all that weight around on your shoulders. Sometimes it's good to just talk to someone. Even if they're not as tough or smart as you."

"Can I be dismissed?"

He nodded and I went out.

I walked back into the kitchen. The dishes were already done, so I went to the bookshelf in the game room to look through the books, and right then somebody pulled into the driveway—I knew 'cause the headlights flashed through the curtains, lit up the shelf I was looking at. I turned around.

Demarcus went to the window and looked out at the driveway. "Les is bringin' in another newbie, son."

"Who?" Reggie said.

"Yo, he a *big* son of a bitch."

Tommy and Reggie went to the window too. But I stayed right where I was. The only thought going through my head was how I knew they were gonna throw new dude in *my* room. And how all my solo time was pretty much ancient history. I turned back to the books, listening to everyone talking all loud behind me.

Tommy said: "Dude, another black guy. How come we can't get a Caucasian for once?"

"Y'all never do nothin' wrong, that's why," Reggie said.

I pulled a random book off the shelf and turned around.

"White cats is too scared to do anything wrong," Demarcus said, tapping Tommy on the back of his head.

"Or maybe we just never get *caught*," Tommy said, pushing Demarcus's hand away. "You ever think about that?"

Reggie shot back: "Then why's your dumb ass standin' here right next to me, then? Explain me that shit, Socrates."

Everybody broke up except me. I was too busy thinking about what kind of buster was gonna be sharing my room, and how I was gonna have to tell him the rules for the room, like the light stays on as long as I want at night so I can read whatever book I'm reading.

The one I pulled off the shelf was called *The House on Mango Street*. I flipped it over and scanned the back to see what it was about. Jaden walked out of his office and made straight for the front door. Pulled it open. A couple seconds later Lester walked in with the new black kid in tow, and when I saw who it was I damn near dropped my book.

Rondell.

We looked right at each other for a sec, and then he looked down at the rug while Lester introduced him to Jaden.

After Lester waved to us and headed back to his van, Jaden took Rondell's bag from him and launched into the same spiel he'd given me on my first day—the one he apparently gives every damn person. "Rondell, huh? I like that name a lot, bro. It's unique. Ha ha! Listen, you wanna meet the guys now, or would you rather settle in for the night and do the whole introduction thing in the morning?"

Rondell didn't say anything back.

Jaden opened his file, flipped through it for a few seconds and then closed it back up. "Tell you what, Rondell," he said. "Why don't we just do it tomorrow, then. Start fresh and all that good stuff. Ha ha! Come on, I'll show you what room you'll be in and where you can stash your stuff."

I couldn't believe it, I was gonna be sharing a room with the same damn guy I had in Juvi.

Jaden walked back through the hall carrying Rondell's state-issued bag, full of his state-issued clothes, but before Rondell followed after him he looked up at me again and said: "Mexico."

I shook my head at his dumb ass for still calling me Mexico, but when he was a few steps by me I said: "Rondell."

I don't think his deaf ass heard me, though.

I stayed out in the game room for another hour or so, to give the kid some space. I watched Reggie destroy Tommy in foosball and Demarcus try to cook a frozen Hot Pocket over a burner with a spatula. When I finally made it back into my room Rondell was already curled up in his bed, snoring. Just like how he did back in Juvi. I had to put my pillow over my damn head just to fall asleep.

July 6

It didn't take long before I figured something out about me and Rondell: we're pretty much exact opposites in everything. Rondell's a musclehead and slow-looking, and I'm thin and fast. Rondell's basically allergic to books, and all I *do* in here is read. Rondell's a damn Bible thumper, and I think anything having to do with God is a fairy tale.

Sometimes when we talk I can spin Rondell around so bad his black face scrunches up and turns purple he's so confused. Like a couple days ago. I was minding my own business, reading my new book, *The Old Man and the Sea,* when Rondell strutted in our room, rapping: "I blow from the word go / Yo, check my flow, my show / I make dough while other punks cop fool's gold."

I looked up at his dumb ass, shaking my head, and tried to go back to my book. But it's basically impossible to concentrate on the words in your book when somebody raps as bad as Rondell.

"Yo, Mexico," he said, interrupting me again. That's pretty much all he does, by the way, is interrupt me from whatever I'm doing. "Yo, wha'chu readin'?"

I closed up shop on my book and sat up, the soles of my state-issued sneaks right there on my blue bedspread (Moms would kill me if I tried that back home). "A book, homey. You ever tried some crazy shit like that?"

"Like what?"

"Reading a book?"

A big grin came over Rondell's face and he went over to his nightstand, slid open the drawer. He held up a well-worn Bible and pointed at the cover: "This the only book I gotta read right here, Mexico. Every answer a human person might be lookin' for is right here in these pages. That's my word."

"I see it's been workin' pretty good for you so far."

An empty look went over his face. "Wha'chu mean?"

"I'm just sayin', Rondell. You get your answers from the Bible. I get mine from in my head. But we both ended up in this stupid-ass group home, right?"

Rondell shook his head and patted his Bible. "It's all part of God's plan, Mexico. You just gotta have faith in the word and let the spirit take you somewhere."

I rolled my eyes, said: "And why the hell do you call me that?"

"What?"

"Mexico."

Rondell shrugged.

"And why do you say 'what' after every single frickin' thing I say?"

Rondell sat there dumbfounded for a sec, and then he said: "Huh?"

"Forget it," I said, reaching for my book. It's basically impossible to have a conversation with a guy like Rondell. We might as well be speaking two different languages.

Rondell flipped open his Bible and pretended to read—though, as we all know by now, that was a straight lie.

I put down my book again and said: "First of all, man, I'm only *half* Mexican. My mom's white. Second of all, I was born in Stockton, California. *America.* Not Mexico. And third, I don't even speak Spanish. So your little nickname for me doesn't make a whole lot of sense, does it, partner?"

"I'm sayin'," Rondell said. "The whole world's right in these pages." He pointed at his open Bible, nodding, like he hadn't heard a word I just said. "I carry it with me every single place I go, Mexico. That's my word."

I stared at him, amazed.

We both went quiet for a few minutes. I turned back to

my book, and Rondell pretended to read his Bible. After a while, though, he closed the cover and said: "Hey, Mexico."

"Hey, Africa."

"You could read this whenever you want." He slid open his nightstand drawer and put the Bible back, slid it closed. "You don't even gotta ask or nothin'. Just grab it. I don't care none."

I got this weird feeling about Rondell after he said that. I actually felt sorry for him. Because as much as he gets mad sometimes or puts his shoe on your neck like he did with me in Juvi, I wondered if his whole life people had been making fun of him behind his back. For how dumb he is. And maybe people took advantage of him too. Like with money or getting him to do stuff that's illegal, stuff they wouldn't do themselves, and he just didn't know better. It actually made me feel pretty bad about life for a quick minute, and I stared at the rug by his feet.

When I finally looked up at him I said: "That's cool, man. About your Bible or whatever."

He smiled.

"But if you try to read this one, dawg, I'll kill you, 'cause I'm almost done and I wanna see what happens."

"Oh, you ain't gotta worry about that none," he shot back, shaking his head. "I only ever read my Bible. Not nothin' else."

I nodded at him. "Good."

"Good, what?"

"It works out, then."

"What does?"

Right then I decided Rondell wasn't such a bad guy. Even if he was dumb as hell and couldn't read a word and put all his simpleminded belief in a stupid thing like the Bible and called me an ignorant name like Mexico . . .

Still.

He wasn't as bad as some other people I've known.

July 8

Me and Rondell were sitting outside today, on the far cinder block, eating cheese sandwiches, when Mong came walking out of the house and sat on the block right across from us. He didn't say anything either, just posted there staring at me and smiling. Fingering the tooth around his neck. I stopped chewing mid-chew, looked back at the guy. Okay, dawg, I told myself. Here it is. The shit's finally gonna go down.

I looked at Rondell, who was concentrating his whole mind on eating his sandwich, and then turned back to Mong. "Wha'chu need, man?" I told him.

He laughed a little, kept his eyes stuck on me.

I shrugged, said: "Lemme know—"

"Why do you read all those books?" he interrupted.

I looked at him all confused. "What?"

At the time I didn't realize how I was saying to Mong exactly what Rondell always says to me. And how most of the time when you tell somebody "what" you're not really asking a question, you're just saying something while you try and think up something better you could say later.

Anyways, I'd just turned toward the house when Reggie and Demarcus came out and started walking into the backyard. But when they spotted Mong sitting with me and Rondell they stopped cold. They looked at each other. Then they turned around and went back inside.

"Those books," Mong said, staring me right in the eyes. Still smiling. "Why do you read them?"

I didn't know if his psycho ass was making fun of me

or what, so I just sat there a minute, thinking. I took another bite of sandwich, chewed it up and swallowed. I looked down at the second half and realized I didn't feel that hungry anymore. I was just about to wad it up in my plate to throw away when Rondell tapped me on the arm, said: "Hey, Mexico."

I looked up at him.

"You ain't gonna eat that second part?"

"Nah."

"Could I get it?"

I handed him the rest of the sandwich and the plate and he took a big-ass bite, sat there chewing and looking at Mong like he was just noticing him for the first time.

I turned back to Mong myself, told him my answer: "To see what happens." Then I shrugged, trying to think if I should've even answered him in the first place.

Mong didn't say anything back. He just stared at me, smiling, hardly even blinking.

"Why you wanna know?" I said.

But he didn't answer me. He just stood up and walked back toward the house.

I watched him open the door, slip back inside, close the door behind him. I stayed looking at the door for a few minutes, trying to figure out what the hell just happened. Like, was dude clowning me for reading? Look at the bike thief nerding out with all his stupid books! Or was he just such a psycho he didn't even know what he was saying anymore? Because who the hell would do that? Come up to somebody they don't even know and ask why they read books? It doesn't make no kind of sense, man.

I turned to Rondell shaking my head, said: "Yo, what's up with *that* guy?"

But Rondell just looked at me with a blank face, wadding up the plate I'd just given him, and told me: "Who?"

July 9

I woke up in the middle of the night, and when I opened my eyes there was Mong. He was standing over my bed again with his arms crossed, only this time he wasn't smiling.

"Jesus Christ," I said, flipping over so I could face him. But after the first couple seconds I realized I wasn't as spooked as the last time it happened. "What the hell you want *now*?" I told him.

When he uncrossed his arms and went to reach his right hand into his pocket I was sure he was going for a knife. Without thinking I bolted upright and swung for his face. Hard as I could. He ducked it, though, backed off holding his hands up.

"What the fuck!" I said.

"Calm down," he told me, and then I saw he didn't have a knife in his right hand, he had a folded-up piece of paper, which he tossed in my lap.

I picked it up, watching him the whole time. Slowly unfolded it. Looked down at the words. It was a letter from the president of all the San Jose group homes, addressed to Lester. It said the state was going to increase funding for the entire program, which would affect the sentence lengths of both current and future residents.

I looked up at Mong, my heart still beating all fast. He was just standing there with his arms crossed again, watching me read.

I went back to the letter. It said what Jaden was talking

about before, how current resident sentences would all go full term from now on, and in some cases they could even be extended for consistent misbehavior.

I looked at Mong, back at the paper.

It said with the extra resources they planned to increase the rehabilitation side of the program, including more one-on-one therapy sessions and educational and career counseling.

Pretty much the last thing I wanted was more damn therapy. I handed the letter back to Mong, said: "So?"

He folded it up and stuck it back in his pocket. "I'm leaving," he said. "One week from today."

"What's that got to do with me?"

He shrugged, peeked over at sleeping Rondell. "Maybe it's better with two people," he said, turning back to me.

I stared at him, confused as hell. I knew dude wasn't asking me to go with him. Last I heard we pretty much hated each other.

He crossed his arms again. "I'm asking you because I trust you."

My eyes straight bugged. "You *trust* me," I said.

He nodded. "I have a place we can get to in Mexico. On the beach. I have a ride for us. If you want, once we get down there we can go our separate ways."

I pictured him stabbing me in the back on a beach in Mexico, me falling to my knees, blood pooling all in the sand. "Nah, I'm good," I said, leaning back on my elbows, letting my head go against the wooden headboard. "I can't be doing all that."

"You can do anything you want," Mong said.

I shook my head, thinking about everything. The letter addressed to Lester. The extra therapy sessions and people's sentences. Mong standing above my damn bed again, only this time asking me to go on the run with him. "Nah, man," I said.

He smiled and kept staring at me.

There were a few seconds of quiet between us. I looked over at Rondell, who was still sound asleep. I looked at his Bible sitting there on his nightstand. Then I turned back to Mong and said: "I know how you could get money, though."

His smile got bigger. "We can get work in Mexico too," he said. "At this resort they have. And it's a different country, where nobody will know us."

"*You* could get work there," I said. "Not me."

Mong kept right on smiling, though. He pointed at me and said: "I'll give you three days to tell me if you're going." And then he turned and left the room.

"I just told you," I called after him. "I can't." But he was already out of my room.

I sat there shaking my head, trying to think. And then I heard the springs in Rondell's bed crunching as he rolled his big ass over. "You gotta take me with you, Mexico," he said.

I turned to look at the shape of him through the dark. "I thought you were asleep."

"Nah, Mexico. I been awake this whole time, that's my word." He went on his back and put his hands under his head, his big feet tenting his blankets way past where his bed left off. "I been in places like this since I can remember. I just don't wanna do it no more."

"I don't even think I'm going," I said.

"But if you do."

But if I do.

He didn't say anything else. He rolled over onto his stomach and immediately started snoring. I stayed awake awhile, though, letting Rondell's last line float around in my head some.

But if I do.

But if I do.

I put my hands under the back of my own head, like Rondell always does, and stared up at the ceiling. I pictured my mom's face when she drove me to Juvi. The way she kept looking in the rearview mirror, or at her side mirror, even though there weren't any cars around us. I pictured her eyes when she finally looked at me outside Juvi, just before the guards took me away. Sometimes the look in a person's eyes can tell you what they mean just as good as words. I never admitted this before, but I think I know what she meant when she looked at me. Even back then I did. It was relief. It was like me going was a big weight lifted off her shoulders. Like she'd been holding her breath underwater and she finally got to come up for air.

Maybe it'd be better if I went to damn Mexico, I thought, laying there across the room from snorin'-ass Rondell. Even if Mong stabbed me on the beach and I had to watch my blood go into the sand. Life for everybody else would probably be easier.

I remembered that first night back at the pad after the judge said my sentence. How I came in from me and Diego's room and saw my moms sitting on the couch in the living room, perfectly still. The TV was on, but she wasn't watching it—she was staring out the window. And when the light from the news show flickered over her face I could see tears going down her cheeks. They were streaming out from her eyes and rolling off her chin onto her shirt. And she wasn't wiping them off or nothin'. Just letting them do whatever, like she didn't even know it was happening.

Seeing her like that, man, it was like somebody shot me in

the damn stomach with a gun. My whole body went numb like I was dead. But I wasn't dead. I tiptoed back into me and Diego's room, climbed under my bed and curled up on my side on the floor. And that's where I fell asleep that night. Under the bed. The next morning I got up and took my shower and ate breakfast and went to the levee with my fishing pole and then when I came home I went right back under my bed and slept there again. I slept under my bed every night until it was time for Moms to take me to Juvi. I remember thinking how lucky I was Diego was away for that week. Or else he would've kicked me out from under the bed and told me I was acting like a little bitch. But at the time I seriously didn't feel like trying to be anything else.

Here's the thing: even if it would be for the best, me going with Mong to Mexico, even if it made it easier for my moms and everybody else in my family, I seriously don't think I can do it. I'd never be able to come back. Ever. And besides, shouldn't I have to stay here and suffer doing the time they gave me? Even if it goes the whole year and I gotta do two times as many counseling sessions? Shouldn't I have to pay for what I did? Wouldn't it be messed up if I just left the Lighthouse and Jaden and the sentence they gave me and went to another country to start over, like Mong said?

Still, though, I keep thinking.

But if I do.

July 16

On the night Mong decided we should bust out we tried to make like everything was perfectly normal. Only thing different was me and Rondell didn't change out of our street clothes when Jaden called for lights-out. We just climbed in bed and pulled the covers over our jeans and sweatshirts and dirty-ass kicks.

When Jaden came by for his nightly room check we closed our eyes up quick like we were already passed out. He walked in, did his normal circle where he checks everything off on a clipboard and then walked back out to get ready to leave for the night. Right after he left I heard Rondell snickering like a little girl.

"Shut the hell up, Rondell!" I whispered.

"I'm tryin'," he whispered back.

"Well, try harder. Put a pillow over your damn head or somethin'."

It's not like I was that freaked out or nervous or whatever, I just didn't want shit to go wrong before we even *did* anything.

Rondell did what I said, he put a pillow over his head, and for the next two hours we waited for Mong's signal (two loud finger snaps from the hall) fully dressed, bags packed, swiped screwdriver stashed between my two mattresses.

I laid there quietly, staring at the paint-chipped ceiling and thinking about stuff. Like my rowdy school cafeteria at lunchtime and me and Diego's secret fishing spot along the levee and riding Diego's dirt bike to the store for moms and my grandma's old arthritis hands patting down tortillas on the griddle in Fresno. I thought about the day Gramps had us out there in the fields from sunup to sundown, bent over picking berries. How after less than an hour I was so mad tired

I didn't think I could do it even ten more minutes. But somehow I made it through the rest of the day. All these random things, they just kept flashing through my mind, and I let 'em. But after a while this idea popped in my head: I bet when people get old there's only a couple actual moments they could look back on and say, Yo, that moment changed my life forever. And most of them probably aren't even the person's choice. Somebody gets hit by a car or gets fired from a job or wins the lottery or their pops gets blown to pieces by a grenade in some stupid war. But tonight was the opposite kind of moment. I was making a conscious choice. The second I broke out of the group home and started for Mexico, my life would be changed forever. And it would be because I *wanted* it changed. I knew I could never come back after this. They'd most likely throw me in *real* prison. And I heard some pretty bad things about that. Shit like you don't even wanna know, man.

Right in the middle of all my thinking I heard two loud snaps in the hall.

I jumped out of bed and scooped my bag. I turned to Rondell ready to make shit happen, but you wouldn't believe what I found: his crazy ass was actually asleep. No lie, dude was out cold, snoring and twitching, drooling on his damn mattress, probably dreaming about chillin' with one of the disciples.

I stood there for a sec trying to think what kind of fool could fall asleep right before he broke out of a damn group home and went on the run.

Only Rondell, man.

I reached down and shook him awake. "Come on, Rondell! Get up, man! We gotta go!"

But I'll give the guy this, he didn't need no transition time. He whipped off his covers, slid out his own bag and was pulling open the window over his bed before I could even get the screwdriver out from between my mattresses. He went right to work on the bars. We'd already unscrewed most of the bolts securing them to the house, so all he had to do was get the last two. When he did I helped boost his big ass through the window and watched him fall into the bushes outside. A couple neighborhood dogs started barking. I dropped both our bags out after him.

I paused for a sec at the window, and Rondell looked back up at me. "Ain't you comin'?" he said.

"Yeah," I said. "I just gotta do somethin' real quick. Go round the other side like we talked about. I'll meet you guys there."

Rondell nodded and took off with both our bags.

I replaced the bars on the window, redid the two bolts and closed the window back up. Then I snuck out of our room and down the hall toward the office with Jaden's keys.

About the Keys:

For the week since I told Mong me and Rondell would go with him, I'd been studying Jaden with his keys. Like I knew he had eleven keys on his key ring, and that he wore the key ring on his side belt loop. I knew the five keys with yellow rubber at the top were Lighthouse keys. I knew the two I had to get, 'cause one was the longest and one was the shortest, and that he didn't use either one after dinner, when the night watch came on. And I knew the only time he took off his key ring was when he played one of us in foosball.

That's why after dinner tonight I went up to him in front of all the other guys in the living room and said: "Yo, Jaden. I bet you couldn't get with me on no foosball."

He looked up at me shocked 'cause I'd never asked to play a game with *nobody* in the house, much less a counselor.

And then he got this grin on his face that I knew meant he thought I was finally coming out of my shell, which made me wanna laugh in dude's face.

But I didn't laugh.

He set down his clipboard and told me: "Wait, did I just hear that right, bro? You saying you want some of *this*?"

"You ain't all that," I said, playing the role, even though whenever Jaden talked shit it just came off like he was trying way too hard and actually made me feel sort of bad for the dude.

"Hey, Tommy," he said, standing up. "Ring the bell, bro. School's about to be in session."

Everybody followed us to the foosball table and Jaden took off his keys, like he always does, and set them on the counter right behind him. We both grabbed the duct-taped handles and Tommy dropped the ball. Our dirt-stained men twirled and stopped on a dime and the rusted metal rods slid in their holsters all smooth and the sound of the ball smacking the wall was like the pop of a BB gun. As we went at it I thought of how many kids before me had slid their goalie in front of this goal. How many kids before me had stood in my exact spot, playing their counselor, while the other residents talked head on the side, waiting their turn. It made me feel like a straight-up cliché, man. Which happens sometimes. I'll find myself doing something that I know every older person in the damn world has already done, like Diego and his boys, and all the kids younger than me will eventually end up doing too. When shit like that hits it makes me think there's pretty much no reason to be alive, because everything you can or will do has already been done by at least ten thousand other people already. And if you're not original then what the hell are you alive for, man? I know, I know, you're probably thinking I'm not looking at shit right and that I should go borrow Rondell's Bible or whatever to see how God says to do it, but I don't even care, man. That's just me. I only really wanna spend the energy it takes to be alive if I'm original. That's how my mind thinks.

Anyways, it was a pretty close game, but I made sure I lost in the end. Jaden slapped my hand and told me it was a pleasure doing business and then Rene took my spot and Tommy dropped the ball again. I waited almost till the end of the game before I swiped the two yellow keys I needed from the ring and put it back real quick. Reggie saw me do the whole thing, but all he did was laugh and shake his head. And I knew he wouldn't rat on me. At least, not right away. People don't really rat on each other in a group home unless it's something that directly affects them.

Jaden played a few more guys and then it was supposed to be my turn again, but I said somebody else could take my spot.

"What's the matter, bro?" Jaden said. "You a little nervous of me now?"

"Nah," I said, fingering his two keys in my pocket.

"You sure?" Jaden said. "You look kind of pale, bro."

I shook my head, said: "Nah, how 'bout this. We could maybe play again tomorrow night. I guarantee you won't beat me tomorrow."

"You bros hear that?" Jaden said, looking at all the guys. "Miguel loses eleven–eight and now he's throwing around guarantees. All right, then, you got yourself a deal. Tomorrow night."

Everybody made their little jokes about my challenge and then Rene took my spot. Tommy dropped the ball and the plastic foosball men started spinning all around again.

Back to the Escape Part:

Anyways, I peeked in the living room, found the night-watch guy lounging in front of the TV, sipping coffee from a thermos. Popping chips in his mouth one at a time and wiping his greasy fingers on his pants. I could smell weed coming off his clothes too. And his eyes were all dopey.

Get past the fat stoner, I told myself, and I'm a free man again. Just the thought of being able to go wherever, whenever made butterflies come into my stomach.

It isn't until you're sentenced to a place like this, by the way, that you can know what kind of busters they got working night shift. This mustache-faced fool had a big-ass beer belly, a tight Batman T-shirt with sweat stains under both arms and a damn feathered mullet. He didn't take his eyes off the TV even once the whole time I was watching him. He was just giggling at some old episode of *America's Funniest Home Videos*. Still, man, it wasn't gonna be easy getting past the living room without him catching me in his peripheral.

Another couple minutes went by before I decided I had to use my mind on him. I squinted my eyes up real tight and thought crazy hard and after only a minute or two something happened: the guy bent over choking on a chip. Coughing and pounding himself on the chest with the inside of his fist and sucking down coffee to try and wash it down.

I snuck by easy, keyed open the office door with the long key and quietly pulled it shut behind me. Locked it. Pulled out the short one to open the drawer where Jaden keeps the petty cash. And there it was, man. Right inside the petty-cash tin. Didn't have to go searching or nothin'. The fat leather envelope—full of cash for Alcatraz and that fancy restaurant Jaden told us about—was just sitting there on top, waiting for me. It had the name "Lighthouse" on the front and the house address and phone number. I unzipped the zipper and looked inside. Flipped through the bills. Felt the weight. I counted it real quick: $750. I'd never held so much damn paper in my life.

I zipped it back up, shoved the whole thing in my jeans pocket and stepped to the window. Pulled it open, unscrewed all the bolts on the bars and tossed everything into a flower bed outside. I was just about to climb out myself when I turned and peeped Jaden's desk. I stared there for a few seconds and then looked over at the spot on the wall I always looked at whenever I sat in here, the cocoon or whatever. I thought about how I'd never see it again. It's so weird how a little thought like that, about a cocoon shape on a wall, can make your entire body feel all like Jell-O.

I told myself I should go on already, pull myself through the window and be out, but something inside my head was stuck.

I hurried back over to the desk, pulled open a different drawer and riffled through all the resident files looking for mine. I found it, yanked it out and tucked it under my arm, closed the drawer. I stood there for a few seconds, thinking, and then I opened the drawer back up, riffled through the files again and pulled Mong's and Rondell's, too.

Right then there were footsteps outside the office door and the sound of keys rattling.

I slid closed the drawer quietly, tucked all our files in my bag and damn near dove headfirst through the window, into the flower bed. I got to my feet next to the window bars and ducked around the side of the house to meet Mong and Rondell.

"Where were you?" Mong said when he saw me. "We almost just left!"

I pulled the petty-cash envelope out of my pocket and held it up.

He stared at it a sec and then a look of understanding came over his face and he nodded.

"What's that?" Rondell whispered.

"The petty cash," I whispered back, peeking around the corner for the night-watch guy. But he wasn't there. The window was completely empty.

"The what?" he said.

"*Money*, Rondell! American currency!"

"Oh, damn. Good thinkin', Mexico."

"Hello?" the night-watch guy finally yelled from the window. He couldn't see us, though, and ducked his head back in the house. The front-porch light came on, and more dogs started barking.

"Let's go!" Mong said, pulling his hood over his head.

Me and Rondell pulled our hoods up too, and we all took off sprinting down the street.

Before we rounded a corner I looked back over my shoulder and saw the night-watch guy bumbling into the road in front of the house. But he didn't chase after us, he just stood there with his cell phone pinned against his ear, probably calling the cops.

And the house looked so different from the outside, like you'd never know it was a group home full of bad kids unless you were sentenced to be there. But at the same time it stood out too. It was faded yellow with black trim while all the other houses around it were white or gray or beige.

Jaden wasn't lying, I thought, as me and Rondell followed Mong down a side road and I turned my eyes forward again. I hadn't really thought about it, but our pad really *did* look like a lighthouse.

We sprinted through the streets of San Jose in our black sweatshirts, hoods up, hands all sharp like we were competing in the damn summer Olympics. We heard sirens in the distance as Mong led us through a couple dark weed-infested alleys, over a narrow wooden bridge, through a fenced-off construction site, down a long empty boulevard and into a big mall parking lot. We zipped past a few sleeping cars and ducked behind a trash Dumpster. Threw our bags down and bent over gasping for air and laughing. Hearts beating in our throats.

There probably wasn't anybody following us once we cut out of our own neighborhood, but what the hell, man: if you're gonna break outta some place like a group home you might as well break out running, right? Plus our adrenaline was going like crazy.

I pulled my hood off when I caught my breath and Rondell did the same, but Mong kept his up. And he couldn't seem to catch his breath at first, or stop coughing.

"You all right?" Rondell asked him after a minute or so.

Mong looked up at us and smiled. "*Of course* I'm all right," he said. "I'm free."

When he finally got his breath he reviewed what was supposed to happen next again—though by this time I pretty much had it memorized. He'd gone over it with us every single lunch for the past five days, outside on the far cinder block. How his cousin would show up in her red Acura and drive us all the way down to the Mexican border. How some guy he knew from Juvi would pick us up from there and take us to this resort near Rosarito. How we could get work there right away, on the local fishing boats, live for mad cheap and meet all kinds of tourist girls from everywhere in the world.

While he was talking I thought in my head how weird it was that some Chinese kid knew ten times more about Mexico than I did. And I was supposedly *from* there. Or at least my family. That shit didn't seem right to me.

"Soon," Mong told Rondell, "you guys will be living brand-new lives on the most perfect beach in all of Mexico."

"And you too," Rondell said.

Mong spit in the bushes and turned his eyes on *me* this time. Only me. "Yeah," he said, that crazy smile he gets slowly coming over his face. "And me too."

July 16/July 17

We've been waiting for Mong's late-ass cousin all the way into the next day. Like three punk little kids waiting on Santa Claus with a plateful of cookies. Our backs up against the dirty-ass trash Dumpster, butt cheeks falling asleep, hardly talking 'cause we hardly even know each other. I keep looking at Mong, wondering if he even *has* a cousin. Or if he just made the whole thing up to get us to go on the run with him so he can stab me in the back when I'm sleeping.

After the first hour I got so pissed off just sitting here I said: "Yo, Mong!"

He didn't even look at me, though. Just kept staring straight in front of him and said: "She's coming."

Then the next couple hours I got mad paranoid. Like the first time Diego smoked me out at the levee. I swore every set of car tires I heard on the street was the cops scouring the neighborhood looking for us. I even held out my hands at one point and couldn't believe how much they were shaking. Like I was some kind of tweaker coming down from a three-day run.

After that I got pissed off again and spent my time brainstorming what I would do if ol' girl *never* showed. Like maybe I could hitch a ride down to Mexico on my own. Or up to Canada. Or across to Stockton, where I could live on the levee and Diego could visit me every day and bring me scraps of food. I even thought maybe I could sneak back into the

Lighthouse and pretend like I was there the whole time, they just didn't see me.

"Mong, man," I said as soon as the morning started chasing off night and the sky changed to lighter.

"Don't worry" was all he said back, though. And still he didn't look at me. Just reached up to touch his brown tooth necklace.

Rondell, on the other hand . . . Man, that dude hasn't gone through *none* of these emotional ups and downs during our wait. Wanna know why? 'Cause about twenty minutes after we got here, homey passed his ass out cold, head hanging all forward, mouth open. One thing I've learned about Rondell is he can catch Z's pretty much anywhere, anytime. In any position. Maybe the bigger a kid you are, the more you gotta close up shop.

And Mong just keeps peeking his shaved head around the Dumpster every ten minutes or so, to make sure we don't miss his cousin's car. All night he's been doing that shit, but still there's no sign of this supposed cousin.

At this point, man, I'm so pissed and confused I'm not even pissed and confused anymore. I'm just sitting here writing every little thing down in my journal, like the judge said for me to do. Though I doubt me writing about busting out from a group home is what his old ass had in mind.

July 17—more

Hours and hours went by and there was still no sign of Mong's cousin. And when it got to be past ten, and all the stores started opening and the parking lot started filling up with cars, Mong finally went off to find a pay phone. I wasn't even pissed or paranoid anymore, I was just mad loopy from having stayed up a whole night leaning against a trash bin thinking about what was gonna happen next.

Soon as Mong left I reached into Rondell's bag for my new book, *Of Mice and Men,* thinking maybe I could try reading a little. Even though I knew I wouldn't be able to concentrate.

The only problem was Rondell woke up while my hand was still deep in his bag. We stared at each other for a few seconds and I laughed and said: "Well, look at this, Rondell. Somebody just got caught with their damn hand in the cookie jar."

I figured he'd have a little something to say about me stashing all the books I'd swiped from the Lighthouse in *his* bag. But he didn't. The thought probably never even crossed his mind. All he did was reach in right after me and pull out *his* book, the Bible, and open it up so he could pretend like he was reading just the same as me.

What Happens When You Get So Damn Bored You Can't Even Think Straight:

I swear to God I tried to concentrate on what was happening with the characters I was reading about, but after a while I couldn't help myself. I was so tired and confused about what was gonna happen next I just wanted something to happen now. So I turned to Rondell and said: "Yo, how's that workin' out for you, homey?"

"What?" he said, looking up at me.

"Staring at a bunch of words when you ain't got no clue what they say?"

Rondell closed his Bible up slowly, keeping a finger on the page he was at. "Wha'chu tryin' to say, Mexico?"

"Nothin', man," I said. "You just always got that damn Bible open, and I know you can't read for shit."

Rondell looked at me confused as hell for like ten seconds.

Then his face went serious and he lunged for me, grabbed my neck in his huge right paw and squeezed. "Who says I couldn't read!" he yelled.

I tried to answer but I couldn't breathe, much less make a sound. I clamped onto his thick black arm and tried to push it away but I couldn't budge him.

"I could too read!" he shouted.

I squirmed and kicked and tried to bite, but I couldn't get loose. All the blood rushed to my face, my eyes damn near bugging out of my head. "Okay," I mouthed without sound, scared he might take shit too far and choke me to death. "Okay, okay, okay, okay, okay."

He let go of my neck, but continued staring at me with this intense look.

I gasped for breath and reached up to feel my numb neck, the thick dents his fingers left in the skin. "Goddamn, Rondell!" I shouted, punching him in the arm as hard as I could. "You almost choked my ass to death!"

"You was tellin' lies, Mexico," he said, hardly registering the punch.

I stretched my neck and opened and closed my jaw. "Jesus, man!" I didn't know he'd get *that* stressed about me saying he couldn't read. It wasn't like I was telling dude the end of some movie he didn't watch yet. He knew he couldn't read.

He kept on staring at me.

I put my eyes on the asphalt under my feet and took a couple deep breaths to pull myself together. There was an ant trying to carry off some kind of crumb that was three times as big as his dumb ass. He kept dropping it, picking it up and moving it a few inches, then dropping it again. I shook my head and looked back at Rondell. "Look, man," I said, trying to calm the guy down, "I didn't mean you couldn't *read* read. I was just sayin' the Bible's hard to interpret. People study that shit their whole lives and still don't get what it says."

" 'Cause I could read," he said, opening his Bible back up. "You shouldn't tell rumors about people when they can read, Mexico. That's how people get a beat-down."

"You just heard me wrong, Rondell. I didn't say—"

"See that sign over there?" he said, pointing to the lit-up store sign a few yards to our right. "I could read them words just fine, Mexico. It says, 'The' and 'Gap.' "

I nodded my head and said, "All right, Rondell. You can read, then. That settles it." I picked up my book again, hoping we were done, but we weren't.

He stared at the side of my face for a while and then said: "I could read them two words like it wasn't nothin', Mexico. 'The Gap.' You shouldn't tell rumors about people that ain't true."

"All right," I said. "Jesus Christ, you can read, okay?"

"The Gap," he said again, under his breath.

I looked up at the sign again, and then at Rondell. "Got it," I said.

The sign actually said "Old Navy," but I didn't feel like getting into it with the dude anymore. He was too frickin' strong and high-strung to argue with about something that didn't even matter. What the hell did I care if he was a damn illiterate or not? I was just trying to have a conversation.

I stared at my book for a minute or so, making like I was already back into the story, but when I looked up Rondell was still mad-dogging me. Over his shoulder, I could see Mong making his way back. *"Finally,"* I said. "Yo, here comes Mong, Rondell. I sure hope he tracked down his damn cousin, don't you?"

But Rondell wasn't having it. He stayed staring at me and held up his Bible, said: "Besides, Mexico, when it comes to the Bible you don't gotta read it like no regular book. You just open up the cover and *it* reads *you*. And you just know what you gotta do."

I closed my book and tossed it back in Rondell's bag. "Look, Rondell," I said. "I'm sorry about what I said, okay? I really am. But will you please just shut the fuck up already? You're driving me crazy."

Rondell gave me a blank look for a couple seconds, and then he said: "Wha'chu tryin' to say, Mexico?"

All I could do was cover my face with both hands and take a long deep breath. And when I looked up again, Mong was standing in front of us, nodding.

"She's coming," he said.

July 17—more

About four hours later, a red Acura pulled into the mall parking lot, and this hipster-looking Asian girl stepped out and shielded her eyes against the sun as she looked around.

"There she is," Mong said, and we threw our bags over our shoulders and ducked out from behind the Dumpster.

At the car, Mong's cousin held up her hand for us to stop and said: "All right, nobody gets in without telling me their full name, first and last."

"Miguel Castañeda," I said, saluting her.

"Rondell Law," Rondell said, saluting her the same as I just did. "Gots two *L*s at the end of the 'Rondell' part, ma'am." He turned and looked at me all proud, like he was some sort of damn spelling-bee champ.

"Okay, two things," she said, pulling off her sunglasses.

"First, nobody I'm driving calls me ma'am. It makes me feel like an old lady. I'm just plain Mei-li. Mei-li Chen." She spelled her first name out for us, dash and everything, then she turned to Mong and said: "Second. Cousin, look, I'm sorry I'm late. But I had to really think about this, 'cause I'm not so sure it's on the up-and-up."

"I told you—"

Mei-li put her hand up to cut Mong off. "But I think I figured out a compromise. You're just gonna have to trust me, okay?"

Mong gave her back a blank stare.

"Mong," she said, all long and drawn-out, tilting her head to the side. She reached out and touched his brown tooth necklace. "You still have it."

They looked at each other for a sec, and then Mong looked away.

"Mong," she said, "are you gonna trust me?"

He shrugged.

"Okay. Good." She looked at me and Rondell and smiled perfect white teeth.

Mei-li:

I watched the girl put her sunglasses back on and fumble with her car keys. Watched her push a few strands of hair out of her face with the back of her hand. And, man, I gotta state it for the record: Mei-li was probably the hottest hipster Asian chick you could ever meet. She was around nineteen or twenty with short choppy green and black hair and big round eyes. She had a silver eyebrow ring and wore a skull-and-bones necklace, a white wife-beater and black Dickies with a chain going from her wallet to her belt. There were two Chinese characters tattooed on the inside of her left wrist and one on her shoulder.

With most girls who dressed like that I just figured they were witches who might cast a mad medieval spell on your ass, but with Mei-li it was different. I bet you could shave ol' girl's head completely bald and dress her ass in garbage bags and she'd still be fine as hell.

She slipped into the driver's seat, pulled closed her door. As Rondell climbed into the backseat I turned to Mong, who'd been watching me stare down his cousin the whole time. "What?" I said.

He didn't say anything back, though. Just looked at me for a couple more seconds like his old psycho self and then ducked into the other front seat.

I waved dude off and looked around the parking lot, at all the people going in and out of cars and stores and walking with shopping bags full of brand-new stuff. I saw this group of kids around our age carrying skateboards. They were laughing and pointing at one kid sipping on a big McDonald's Coke. You'd probably think it made me feel bad about myself. Because they weren't running from the cops. They were just out in the open, laughing, having a good time. And maybe it *did* make me feel a little bad. But mostly I just felt excited. Like me, Mong and Rondell were getting away with some bank robbery or something. And nobody knew. Like we were outlaws from back in the Wild West days. Riding out of town on horses, toward Mexico, with all the money.

It's how we were different from other people.

Original.

I slid into the seat behind Mong's cousin and closed the door. Mei-li turned the key in the ignition and some punk music started blaring out of the speakers, but she only lowered the volume a little as she put the car in reverse and backed out of the parking space.

"All right, boys!" she shouted over the screeching guitar solo. "Here we go!"

We got out of the parking lot okay, and Mei-li used her blinker and moved us onto the main road all safe and sound, but when we got up to where you could merge onto the freeway she didn't take the on-ramp going south like she was supposed to, toward Mexico. She got on the one going *north*!

Me and Mong both whipped our heads around, watched the southbound on-ramp fade into the distance.

"Mei!" Mong shouted, turning to her.

"Oh, by the way," she said, lighting a cigarette, not looking back at Mong, "I'm taking you guys to Mexico. Just not yet. That's the part where you're supposed to trust me. First we're going to Guerneville, up past San Francisco, so Mong can see his *gung gung*." She rubbed Mong's shoulder—even though he seemed crazy pissed—and glanced at me and Rondell in the rearview.

I was so shocked it felt like my entire body went numb.

"This is shit, Mei!" Mong shouted, his eyes looking like he could kill somebody. And then he turned and stared straight ahead.

Mei-li pulled her hand off Mong's shoulder and blew her smoke out the window. She looked at the side of his face and said: "He knows how sick you are, babe. He's worried. It's the least we can do if you really plan on running off to a whole other country."

Mong didn't say anything else, just kept staring ahead, and after a few seconds a little smile actually came onto his face—the one he does where his mouth forms a regular smile, but his eyes look totally empty, like he's thinking about something psycho. He picked at the seat belt Mei-li had made him put on and didn't even turn to look at his cousin.

I was pissed too. I thought we were going straight to Mexico, where my brand-new life was about to start. Like a second chance. A do-over. But at the same time I wasn't as stressed as Mong. I figured we'd still get there eventually—long as we kept ducking the cops. And how much did cops even care about group-home kids anyway? They probably had bigger things to worry about, like murders and rapes and terrorists sneaking onto airplanes. But more than anything I was just confused about this "gung gung" person and what Mong's cousin meant about Mong being sick.

"Here's the deal," Mei-li said, her eyes back on the road now. "I know you guys aren't *all* on weekend pass. Three at one time? All of you hiding behind a Dumpster like fugitives? Uh-uh. I'm not *that* naïve. I have a boyfriend who's cheated on me three times. Sadly, I've been made aware that the world's made up of mostly BS."

Mei-li shook her head. She ejected the CD we'd been listening to and slipped in a different one. "Anyway, I figure since I'm doing you guys a solid by picking you up, aiding and abetting and all that, it's not too much to ask for a little something in return. Mong here sees his *gung gung*, spends a few quality hours with him, maybe sits down for a nice dinner, then we turn around and head for Mexico. Simple as that."

The car went quiet for a few minutes as Mei-li merged over a couple lanes and onto a different freeway. I looked at Mong sitting there, smiling, and tried to think what Mei-li meant about him being sick. He was little, yeah, and he had those nasty scars on his cheeks, but dude seemed strong and scrappy as hell. I should know since I'm the one who fought him my first day.

I turned to Rondell. Guy was out cold again, baby Afro pressed all up against the window, mouth wide open. I couldn't blame him this time, though. We were all tired after sitting against a damn Dumpster for an entire night.

Then I looked out the window, at all the cars driving next to us. I thought how weird it was that none of the drivers—not the guy in the suit or the old man with giant sunglasses or the guy with the backwards hat or the fat woman eating a bag of chips—knew us three were on the run. That once we went to Mexico we could never come back to this freeway again for the rest of our lives. We could only drive on Mexican freeways.

I pulled out my journal and pen and started writing about everything I was thinking.

Mei-li saw me scribbling away in her rearview and said: "Wait, Miguel, don't tell me you're a writer."

I looked up at her and shrugged, said: "I guess so."

"I *love* writing," she said back. "I took a class last semester with this crazy old hippie, Professor Weltzer. He was funny, made everybody call him Rick. Anyway, what do you write? Poems? Short stories? Screenplays?"

I shrugged again. "Nah, I'm supposed to do this journal thing for some counselor. But I just put whatever comes in my head."

"That's so interesting," she said. And then this excited look came over her face and she said: "Hey, maybe if I tell you stuff, maybe one day you'll write a story about me!"

"I probably could," I said, though I didn't really get how she meant.

"I would love that," she said. "Nobody's ever written a story about me before." Her face went into a big smile as she checked her side mirror and changed lanes to get around this little Indian dude in an old beat-up truck.

I looked up at Mong, who was still staring straight ahead with his crazy blank look. It was like he was so pissed off he couldn't even hear what we were saying. I wondered why I wasn't as mad as him. Us not going straight to Mexico was happening to me, too. I almost felt like a sellout for not being madder.

Mei-li turned down her music some, said: "I guess the first thing you're wondering is why I'm still with my boyfriend, right?" She pulled in a drag and blew her smoke out at the roof. "After he cheated on me, I mean."

I looked at her in the mirror.

"Wait, aren't you gonna write it?"

"Oh, right," I said, and I looked down at my journal and wrote how she had a boyfriend that messed around on her. I didn't know why I was supposed to write everything, but I could tell she liked thinking I was a writer, so I decided to be one.

"Look," she said, "what I've come to realize over the past year is that life's not as black-and-white as some people would like to believe it is. That's something you should maybe put about me. For example, lots of girls say if a guy ever cheated on them they'd end the relationship right there on the spot. But it's different when it actually happens to you. Besides, I *did* break up with Jay the first time. But he kept calling me and leaving these long messages about how sorry he was and how much he missed me. He sent flowers and cards and boxes of candy. After a few weeks I picked up one of his calls, let him convince me it was a good idea to meet for coffee. We went to a Starbucks down the street and we talked and cried and shared a piece of carrot cake and then talked and cried some more. The next night we met at the theater and saw a movie. It was an awful romantic comedy, but we couldn't stop laughing. Two nights after that we went to dinner for my birthday. Then I realized we'd just sort of gotten back together—without ever saying we were getting back together. Know what I mean?"

I nodded, but she didn't look back at me. I didn't *really* know what she meant, but I decided I could figure out that part later. For now I just had to write everything down.

"By the time it happened a second and third time I was totally jaded about relationships in general. Besides, I'm transferring to UCSD at the end of the summer. It's not like I ever saw Jay and I getting married and having babies and doing the whole white-picket-fence thing. We're just passing the time together. And sometimes it's just easier when you have another person, you know? When you're not alone."

She pulled in another drag and looked at Rondell in the rearview mirror. Then she looked at me. "God, that sounds so sad, doesn't it, Miguel?"

"I guess so," I said, though I was too busy writing to really think about it.

"But maybe that's what growing up is. I mean, first they take away Santa Claus and the Easter Bunny. Then they shatter the idealized vision you have of your parents. And finally they come looking for you! 'Hey, little Asian girl: You know this life you were leading? The one you always thought was so special? Well, actually it's not that special at all. Actually you're just a lonely, flawed person like everybody else. You'll have some good times and you'll have some bad times, but mostly you'll just have a lot of boring times. Mostly your days will just be painfully uneventful.' Hey, maybe if you boil it all down, Miguel, *that's* what life is. Uneventful."

She paused for a couple seconds, thinking about what she'd just said, and then she told me: "You could maybe have one of your characters say that if you want. You have my permission."

"That's cool," I told her back, still writing.

After I wrote the word "permission" I shook out my cramping hand.

Mei-li caught my eyes in the rearview and said: "What about you, Miguel? I wanna know, how do *you* see the world?"

I looked back down at my journal, at all Mei-li's words I'd just written down, and I shifted in my seat. I wanted so bad to come up with something just as deep, something that would impress Mei-li and show her how smart I could be. But nothing was coming into my head.

"I don't even know," I finally said, shifting in my seat again. "But maybe when somethin' really bad happens in your life . . . maybe then you wish you could make it go back to being boring." I stared at the back of her headrest and pictured my moms looking at me that last time, and the guards at Juvi, waiting, and my bro Diego holding open the door of the fridge, pulling out the milk. I cleared my throat, said: "Maybe boring isn't so bad compared to other stuff that could happen."

Mei-li nodded as she put out her cigarette. "I think that's true, Miguel," she said. "I think that makes a whole lot of sense."

The car went quiet for a while as she sat there thinking. Rondell almost choked on his own breath and opened his eyes for a sec. But all he did was shift his head around and fall right back to sleep. Mong was still staring ahead like a zombie.

Mei-li's face looked sort of sad in the rearview, like she was remembering something from her past too. I wondered why she'd just told me so much about herself. I didn't mind or anything, I'd just never had somebody do that before. Especially a girl.

Then she sighed and said: "Sometimes I wonder if growing up isn't the saddest thing that can happen to a person."

July 17—more

Mei-li drove us on the 280 for what seemed like hours. Past San Jose State and Kelley Park. She rolled down her window as we cruised through Felt Lake, then Crystal Springs Reservoir near where my moms grew up. Traffic slowed as we got into lower San Francisco near the airport. And in the actual city it became so thick I could've hopped out and walked faster.

After a long stretch without any talking, Mei-li turned down her stereo again and looked at me in the rearview. "Hey, Miguel," she said. "I hope I don't come off as bitter in your story. I'm really not. I still believe in 'true love' and 'meant to be' as much as anybody else. Maybe more."

We caught eyes in the mirror and she said: "Make sure I don't seem so bitter, okay?"

"Okay," I said. It'd been so long since we talked I was surprised she was still thinking about that.

For some reason right then I wondered what it'd be like if *I* was her boyfriend. And not that punk who cheated on her. I tried to think of me up there in the front seat with her, where Mong was. Or maybe even driving. Her hand on the inside of my knee as I shifted gears. Or kissing on my ear. I'm not gonna lie, I felt shit getting all hyped in my jeans, so I shifted around some. Made sure nobody could peep my situation.

Sometimes I seriously don't get how a guy who has a fine girlfriend like Mei-li, or some of the girls Diego gets with, could even *look* at other girls, much less mess around. Staring at the back of Mei-li's head, her short green and black hair, I tried to think for the first time about the girl's side of things when it came to Diego. But it made me feel pretty bad about shit, and I don't like feeling bad when it comes to anything Diego-related, so I put the whole thing out of my head.

Mei-li looked at Mong—who was still staring straight ahead in his trance—and then at me in the rearview. "Hey, Miguel, since we're in all this traffic—I mean, we're not getting anywhere anytime soon, I don't know—how 'bout if I tell you my all-time favorite story about true love. From all the way back in China. Maybe you could even write *this* story someday." She turned around and looked at me.

"That's cool," I said, and I got my pen ready, all happy she was gonna tell me more.

"Cool," she said, excited. "I'll talk slow so you can write it all down. By the way, I don't know how this drive became 'sponsored by love' or whatever. I know guys don't really like talking about this stuff as much, right?"

I shrugged. "I don't care that much."

She smiled, said: "Writers are different, I think. You guys are so much more sensitive."

I shrugged again and looked down at my journal. But inside it felt kind of nice what she said about me.

Mei-li turned back around and rolled up her window, then she turned off the music completely.

Mei-li's Story About True Love:

"Once upon a time," she started, "years after things started changing in China, there was a beautiful and talented young singer in Shanghai. She was half Chinese, half Vietnamese. As a child this girl won lots of little competitions all around the city. Almost every one she entered. And as she got into her teens, she only got better. Everyone who knew her, especially her own family, believed she was destined to lead a special life."

Mong turned to his cousin and glared at her.

Mei-li shrugged and said: "Come on, Mong, it's such a beautiful story."

Mong shook his head and stared straight ahead again.

She slipped another cigarette from her pack, lit it with the car lighter, pulled a drag and let her smoke out slow. "Anyway," she continued, glancing at Mong and then turning back to the freeway. "Only a few miles away a handsome young man had just returned home to China from America, where he'd attended law school. His ambition was to find a beautiful and intelligent wife and start a family of his own. The man was the only son of one of the most respected families in all of China. But he was shy. Much too shy to meet women on his own. He could only do it through a matchmaker. So his mother called upon the most popular one in the city. The problem was the young man was even more picky than he was shy. He rejected the first twenty-three women the matchmaker brought for him to meet—meaning he rejected their families, too. Remember, this is China we're talking about. He declared he would rather be alone forever than marry someone he didn't love body and soul. Just as he was about to give up hope, the matchmaker and his mother talked him into meeting one last girl. A beautiful young singer.

"The young man met the girl in a crowded noodle shop in the middle of Shanghai and fell instantly in love. There was only one problem: the girl was still young, eighteen, and much more self-centered than most Chinese girls. Her promising singing career was all that interested her. After arguing with her mother and father for two straight days, she rejected the young man's proposal. He and his family were outraged, but did he let this rejection discourage him? Not for a second, Miguel. He knew the girl was the only one he could love. Ignoring the pleas of the matchmaker and his mother to continue meeting other women, he wrote the girl letters. Every single day, without fail, for over two years."

Me and Mei-li locked eyes in the rearview as she stubbed

out her cigarette on the top of a Starbucks cup, slipped the butt in the little drinking hole.

I stopped writing for a sec and thought of my parents' story. Or at least what Diego *told* me their story was. The only reason they got married was 'cause my pop got Moms pregnant. They were eighteen and sixteen when they walked down the aisle in Vegas, told each other "I do." My pop rockin' hair halfway down his back and a full beard. Premilitary. A hippie Mexican. Mom's white stomach already ballooning out. They'd only known each other for seven months. My pop once told us at the dinner table it was a case of "slumming gone too far." Not exactly the true-love story Mei-li was talking about.

"So he writes her these letters," Mei-li went on, lighting another cigarette. "And the whole time he never so much as *looks* at another woman. After eighteen months of constantly hearing her mother and father tell her she's ruined the best chance of her life—not only for her, but for their entire family—the girl finally agrees to respond to one of the young man's letters. And then she responds to another. And another. And soon they have a friendly correspondence going. They've become pen pals who live only three train stops away. Their letters are very simple, explaining what happened that day, complaining about family members or politics or the weather. Normal things. But when the girl turns twenty, she finally gives in to the pressure from her family and decides to become more serious with her life. She now believes she can do both: singing *and* a family. The first person she thinks about is the young man. The last letter she ever wrote him contained only one simple line: 'I'm changing my answer to yes.' They were married ten days later in the small Chinese city of Yixing, in front of over two hundred people. Six months after that she became pregnant with their son.

"At that same time the girl's singing career was at its highest point, and she was invited to compete in the biggest singing competition in all of China. She breezed through the three qualifying rounds and made it all the way to the national finals with only three other girls. Think of *American Idol*, Miguel, only with Chinese girls singing traditional Chinese songs. After all the girls performed in front of the big ballroom crowd, the judges approached the girl backstage and told her she was going to be named the winner. But first they had to ask her a couple questions. The winner, they explained, could not be married. Not officially, anyway. However, two of the previous winners had been 'secretly' married. She would simply have to sign a release form that allowed them to say she was single while she was out on tour and when they promoted her recordings. The young man, who was backstage at the time too, put his hand on his new wife's elbow and asked to speak with her in private. As I said, he'd studied law in America, and he advised her not to sign the contract. He was very traditional in this way. He claimed she would be entering into a dishonest agreement."

I shook my cramping hand and kept writing. I don't know why, but I was totally into Mei-li's story about China and wanted to get down every single word she said.

She kept going: "The girl didn't know what to do, Miguel. She went back and forth between the judges and her husband, asking questions, listening to their advice, and then she slipped off to an empty room to think by herself. See, not only was the girl married, she was also *pregnant*. And she knew a woman could only be 'secretly' pregnant for so long. In order to sign the contract, she would have to defy her new husband *and* get rid of his baby. It was simply too much to bear. When she returned backstage she walked right up to the judges and told them she would not be able to sign the contract. They said they were very sorry to hear it and gave first prize to another girl."

Mei-li pulled another drag off her cigarette. She blew her smoke out the side of her mouth and sat there quietly as we inched along in traffic. I waited for her to keep going with her story, but she didn't. She just sat there, smoking and driving, staring out her windshield. Mong stared forward too.

"So what happened then?" I finally asked.

She looked at me in the rearview and smiled. Blew more smoke at the roof. "I'll let Mong tell the rest, Miguel. He knows the story much better than I do. I just wanted to tell you how they met. How the young man courted the girl like men used to. Because he believed it was true love. I don't care what anybody says, the young man's love for the singer was the basis of every single decision he ever made."

"But did she still get famous?" I said. "Did they stay together and have the kid?"

Mei-li glanced at me in the rearview and smiled, then she put out another cigarette on her Starbucks cup and rolled down her window. "God, this traffic is *killing* me," she said. "Hey, I got an idea. Why don't we stop off and grab lunch before we do the rest of the drive? That sound okay to you guys?"

Mong didn't say anything.

Rondell didn't even lift his head from the window.

I looked down at my journal full of Mei-li's words, all confused as hell. Why would somebody tell a story like that and not finish? It's a straight-up blue balls situation, right? But at the same time I knew we had more driving to do. Maybe she was just taking a break and would say the rest later.

"Uh, hello?" she said, looking right at me in the rearview. "Miguel? Lunch?"

"Yeah, that's cool," I said.

"Great," Mei-li said. "I know a little pizza place. You guys will love it. And maybe when we're done eating traffic won't be so bad."

She zipped us off the main road and down a few steep side streets. At the bottom of the hill she moved slowly down a narrow one-way road, looking for a place to park.

This chubby blond hostess led the four of us to a table near the back of the restaurant. We were quiet as we sat down and she handed us each a menu and told us the specials. I was right across from Mei-li. Mong and Rondell were next to us.

After the hostess walked away, Mei-li said: "Why don't we just get one big pizza and share it? Pepperoni okay with you guys?"

"That's cool," I said, looking to Mong and Rondell.

"That's cool," Rondell said.

Mong didn't say anything.

The waitress came over and asked us for our order, and Mei-li told it to her. As she talked I watched her mouth move, realizing I'd never met a girl like her before. One who's not only fine but also older and confident. One who tells you stories about people in other countries.

I peeped her bare shoulders on the slick—the skin so brown and soft-looking. Her smallish boobs and how you could sort of make out where her nipples were through her wife-beater. Her petite collarbone. Her perfect nose and long eyelashes. Dark brown eyes. Even though her ears were pierced like six times each, not all the holes had earrings.

Then I peeped Mei-li's face as a whole. It was so damn pretty it made something inside my chest ache—like when you look in the eyes of a little baby in a stroller at the park.

But then I started getting sort of pissed off, too. I realized how I'd probably never meet somebody like Mei-li ever again. It finally hit me what it meant that I'd have to live the rest of my life in Mexico. Where my grandma and grandpa were born. Which wasn't bad in a respect kind of way. I'm not saying that. But I was born *here*. In America. And that's where I wanna live too.

Thinking all this made my stomach clench up on me. Like how it did that first night in the Lighthouse. Only different. 'Cause now it only happened when I looked straight at Mei-li's face.

The busboy came by and dropped off our Cokes and put a basket of bread in the middle of the table. Rondell grabbed a piece right off, but me and Mong didn't touch it.

Mei-li pushed her chair back and stood up. "I need to go pee, you guys." She looked over her shoulder as she left, said: "Don't even *think* about talking shit while I'm gone." Then she skipped around the corner toward the restrooms, out of sight.

Mong immediately slid back his chair and stood over me and Rondell. "I'm leaving," he said.

"What?" I said.

"What?" Rondell said too.

"You guys can come or you can stay," Mong said. "I don't care. But choose right now."

Me and Rondell looked at each other, and then I looked at Mong. I couldn't believe the guy. He wanted to just bail out on our whole plan. I told him: "Wait, man, she's still gonna take us to Mexico. Just not yet."

"No, she's not," Mong said.

"What?" I said.

"What?" Rondell said.

I stared at Mong, trying to figure out why his cousin wouldn't do what she just said she would. She seemed way too nice for that. Plus I'd believe Mei-li over Mong any day.

97

"There's no time," Mong said. "Just choose."

There were a few seconds where all three of us stayed perfectly still, staring at each other, trying to think.

Then, I don't even know why, but I stood up.

Rondell looked at me and then he stood up, too. Dropped his half-eaten bread back in the basket.

"Back door," Mong said, moving away from the table. He walked quickly toward the open back door, me and Rondell following after him.

"Wait," I said, stopping at the door.

I hustled back to our table, slipped the leather petty-cash envelope out from my pocket, unzipped it, pulled a twenty, and dropped it on the table by where Mei-li had been sitting. I stared at her chair for a sec, then pulled another twenty, dropped it on top of the other one. For gas money.

I moved back toward Mong and Rondell and we all ducked out the back door and took off running through the alley, down the street. Me and Rondell following Mong. Exactly like the night before, when we left the Lighthouse. Hands slicing air like we were running a race.

Only this time we were in the middle of San Francisco.

And this time we didn't have a plan.

July 17—more

We sprinted down Bay Street, no idea which way we were going or what for. Down steep asphalt hills, in and out of cars and buses and trolleys. Through sidewalk traffic of business-suit dudes, packs of joggers, camera-strapped tourists, women on cell phones pushing double-decker strollers. Some people turned to watch us run by, and I wondered what they saw. Just normal kids running? Or group-homers? Escaped prisoners?

And how'd I become a part of what they saw when just four months ago I was sitting on a couch back in Stockton with my big bro, breaking apart Oreo cookies, eating them icing first like any other regular kid?

Your whole life, man, it can change in one minute.

Mong led us down to this part where there were a bunch of piers along the water. I looked back and there was nobody chasing us, but it felt like we'd be caught any second. By Mei-li. Or the cops. Or the night-watch guy or Jaden. I couldn't calm down about us getting caught and being sent back to Juvi.

And it's all because of Mong.

We headed down Pier 39, zipped around a grassy hill where homeless people were lounging with trash bags full of cans and plastic bottles, and onto this wooden section that overlooked the water where seals barked and swam around with each other or perched on big floating crates.

We leaned against the fence to catch our breath. Mong started coughing again. And this time he even went down on one knee and puked, right off the pier, into the water. Me and Rondell looked at him, and I said, "Yo, man, what's wrong with you?"

He didn't answer. Didn't even look at me.

"What happened back there with your cousin?" I said, tired of him not answering people. "Why'd we just leave her? She said she was still gonna take us."

He just stared at the seals.

"PS," I said, ready to smack the little smirk right off his face, "I ain't gonna just follow your dumb ass wherever you wanna go. You already fucked up our ride to Mexico."

Mong looked up at me more serious, said: "What'd I do?"

"You heard me," I shot back, staring dude down. I knew I was about one step away from something happening, but I pointed at him anyway, said: "I'm gonna tell you now, man, I ain't like everybody else at the damn Lighthouse. I ain't scared of some Chinese punk bitch—"

He leaped at me, tackled me onto the wood and smacked me in the jaw. But like I said, this time I was ready for it and snuck in a punch of my own. Socked his ass right on one of his cheek scars. We wrestled around on the ground, holding back each other's fists, trying to claw at each other's faces and kick, but Rondell took both our foreheads in his huge hands and pushed us apart.

"Stop it!" he yelled. He shoved me back like fifteen feet and pinned Mong to the ground, his face right up against the damp wood. "Just stop it!" Rondell shouted again, pointing back and forth between us.

Mong smiled and puked again, right in front of his own mouth.

Rondell backed up a little with this grossed-out look on his face. He checked his hands to make sure no puke got on him and then he looked back and forth between us. "Come on, man. Y'all gotta just stop it. It ain't right."

Mong laughed. "Nobody can change my mind."

"Yo, nobody gives a *shit* about your mind," I shouted back.

"It ain't right, though," Rondell said.

In the distance, a grip of seals were scattered around the wooden crates, barking every once in a while and nosing each other in the stomach. They had no clue who I was or how something inside me was changing by the minute, getting more and more angry and confused. They didn't know how I was becoming what people probably thought if they ever read my file, saw what I did.

I stared at the seals for a sec, trying to decide what I

thought about that. 'Cause I was actually *happy* Mong was sick. I swear to God. And what does that say about me?

Here's the thing: Maybe it's a waste of damn time to fight what's in your file. Maybe you're destined to end up being that person no matter what.

For some reason I pictured Mei-li coming out from the bathroom right then, seeing our empty table at the pizza place. Her face all surprised and sad. Maybe it was best that she wasn't sitting with me in the car, her hand on my leg, my girl. She probably wouldn't like who I was anyway once she got to know who I am now.

"You stopping it?" Rondell shouted at me.

I turned to look at him but didn't answer.

"*Are* you, Mexico?"

"Whatever makes you happy," I said.

He looked at Mong. "Are *you*?"

Mong smiled big. He put his right hand in his own puke and wiped it all over his face and then spit in my direction and laughed.

"Jesus," Rondell said, jumping away from Mong.

I crinkled my face up and told the guy: "Yo, man, you're disgusting."

Mong stood up, still laughing, and leaned against the fence to watch the seals. He wiped his face on his sweatshirt, spit in the water.

Rondell looked to me, but I just did the same thing as Mong, stood against the fence, a ways down from him so I didn't have to smell his puke. Rondell looked back and forth between us for a minute or so, and then he went up to the fence too. And we all just stood there, staring at the water, nobody talking.

While we stood there, I watched all the different people

who came to watch the seals. Sometimes a whole family would step up to the wooden fence overlooking the water. They'd point at the seals and laugh or say how cute they were. The dad would put on a voice and pretend it was the seals saying stuff. Or the mom would position her kid in the perfect spot and snap a digital picture with seals in the background, and then they'd all hover around the little camera screen joking about the kid's eyes being closed. Or some old homeless-looking dude would just stand there solo like us, watching. All by himself. Dirty-ass flannel and beard blowing around in the wind. But after a while they'd all get tired of watching seals and move on. All except me, Mong and Rondell. We stayed there for like two hours. Not saying shit. Just standing next to each other, thinking our own thoughts. About how we got here and what we were gonna do now. I kept thinking how Jaden was supposed to take us to San Francisco in a few days anyway. We could've just waited for a ride. Or how back in the day my pop promised to bring me and Diego here for our first time. Just as soon as he got back from the war. But he never got back from the war, so we never came.

Well, here I am, Pop, I told him in my head. I finally made it to damn San Francisco. All on my own, too.

Ain't you proud?

Mong wiped his face on his sweatshirt again and stepped away from the fence. He seemed totally back to normal. Super calm. Like nothing even happened between us. In a mellow-ass voice he told us how we should go south toward the border. Along the coast as much as we could because then we could sleep on the beach where nobody would bother us.

Me and Rondell straightened up too.

Mong started walking back the other way, down the pier, and me and Rondell just sort of followed him. For now, at least. I told myself I'd go along with the guy until I came up with a better plan, and then I'd jet out on my own, roll solo. But for now he at least knew the city better than me.

As we walked Rondell tapped Mong on the shoulder and said: "Hey, Mong."

"Yeah."

"We still tryin' to get to Mexico, right? To them fishin' boats?"

"Yeah," Mong said.

"Good." Rondell turned his big Afro head my way and grinned, said: " 'Cause this whole time we was sittin' there, Mexico, next to them seals, I been thinkin' 'bout that. How I really wanna be a fisherman now."

"That right?" I said.

"Yup."

"Well, you already *look* like a fisherman, Rondo. You got that part down."

Rondell looked straight ahead and got this excited look on his face. "You really think so?"

"Yeah, man," I said. "Most fishermen are big and black just like you. And they got nappy-haired Afros like yours. Almost all of 'em actually. All you're missing is the damn pole and bait."

Mong looked at me out of the corner of his eye, and it almost seemed like he was grinning at what I said. Which was so weird, man, considering we were just in another fight. I'd never met a person who could go from one extreme to the other in such a short amount of time. I bet Lester used to take him to some counselor who specialized in split personalities—schizophrenics or whatever—'cause Mong definitely had some advanced shit like that.

"I bet I catch the biggest ones you ever seen," Rondell said as we kept walking. "That's my word, Mexico."

I looked at Rondell and I couldn't help it, man, I sort of

cracked up a little. Inside. I don't think I'd ever seen a dude his size look so happy. And just 'cause I told him he could probably be a fisherman.

We backtracked the other way, on Lombard this time, took it all the way to Fillmore and cut over toward the water. I had no idea where we were, but I read all the street signs like my old man taught me. It wouldn't make sense, I knew, but it was a distraction and made me quit looking over my shoulder for cops every three seconds. We turned onto Marina and walked along this nice park where a bunch of white kids were playing soccer and Wiffle ball and the grown-ups were bunched together on blankets, talking and cutting off hunks of cheese to put on fancy pieces of bread. And this giant red bridge towered over everything in the background. It was that famous one in all the postcards and T-shirts about San Francisco. I'd never seen a bridge so big.

We stayed on the road all the way until it turned into Mason and then Mong had us cut through a part of the park called Crissy Field, where hippie-looking people were playing Frisbee and Hacky Sack with no shoes on. We walked out onto the sand and then Mong stopped cold and dropped his bag. He wiped his mouth with the arm of his sweatshirt and stared up at the bridge, which was right in front of us now, a huge mass of steel and cement and wires. It made you feel like an ant.

We stayed like that awhile, him looking at the bridge and me and Rondell looking between it and him, none of us really saying anything. Eventually Rondell sat down on this piece of driftwood and stared out at the water. I sat down too, ran my fingers through the sand. Mong squatted next to us. It was kind of disturbing, us just sitting there next to each other, like nothing ever happened between me and him just a while ago. I still felt the sting of his punch on my right cheek, the ringing in my ear. But at the same time if he was really schizophrenic like I thought, it would make mad sense, right? I thought how there were actually *two* Mongs: Psycho Mong and Mellow Mong. Right now he was being Mellow Mong. And it was only the other one I actually had a problem with.

He pointed up at the bridge, said: "Know what that is?"

"A big-ass bridge," I said.

Neither of them laughed, though.

"It's the Golden Gate," Mong said.

"Oh, yeah," I said. "I heard of that bridge. It's famous."

"I heard of it, too," Rondell said.

I patted him on the shoulder, said: "Sure you have, big guy."

"Wha'chu mean?" Rondell said. All I did was laugh, so he looked back at the bridge and tilted his head a little, said: "Why's it all red like that?"

I gave the guy a little round of applause. I don't even know why, man. I guess when I get bored I like to mess with Rondell for some reason. "Yo, nice work, dawg," I said, patting him on the shoulder again. "And here everybody's been sayin' you still ain't got your colors down."

He brushed my hand away, said: "I know what's red and what ain't, Mexico."

Mong sat all the way down with us, wrapped his arms around his knees. "My dad said it's made up of so much steel that by the time they finish painting all the way to the end they have to start right back at the beginning again."

We all stared up at the giant bridge, Rondell pointing at it because who knows why, and then Mong said: "A lot of people commit suicide off it, too."

"Yeah?" I said.

Mong nodded. "It's so high the impact of hitting the

water mostly kills them. But if it doesn't, they just drown anyway."

"Tough way to go, man," I said, glancing at Mong. Even Mellow Mong was morbid as hell.

"You think so?" he said.

"Hell yeah, man. Jumpin' off a damn bridge?"

Mong turned to look at me. "How would *you* do it?"

I shrugged. "Maybe knock down a bunch of pills. Gas the car up while it's still in the garage and take a snooze. Something that wasn't all messy."

"I wouldn't do it at all," Rondell said. "My auntie Reina told me people who kill theyselves can't make it into the kingdom of heaven."

"You ain't exactly a shoo-in either way," I said, tossing a stick toward the tide.

"Wha'chu mean?" Rondell said again.

If you haven't noticed, that's pretty much all Rondell ever says to anybody. Wha'chu mean, Mexico? Wha'chu mean, Mong? The shit's actually mad annoying.

I shook my head, said: "Forget it, man."

"I think dying in the water is perfect," Mong said.

"I guess you ain't never heard of no sharks."

Mong just stayed staring at the bridge, this far-off look in his eyes. He probably didn't even hear what I just said.

"Maybe I'd take pills too," Rondell said. "I mean, if I really had to do it. So I could just go to sleep forever and ever."

I turned and looked at Rondell for a minute. Sometimes when you catch the dude thinking he almost looks like an innocent little kid. Like he couldn't hurt a fly. I'm serious. Once you get past how big and strong he is, I mean. And that I only know him from Juvi and the Lighthouse.

"Nah, Rondo," I said, picking up another stick and tapping

it against my knee. "You're better off just listenin' to your auntie, man."

Rondell looked at me, said: "Wha'chu mean, Mexico?"

I smiled and stayed looking at him, wondering if he could tell that for once in my group-home life I actually meant what I just said.

Us Looking for a Bus Station:

We cut through this old-school cemetery and back out onto a street that led us to the first part of Highway 1, where we stood at the side of the road and tried to hitchhike. But nobody picked us up so we kept walking. We followed along the side of the 1, through this grassy Presidio area and a fancy golf course and then down Fourteenth Ave. Then we ducked through Golden Gate Park, and when we got to the other side, we were on Nineteenth Ave.

It was hot as hell and we were all exhausted from being up so long, but still we just walked and walked and walked. And none of us complained any. Even though we hadn't eaten anything and we were worried about getting to Mexico and how Mei-li said Mong was sick.

As we kept walking, wiping forehead sweat every five seconds and constantly looking over our shoulders, I thought about that, why none of us complained. Maybe it's just 'cause we're young and don't know any better. Or 'cause we were thinking so much about how it'd be in Mexico. Or we were too stressed about getting picked up by some cop car that would eventually come creeping up over the hill behind us and flip on their lights. Or maybe us three are just tougher than how some people might be. But after a while I came up with this other theory.

Maybe the real reason we didn't complain none is 'cause secretly, unconsciously or whatever, we thought we *deserved* to suffer. For real. We'd all done something bad to be put in a group home in the first place, right? And then last night we just walked out. Cut short our sentences, made plans to live somewhere else where we could start over fresh and have a better life of freedom and fine-ass tourist girls from all around the world. But shouldn't we still have to pay for what we did? Shouldn't we have to suffer somehow? Maybe us going on this never-ending walk like this, with no food or water or sleep, with the sun burning down on the backs of our necks, maybe that was the only way we could think of to make the world seem balanced again. Otherwise you could just do any damn thing you wanted in this life, and I don't think that shit's true.

Eventually we cut into the heart of some college campus 'cause Mong said there might be a bus station somewhere inside. All the college kids wandering around made me think of Jaden's goofy ass. How he said those were the best days of his life and maybe I could go too 'cause I got good grades. They were roaming around with backpacks and flip-flops or sitting on little grassy hills eating lunch or laying out in the sun on towels with books in their hands or sleeping. It's easy for a guy like Jaden to *say* you should go to college, because he fits right in. And that's his job, to say other people could too. But walking around looking at everybody, I felt a million miles away from all them. From college. Like it was in a completely different galaxy from a kid like me.

When we finally found the station we stood in front of the counter and stared at all the possible places to go. This gray-haired lady with big thick glasses sitting in the booth turned on her mike and said: "Where you fellows headed?"

"South," Mong said.

She smiled. "I'm gonna need you gentlemen to be a little more specific."

"Something cheap that goes along the coast," Mong said.

She looked down at a paper in front of her and then back up at us. "Got a bus like that just pulled into the station," she said. "You guys hurry you can still make it."

I stepped to the window with the leather petty-cash envelope, paid her for three tickets, and we hustled around the corner to where the buses were, trying to make it on ours before it left. We found bus 47 and stood at the bottom of the entrance with our tickets in hand. Before we climbed aboard with our bags I asked the skinny black driver: "How long till we leave?"

He looked down at his watch and said: "Be pullin' her out in exactly six minutes."

He reached for my ticket, stared at it for a sec and looked at me, handed it back. "All the way to UC Santa Cruz, huh?"

"Or as far south as we can get that's still by the beach," Mong said.

The driver nodded.

I looked at Mong, wondering how he knew so much about geography. Not only San Francisco and Santa Cruz but Mexico, too. Maybe Rene was right about him being kind of smart.

As he and Rondell climbed onto the bus, I went back to the waiting area and bought candy bars and Cokes and chips from the vending machines. Then I went onto the bus too, took a full seat next to them in the back and let Mong and Rondell pick whatever they wanted. Me and Rondell dug in like it was the first time we'd seen food in a damn month, but Mong didn't eat a bite. Instead he just stared at me with this little grin on his face—and not the psycho one I was used to either, just a normal one. "You liked her, right?" he told me.

"Who?" I said, though I already knew who.

"Come on, you can tell me. I won't be mad."

I studied him for a sec. I didn't know if he was being true about not getting pissed off so I just didn't say a word about his cousin. Instead I asked him: "Yo, man, what a *gung gung*?"

He laughed to himself. It was the first time I'd ever seen Mong laugh without being all psycho about it. You'd almost think he was a regular Asian kid with a shaved head if it wasn't for the nasty scars on his cheeks. He took a sip of his Coke and wiped his mouth on the arm of his sweatshirt. "It's a Chinese person's grandfather," he said. "On the mother's side."

I nodded my head but didn't say anything else. I looked over at Rondell, who was chewing away at a candy bar, watching us.

After a minute or so, Mong tapped me on the shoulder and said: "She'd probably like you too. Except you're so much younger. And you're Mexican." He took off his sweatshirt and balled it up, set it between his shoulder and the window. "But who knows," he said. "Maybe she wouldn't even care about that."

Instead of saying anything back I shoved the rest of my second candy bar in my mouth and chewed. Washed it down with Coke. Rondell burped so loud a couple people turned around to look at us.

He said excuse me, though, and they all looked forward again. When the driver started the engine and it began rumbling under our seats I put my hood back up, and Mong leaned his head against his sweatshirt and closed his eyes. I looked back at Rondell, who was asleep with his mouth wide open, half a candy bar still in his big-ass right hand.

I leaned my head against the window too.

All three of us were dead asleep before the bus was even out of the parking lot.

July 18

For the third time this month I woke up with a damn dude in my face. But this time it wasn't Mong, it was the skinny black bus driver.

"Wake up," he said, kicking the bottom of my seat. He kicked the bottom of Mong's and Rondell's seats, too. "Last stop along the coast, like you guys said."

The three of us sat up all groggy, stretching our arms and looking all around. It was dark out, and at first I couldn't see anything except the massive black ocean across the street. "Where are we?" I said, all disoriented.

"Davenport," the driver said. "Last stop along the beach. Unless you wanna head up to College Station with the rest of us." He motioned toward the five or six college-looking kids still on the bus, sleeping. "But y'all don't really seem like the studious type."

"We'll get off here," Mong said, rising out of his seat with his bag.

Me and Rondell followed him off the bus, and then we stood there watching it pull away.

It was dark as hell and the foggy sky was full of blurry stars. On one side of the road was nothing but sand and ocean, on the other it was these steep green cliffs full of baby trees and wild bushes. It almost didn't even seem like America anymore.

"We're north of Santa Cruz," Mong said.

"Yo, I been to Santa Cruz before," I said. "With my dad and my bro. But I don't remember it bein' all like this."

"We're still a few miles away."

"What we gonna do now?" Rondell said.

"I'm thinking," Mong said.

I listened to the muffled crashing of waves, like the sound you hear inside those big shells you're supposed to put up to your ear at gift shops. I watched specks of moonlight sparkle off the water's surface whenever a small swell rolled toward shore. Like some little kid had sprinkled glitter everywhere. The air was heavy and wet, smelled like seaweed and salt. I thought about the time me, Diego and my old man went to Santa Cruz the weekend before he got shipped out. Pop took turns throwing me and Diego deep passes while we stood in knee-deep water with our shirts wrapped around our heads like do-rags. He'd throw 'em just a little to the side so we'd have to dive into a wave to catch it. And me and Diego would fight for the ball, pushing and pulling and shoving each other under. I remember we stayed out there for hours and hours that day. Till the sun started going down and everybody packed up to leave. It was probably one of the best days me and Diego ever had with the old man.

About a year later, after Diego got his permit, we drove up there again, just us two, and threw the football in the water and almost drowned trying to swim out to the pier. But on the drive home we both agreed it wasn't the same no more.

Mong picked up his bag from the dirt. "Okay," he said. "We can get food and the stuff we need from that store over there." He pointed down the road with his free hand. "Then we can build a fire on the beach and eat and sleep. We need rest. First thing tomorrow we'll figure out how to get further south."

Me and Rondell nodded.

"How much money do we have?" Mong said.

I pulled the leather petty-cash envelope out of my pocket

and counted the cash up in my head. "Six hundred forty dollars," I said.

"Damn," Rondell said, "that's a grip."

"We gotta save as much as we can, though," Mong said. "It's gonna take longer to get to Mexico now."

We looked all around, at the beach and the cluster of stores down the way and the trees and bushes behind us climbing up the steep cliff. After being in a city all day it felt like we'd woken up on the set of a damn horror flick or some shit. Like any second some masked dude would pop out from behind a tree and start chasing our asses around with a machete.

Yo, bring it, I thought. And then I laughed at myself for playing hard when really I kept looking all around, kind of spooked.

Mong set off toward the stores, and me and Rondell followed him, the three of us walking single file along the dirt shoulder of the random two-lane highway.

Me and Rondell's Surprise Shopping Spree:

The plan was to just pay for the stuff we needed, but it turned out this old white guy working the register was a straight-up racist. And that changed everything.

The second we walked in, the guy (whose face was wrinkled and blotchy and looked mad fake, like he was just a regular guy wearing an old dude mask) left his spot behind the counter and started following us around with a crooked little grin like he didn't trust us. He folded his arms and told Rondell to get away from the nectarines unless he planned on buying every single one his grubby hands touched. Then he turned and asked me if I had any money. "And I'm not talkin' 'bout no pesos, either, compadre. We don't take but dollars around here."

I looked at dude like he was out of his mind. I've had

people talk shit about me being Mexican before, and I know how it happened with my pop when he was going for a higher job in the military, but most people are kind of on the down low about it. They say shit all under their breath. But not this dude, he was right out in the open.

Mong got up in his face, pointed a finger at his veiny white forehead and said: "You say any more like that and we'll just take whatever we want, leave you tied up in a freezer somewhere."

Me and Rondell got closer, and I looked in Mong's face. It was just like I thought, his psycho self had entered the building.

"Oh, really," the guy said, walking back toward the counter. "Tell you what, Kung Fu Theater. Why don't I just call the cops right now. Let's see how *they* feel about you waltzing into my store making threats."

Mong signaled for me to get the stuff we needed and followed the guy to the counter. "I don't think that'll be necessary, sir," he said.

I grabbed a basket and stayed there watching. I'd seen Psycho Mong mess with almost every kid in the Lighthouse, heard stories about him breaking residents' arms and all that, but I'd never seen dude go after an adult. For some reason I gained a little respect.

". . . need to get somebody to come down here and take out the trash," the guy was saying, picking up the phone.

Mong snatched the phone right out of his hand, pulled the wire clear out of the socket. Then he fired the phone at the wall, shattering it to pieces. Mong may have been sick like Mei-li said, but he wasn't so sick he couldn't fight people or destroy their shit. My only thing was if he might take it too far. 'Cause even though store dude was racist as hell, he was also *old* as hell, and I knew how some old people could be just 'cause they don't know no better, or 'cause they were raised in a different generation or whatever.

Mong looked up at me.

I picked up a second basket, handed it to Rondell, and we hurried up and down the aisles throwing stuff in: hot dogs and ketchup and matches and skewer sticks and paper towels and six-packs of Coke and apples and nectarines and six-packs of beer and charcoal and lighter fluid and beef jerky and powdered donuts and chocolate donuts and orange juice. Every few seconds I'd look up to make sure Mong wasn't actually hurting the guy, but mostly I was just concentrating on ganking whatever came into my head. It was like me and Rondell were on a damn shopping spree, the kind you always dream about when you're a kid.

Only this wasn't no dream. We knew we weren't paying for shit.

By the time me and Rondell got back up to the counter Mong had old dude gagged and tied up in telephone cord. And the knots he made were mad professional, like he'd been doing them on people all his life.

"Got what you need?" Mong said.

I nodded, though in my head I was a little spooked at seeing the guy all tied up like that. It's one thing to swipe supplies, but it's something else when you tie up an old man and leave his ass there to starve.

Mong turned to dude, said: "You shouldn't talk about people's races like that, sir. Especially when the people you're saying it to don't have nothing to lose. Like us three."

Mong looked at me and pointed to the guy. "Tell him."

I moved forward a little, unsure of what he wanted.

"Yeah, man," I said, "and why would you say if I had pesos for? I'm from America, just the same as you are. That shit's ignorant."

"That's right," Mong said.

The guy tried to say something back, but all that made it through the rag in his mouth were these crazy low muffled noises. Like when you shout something into your pillow.

Rondell leaned against the counter and started unwrapping a piece of chocolate. I couldn't believe the guy. Here we were, messing with some old man who Mong had all tied up and gagged, and Rondell wasn't even paying attention.

I turned back to racist dude's wrinkled white face, his thinning gray hair. You could tell by his expression he wasn't being Mr. Tough Guy anymore. He was just scared, like a little kid. Maybe old people revert back to when they were young when they get scared. His eyes darting back and forth between me and Mong. His loose cheek skin quivering. For some reason that shit made him seem even worse to me. If you're gonna say something bad about somebody's race, man, then you shouldn't act like a damn baby when they tie your ass up. You should just man up about it.

"All right," I told Mong, "let's let his old ass go now and get outta here."

But Mong didn't let him go. He grabbed the guy's ear and made him turn back around. And he did the shit all mellow-like. He didn't even seem pissed anymore. He made you think of someone in the park training their puppy how to sit or roll over. "I'm not gonna throw you in the freezer this time, sir," he said. "But I want you to think about what happened here tonight. Try to improve yourself as a person, okay? And the next time the three of us come in here to shop, I expect to see a changed man."

Then Mong slapped the guy in the face.

I totally jumped, not expecting it.

The guy cringed and kept his head to the side like that for a few seconds. And then he lowered his eyes to the ground and sort of cowered in front of Mong.

Mong looked at me with a big smile, but I couldn't smile back. "Wanna smack him?" he said.

"Nah, man," I said, frowning. "I'm cool."

"At least kick him or spit on him. People shouldn't talk like that about people's races."

I looked back at Psycho Mong without saying anything. He was taking shit way too far now. A racist comment shouldn't lead you to tie somebody up and slap their ass around and say for me to kick or spit on him. But at the same time I didn't say anything 'cause I don't think you can explain your opinion to people when they're being all psycho.

I looked down at old dude. He had his eyes closed now, and he was actually shaking. His whole body.

Mong reached into the guy's pocket and pulled out his cell. He flipped it open and snapped it in two, tossed both pieces to the ground. Me and Rondell loaded all our groceries in our bags and zipped 'em back up. I stepped up, grabbed some scissors off the counter and cut the cord on dude's hands. He flexed them.

Mong shot me an irritated look.

"Come on, dawg," I said. "He understands now."

I tossed the scissors down a food aisle and we all tore out of the store.

Outside, I kept expecting to hear a cop's siren wailing away in the distance, racing toward us, flipping on its spotlight and calling for us to "Freeze!" over their loudspeaker. But no cop cars were coming.

We sprinted the other way, across the street, hopped an

old rusty guardrail and ran along this grassy part near the beach.

About a mile or so down Mong veered us across this little bank, past an old unused road with mad weeds shooting up where paint used to be, and into the thick sand. We jogged heavy-footed, carrying our bags packed full of groceries, for another ten minutes or so, toward this cliff part, and then Mong threw his bag to the side and collapsed into the sand on purpose. He gagged a few times and held on to his stomach, rocking back and forth and searching for his wind.

Me and Rondell stopped too, bent over trying to catch our breath and looking at Mong and all around us to see where we were. But we were nowhere.

Mong rolled onto his back and stared into the sky. Even though he was still sucking in short, desperate breaths, a little grin came on his face.

None of us said anything for a while, but we were all sort of grinning now, and looking at each other, still listening for sirens though no sirens would ever come. Behind us the ocean hummed and sometimes crashed onto itself with a slapping sound like if a long line of people all hit their knees at the same time. Rondell started laughing for no particular reason and went on his back just like Mong, stared at the sky too.

I knew something important had just happened in that store. With the old racist dude. We'd crossed an imaginary line. Gone beyond just leaving the group home where we were still supposed to be. Now we'd assaulted somebody and stolen from their store. Soon as he found a way he'd call the cops and give our description and they'd be out looking for us for real.

I tried to think how I felt about what was happening.

Being wanted by the cops and trying to flee the country. The old me would've probably just turned myself in already. Or I never would've left in the first place. But what happened in Stockton had completely changed who I was. Made me into a totally different Miguel. One that actually *wanted* to cross imaginary lines because I now knew nothing in this world really mattered.

Growing up, Diego was always the crazy one. Starting fights and jacking beers from the bodega across town and messing with mad girls. My folks were always worried *he'd* be the one who would end up in trouble one day. My pop used to sit him down every other week so they could have talks about his grades and his bad behavior in school and his choice of friends.

I looked at Mong and Rondell laying there, staring up in the sky. How strange that it was *me* sitting here on this beach with them. Everybody always thought it'd be Diego, including me and Diego. But it wasn't.

It was me.

But then again, I thought, looking into the sky to try and see what Mong and Rondell were seeing. Maybe it's *not* that strange. People always think there's this huge hundred-foot-high barrier that separates doing good from doing bad. But there's not. There's nothing. There's not even a little anthill. You just take one baby step in any direction and you're already there. You've done something awful. And your life is changed forever.

And here's the thing: it's not even that your life changes because of what you *did*, I don't think. Even if it's damn murder. Sticking a knife through somebody's chest and watching in their terrified eyes as the life drains out. Nah, man, it's not even that. People change because they discover that this supposed line between being a good person and being a bad person doesn't actually exist. They realize that shit's straight make-believe. Like the tooth fairy. Or even Jesus. I promise, man. Go on and take the nerdiest damn dude you know. Even *he* could cross to the other side.

It reminds me of when you stand right up near the tracks watching a big-ass Amtrak train barreling toward you. And you think, Yo, I could just take one little step forward, onto the tracks, and I'd be dead. And deep down you assume there's some kind of line there you could never cross. A barrier. Something that wouldn't ever let you take that step even if you tried. But guess what? There's no line. You can do anything.

You can step.

You can die. . . .

Eventually I stopped thinking so hard and Mong and Rondell sat up and our eyes all focused on the same thing. A few feet in front of us was this hole in the side of a medium-sized cliff that ran right up along the sand and rocks. All you could see was the hole, and it wasn't that big or anything, but you could tell right away it was a cave.

I finally let go of my bag and hiked up toward it. Rondell left his bag too and followed me. We both looked into the mouth of the cave. It was dark and you couldn't see much, but you could sort of make out what size it was and how deep it went. Because it was high tide, when a bigger-sized wave broke and rolled with the tide toward shore, some of the water sucked up into the bottom of the cave, shot around like the inside of a washing machine and then sucked back out to sea.

Mong hiked up toward us and looked in too.

After a few minutes we all started crawling down into it, without even saying we were. We struggled all the way to the bottom and then just sat there with our backs against the cave wall, breathing. Crowding in on each other. Whenever the water came in, which wasn't that much, we'd just step our shoes up on a big rock or a part of the cave wall until it went back out.

"This is exactly how I picture Mexico will be," Rondell said.

It was mad dark at the bottom of the cave, but I could sort of make out Mong nodding his head.

"I bet no police could ever find us in here," Rondell said. "Long as they looked too. Probably we could hide in here for the rest of our lives."

"Yeah," I said, "but, Rondo, man, then you'd never get to be a fisherman." I was grinning, but he probably couldn't see my face.

"Wha'chu mean?" Rondell said.

"You told us you wanted to be a fisherman, remember?"

"Oh, that," Rondell said, laughing a little. "Nah, I bet I could catch 'em right from here, Mexico. I bet they's lots of good ones that come right up into this cave."

I smacked him in the arm with the back of my hand. "Come on, dawg," I told him. "That doesn't even make sense. How you gonna cook 'em? What're you gonna use for seasoning? Fish need mad herbs and shit."

Rondell was quiet for a few long seconds. That's how I knew his goofy ass was taking me serious. "Maybe I could just have 'em cold," he said. "Not all kinds of fish gotta get cooked, right, Mexico? Ain't that what sushi is?"

I was impressed, it was the first damn time I'd ever seen Rondell actually put two and two together. "All right, all right," I said. "So your whole life now, Rondo. It's gonna be eating sushi in a cave. If that's how you wanna do it."

"Maybe," he said.

121

We were all quiet for a while, listening to the sound of the ocean and each other's breathing, and then Rondell started climbing back up out of the cave, saying he had to go to the bathroom.

"Don't forget the paper towels," I said.

He stopped and turned around, said: "Wha'chu mean, Mexico?"

"Nothin'," I said. "Just don't do it too close to our bags. All our food's in there. Go down the beach a ways."

"I already knew that," he said, pulling himself out of the cave and walking off.

Soon as we couldn't hear Rondell's footsteps anymore Mong said he was gonna make a fire, but he didn't go anywhere. He just sat there taking deep breaths and looking up at the opening of the cave. Fingering his brown tooth necklace. Every once in a while he would cough or spit between his shoes. I wondered if he even thought about what he'd just done at the store. Tying the guy up and gagging him and smacking him in the face. I knew I couldn't spend too much more time with somebody who actually got off on that kind of thing. Soon as we got to that place in Mexico, I decided, I was gonna go on my own. No more Psycho Mong. No more short-bus Rondell.

Mong turned his head suddenly and puked against the cave wall behind him. Then he puked again and coughed like he was coughing out his damn lungs. He puked one last time and spit and then made this pissed off growling noise as he wiped his mouth on the sleeve of his sweatshirt.

"Yo, you all right?" I said.

"I need to go make a fire," he said back. But again he didn't move.

I thought about what Mei-li said about him being sick. And how he seemed to be getting worse. And then my curiosity started going and finally I just asked him: "Yo, man, what do you got anyway?"

I could see the outline of his face turn to me, but he didn't say anything back.

We both lifted our feet when a little water from the tide came rushing in. After it drained back out I said: "Your cousin said you were sick, right? I'm just asking, what kind of—?"

"What'd you *really* do?" he interrupted.

I stared back at him, caught off guard. "What do you mean?"

"To get locked up in the first place," he said. "What'd you do?"

I shrugged and thought about his question for a few seconds. Wrapped my arms around my own chest and looked up at the light coming in through the opening of the cave. And I'll be honest, a part of me wanted to just say it. Let the shit out finally, to some Chinese kid I'd probably never see again once we got down to Mexico. But when I opened my mouth nothing came out. And my chest felt hollow, like when you break open a chocolate bunny on Easter. Actually, more hollow than that even. So hollow I wasn't even in my own body anymore. I was hovering up above, near the opening of the cave, watching to see what I'd say. Which words I'd use to explain the horrible thing I did. To my own family.

"What'd you do?" Mong said again.

I turned to face him, nodding my head up and down, said: "Stole a bike, man."

The part of me that was floating over me shook its head and whispered about what a little bitch-ass I was that I still couldn't even face what happened and just say it. But I didn't give a fuck about that part of me. I was the one who had to live the rest of my damn life.

"No," Mong said, "I mean what'd you *really* do?"

I looked right back at him. I could almost make out his eyes now that mine had adjusted to the dark. Could almost see the scars on his cheeks. "That *is* what I did," I said. "I stole a bike. Just like everybody says I did. One with a little pink basket in front for my panties, and tassels."

He reached out and touched his fingers to the cave wall, and then leaned back again. "All right," he said. "You stole a bike, then."

"What, you don't believe me?" I said.

"Not really."

"How come?"

Mong shrugged. "That first night when I was watching you sleep. When you woke up and looked at me, I could just tell. You did something bad. Something that's gonna stay with you forever."

I stared back at him, confused as hell. How could he know what I did from just me waking up? Plus, if you think about it, the dude was really my enemy. We'd already been in two fights and he'd spit on me. I remember wishing as hard as I could that something bad would happen to him. And now he was sick.

He coughed again, spit between his legs. "I'm gonna make a fire," he said, and this time he actually pushed off the wall and stood up, started climbing toward the mouth of the cave.

Just before he pulled himself through, though, I told him: "I just wish I could stop thinking about it, man. That's all."

Mong paused and turned to look at me over his shoulder.

"I try my ass off, you know? But I just keep thinking about it. Over and over."

Mong stayed there for a long time, looking down at me.

Staring at the air above his head, I went dizzy for a sec and had a fully awake dream about diving off Mong's bridge in San Francisco. I was falling toward the water with my eyes closed and my hands extended in front of me like an Olympic diver. I looked like a bird going down for prey or a big kite taking a nosedive. I felt the wind pushing into my face and then the surface of the cold bay as it sucked me in and held me under until my lungs were full of water and I was dead.

"I'm gonna go do the fire," Mong said.

I closed and opened my eyes, still alive, still having to remember.

I heard Mong's footsteps walking back to where we left our bags. Heard Rondell's voice and the sound of somebody tearing open our bag of charcoal. And I heard somebody say my name: Mexico.

What Happens to Somebody's Mind When They Sit at the Bottom of a Cave:

I stayed down there alone and made like it was my cave all along, from the beginning of time. Like God or whoever put it here just for me to find, tonight, and now I had to stay down here and think about what I thought, long as it took. But at the same time, even in my own cave, I still felt out of place. And I'm not just talking about tonight. I'm talking about all the damn time, in my own body, ever since that day in Stockton.

You know how when you're a kid and you get a new badass rubber football for Christmas, and then when you wake up the next morning it takes a few minutes to remember why you're so excited? It's like that for me, only the opposite. When I wake up, everything's normal for a while. I'm just plain Miguel. And then suddenly it hits me what I did. It punches me right in the ribs. It screams in my ears how everything *isn't* normal anymore, it's fucked.

125

I sat in the cave a long-ass time, lifting my feet whenever the water came in, imagining myself falling to the kitchen floor again in Stockton. For the hundred-thousandth time. Falling flat on my back, slamming my head against the wooden cupboard. The wind knocked out of me and my head all wet with my own blood. I stared at the dark cave wall and saw everything happening all over again. From every angle. In slow motion. Speeded up. Me falling and the sound of my head hitting the cupboard and the big knife in my hand. And the kitchen table turning over. And me falling and hitting my head. And the big knife sticking straight up. The blood gushing from my head, pooling on the cracked tile.

And his eyes—on mine, and then not.

His eyes.

On mine.

And then not.

Against the dark cave wall those twenty seconds played like a movie. A video some teacher was showing at school. And I just sat there in the back row watching it. This surge of aloneness rolling through my entire body, numbing the tips of my fingers and making my skin sweat even though I wasn't moving, and everything trying to push itself out from the back of my eyes.

And I know how people say you should just let it all out, even a guy. But what the fuck do *they* understand? 'Cause all I know is the only way I could go on living for even one more hour is if I kept everything exactly where it had to be. Inside. I clenched up every muscle and held it there with all my strength. Like I'd done every other time. I shoved it back down my throat. Gagged on it. Swallowed it back into my stomach like poison.

And right then I decided something: I didn't care if I *ever* left this cave—like Rondell said, only different. I didn't care if

I ever really made it to Mexico. Or if I met another cool girl like Mei-li. Or even if I lived or died. I didn't care about nothin' or no one and I never would again. 'Cause I didn't deserve to. And just like what Mong said to the store worker earlier, I had nothing left to lose. Those weren't just words he was saying, they were the truth.

It took me being in the bottom of a cave to truly understand what he meant. In the middle of the night. The middle of nowhere. I really had nothing.

I dreamed about me staying in the cave for the rest of my life. Eventually starving to death. How years from now a couple adventure-type kids would find my bones. How the news channels would all do a story about the mysterious skeleton found at the bottom of a cave. Who was it? Why'd he just stay in a cave until he starved to death?

After a while, though, I took a deep breath and wiped my eyes with the back of my hands.

I squeezed my own arms hard as I could to show I was still real. And then I climbed out through the mouth of the cave and went to go help Mong and Rondell do the food.

When they said they had it covered I went to my bag and got my journal out. I went a little ways down, closer to the water where I could see better, and wrote and wrote and wrote. And now I think I've said every single thing that's happened since Mei-li told her story about those two people in China.

July 19

Me and Rondell killed about five hot dogs each, mowed through half a pack of beef jerky, some donuts and were working on our second six-pack of beer. Mong, on the other hand, he'd hardly touched a thing. He claimed he wasn't hungry because he was thinking about how we were gonna get to Mexico, but that was BS. Twice I watched him sneak down the beach and I'd put money down he was throwing up. I didn't know what was wrong with dude, but it wasn't no regular stomach flu or food poisoning. I felt bad, too, 'cause of how I'd used my mind on him. I mean, we weren't best friends or anything, and he was mostly a psycho who I was definitely gonna part ways with the second we got to Mexico, but still. People should never wish medical stuff on other people.

We stayed sitting around the big pile of glowing charcoal, talking—me and Rondell mostly. Us drinking beer, Mong sipping a can of Coke. We talked about Juvi and the way Jaden called everybody "bro" and how it might be down in Mexico. We talked about old girls we'd known and the racist store worker and if because of him the cops would be out looking for us tomorrow. We said how if we had our pick we'd all live in houses right here on the beach like this, where you could hear the waves breaking on the sand and smell the saltwater air coming in through your bedroom window when you climbed your tired ass into bed at night. And then I don't even know how but we got to talking about what made us scared.

Rondell said the devil. Sometimes, he explained, the devil came right up into his head, at the weirdest times, made him do things he'd never think of on his own. He told us about the time he beat up some man in a suit standing outside a church. For no reason. The devil just went into his head and twisted his thoughts around as he was walking toward the guy. Next thing he knew he was wailing on the guy's bloody face. Right there on the sidewalk, in front of everybody. Took three cops with billy clubs to finally pull him off. The suit guy ended up spending four days in intensive care with all kinds of injuries, including a fractured skull. It was the first time he ever got arrested, Rondell said. He was only eleven.

I stared at him after he was done telling his crazy-ass story, thinking how maybe that's the reason he carried a Bible around everywhere he went. Maybe he thought it would fend off his imaginary devil problems.

"Now I'm scared like hell of hearin' the devil," Rondell said. "I never know when he's just gonna come runnin' up in my head and mix everything up."

Me and Mong sat there a sec, nodding, letting Rondell's words have a little space. We all sipped our drinks and stared at the glowing charcoal. I considered how Rondell was more messed up than I even thought. Maybe even as messed up as Mong if you looked at it a certain way.

But what'd that shit say about me, then? I mean, I was right there with 'em.

"What about you, Mexico?" Rondell said.

I took a sip of my beer and pointed the can at him. "Don't laugh," I said. "I'm serious. But it's damn spiders."

Rondell looked at me with his eyes all bugged. "Spiders?"

"Spiders."

He slapped his jeans-covered knee and put a fist to his mouth. "Nah, Mexico," he said through his laughter.

Mong gave me a weird look like I had to be just playing, but I wasn't.

"I promise, man. Those little bastards freak me out. Bring on a damn panther or cobra snake, put me in a ring with a big-ass bull, I don't even care. But if I catch a daddy longlegs creeping across my bedspread one night—yo, I put this on everything, I'll go crash on the living room couch for a week."

Rondell threw a piece of seaweed at me, still cracking up. He took a swig of his beer and said: "You's a scaredy-cat, Mexico. I let spiders crawl all on my hands and arms."

"You also let the devil crawl all over your brain," I shot back.

Rondell's face went dead serious. "Wha'chu mean by that, Mexico?"

"What I just said, Rondo." I glanced at Mong, then went back at Rondell. "Dawg, you gotta take a couple Q-tips to those ears, man. You got mad wax buildup."

"Just what'd you tell me, then?"

"Spiders freak me out."

"Oh."

"That's all I'm sayin', Rondo."

"Why didn't you just say it then, Mexico? You don't gotta bring up me and the devil like that. It's blasphemic."

I smiled. "Uh, you mean 'blasphemous'?"

"Wha'chu think I just said?"

I shook my head at the poor kid, told him: "Lemme ask you somethin', Pope John Paul, what do you think that word even means?"

Rondell sipped his beer and looked at Mong, then he looked back at me. "Means when someone brings in the devil when they supposed to just be talkin' 'bout spiders."

I spit out a mouthful of beer I laughed so hard. I pumped my fist and told him: "Rondell, man."

"What?"

"You my man, dawg. For real."

At first he tried to be serious, like maybe I was still messing with him, which I was, but then a smile slowly came over his face and he said: "But that's just what it means, Mexico. Don't play like I ain't never knowed what 'blasphemic' is."

Even Mong was chuckling now.

When we all finally stopped laughing I asked him the question, too: "Yo, what about you, man?"

Mong shrugged, said: "Nothing."

"Come on," I said. "You gotta be scared of *somethin'*. What about terrorists or earthquakes or herpes."

He shook his head and looked at the label of his Coke can. "I think we're all just passing through in this life. We're only temporary. When I learned that I realized there's no reason to be scared."

I nodded for a little while, staring at the sand by Mong's feet, feeling the alcohol warming my insides. I looked up at him. "I'm not gonna lie, man, you kind of lost me a little. And if you lost *me* that means Rondo over there probably thinks you're talkin' about the devil again."

"Wha'chu sayin' with me and the devil?" Rondell said, shooting me a dirty look. "That shit ain't right, Mexico."

I waved Rondell off and turned back to Mong. "How long you thought that way?"

Mong shrugged. "I just woke up one day and realized it. Like I told that guy in the store, I have nothing to lose because nothing belongs to me." He paused a sec, picked up a stick and spun it around in his fingers. "I don't even know what it feels like to be scared anymore. It's complicated."

Me and Rondell stared at him, confused. But at the same time I believed him too. Maybe it explained some of the crazy things he did. And how calm he seemed even when we were in a fight. *Nobody* looks that calm during a fight. Not even Diego.

As we sat there in the sand, me and Rondell finished another beer each, cracked open a couple fresh ones. I hadn't touched a drop of alcohol since the last time I chilled with Diego on the levee, so I was buzzing pretty hard. It felt nice and warm and mellow. It made me feel like us three were on some kind of important journey to save America from evil. Like a brand-new kind of war. No fighting or bombing or invading other places, just living out in the open, on the beach. The opposite of being in jail. We were totally free. People think they're free just being in this country, but it's more than that.

I looked up at Mong and Rondell all inspired as hell and said: "Yo, I gotta go write in my journal, man."

When I stood up I realized I was more than just buzzed. I was drunk.

"Why you always writin' in there for, Mexico?" Rondell said.

"Well, Rondo," I said, swaying a little, "maybe it's 'cause a court-appointed judge told me I *had* to."

"Yeah, but, Mexico," Rondell said, "that judge ain't gonna be with us down in Mexico."

I stood there looking at him for a few seconds. I couldn't believe it, Rondell had actually just stumped my ass. I almost wanted to tackle the guy into the sand and get his big head in a vise grip for saying something that actually made sense. Instead I just swayed in the wind and sipped my beer, thinking how beer had the exact opposite effect on us two: it made me all dumb as a rock and him halfway literate.

I waved them both off—the big black, drunk-ass Einstein and the little Asian Buddhist psychopath. I scooped up my bag and pointed at Rondell. "Maybe I just still wanna do it. You ever think about that, homey? Maybe someday I'll bury my journal somewhere in Mexico and hundreds of years from now some archaeologist will come along and dig it up and people will know how we all lived in this era—or at least you, me and Mong. And when they read about you, money, they'll find out how the devil twists your thoughts and how you eat hot dogs by leaning your head back and dropping the whole damn thing into your big-ass mouth and how pretty much all you do when you're not eating is piss and shit and sleep and say, 'Wha'chu mean by that, Mexico?' "

Rondell and Mong both grinned a little, and then Rondell shot back: "You gonna tell 'em I'm handsomer than you, too, Mexico?"

Mong actually laughed out loud after Rondell said that one, which made Rondell think what he just said must've been the funniest thing in the history of mankind, and he laughed so hard he actually fell over into the sand.

"I already did, Rondo," I said.

"Did what?" Rondell said, sitting back up, still laughing.

"Said how handsome you are."

His face got a little more serious. "You really said that about me, Mexico?"

"Hell nah, I didn't say that, Rondo! This shit I write in here ain't fiction. It's true to life."

They both laughed a little more, and I shifted my bag from one shoulder to the other and spun around and left.

I walked through thick sand and giant clumps of fly-infested seaweed to try and find a spot with enough light that I could see what I was doing.

I cruised all the way back out to the street, sat on a rock underneath one of the few streetlights and pulled out my journal. Every few seconds I'd look for cop cars even though we were a long ways from the store and I supposedly didn't care.

I stared at the cover of my journal, thinking about what Rondell had just said about no judges being in Mexico. The guy was right, technically I didn't have to write in here anymore, but for some reason I still *wanted* to. Maybe it was 'cause I'd already started or 'cause I thought we should have a record of us getting to Mexico. Or maybe it was 'cause of all the books I was reading. And how much I liked 'em, and how me writing in this journal was really just a way for me to make like I was writing my own book—except everything that happens in it is true instead of made-up stories. And I don't wanna waste time saying a bunch of shit about how I *feel* and how everybody else *feels,* like a damn girl's diary does. Maybe I just wanna put what happens. And what people say.

Miguel Castañeda: author.

Yo, you better recognize.

Actually it really doesn't matter *what* the reason is. Or what anybody else thinks. Or how I do it. I just wanna keep going with my journal.

So I am.

I didn't end up writing in my journal right away, though. I set it to the side of my bag and pulled out Mong's, Rondell's and my files instead, the ones they had no clue I even had. The three folders had gotten pretty messed up in my bag, all folded over and crushed by clothes and some of the food we'd swiped. I smoothed them out, picturing Jaden and Lester sitting in their offices, sipping coffee and reading about us. Deciding who we were just based on what it said.

I opened Mong's first and read it cover to cover. And I was completely shocked about what it said:

Under education: Mong attended private schools through junior high school, all in Santa Monica, ranked top five in his class with a GPA of over 4.0 at the time of his parents' death. After being sent to live with extended family, enrolled in a public school in Guerneville, California. Severe drop in grades, attendance and behavior. Held back in ninth grade. Teachers labeled him: "aloof," "withdrawn," "violent," "at risk."

My eyes bugged as I flipped to the next page. I looked back at where Mong and Rondell were, but I couldn't see them from my spot on the street. Suddenly I was sober as hell. I knew I was reading some shit I wasn't supposed to be

134

reading, but it was so fascinating to find out about someone you've been around for over a month.

I turned back to Mong's file and kept going:

Under health issues: Shot in face from point-blank range at age fourteen. Bullet entered one cheek and exited the other. In hospital for four months, multiple surgeries, months of physical therapy. Ultimately recovered with major scarring around face and reconstructed teeth. At sixteen diagnosed with major kidney disease. Now "advanced." Must be taken to health clinic every forty-eight hours for hemodialysis. Currently on waiting list for donor and kidney transplant. Outlook uncertain.

Under criminal history: Arrested at fourteen for arson, set fire to family house in Los Angeles. Arrested at fifteen for first-degree assault. Arrested at fifteen for vandalism and disorderly conduct. Arrested at sixteen for first-degree assault. History of substance abuse. Clinically depressed, severely antisocial, suicidal tendencies.

Under Mong's family history: Father Chinese, graduated Harvard Law. Mother half-Chinese/half-Vietnamese singer from Shanghai. Moved from China to Santa Monica, California, a few years after marriage. Mother diagnosed with bipolar disorder. Showed improvement as a result of medication, relapsed after second miscarriage. Father moved wife's entire family from China to California to form support system. Mother refused to leave house, stopped all communication with husband and family. Mong raised by nanny. Family therapy, couples therapy, but marriage ultimately failed.

September 13, 2006: Father shot wife in back of head while she slept, killing her instantly. Father shot Mong in face, intending to end his life also, then placed gun in own mouth and committed suicide. Mong survived with major injuries to head and face. Copy of father's suicide note written in Mandarin (translated):

"Our family was no longer happy in this life. We will try again in the next one. Things will be better."

Five months in UCLA Medical Center, multiple surgeries. Mong moved up to Guerneville, California, to live with extended family: grandmother, grandfather, aunt, uncle and cousin.

Holy shit, I thought as I closed Mong's folder. My life was twenty times better than Mong's. His old man had actually killed his moms and then tried to kill *him*. Mei-li's whole story of "true love" was actually Mong's damn life. He had to have been the baby the singer had in her stomach that made her not able to win the contest. Holy shit.

And how could all that shit happen to somebody and then they get a kidney problem too? How's that even fair? To have so many bad things happen in one life? No wonder Mong never ate anything and was always tired and throwing up all over the place. No wonder he was so pissed off and wanted to fight everybody.

I sat there for a few minutes, completely stunned. I didn't even know what to do or think. I stared down the empty highway not really seeing anything but going over Mong's life in my head.

Without even thinking I picked up Mong's file and ripped it into a thousand little pieces, got down on my hands and knees and dug a huge hole by the side of the road. I buried everything I'd just read and covered it with dirt and sand and gravel, patted it all down with the underside of my fists so nobody could ever read his life again.

I grabbed Rondell's file, opened the cover:

Under education: Held back in first grade, again in third grade. Placed in special-ed program in fifth grade, dropped out of school entirely halfway through school year. No further public school records. Placed in vocational school program in Juvenile Hall, failed to turn in work.

Under health concerns: Born extremely premature, underweight, with critical addiction issues. Underdeveloped lungs. Small head circumference. Mild learning disabilities. Health improved dramatically during adolescence. Now far above national average in height, weight, strength. Nationally ranked AAU basketball player at time of first arrest.

Under criminal history: Arrested at eleven for assault. Arrested at eleven for grand theft auto. Arrested at twelve for assault. Arrested at thirteen for assault with a deadly weapon. History of alcohol and substance abuse. "Aloof," "antisocial," "deeply religious."

Under family history: Born to a crack-addicted mother, father unknown. Great-grandmother took him home from hospital, raised him in projects in Oakland, California, until she died of melanoma when Rondell was six. Placed in foster care for a year and a half, until aunt and her partner adopted him. Social services took him away a year later under suspicion of male physical and sexual abuse. Placed back in foster care. In and out of various foster families for next three years until first sentenced to Juvenile Hall. In system ever since.

I closed up Rondell's file and tore his to shreds too. Got back down on my hands and knees and dug another hole, right next to the one I'd dug for Mong's file. I buried his pieces at the very bottom, covered it and packed everything in with the underside of my fists.

I grabbed my own file, stared at the cover:

"Miguel Castañeda."

I wanted to open it so bad, to see what they said about me. How they explained what happened in Stockton. Or with my dad. Or what they'd say about my moms and how she feels about me now. Or my grandparents in Fresno. But at the same time I was scared. Maybe I didn't really wanna read what somebody wrote about me. What if they got something wrong? Or if I read about my moms not ever wanting to take me back? Or something about Diego that pissed me off?

I sat there at the side of the road for a long-ass time, staring at the file, trying to decide what I should do. I took deep breaths preparing myself so I could read it. Peeked open the folder, flipped to the Crime History part and read the first couple words about what I did.

Then I slammed closed the damn thing and ripped it to shreds. And instead of digging a hole this time, and burying it in the ground next to Mong and Rondell, I threw my pieces up in the air and let the wind carry 'em all over the place. Little scraps of my life blowing away from me, blowing down the road, into the sand, across the street. I sat back up on my rock and watched them go everywhere, and then I zipped up my bag and went over everything I'd just read about Mong and Rondell in my head. The ocean still buzzing behind my back. And then I thought how the ocean would *always* buzz like this. Long after us three were gone. And the moon in the sky too. It would always come climbing up above the clouds when nighttime came around. And like Mong said, we were just temporary. People. We were just passing through.

But even so, I decided something sitting there: me, Mong and Rondell might be temporary, but while we were here we were more than just what some file could say. We were real people too, just the same as anybody else who was alive. If somebody wanted to know about us they should meet us face to face instead of just relying on typed words.

I unzipped my bag, pulled out my journal and started writing everything down.

When I was halfway done I grabbed my bag, got up and

went over to where Mong and Rondell were laying on their backs in the sand, both their bags underneath their heads as pillows. Mong shot his head up and opened his eyes when I got up to them, but when he saw it was just me he slowly lowered his head back down, closed his eyes again.

I laid on my back right next to them, bag under my own head. I stared up at the moon for a little bit, at all the stars in the sky. It made me think of when me and Diego used to lay on our backs near the levee some nights and look straight up in the air. Sometimes we could see stars for days. And now I was laying here with Mong and Rondell, doing the same thing.

I flipped over and opened my journal.

The last thing I can think of before finishing my writing is if I'm being disloyal to Diego by looking at stars with anybody besides him.

July 20

Before I got put away, Moms always went after me and Diego for fighting so much. She'd pull me aside when I was on my way out the front door for school, or she'd grab Diego off me in the hall, screaming us down, but mostly she'd just try to bring it up all casual when we were sitting around the TV after dinner. Like it wasn't a big deal. Like it didn't completely tear her apart every time she saw it.

"Tell me something, boys," she'd start, "why are you two always going after each other? Every time I turn around. Can somebody please explain this to me?"

Neither one of us would give her much of an answer, though. Diego would shrug, or I'd glance at my big bro and tell her: "We don't even know, Ma. Just happens."

And it's true, things sometimes just get out of hand when

me and my bro are together all day. Especially since our old man has been MIA. We get in these wild fistfights at the levee or wrestling matches in the backyard or Diego will pin me against the floor in the bathroom and try to make me say mercy:

"Say mercy, Guelly!"

"Hell nah!"

"Come on, Guelly, just say mercy and I'll let your bitch ass go!"

"Hell nah!"

According to Diego, it isn't that big a deal, though, 'cause we never hit each other in the face. He says you only punch somebody in the face when you're really trying to hurt 'em, in a *real* fight, and if we're not really trying to hurt each other then technically we're just "fooling around"—no matter how crazy serious we might seem at the time.

"It just doesn't make sense," Moms will say, flipping the channel to a baseball game or some reality show we all like. "You two love each other. As much as any two brothers I've ever known."

She'll turn to look at us with this concerned face that kills me, then go back to the TV shaking her head, legs curled underneath her on the couch, the way she's always liked to sit. Me in the rocking chair on her right, watching her.

"It's just how brothers are, Ma," Diego will say, kicking his feet up in Pop's old La-Z-Boy. "You even said so yourself. Dad and Uncle Armando were the same way coming up. They'd get in scraps all the time, right? But when it came down to it, they had each other's backs."

"That was different, Diego," Moms'll say. "Nobody ever got *hurt*. Look at your brother's eye, baby." She'll reach out and take my face in her hands, turn it so Diego can see my latest war wound in the light. "Look at this gash. Your Dad and uncle never drew *blood*."

"Come on, Ma," Diego'll say, waving her off. "That was just a freak head butt. It wasn't on purpose or nothin'."

"We were playin', Ma," I'll add, so Diego knows I'm taking up for him again.

"See?" Diego will hold his hands out all innocent-like.

And that's when Moms will force a smile and shake her head, pretend like she knows it's not as big a deal as she's making it out to be. But I can usually see it in her eyes: she's genuinely scared about how we are with each other.

"What am I gonna do with you two boys?"

"Tell you what," Diego will say. "Me and Guelly'll try and cool it a little, all right, Ma? He'll watch that mouth he gots, and I'll cut the kid some slack. That work for you, Ma?"

"We'll chill," I'll add. "We don't wanna make you worry or nothin'."

She'll roll her eyes and shake her head, say: "I've heard *that* one before." Because she has. A grip of times. But still she'll drop it. And we'll all three of us just sit there watching TV together, not really talking anymore. Or she'll change the subject to something about school. Or me and Diego will cruise into the kitchen to rummage through the fridge and cupboards for something else to eat.

But that's just how it is with me and my big bro. We hang together all the time, so occasionally we get on each other's nerves, right? Plus Diego's got this crazy temper. Sometimes when he's bombing on me he'll even forget about his rule, how we're not supposed to hit each other in the face. But I always bomb right back. I know he respects me way more if I stand toe-to-toe and fight.

And most times when we get tired we'll just stop mid-brawl and lay on the floor next to each other breathing all hard.

"Dude, Diego," I'll say, between huffing and puffing, "I think you caught me, man. In the liver. With that last body shot."

Or he'll say: "Yo, Guelly. Peep the back of my neck, man. That shit bleeding?"

"Nah, it's just red."

"What up with them fingernails, dawg? You gotta cut that shit."

And then we'll just lay there, still breathing crazy hard, laughing at each other's wounds.

Like since we were kids.

July 21

I cracked open my eyes early this morning when the sunlight crept over the cliff to the east. I sat up and stretched, yawned, walked over between two big boulders to pee. Even though it was the middle of the summer, and I had a sweatshirt on, it was still pretty cold. I held my arms in close to my body and blew warm air into both my fists.

When I came back I looked down at the huge black mound of human body that is Rondell, laying there all curled like a baby. Surprise, surprise, I thought, still asleep. I looked up, spotted Mong down on the beach, in water up to his ankles, staring out over the horizon.

I kneeled next to Rondell and rolled his big head to the side a little so I could get my book, *Of Mice and Men*, out of his bag. Dude was so comatose he didn't even change his breathing.

I read the last couple pages on my stomach, facing the water. The ending was pretty damn sad. But I liked how short the book was. And I liked the characters—made me think of me, Mong and Rondell, and how we were kind of living off the land too. And Rondell was sort of like that dude Lenny except he's never killed an animal just by petting it—at least, not that I know of.

When I closed the book I glanced over at Rondell for a sec, going back over what I'd read in his file last night. He didn't seem like a kid who'd had all that bad stuff happen to him. He just looked normal. Except the fact that he's so damn big and not that smart. I looked down the beach at Mong, though, just standing there in the water, staring out at the ocean in one of his trances, and I could actually *see* it. Mong was touched by all the shit he'd been through.

I moved Rondell's head again, stuck the book back in his bag and pulled out the next one in my stack: *The Catcher in the Rye*. I know pretty much every-damn-body in the damn world's read *The Catcher in the Rye* at some point. But not me. I think it was assigned in my English class last year, but I never got around to it.

I read the first twenty-something pages, and right off I knew why it was so popular. It was the way the kid, Holden, talked about stuff. And how he seemed so honest about everything that was going through his head. The only thing I wonder about sometimes, though, is why some rich kids like him complain about their lives so much. I know everybody's situation is hard in its own way, but when you look at a kid like Mong or Rondell, when you read their files and think about how they never even say a *word* about it, they just deal, and then you start reading about some prep school kid like Holden, and how the whole time he keeps complaining and complaining . . . I don't know, I just think about that sometimes. I'm not saying the book's not good so far. I like it a lot. I just wonder how this Holden kid would be if some *real* bad shit went down, like he was born to a crackhead mom or his dad shot him in the damn face.

By the way, reading on the beach, early in the morning like this, with birds chirping and flying all over the ocean looking for fish, a little bit of beach dampness covering everything in sight, including you—it's probably the coolest thing you could do with a book. Trust me.

The reason I didn't read so much back in Stockton is 'cause I figured I was too busy living my own life. Why would I read about different characters' lives all the time when I had a damn life of my own: me and Diego cruising the hood, fishing off the levee, playing ball at the park, looking in people's windows and watching them sleep. But now I know it doesn't matter. You maybe even get *more* from a book if you have a life of your own, 'cause you can relate.

Anyways, I read until Mong came back from the water and Rondell woke up and then we gathered up all the stuff we were gonna take with us—some of the food and the matches and the leftover beers and Cokes—and shoved it all in Rondell's bag. We didn't say much as we took off walking, just that we were gonna go along the highway to see if we could hitch a ride to Santa Cruz, where Mong said there'd be a major bus station. He also said we had to watch out for cop cars in case they were looking for who tied up and robbed that old store dude last night. The place was miles back from where we were, but cops can spread the word about what happens in different places mad quick through their system.

And I don't know why, but I didn't care as much about following Mong anymore. Maybe it's 'cause it didn't matter who was leading who anymore. Or because it was only temporary, until we got to Mexico. Or because of what I read in his file. But I hardly even thought about it now.

We walked along the narrow side of the road single file, holding out our thumbs and watching for cops. Twice in the first two hours we had to duck off the side of the road when we saw a black-and-white moving toward us in the distance. But they never saw a thing and we just watched 'em roll on by. The problem was for the longest no regular cars slowed for us either. It was three hours into our walking before a stock-looking black car finally pulled to the shoulder in front of us and slowed to a stop. I was happy as hell too, 'cause the whole pedestrian thing was getting mad played out, but then Mong sort of hesitated.

"Shit," he said.

"What?" I said.

"What?" Rondell said.

"I think that's a cop," Mong said.

My stomach dropped.

Sure enough, right after Mong said it a big Mexican cop wearing sunglasses got out and leaned against his trunk, waiting for us to get up to him. I looked at Mong to see if we should run but he motioned with his head for us to keep going.

"Gentlemen," the cop said.

"Hey," we said back.

He pushed off his trunk and crossed his arms. "You know it's not real safe to hitch a ride these days, right?"

We all nodded and looked at the pavement.

"Where you headed?"

Mong smiled and looked up, said: "We're gonna go ride the roller coaster in Santa Cruz."

"That right?" the cop said, nodding his head and staring

at each of us, one at a time. Then he didn't say anything for a second and neither did we. He reached in the window of his car and pulled out a folder, started looking through some papers in there, peeking up at us every couple seconds.

The guy was rocking a pair of those shiny cop sunglasses, and on both of the little lenses I could see me, Mong and Rondell standing right there in front of him—a Chinese kid with damn bullet holes in his cheeks, a skinny cholo-looking kid, and a giant black kid with a baby 'fro. Add to the fact we all had on the exact same stock sneaks, the same jeans, same black sweatshirts, same bag slung over the same shoulder.

I was surprised dude hadn't *already* thrown our asses in the back of his undercover cop car.

"Gonna spend a day in the Cruz, eh?" the cop said, closing his folder again. "Sounds like a blast."

"We're excited," Mong said.

"Okay, lemme get your names real quick and hopefully I can send you on your way."

"How come you need our names?" I said, maybe a little too fast.

He smiled and put his folder on the roof of his car, pulled a little notebook and pen from his shirt pocket. "Just standard procedure, gentlemen." He pointed at me to go first.

I looked at Mong and Rondell real quick, then turned back to the cop, said: "Marco Sanchez." I watched the cop scribble it down.

He pointed at Mong.

"Yao Chang," Mong said.

The cop scribbled down the name Mong said too, and then pointed to Rondell.

"Rondell Law," Rondell said. He pointed at the cop's pad of paper and added: "Gots two *L*s at the end of the first part,

Rondell." He looked at me all proud of himself as the cop scribbled down his name.

Me and Mong both looked at Rondell with our mouths hanging wide open.

"You guys just sit tight for a minute," the cop said, and he went around to his door, reached in for the radio and held it up to his mouth. He looked back at us all skeptical, then picked up his folder and started riffling through his papers again.

Mong tapped me on the forearm, motioned with his head toward the beach.

I nodded, turned to Rondell and whispered: "Good one, homey."

"What?" he said.

Soon as the guy turned his back to us again, Mong broke for the beach. I grabbed Rondell's arm, pulled his big ass with me, and we all hit the sand racing south toward Santa Cruz, our bags still slung over our shoulders and bouncing with every step.

The cop spun around, yelled out "Hey!" and sprinted around his squad car. He chased us down the beach for a ways, but when he saw he wasn't gonna catch us on foot, he spun around and ran back toward his car.

Mong slowed and turned to us out of breath. When he stopped, me and Rondell stopped too. Mong coughed and spit, said: "We gotta go back. The other way." He was having trouble catching his breath.

"To where the cop is?" I said.

"He's gonna call on his radio." He spit and bent over for a sec, looked up. "They'll have cops looking for us. All down the beach."

"Shit, that's true."

Me and Rondell leaned over too, trying to get our wind. "We gotta go back," Mong said, standing straight up and spitting. "We gotta go past where he is and wait. Maybe till nighttime."

I nodded. Then I turned to Rondell and punched him in the arm as hard as I could.

He frowned, grabbed his arm, said: "Ouch, Mexico."

"What the hell were you thinkin'?"

"Wha'chu mean?" he said, rubbing the spot where I hit him.

"You gave him your *real* name, Einstein."

"He told me to say it." Rondell stared back at me, baffled, then turned to look at Mong. It was amazing, the guy genuinely had no idea what he'd done wrong.

"It wouldn't have mattered," Mong said. "He was looking for our description. I was wrong to use the road in the first place."

"Still," I said, frustrated as hell.

"He told me to say it," Rondell said, shrugging.

I looked down at my sweatshirt and jeans and told Mong: "Yo, we need different clothes."

Mong nodded. "Tomorrow."

He started creeping back the other way, along the cliff, and me and Rondell followed him.

We snuck around to the small cliff that stood between the ocean and the highway where the car was, peeked around at the cop. He was sitting in his front seat with the door wide open, radio up to his mouth. He lowered it into his lap, listened, raised it and said something else, then he just sat there for a couple minutes. Cars occasionally sped by on the highway, a backpacking couple on mountain bikes pedaled past. It was much warmer now, because the sun was up higher over the mountains. But behind us, over the ocean were evil-looking black clouds that seemed headed our way, made me think it might rain soon.

I looked at the road just as two normal-looking cop cars pulled up next to the guy and cut their engines. Three cops got out, slammed closed their doors. They huddled next to the Mexican cop, talking. One had a cup of coffee in his hand. Then three of the four started climbing back down to the beach again.

Me, Mong and Rondell scurried into a big cluster of boulders, out of sight. They walked by, carrying their walkie-talkies, sunglasses now up on the Mexican one's head. He looked around and talked to one of the other cops, then into his walkie-talkie. Another cop, a female one, turned to face the water. She kicked at a shell and looked up at the dark clouds over the ocean.

I was nervous watching them, but at the same time there was no way they could see us. And they were more talking on their radios than actually looking. They probably figured we were still booking it down the beach, a long ways down there by now.

Rondell tapped me and whispered: "Hey, Mexico, I get it now. I shouldn't have told 'im my real name, right? That's why you said you was Marco."

"Whatever," I whispered back. "It's over now."

"I get it, though," he said. He turned to Mong, said: "I get it now, Mong."

"It's okay," Mong said, patting Rondell on his shoulder.

I thought how weird it was that Mong never got frustrated with Rondell like I did. He was always nice to the guy, which almost made Mong seem like a regular person.

Rondell turned back to me, started whispering something else about this incredible discovery he'd just made about saying his real name, but I put my finger up to my lips so he'd stop making noise.

He nodded his head and smiled, said: "Okay, Mexico, but I get it now." Looking at Rondell's face, you'd think he just found the cure for damn cancer.

"Sorry," he said.

"It's fine, Rondo," I said. "You just gotta *think*, man."

"I know." He hung his head.

"It doesn't matter," Mong said.

"We'll be all right," I said, trying not to be so pissed.

Rondell nodded and patted me on the shoulder.

Me and him glanced at each other real quick, and then we looked back at the cops with Mong. They stood there a while longer, gazing up at the black clouds now coming in over the choppy ocean, pointing. One of them said something else into his walkie-talkie and then they all hiked back through the sand and over the guardrail to their cars.

The three of us snuck up to the cliff again, watched them climb back into their driver's seats and take off down the highway, the lead car's lights spinning but making no sound.

July 21—more

We hiked through thick sand the opposite direction of Santa Cruz to lay low for the day, stopped about a mile past where the Mexican cop had asked our names. We ducked into this perfect little crevice, between a few big boulders and the face of a rugged-looking dirt cliff that shot up over the sand about two times higher than my apartment building back in Stockton. If any cops were gonna find us now they'd pretty much have to scour every section of the beach, and even then they might miss our hiding spot.

Plus me and Mong agreed we probably weren't even that important to them in the grand scheme of things. Yeah, they most likely linked us to the tied-up store worker, got our descriptions, and maybe they even knew we were from the Lighthouse, but it's not like we'd hurt anybody really. And all we took from the store was food. We didn't go into the cash register and steal all the old dude's money.

Just to be safe, though, we decided to wait until dark to continue down the beach toward Mexico. Mong guessed it would take at least six or seven hours to walk all the way to Santa Cruz in the dark, but we'd learned our lesson about hitching. Wasn't worth the risk. And anyways, who would be crazy enough to pick up three group-home-looking kids in the middle of the night?

Shit, *I* wouldn't.

The Storm:

We were in a tight space together for a pretty long-ass time, but we didn't talk too much. Rondell mostly slept. Mong just stared out at the ocean without blinking like he was meditating. Sometimes fingering the brown tooth around his neck. I read some of my book and then wrote in my journal and then went back to reading again. Occasionally I'd look up at them, though, and think about what I found in their files last night. But it didn't make me feel closer to them like you might think. Actually it was the exact opposite. It made me feel farther away. I didn't see them as random kids anymore. They were real. And I think it's harder to be close to people when you know they're real. Like, if it's just some dude you're sharing a Juvi cell with you start to know how they act and what they say and how long they'll sleep for. You know they did something bad to get put away, same as you, and that they damn for sure don't wanna be there. But when you find out about all the stuff they've been through in their childhood and their health problems and what crimes they committed, it becomes totally different. They turn into real people. And it makes it way harder to talk to them, because now if you just talk about ordinary stuff like the weather or what day it is you know you're both being mad fake. Which I hate.

Anyways, that's what I found myself thinking about at one point, between reading my book. I don't even know why.

Speaking of the weather, as we sat there tucked away all afternoon I watched the thick rain clouds I'd seen earlier creep slowly toward shore and us. They looked like giant puffs of dark gray smoke, like there was a huge fire in the middle of the ocean, but the ocean wasn't red and orange with flames, it was gray and hazy and choppy. And the clouds made the sky grow dark even though it was still day. Then the wind picked up and a little rain started coming down.

At first it was just sprinkling, and the rocks and cliff mostly protected us. But even being just a little wet made the wind feel freezing cold. All three of us hugged our own knees and chattered our teeth a little. Rondell was awake now. Mong stopped holding out his hand to let drops fall in his palm. I'd put away my book and journal so they wouldn't get wet and just sat there on my bag, holding my legs up tight, watching everything.

The ocean surface had thousands of tiny white waves breaking in every direction now. A few brave seagulls were still waddling around in the sand or flying over the shallow part of the bumpy water, looking for fish. I wondered how it was even possible that a bird could still fly when it was raining. I'd never seen it before. But there were two of them, still struggling through the air, scavenging for food or whatever.

Even *they* disappeared, though, when the black clouds made it directly over us and the sky opened up and poured rain and thundered so loud it made us three jump a little every time. We got soaked 'cause the boulders couldn't protect us much from the heavier rain—which was loud as hell coming off the cliff. The wind whistling through the rocks. It sounded like we were underneath a huge waterfall or something. To take my mind off how miserable I felt I pretended that's exactly what it was. Me and Mong and Rondell were on some tropical island like Hawaii, and there was a waterfall above us. We were taking a break from hiking through the forest, totally in nature. It was before people even had houses. Everybody just lived in grass huts on the beach and had to fish every morning to get their food. And me and Mong and Rondell were hiding out watching the ocean to make sure nobody came floating up in a raft to try and invade our island.

It was a stupid-ass thing to think about, I know, but when you're soaked and freezing cold and the wind is whipping all in your face, you'll pretty much think up anything to take your mind off it.

Then suddenly the rain went soft again. And the wind died down. And eventually it cleared up altogether above us and the sun even came through the clouds making this giant real live rainbow appear over the ocean. It was the first one I'd ever seen that wasn't in a book or a magazine or on TV. It was amazing.

It warmed back up a little and Rondell fell back asleep and so did me and Mong for a while, even though we were still wet and uncomfortable. And when I woke up the sky above the ocean was completely clear and the sun was blood-red and falling behind the surface of the water. I watched the sky go light pink and then red and orange and then dark blue and purple. And when the sun disappeared completely from our view the colors faded too, and it became nighttime.

Rondell opened his eyes and stretched.

Mong said we could start walking south again.

The three of us picked up our bags, slid out from our spot and moved around our stiff arms and legs. Then we started walking toward Santa Cruz again, this time along the beach with clothes that were still wet.

July 22

To pass the time during our long walk, we decided to tell stories. At first the plan was to tell each other ghost stories 'cause it was so dark and eerie walking the long stretches of abandoned beach. Like any second some drugged-out bum might jump us. Or some crazy serial killer who sits all night with an axe leaned against his shoulder, waiting for victims like us to come strolling by gazing at the damn stars. But the ghost-story idea didn't fly 'cause none of us actually *knew* any ghost stories. Maybe Mong did, but he wasn't saying anything at all. He was being Silent Mong, my new name for when he walks right next to you but acts like he doesn't hear a word anybody's saying even when they ask him a direct question.

Anyways, me and Rondell ended up just telling random stuff from our lives.

The Story About Rondell's Horny Cat:
Rondell told us about a former foster mom's crazy cat that never got neutered and always sat in their sixth-story window meowing at female cats that pranced by on the street below. One day, Rondell told us, the cat lost its mind after seeing this one particular calico and started tearing around the house pissing and shitting everywhere and knocking things over, and then it jumped right through the screen and out the damn window. It ricocheted off a tree and somebody's

awning and fell into a thorny-ass rosebush, where it started yelping like a dog. The female cat raced off down the street, spooked as hell.

Rondell said when his foster mom looked at the hole in the screen she covered her ears, screamed her head off, and started running in place with mad tears streaming down her face. When she finally got herself together she and Rondell and a couple of his other foster brothers and sisters rumbled down the stairs and out the front door to see if the cat was still alive. It was, but just barely. And it wasn't yelping no more or making any sound at all. Poor thing had two broken legs and a dislocated shoulder, and its fur was all shredded-up and bloody 'cause the thorns. She pulled its little broken body up out of the rosebush and handed it to Rondell and they all ran down the middle of the street for ten blocks to the vet's office, but all the vet did was explain the injuries and put the cat to sleep.

"It was real sad," Rondell said, shaking his head. "We was all of us cryin' in that man's office."

Rondell looked mad serious about the memory of the poor cat, so I did everything I could not to laugh. Pinched my own side and bit my lip. But I couldn't make my grin go away.

"We gave him a little funeral," Rondell said. "The lady told a speech and asked us did we wanna say anything too."

"I hope you paid your respects, Rondo."

"Course I did, Mexico," Rondell shot back. "I said about everybody he made happy when he was still here. And when he went in their laps and how he had such soft skin."

"You mean fur."

Rondell looked at me. "That's what I said."

I started cracking up a little behind my fist. I kept picturing the cat leaping its little ass out the window after the girl one, whipping around in the air like a damn helicopter blade. I peeked at Rondell, but he didn't seem like he was paying attention to me.

"Know what the saddest part is?" Rondell said.

I made my face go straight. "What?"

"After I said my thing about his fur, and someone else started talkin', I kept thinkin' how he could never go to no heaven. Not even a cat one."

"Yeah?" I said, on the verge of busting up again. "Why's that?"

"It's 'cause the little guy committed suicide. I already told you what my auntie said 'bout people committin' suicide. It's for animals, too. That's my word."

"All for the chance at a little tail," I said.

And after I said it Rondell looked at me and we both sort of started cracking up together, even though we both knew technically a cat getting hurt wasn't something people should really be laughing about.

The Story About Me and Diego at the Beach:
I told them about when me and Diego went to the beach by ourselves, the first and only time after my pop passed. Diego had just gotten his license and he begged our moms to let us have the car for the day. She wasn't exactly stoked on the idea, but eventually, after we helped vacuum and dust the whole apartment, she handed Diego the keys and told us to be super careful and drive in the slow lane.

First thing we do is pop in some hip-hop, I told 'em, switching my bag to the other shoulder.

We were walking along the solid part of the sand, where it was dark and packed tight 'cause the tide had just been there. Mong was closest to the surf, Rondell was in the middle and I was toward the cliffs. As I started going into my story I could actually see me and Diego in the car, rolling down our windows and pointing to girls on the side of the road. It made me wish I was right back in that time for real.

Here's how I told it to 'em:

So our moms never let us listen to rap when she was in the car, right? So you know we gotta blast that shit the whole two-hour ride. When we finally get into Santa Cruz we park downtown, walk to the beach with all our stuff, and my bro Diego goes: "Wherever you want, Guelly. Your pick, little bro."

I stand there scopin' the scene for a minute and tell him: "How 'bout over there, D? By the lifeguard tower."

But he frowns my shit down, points instead at this group of girls laying out in bikinis. "Or maybe we should go see what's up with them heinas. You feel me?"

I laugh and follow him over there.

That's somethin' you gotta understand about my bro, man. Isn't a minute that goes by when he isn't on some kind of female mission. So we go over there, set up shop right next to 'em, and me and Diego pull off our shirts and start tossin' the football around. And my bro's totally playin' for their eyes, right? He's tacklin' my ass into the sand and talkin' mad head like we're on some NFL-type shit. But I don't even care 'cause we're at the beach, man. And it's actually fun as hell messin' around with Diego like that.

Isn't long before the girls start payin' attention to us either. Or at least Diego. One of them sits up, taps her friend on the back and points. And pretty soon they're all kind of watchin' us on the slick. And Diego has mad sixth sense for that kind of thing, right? So he decides to go on some next-level shit. He catches a long toss from me, cups the football under his arm and points to this buoy floating out past the waves.

"Yo, Guelly," he says. "You think you could swim all the way out there and touch it?"

I look to where he's pointing and then back at him. "I don't even know, D. Looks kind of far."

And then outta nowhere he tosses the football to the side and takes off sprinting toward the water, dives under and starts swimmin' freestyle like he's damn Michael Phelps.

I stand like a statue for a quick sec, watchin' him. But then I tell myself to come on, man, and run in after.

Once we've been swimmin' awhile, though, I start thinkin' 'bout how I ain't so sure I'm that good of a swimmer. So I slow my dog paddle down and yell up to Diego: "Yo, man! D! I don't know if I could make it all the way!"

But he turns around treading water and gives me this irritated look. "You ain't gonna bitch out on me, is you, Guel?"

And this is my big bro we talkin' 'bout, right? Course I'm not gonna bitch out on Diego. So I just put my head down and keep on swimmin', hard as I can.

Not ten more minutes go by, though, when Diego pulls up and I run right into his ass. We both tread water, staring at each other, our eyes all bugged in fear, and he goes: "Yo, I don't know if I could make this either."

I look out at the buoy and then back at the shore. Yo, I put this on everything, Rondo, we're right in the damn middle. And I'm not even gonna lie, I panic. Start hyperventilating and reaching out for Diego's shoulder and trying to keep my head above the water so I could breathe.

But he's brushin' my hand away, thrashing around to keep his nose and mouth up too.

"Shit, D!" I shout, all out of breath. "What we . . . gonna do?"

"Call for . . . help!" he shouts back.

And we both start waving our damn hands around,

yelling our heads off for the lifeguard like little girls. Diego puts two fingers in his mouth trying to whistle, but when he does he just sinks underwater and no sound comes out. He thrashes his way back up and gulps for air.

But the lifeguard finally spots us. She stands up, focuses our shit in her binoculars. And them girls on the beach, man, they're all standin' up now too, realizing our dumb asses are in mad distress. Random people on the beach stop walkin' their dogs or whatever to see what's gonna happen to the two Mexican kids 'bout to drown. And me and Diego are out there shittin' our pants, splashing around to keep above water.

The lifeguard sets down her binoculars and reaches for her electric megaphone. And check this out, yo: She wags her finger at us. Announces over the whole damn beach: "No! Just stand up! Just stand! Up!"

And that's exactly what we do, man. Me and my bro. We reach our feet down and touch the damn bottom. I swear to God, yo, we actually stand up, just like she said. The water's only up to our necks. And you know what we do then? We *walk* back to the beach, man. I put that on everything. We were on a big-ass sandbar.

"You swear," Rondell said, damn near shoving me over in disbelief.

"I'm telling you."

"You *walked* back to the shore."

"*Walked.*"

Rondell laughed. "You crazy, Mexico."

"When we got back to our towels I asked Diego did he still want to throw the football around, but he waved me off, man. Said we had to get the car back to Moms. It was the first time I ever saw Diego leave some place without getting a girl's digits."

Me and Rondell laughed and said a few more things about it, and then we turned to Mong thinking maybe he'd wanna tell a story of his own, but he was just walking alongside us with no expression on his scarred-up face. It was like he hadn't heard one word of my story about almost drowning.

Me and Rondell looked at each other, and I shrugged. "Yo, earth to Mong," I said, but dude still didn't look at me.

I turned to Rondell, told him: "It's okay, man, he's just in Silent Mong mode right now."

Rondell smiled big and nodded his head some, and we all three of us kept walking along the wet sand, a half-moon pasted on the sky over us and shining in the black ocean.

A few minutes passed and then Rondell jumped in and told a story about this three-legged dog that was at another foster house he lived at, and I told a couple more about me and Diego. And before we knew it we'd made it all the way to Santa Cruz.

After only a couple wrong turns Mong led us to the bus station and I paid for three one-way tickets to L.A., the farthest south we could go in one shot. We went to a twenty-four-hour burrito spot and ate carne asada tacos while waiting for our bus to come. Then we climbed aboard and each grabbed our own seat in the back and leaned against the window. Mong and Rondell fell right to sleep, but I stayed up for a while, thinking about Stockton and Diego and all the funny shit that's happened with us. I had this bad longing to be back there that sat in my stomach like a twenty-pound weight. Out of nowhere I felt incredibly alone and lost on the bus, and I had no idea what I was doing or why or which way was which. My breathing even got rushed. It felt no different than when me and Diego damn near drowned in the ocean that day I'd just told Rondell about. Just find the sandbar, I kept telling myself. There's gotta be a sandbar.

But there wasn't no sandbar.

I stared out my window as we moved through Santa Cruz, past all these homeless long-haired hippies sleeping near this dried-up fountain and down a sleepy neighborhood street where tree leaves scraped the top of the bus and all the houses looked like the olden days.

We veered up the southbound on-ramp and merged onto the quiet highway. Even though the sun was starting to creep up into the sky in the east, it seemed like everybody was asleep on the entire bus except me. And I just sat there, watching the light wash over the mountains, the way it had a million times before. And the way I realized it would a million times after. I reached into my bag and pulled my journal, started writing all the stuff that was happening to us.

What Rondell Thinks About, Part 2:

About an hour into the bus ride, Rondell woke up and looked over his seat at me.

I stopped writing.

"Hey, Mexico," he said in this half-asleep voice that sounded all froggy and inhuman.

"What's up?"

He smacked his lips a couple times and closed his eyes halfway, making me think he was *still* asleep. Like he was sleeptalking or something. He took a deep breath and sighed. "Mexico," he said again.

"What?" I said, kind of irritated. If he wasn't gonna say anything I wanted to finish my journal stuff so I could go to sleep too.

"I bet he could see us now," Rondell said.

"Who?"

"God."

I raised an eyebrow at the guy, trying to think what the hell he was talking about *now*.

"I bet he could see everything 'cause we ain't in Juvi no more. We ain't even under no roofs."

Right then I sort of remembered back to the first conversation me and him had when we were roommates. When he'd asked me did I think God or whatever could see us when we were locked up and I told him that thing about Santa Claus. I couldn't believe he was still thinking about that.

Rondell opened his eyes a little wider and told me: "I just figured out alls I want out of anything, Mexico."

"Go 'head, Rondo. This oughta be good."

"I wanna be see'd by him. That's it. So he knows I'm here too, just like other people."

"Okay," I said, closing up my journal.

"I was in there a long time, though. I been hopin' maybe he ain't lost track of me." Rondell looked down at my journal and then he looked back at me. "I'm fittin' on asking him 'bout that. When my time comes to go up there."

"Asking him what?" I said. I was actually kind of interested in what Rondell was gonna say for once. It felt like he was getting at something important.

He wiped a hand down his face and yawned. "If he could see people when they locked up. I had this one guard told me when I was little. He said God couldn't see nobody who was in jail. I said back how God could do *anything* 'cause he all-knowin' and all-bein', but the man just shook his head at me."

I stared back at Rondell, wondering why some people thought so much about religion and others didn't think about it at all. Like me. I wondered who was better off about that.

"And also if cats can be in heaven," Rondell said. "I'm

maybe gonna ask him 'bout that one too. And dogs. I got things I wanna ask him, Mexico. If I ain't too nervous, I mean."

Then Rondell shrugged and his eyelids started falling down his eyes even though he was still sitting up. He jerked and smiled, yawned the biggest yawn that's humanly possible and went down on his seat again. On his back. Started snoring right away.

I looked at him over his seat back, cracking up to myself. I thought how if there was really a so-called God he *better* be seeing Rondell. Even when the guy was locked up. It'd be entertaining as hell. Plus it'd be messed up if somebody who was God only cared about seeing people who did everything right, or rich people, or smart people. He should see people like Rondell, too. Rondell's life shouldn't mean any less than anybody else's.

I leaned back and looked out the bus window. At the cars flashing by on the other side of the freeway. At the houses and car dealerships and off-ramps and gas station signs and hamburger places and big green trees. It was so weird thinking how I was actually alive to look at it all.

July 22—more

The bus dropped us off in Santa Monica in the late afternoon, and we wandered around for a while in clothes that were still a little damp from the storm. We checked out a bunch of stores and then sat on a curb to watch people on the streets. They seemed different than where we just were. The girls were dressed up more and all of them had on big sunglasses and fancy bags and led around these tiny leashed dogs that looked like little hamsters. The dudes had short spiky hair and big collars and flip-flops and they all walked around like they were supposed to *be* somebody, but I'd never seen none of 'em on TV.

By the way, everybody says L.A.'s supposed to be about movie stars cruising the streets with their agents and paparazzi hanging out of car windows snapping photos and models sipping tea at every café you go by. But me, Mong and Rondell sat on that curb for almost two hours and we didn't recognize one person the whole time.

Finally we ate at another cheap burrito spot and went into Ross Dress for Less to buy some new gear. We each got a couple cheap shirts and some different kicks and Rondell got a bigger sweatshirt, one that fit him better. I got a pair of baggier jeans. After we paid for everything we threw our old group-home gear in a Dumpster and wandered around some more until we ended up walking into this hoop gym in Venice Beach.

We went in all hesitant, looking back and forth at each other, not sure it was cool to even be in there if you weren't a regular. But nobody said anything, so we sat up in the bleachers and watched the guys play. It was a hundred percent black inside, all of them bigger than me and Mong put together. And they could play, too. Guys were raining Js from deep, doing spin moves through the lane and throwing down in traffic. Some guys had finesse, but others were big Shaq Diesel types who could toss somebody around without even trying. And all of 'em were jawing after damn near every trip down the court.

I was loving it just watching. Hoops has always been my sport, man. Back in Stockton me and Diego would hit all the local runs during summers. I never played for a school team or anything, but guys would usually pick me up if they'd ever seen me ball before. I'm quick and got a pretty decent handle and I can shoot threes for days. Ball is one of the few things, other than school, that I can do better than my big bro. So I always wanted to play.

Anyways, we watched a couple good runs, and then the crowd started to thin out. Guys went to the side to unlace their kicks, change into clean shirts. Some jetted right out the front doors. We were about to beat it too, when this dude with ratty dreads came off the court and asked us did we wanna run.

Me and Mong and Rondell all looked at each other, peeped our new jeans, looked back at the guy.

"I'm sayin'," the guy told us. "We ain't got a full ten. We need y'all."

I secretly wanted to play, 'cause it'd been a grip since I even *touched* a ball. But at the same time, we didn't have hoop clothes and these guys were mad big and skilled. I looked at Mong, who cracked his fingers and then hopped down from the bleachers. "Yeah, we'll play," he said, motioning for me and Rondell to get down too.

"That's what I'm *talkin'* 'bout," the guy said, holding out his big right hand. "I'm Peanut Butter, by the way."

"Wha'chu mean?" Rondell said.

"Peanut Butter," the guy said again. "That's my name."

We all slapped hands and then they made teams, keeping us three together. After they told us who to guard the guy Peanut Butter tossed the rock in to the other squad and we started playing. I got stuck checking this tall athletic dude people were calling Slim. On the very first play he whipped a no-look to Mong's man, who cut through the lane for a finger roll over the rim. Next time down Slim hit a deep jumper from the corner with my hand all in his face. He ran back the other way, slapping hands with his teammates and calling out: "Water!"

It was cool watching these guys from the side, but playing was a whole other deal. They were even bigger and faster up close. It was miles away from the barbecue games I could hang with back in Stockton. My man could pretty much scoot past me any time he wanted. And he did for three out of their first five buckets.

Then big Rondell decided he was gonna do something about that. And this is the part that's sick.

Rondell Shocks Everybody in the Gym, Including Me and Mong:

Next time down the guy Slim took me baseline again, but just as he was laying the rock up over the rim, Rondell came out of nowhere and swatted his shot out of bounds. "Get that shit!" Rondell shouted as he came back to the ground wagging his finger. "You done gettin' them easy ones, black."

Guys on the side erupted, laughing and clowning and calling Rondell Mutumbo.

"That's it, Mutumbo, don't let nobody come in your house."

"I see you, Mutumbo. Found the fountain of youth out there in Africa, didn't you, boy?"

In all the talk it took everybody an extra few seconds to notice Mong laying on his back on the ground at half-court, chest heaving in and out, holding his head.

Me and Rondell rushed over and stood over him. I thought about his kidney problem and wondered if he was gonna be sick right there on the court, in front of everybody. I felt bad for the guy, but I'm not gonna lie, I was more worried it was gonna get us in trouble.

"You all right?" Rondell asked him.

He shook his head no. Kept breathing hard and held his arms around his own middle.

"What should we do?" I asked him, but he didn't answer.

"He all right?" one of the big dudes from the other team said when he got up to us.

I looked at everybody in the gym, then back down at Mong.

"What's wrong with him?" someone said.

"He catch a elbow?" Slim said.

Peanut Butter came over and told everybody to stand back, give him some room. I didn't know what the hell to do. I was so afraid any minute ambulances would come speeding up to the gym, or cops.

But then Mong sort of got his breath back and sat up.

"You all right?" I said.

He nodded and then turned to Rondell, said: "Sick block."

"Thanks," Rondell said, smiling big.

Mong held out his hand, and Rondell yanked him up with so much strength Mong actually left his feet. "I'm too out of shape right now," Mong said, shaking his head. "You guys play without me."

We watched him walk over to the sideline to get somebody to take his spot, but everybody said they were done for the day. Finally this older black dude with goggles put his shoes back on and said: "All right, all right, one more and that's it." He jogged around the court once and pulled the ball out of Peanut Butter's hands, bounced it twice.

I watched Mong wander over to the drinking fountain. He looked better, but I still wondered how serious his kidney thing was. For the first time since I read his file I wondered if you could actually die from having bad kidneys. And what would we do if it happened while we were still trying to get to Mexico?

Once Mong was sitting back in the bleachers we started up again, and Rondell pretty much took over. He swatted another shot, this one off the backboard. He scored a fast-break layup with his left hand, pulled us within four. He stripped his man clean in the open court, raced down the right wing and did this nasty reverse dunk. I couldn't believe my eyes. I'd read about him playing AAU in his file and all that, but seeing it with my own eyes was something totally different. He was the best player I'd ever seen.

Guys on the sideline were going crazy too, yelling and pointing at each other. They stopped calling him Mutumbo and started calling him Matrix. He blocked another shot, hit a jumper from beyond three-point range, drove the lane and finished with this sick tomahawk over two guys.

After the tomahawk, Peanut Butter pretty much gave Rondell the ball every damn time down the court. He'd dribble down, whip it over to Rondell, and say: "Feed the beast!" I hadn't even taken one shot, but it didn't matter. Watching Rondell play ball was like watching those seagulls fly through rain. He didn't even notice defenders draped all over his arms, trying to stop him from getting in the lane. Didn't even register. And he was smooth, too. That was the most surprising thing. Off the court Rondell was big and awkward, he moved molasses slow and couldn't read a word you put in front of him. But *on* the court? Nah, man, on the court Rondell was a damn ballerina. He was valedictorian. Dude zipped up and down the wing on fast breaks like a cheetah, finished at the rim like a bull. Shit gave me goose bumps just watching the guy. I wondered if he could even play in the NBA.

It came down to a super close game at the end. We had game point and they were one behind us, with the ball. This guy everybody called Boo dribbled down the court and tried to dump it into their big man, but Rondell stepped in front of the guy and picked it off. He raced down the other way—just me, him, a defender and the basket. Since he was so far ahead of the pack I figured he'd just flush it home for game, but he didn't. He kicked the ball back to me, set a screen on the defender and let me go in for the winning layup.

"Game time!" Rondell yelled as my shot kissed off the glass and fell through. Then his big ass came over and boosted me in the air, yelling: "That's my boy Mexico right there! Pack your bags, fools!"

The guy genuinely acted like I'd just done something special when really it was him the whole time. He'd single-handedly won the game for us.

Mong came jogging over from the bleachers and slapped the hell out of both our hands. I'd never seen Mong so excited since I met him. He kept patting Rondell on the back the whole time we were walking back to where our stuff was in the bleachers. "You can really play," he said to Rondell. "Amazing skills. You see the looks on those guys' faces?"

"Mexico hit the game winner," Rondell said.

"I know, I know," Mong said, turning to me. "You played great too! Amazing!"

Some of the other guys chimed in. Once we all sat down in the bleachers, they asked Rondell where he played and who was his AAU coach. And when Rondell said he didn't play anywhere, they all looked at him like he was crazy.

"I *can't* play," he said.

"Why not?" Peanut Butter said.

" 'Cause us three's in a group home," Rondell said. "Or at least we was. We just broke out two nights ago. And now we on the run to Mexico where we could fish."

Me and Mong stared at Rondell with our mouths hanging open.

What can I tell you, man. Rondell definitely wasn't no ballerina *off* the court.

"Today?" Peanut Butter said.

"Yup," Rondell said, turning to me and Mong. When he saw the look on our two faces, though, he realized he'd said something wrong and blurted out: "But my name ain't Rondell, though. It's somethin' else."

The conversation didn't go any further 'cause when I stuck my hand in my bag I couldn't find the leather petty-cash envelope. I dug all around, nothing. Ripped it open all the way.

My stomach dropped.

"Yo, the petty cash!" I shouted at Mong. "Somebody took it!"

Mong looked at me, and then we both glanced toward the door where these two dudes in jeans and Timberlands were just sneaking out of the gym.

"Hey!" Mong yelled.

One of them turned to look at us, then they both took off running.

Me, Mong and Rondell sprinted after them, some of the guys from the gym trailing behind us. We sped through the double doors and out into the parking lot. It was so damn bright outside I could hardly see. Me and Rondell weaved in and out of cars after the guys. Mong darted off toward the exit.

We were just closing when one of the guys stopped, threw a wild punch that grazed my ear and then shoved me back at Rondell. Both of us fell over each other to the asphalt. Blood started coming from my scraped elbows, but I sprang back up and threw a punch right back. He ducked it, slugged me in the stomach, cracked me in the mouth.

When I opened my eyes I was on the asphalt again. No memory of falling. Head spinning and mixed up and blood dribbling out my nose and mouth. Rondell grabbing the guy in a headlock, squeezing, pounding him on the top of the head, again and again. The guy slipping Rondell, taking off on foot again.

Rondell pulled me up by my sweatshirt and we raced after. But they were too far ahead now. All we could do was slow up and watch as they sped around a last row of cars toward the parking lot exit. My face stinging and heart pounding. Dizzy like I just stepped off a merry-go-round.

But Mong came out of nowhere. He leaped in the air, kicked the first guy square in the chest with both feet. They tumbled to the ground. Mong up first. The second guy grabbed him, pinned him under his arm, squeezed his shaved head. But Mong spun out of his grasp, delivered three lightning quick punches—boom, boom, boom—all to the guy's face.

Timberland went down on one knee and reached up to touch his bloody mouth.

The first guy was back. He threw a wild right at the back of Mong's head, but Mong ducked it, turned and caught the guy with an uppercut to the chin. Small Chinese kid putting a guy twice his size on the ground, one shot. Then Mong reached down and took the guy's head in his hands and bit into his face. Sickest thing you could ever witness. The flesh breaking in his teeth.

Rondell and me racing toward them.

The guy's screams. And blood spewing out in every direction, down the guy's chest and Mong's face and clothes, splattering across the asphalt in stringy lines. The guy cupped his bloody cheek in his hands and screamed in short bursts, a high-pitched squeal and then silence, a high-pitched squeal and then silence.

Mong pushing him down, kicking him in the back of the head. Dull thud and more blood flying and his body sprawled across the asphalt on his stomach and then curling up. Holding his head and face and still screaming.

171

Mong turned to the other guy, booted him in the ribs and the back of the legs and the ribs again. The guy huddled there on the ground protecting his head and face with his arms. Fetal position.

Me and Rondell finally made it to them. Some of the guys from the gym. Peanut Butter and Slim held down the Timberland guys. Someone flipped open a cell phone and called 911.

I wiped blood off my own face, reached into the screaming one's bag, my eyes darting all around me. I pulled out the leather petty-cash envelope, unzipped to make sure the money was still there, zipped back up. I turned to the screaming guy whose face Mong had bitten. He was holding his hands to his bloody face and kicking now, like a kid in a tantrum. A chunk of hanging flesh he was trying to push back in place. My stomach turned over like I might be sick, but I wasn't. My eyes blurred and stung.

I moved quickly toward Mong, who stood breathing hard, his head turned slightly to the side and smiling. Like he was admiring a painting in a museum. He looked more psycho than I'd ever seen any human ever look. His eyes bulging and red with hatred. But at the same time smiling. Chest heaving in and out and in and out. But calm somehow also.

"We gotta go!" I said.

Mong didn't move.

I put my hand on his shoulder, said: "Mong. Come on, man."

I half expected him to throw a punch at me, too, but he didn't. He turned around, wiping the guy's blood off his face with the sleeve of his sweatshirt and spitting on the ground. He took my arm and looked at my cut, said: "You okay?"

I nodded, staring in his eyes. Something different about this Mong. His eyes still crazy, but everything else too calm for what he'd just done. Nobody could be that calm. Like he'd already forgotten what had happened.

"We should go," I said.

He nodded.

"Should wait for the cops," the guy with the cell phone said.

"Press charges," somebody else said.

"We can't," I said.

Then everybody was talking at once and the second Timberland guy was off the ground and yelling at Mong and two guys were holding him back. And my head was so loopy from getting punched I couldn't think. Just knew we had to be out before the cops came. I grabbed Mong and Rondell by their sweatshirts and the three of us ran back to the gym to get our bags off the bleachers.

As we were leaving sirens wailed in the distance, coming toward us, and this long lanky guy stepped in front of me and said: "Y'all got any transportation?"

We shook our heads.

"Come on, then," he said, waving for us to follow. "Let's get y'all outta here."

We went down the parking lot a ways, to an old Buick. He keyed open his door and we all climbed in and he turned around to face us, said: "So, where you wanna go?"

Rondell looked at me, and I looked at Mong.

"Can you take us to Malibu Beach?" Mong said, glancing down at his swollen right hand.

"We on our way," the guy said, flipping it into gear.

It was the first time I'd felt relieved since the petty cash got swiped. I reached in my bag and squeezed the envelope to make sure I still had it, tried to calm my breathing.

Just as we were pulling out of the parking lot, we saw two cop cars speeding the other way with their sirens wailing. Me,

Mong and Rondell spun around after they passed us, watched them scoot into the gym parking lot.

"I'm Dallas, by the way," the guy said.

We turned back around and I thanked him for giving us a ride, and Mong and Rondell did too. He nodded in the rearview, told us: "I spent two years in a group home when I was a kid. Whole time I wanted to break my ass out, but I was too scared. Least I could do is help somebody else."

He turned on his car radio and tuned in an old Motown song, started singing the words. Me, Mong and Rondell looked at each other, still breathing hard. I reached up and touched my face where I got punched. Checked my nose. Didn't seem to be broken. All my teeth still there. But my lip was split pretty bad. I knew it'd swell up huge by tomorrow. But I got off cheap considering how big the guy was. I always forget how much it hurts to get punched in the face until it happens again.

I glanced over at Mong. The Timberland dude's blood still all over his face. The nasty scars on his cheeks. And he had that calm face still. I wondered how a skinny little Asian kid could beat up two big black dudes like that. All by himself. It didn't even seem possible. It wasn't like he was doing crazy martial arts moves either. He was just scrapping, like any other kid would.

I looked out the window again as Dallas drove his Buick through a yellow light, toward Malibu. I reached into my bag, fingered the petty-cash envelope again. Then I reached up and touched my split lip. The bleeding had stopped, but it was already getting big. Me and Mong sort of looked at each other, then looked away.

And the whole time Dallas kept right on singing with the song on the radio. Like nothing had even happened.

July 23

Mong had Dallas drop us off at this quiet little beach town called Malibu. It's way different from how Venice was. There aren't so many cars or people out walking around or young people. And the stores are smaller with less flashy signs, and all of them have stands outside selling beach towels and sunscreen and Styrofoam coolers.

We got out, stood by Dallas's driver's-side window thanking him for giving us a ride. He nodded at me and Mong, then grabbed Rondell by his sweatshirt, told him he better get his ass on a hoop team and quick. "Even if it's one in Mexico, boy. They got pro teams there, too, you know."

"They do?" Rondell said.

"Hell yeah," Dallas said. "Got one of my boys down there somewhere right now. Gettin' paid, too."

Rondell nodded.

"I'm sayin', though, it's a sin to waste talent like you got." He let go of Rondell's shirt and pushed him away from the car. "A *sin*, boy. You hear me?"

Rondell nodded.

Dallas waved at me and Mong again and then drove off.

We went across the street to this cluster of stores, bought more hot dogs and fruits and donuts, and this time Mong had us buy a bundle of wood instead of charcoal. There was a liquor store next door and Mong sent Rondell in with a list thinking he'd have the best chance of passing for twenty-one. Mong seemed to have our whole night planned, probably figuring it was our last one in America. And it wasn't just him, either. I think we all sort of wanted to go out in style.

Rondell came back from the liquor store with beer and Mong's whiskey, and we took everything across the street, followed Mong a long ways down the beach until he stopped in line with this big blue two-story beach house. He tossed his bag on the sand, said: "This is it."

"This is what?" I said.

"Where my dad used to take me when I was a kid."

"You went to this beach before?" Rondell said.

Mong nodded, pointed up at the big blue house. "Stayed at that place," he said. "Every summer. Just me and him."

Me and Rondell threw our bags in the sand too and looked up at the house. It was the nicest one in the whole row. I tried to imagine how it'd even *be* like, chilling inside such a big place, right on the beach, but I couldn't really picture it. I peeked at Mong and then went back to the house. It seemed crazy that a kid who used to stay in that place could end up down here with me and Rondell, on the run from a group home. If I hadn't read his file, how his old man came from money and was a lawyer, I wouldn't have believed his ass.

Mong started clearing space for a makeshift barbecue pit, me and Rondell trying to help out but really just getting in the way. The beach was quiet, except a few older couples walking by holding hands. Some of them had their pant legs rolled up so they could walk right through the water whenever the tide came up. I watched one particular couple walking an old bulldog. You could tell all three of them had made this walk hundreds of times before. Probably thousands. The woman had a gray ponytail and the guy had a baseball cap and glasses. They weren't really talking, but every once in a while the guy would reach up and rub his wife's back. Behind them the sun was starting to set, like the whole thing was a damn Hallmark card.

As they passed us they both smiled and the old guy said "Howdy." I said "Howdy" back and watched them walk a long way down the beach, touching my split lip and thinking how different their lives were from mine. They were just strolling along the beach, not a care in the world, happy. And me, man, I was spending my last day in the country. This was it. I'd maybe never see an American beach ever again.

For some reason seeing that couple and saying howdy to the guy made me think I should call my moms tomorrow. And maybe Jaden, too. Even if I just left a message. At least people would know we weren't dead or whatever.

Mong showed us how to dig a little hole in the sand and line it with a bunch of small rocks for a homemade barbecue pit. We wadded up pieces of newspaper and scattered them in the hole, put the firewood on top of that and doused everything with lighter fluid. I struck a match and tossed it in, started a giant flame on the paper that quickly jumped to the wood. Then the three of us just sat there awhile, drinking and watching the fire, not really saying anything.

When Mong claimed the wood was perfect, we cooked the hot dogs and ate and drank more. We started a conversation about how crazy it was watching Rondell take over the basketball game, before what happened with the Timberland guys. Mong even ate a lot for the first time since we left the Lighthouse. Usually he just picked a little or ate the corn tortilla of his taco and then pushed the rest of his food away. And he kept drinking, too, pulling sips off his bottle of whiskey every few minutes. I decided he must be feeling better if he was trying to get his buzz on like that.

Rondell was feeling good too. He grilled all his dogs until they were burnt as hell and sucked 'em down whole. When Mong asked him to describe what it felt like to be so good at ball he got a giant smile on his face and shrugged, took a long swig of beer. "In the rest of everything," he said, staring down at his feet, "you gotta sit there and think of all these little things." He looked up at us. "But not with ball, man. With ball you don't gotta think about *nothin'.* It just flows."

"You had that shit flowin' today," I said.

"It's like a rap," Rondell said. "Or when a preacher starts shoutin' 'bout the Testament at church. Or the women sway back and forth singin' and clappin'. And you don't never get tired either. That's my word." He paused for a sec, got a look on his face like he was thinking. "I don't even know why about that part."

"Maybe you love it so much," Mong said.

"And you're so good," I said.

Rondell shrugged. "Everything just flows and flows and you ain't gotta think about nothin'."

Me and Mong nodded our heads. I tried to think if I'd ever felt that way about anything. Loved it so much I could never get tired. Maybe fishing off the levee with Diego. Or reading on the beach. Or writing in this journal like it's a real book. But it didn't seem like the same thing. I looked back at Rondell, who was still nodding his head, looking at the fire. For the first time since I knew him, I actually felt jealous about the guy.

An hour or so after we finished eating, Rondell fell sound asleep on his bag, and Mong motioned for me to follow him closer to the water. I got up kind of hesitantly, though. I didn't know what he wanted all drunk like he was. Which version of Mong would the drunk one turn into?

Me and Mong Have an Actual Talk:
We walked down to the edge, right by the water, and he plopped down with his whiskey bottle, patted the beach for me to sit next to him.

"What's going on?" I said.

178

"Nothing," he said, digging his bottle into the sand so it would stand upright. "I just felt like talking."

I looked the guy over for a few seconds. "You?"

He nodded.

"About what?"

"I don't know," he said, glancing up at me. You could see in his eyes how wasted he already was from the whiskey. "Just talk. Like regular people."

"Like regular people," I repeated, grinning on the inside. "Right. Okay." I kicked a rock out of the way and sat down, still watching him. Took a swig of beer.

"Look how giant it is," he said, pointing his bottle at the ocean. "Sometimes I look out there, and I can't believe it. Ocean water makes up seventy percent of the earth's surface, you know."

"Yeah?" I said. I watched a small swell crumble near the shore and roll up the sand over clumps of seaweed and rocks and shells, then suck back into itself.

"People spend so much time on trivial things they forget to look at the ocean. Look at it, Mexico."

"I am," I said. It felt mad weird how Mong was talking so much. I didn't know how to react.

"Really *look*, though," he said.

I tried for a sec, but I kept peeking at him every couple seconds. I knew how people got when they drank. Like Diego, for example. He *always* wanted to fight. Didn't matter who was around, if it was a girl, an older person, or his own damn brother. He just had to yell or hit somebody. I tried with the ocean a few more times, but after a couple seconds I'd be right back to peeping Mong again.

He spit in front of him, said: "When you look at the ocean, like you and me are right this second, you realize how small we are."

I nodded my head some.

There was a long silence and then Mong smiled and said: "I can't believe how good Rondell was." He laughed, tossed a bulb of seaweed into the water. "I wonder what it feels like to slam one home."

"Shit," I said. "I wouldn't even know."

"Me neither." Mong made like he was dunking a ball with his right hand and laughed a little more. Then he drank from his whiskey bottle.

Seeing him laugh without being all psycho about it made me think how little I actually knew about the guy besides what I read in his file. I took a long pull of beer imagining the dude as any regular kid I might pass in the halls at school. It was probably the first time I'd ever thought of Mong like that.

"Hey, Mong," I said, feeling the buzz move through my body, into the tips of my fingers and toes.

"Yeah."

"I wanted to ask you something."

"All right."

I picked up a smooth black rock, felt it between my thumb and forefinger. "You're gonna be straight with me, right?"

"I'm drunk on whiskey," he said, holding up his bottle. "I'd probably tell you anything right now." He took a long swig and made a big production out how refreshing it was— even though he was still sort of cringing.

I looked at the ocean for a few seconds, tried to think how to put it. I looked at Mong. "How sick are you, anyway?"

He turned to face me. "Very sick."

I was surprised he just came out and said it like that. I flung the rock in my hand toward the water. "You're gonna get better though, right?"

His eyes went to the label on his bottle. "They told me I'd

have to get a new kidney." He paused, flipping the bottle so he could see the other side. "But I was far down on the list."

I stared at the side of his face, at his scars. I'd never known anyone who needed a new kidney before. I thought how maybe somebody in Mexico might have one for him. We could get him into a hospital first thing, and they'd operate and he'd be straight. Maybe that's why he wanted to go there in the first place.

He took another sip of whiskey and then just sat there, staring at the quiet ocean. "I don't really wanna talk about that stuff," he said. "Not tonight."

"Nah, that's cool," I said, picking up another flat rock. I skipped it across the water, watched it disappear into a little crumbling swell.

"Maybe you can ask me something else," he said.

I nodded, thought about everything since we left the Lighthouse. All the walking we'd done and the tied-up store guy and the cave, the guys who took our petty cash. "Okay," I said, "how could such a small Chinese kid like you fight so good?"

"I'm not afraid to get hurt."

"Why not?"

He shrugged and then turned to look me in the eye. "I guess because I don't care what happens to me."

I nodded and looked back to the ocean.

It was a trip to hear somebody like Mong say the exact same thing I'd thought since what happened in Stockton. I wondered if almost every kid in a group home feels that way. Stops caring what happens to them. 'Cause first of all they did something bad to get put away, and second everybody in their family is disappointed, and third you start to wonder if maybe that's really who you are. A group-home kid. A fuckup. And once you start thinking you're a fuckup maybe you automatically stop caring what happens to you.

"But what about with those dudes today, man," I said. "They were big as hell."

"They were big," Mong said, "but they also knew they were wrong to take our money. They knew they deserved to lose."

I picked up another rock, said: "Why'd you bite that one guy in the face?"

Mong looked at me, fingering his brown tooth necklace. "I couldn't think of what else to do."

I frowned and shook my head. "You know that shit was kind of sick, though, right?"

He nodded.

"I mean sick in the head, man. Psycho."

"I understand."

"And you don't care if that's what people think of you? That you're fucked-up or whatever?"

He took a sip of whiskey, spit in front of him and went quiet for a few seconds, like he was thinking about it. "Ever since I found out I was sick I feel like I've been fighting," he said, staring out at the ocean. "Not just people, either. Everything. I thought the more things I could wreck the better I'd feel. But then today . . . Afterwards, I felt . . . I think that was the last one." He turned to look at me. "I don't think I want to fight anymore."

He looked back at the ocean.

I took another sip of my beer, thinking about that. I felt the liquid drain down my throat and into my stomach. The beer was warm now, but I wasn't drinking it for the taste. I was drinking it 'cause of how it made me feel and how all the things I wanted to say came right into my head without me even trying. I turned to Mong. "So why'd you spit on me that first day?"

"To find out who you were."

"And who am I?"

He smiled and picked up another bulb of seaweed. "You're a normal kid who did something very bad. And even though it was just a mistake, you're trying not to forgive yourself."

I frowned at him and shook my head. "Nah, man. You got that part wrong—"

"And you're trying to convince yourself you don't care. But you do care. You care a whole lot. I can see it."

"Ha!" I said, waving him off and making myself laugh. "That's some damn BS if I ever heard it."

"It's what you hate most about yourself," Mong said, grinning at me. "You hate that you care so much."

I laughed some more and sipped my beer. I tried to think up something I could say to show him how dumb as hell his opinions were, but nothing was coming in my head, so I just picked up a rock and fired it into a small wave.

"I'm just being honest," he said. "Did I say too much?"

I shrugged, said: "Whatever, dawg. That's how you wanna believe then that's how you wanna believe. Don't mean you're right, though."

He held out his whiskey bottle. "Cheers?"

" 'Cause actually, if you wanna know the truth, I don't give a fuck about *anything.*"

"Okay," Mong said, smiling big. "Come on, though, cheers."

I looked at his bottle, still shaking my head. I thought about not giving him a cheers. Thought about going back up with Rondell and letting Mong's drunk ass alone for the rest of the night. 'Cause, come on, man. Dude was trying to talk like he knew me. He didn't know *shit* about me. Like Jaden even said, nobody knows anybody. But for whatever reason I tapped his bottle with my can real quick and turned away, took another sip of warm beer.

We both sat in silence for a while. I couldn't stop thinking of what he'd just said, though, so I decided to change the subject. "Yo, man, what's up with that flea-bitten tooth you always got around your neck?"

He set down his bottle in the sand and held up the ugly brown thing so he could see it. "This?"

"Yeah, man. I don't know if you've noticed, but that shit ain't exactly fashionable."

"You don't think so?"

I pointed at it, said: "Look at it. What the hell's it supposed to be, anyway?"

"A tooth."

"I know *that*, man. I'm saying whose is it? And why do you wear it all the time?"

I figured it must have some important meaning or whatever. Like it was his old man's or somebody's who he'd beaten up before. Why else would a person wear a cavity-ass tooth like that? But he shrugged his shoulders at me and said: "I don't know whose it is. I found it on the ground somewhere like three years ago."

He let it fall back to his chest and lifted his bottle to his lips again.

I gave him a crazy-ass look, said: "You don't even know whose tooth it is?"

He shook his head.

"That's nasty, man."

"Why?"

I frowned at him, said: "Well, for one thing it's unsanitary as hell."

He smiled. "You've never had a good-luck charm before?"

"Not one that came out of some homeless person's damn mouth."

He chuckled a little and said: "It's good luck. I've worn it every day since I found it."

I thought about that for a sec. How his parents are dead and he got thrown in a group home and now he's sick. I told him: "You really think it's been lucky, though?"

He nodded.

"How?"

"It's not about what happens to people," he said. "It's how they figure out what it means. It's helped me understand all the meaning."

I took a drink. Picked up another rock and flung it at the tide, thinking about what he said. I wondered if that was what I should do. Find meaning.

After a short silence Mong said: "I wanted to ask you something too."

"Okay."

"What'd you think about what my cousin said in the car when we were going to San Francisco?"

I reached up and touched my cut, felt the swelling. "Which part? She said a lot."

"She was telling us the story about a man and woman in China."

I looked at Mong out of the corner of my eye, surprised he was bringing it up. "I guess she was just saying a random story," I said.

"Did you agree with her, though? That it was true love?"

"How would I know, man? I don't know nothin' about no love."

He frowned at me. "*Everybody* knows about love," he said.

I scooped a handful of dry sand and let it pour out slow through my fingers, shaking my head.

He turned back to the ocean, took another swig of whiskey. "People only think of romantic love, but that's just one kind. Love can be anything. Since I was a little boy, staying here every summer, I've been in love with the ocean."

I didn't say anything back. Dude wasn't even making sense anymore.

"Tonight it's even bigger," he said. "Tonight I'm in love with the whole world. Everything of the earth. The dirt. The sand. The sky. That cave we went inside the other night." He paused a sec and took another drink. Then he looked at me all excited. "Maybe when a person dies they don't really die, Mexico. Maybe they just go back into the earth again."

I shot him a confused look and took a sip of my beer. I didn't really know what he meant.

"What about you?" Mong said "What do you love?"

I thought about his question for a sec. I actually took it serious. "My family, I guess. Especially my brother Diego. And my moms." I looked at him, said: "Yeah, man, my family."

He nodded.

I pictured Diego's lit-up face whenever he'd be reeling in a fish at the levee. Or how he'd roll his eyes at me when he got dropped off at home from some white chick's car. When she'd make her window go down to say one last thing to him. I laughed a little under my breath, said: "Yo, I used to try and be just like my brother. In every possible way. Used to copy his clothes style and how he did his hair. Even copied the way he *walked*. But then I realized I was wasting my time. 'Cause no matter how hard I tried, Diego was always gonna be Diego and I was always just gonna be me."

Mong nodded his head and took a long swig of whiskey.

We both looked back to the dark water. I scooped up another handful of sand and tried to think what else I could add, but everything I thought about had to do with Diego, so I just let the sand pour out and stared at this tiny light coming from a boat way the hell out there.

When I looked back at Mong I couldn't believe it. I saw tears coming down his scarred-up cheek. The dude was crying for no reason. Or 'cause he was so wasted he didn't know what the hell was happening anymore. It made me feel mad awkward too, 'cause whenever a dude cries near me I can't really look at him. I feel like it's none of my business. And I can't talk to him either 'cause all I'm concentrating on is not looking at him. But at the same time, I wondered if it was maybe 'cause Mong was sick or something. Or he was thinking of what happened with his parents. Or how it might be our last day in America.

I snuck a little glance at him and, I don't even know why, tried to think if I'd ever seen an Asian person cry before.

Mong wiped his face and took an especially long swig of whiskey. Then he leaned away from me and got sick. Two crazy long heaves and all this nasty-looking barf came spewing out of his mouth and soaked into the sand. But when he was done he just looked right back at the ocean, smiling like nothing happened. He even laughed a little and took another sip from his bottle, two tears now dangling off his chin.

"Your kidneys?" I said without looking at him.

"The whiskey," he said back.

We both cracked up a little and then Mong said: "I'm happy you're here, Mexico. The first night I watched you sleep, I knew we'd be sitting here, talking about these things."

"Oh, yeah?" I said, looking at him like he was crazy.

He nodded.

"How's that?"

He shrugged. "Sometimes I just know things."

I frowned and pointed at his bottle. "So how's that treatin' you, man?"

"What?" he said, looking at his whiskey.

"Bein' drunker than shit."

"No, I really know things," he said. "Sometimes I think I've known every single thing that was going to happen to me. For as long as I can remember. Even the bad things. It's weird."

I waved him off and went back to my beer.

But I knew I was drunk as hell too. 'Cause my whole body felt fuzzy and I could barely focus on the ocean. It seemed like a part of a movie, like the moonlight shining off the surface wasn't even real, it was special effects. The sand in my hands felt fake too.

"I also knew we'd end up being best friends like this," Mong said. "Before we went our separate ways."

I shot him a crazy-ass look. Best friends? Me and him? Now I *knew* his ass was wasted. How could two people who didn't know each other for shit, who'd been in more fights than damn conversations, even be friends?

"I know what you're thinking right now too."

I rolled my eyes, said: "Yeah? What's that?"

"That we don't know each other good enough to be friends."

I frowned. "Not even close, man."

"You sure?"

I didn't say anything back.

"Don't believe me," he said. "But it's true. You and Rondell are the only friends I have in the whole world."

I took a sip of beer, said: "That's pretty sad, man."

"Sad but true."

I spit toward the ocean. We sort of stopped talking, but

we stayed sitting there and drinking a while longer. I almost wanted to tell him he was me and Rondell's friend too, but I didn't. I just stared out over the ocean, trying to do it like he did, like I was in a trance and I was in love with it even though it wasn't a girl or even a person. But after a while my eyes started drooping and I almost passed out sitting up. Soon as I'd close my eyes, though, everything would start spinning like crazy 'cause I was so drunk and I'd have to jerk them back open.

"Yo, I'm so faded," I told him. "I gotta go crash."

He nodded without turning to me, said: "I'm gonna stay here. I'm not tired yet."

"Okay," I said, stumbling to get up.

"Hey," he said.

"What?"

He stared at me for a few seconds and then looked down at the sand shaking his head. "Nothing."

I shrugged, standing over him. I wondered what would happen once we got to Mexico. Would he get even sicker down there? Could he even die from his kidneys? Or would he go to the hospital and get a new one? It's weird, even though we'd been in a couple fights, and I still didn't trust him that much, I thought he totally deserved to get better. It didn't seem right for someone to get shot by their own dad, get bad kidneys, and then that's it. There had to be more in his future, another chance.

I stumbled up to where Rondell was sleeping, put my bag under my head and laid down. I let my eyes close up shop and tried not to spin. A couple times I had to open them back up quick, though, 'cause I knew if the world turned even one more rotation I'd be sick.

The last time I opened them I looked up and saw Mong

was sitting up by the big boulders—straight down from the blue vacation house he used to stay at with his dad. He was carving something into one of the boulders with a small rock. I watched him for a few minutes, thinking about what a strange kid he was. Sick as hell but still beating up guys twice his size. Shot in the face. In love with the ocean. But watching him scrape a rock into a boulder, over and over like that, with total concentration, I don't know, man, for the first time I saw him in a totally different way. He almost seemed like a little kid. A sad one who'd lost his parents. One that didn't have no friends at the playground and just stood there watching while all the other kids were laughing and chasing each other around the sandbox and jumping off the bars.

I tried to think how I'd be if my own dad shot me. Or if I had bad kidneys. I let my head fall back on my bag thinking about those things. I decided first thing in the morning I'd go see what Mong scraped into that rock.

And right then my eyes closed up.

And I couldn't even tell you if I started spinning that time 'cause right away I passed the hell out.

July 24

I wake up early with a bad feeling and lift my head. Rondell asleep in the same spot. Mong down by the tide taking off his sweatshirt. Mong. In an ocean trance and taking off his shoes and socks and T-shirt. Here's this skinny Chinese boy in jeans stepping into the ocean.

Right away I know what's happening.

I push up off the ground quick and then just stand there, thinking. Head pounding and heart racing. My lip swollen to twice its size, face sore. I step over Rondell and start down the sand toward the water. "Yo, Mong," I'm calling out. "Yo." I'm calling this out 'cause it's just hit me what it is I know. "Yo. Mong."

He turns, looks at me. Knee-deep. Dark bags under his eyes and ribs showing through ghost white Asian skin. He hasn't slept all night.

"Yo, man," I say. "What's goin' on? What're you doin'?"

"Swimming," he says.

I rub my eyes and look at his face again. I know he's lying. My head is killing me and I feel like I might be sick. And then suddenly I am. I lean over and spray puke onto a pile of fly-infested seaweed. Coughing and spitting. Throat burning. I look up and Mong's watching me. But he's not really watching me. He's empty. He's already done this thing in his head.

We look at each other.

The tide reaches his shoes, picks one of them up, carries it a few feet toward Mong and sets it down.

Rondell wanders down to us, yawning. "Wha'chu all doin'?" he's saying.

"Mong says he's goin' swimmin'," I say.

"Swimmin'?"

"That's what he says."

Mong stares at me and Rondell and then turns around and continues moving into the ocean.

"You goin' in your jeans?" Rondell calls out.

Mong doesn't turn around.

"Ain't they gonna get all wet?" Rondell shouts. He turns to me and asks softer. "Ain't they gonna get all wet, Mexico?"

I turn to Mong, shout: "You gonna answer Rondell, or what, man?"

Mong doesn't answer or even turn around.

I take a couple steps toward him, into the water. One of my shoes gets soaked, and I step back. My heart is in my throat now and I have no idea what to do. Everything is out of control.

"Mong!" I shout, but he keeps walking toward the waves. A small one breaks into his waist. The power of the moving water makes it seem like he's walking in place for a few seconds. Then it calms and he's moving forward again. A bigger wave breaks right into his chest, knocks him over. He gets up wiping water from his face and continues walking.

Rondell sneezes and says: "He gonna get his jeans all wet, Mexico."

I turn to Rondell, tell him. "He's not goin' swimmin', man. Don't you get it?"

"Wha'chu mean?" he says.

I turn back to Mong. He dives under the surface and now he's swimming.

I'm stuck watching him. Can't move or breathe barely. My head pounding in my ears and buzzing with the sound of the giant ocean. Seventy percent of the earth's surface. My stomach turning over and dropping out and Rondell's voice in the background, saying: "Wha'chu mean, Mexico? What's happening, Mexico? Where's Mong going, Mexico? Mexico? Mexico?"

I don't have any answers.

Mong is swimming out to sea now, farther and farther.

And the strangest thing. A perfect morning around him. A sky without no clouds and air crisp but not really cold. Birds soaring together in packs over the water, over Mong, making calls to each other and everything around us. The sun climbing over Mong's big blue house behind us and touching warmth on the back of my neck.

"He goin' out too far," Rondell says.

I nod but don't move.

We stay watching like this forever. See him swim, skinny

arm coming up and then slapping down and then the other one coming up and slapping down. Out past the waves now, past the kelp beds. Until I can barely see his shaved head bobbing up and down above the water's surface. And then there's nothing, just ocean and waves. Dark green and gray. Kelp floating in packs past the small swells. The birds white and flying just above the surface, sometimes going in with their beaks. Salt in the air and on my face and Rondell sneezing.

No more shaved head.

Still, we don't move. Or talk now. Or even make a sound. We just search for Mong and find nothing.

After an hour I wake up and turn to Rondell. We look at each other. Confusion in his face.

I tell him: "Come on."

He follows me back to our stuff, and we pack up in silence. Shoving things back in our bags and shifting them around and zipping up.

Then Rondell is staring at me and saying "Mexico" and pointing at my chest.

I look down at myself, and I can't believe it.

Mong's brown tooth on a string, around my neck. I look up at Rondell, his face concerned and so sad. I look back down at the tooth. When did this happen? I felt nothing all night.

What will we do?

I let the tooth fall back around my neck and pick up my bag. I start down the beach, south, in the direction of Mexico.

Right away Rondell follows.

We walked beside each other near the water. Carrying our bags on our shoulders. Not talking. I concentrated on the sand in front of me and kept my legs moving forward. I was like a guy in the marines, marching into war. He wouldn't want to do it or not want to do it, it's just what they told him. I looked at the sand and kept moving and didn't think about anything else.

We passed a group of people with swim caps stretching by the water, talking. They smiled, told us "Good morning."

We passed a little boy and his mom doing a sand castle.

We passed a jogger and lifeguard truck parked with its door open, the man inside pouring coffee from a thermos into a cup.

We walked for hours before I remembered Rondell. I had to tell him. I had to explain. But when I turned to him and opened my mouth to speak, I saw tears running down his face. Big thick Rondell tears. He was crying without sound. He was hiccupping. When he saw me looking he turned away.

He understood.

I looked straight again.

I didn't know where we were going, or how we were gonna get there, or why. None of these things came into my head. I just knew to keep moving forward. And to look at the sand.

I had to do just like the marine marching into war. Keep marching. Don't think about it. Look at the sand. These are your orders. This is what you're supposed to do.

July 24—more

All day long me and Rondell wandered down the winding beach, following the water's outline. Not talking. And then it went dark and we climbed up onto this locked-up lifeguard tower and leaned our backs against the wall facing the ocean. My legs so tired and sore I could hardly move. My feet aching. I sat there and sank into the tower and didn't think.

A dull yellow light shining down on us from the roof showed hundreds of initials carved into the dirty white paint: people's names, people saying who they loved, people's phone numbers, people telling whoever was reading to "Fuck Off" or "Eat a Dick."

Me and Rondell hadn't talked since leaving Malibu, and we still didn't. He opened up his bag and pulled some donuts and the leftover cans of beer and we ate and drank in silence, stretching out our tired legs. I wrote in my journal for a while, pretending last night and this morning were just scenes in a book, not real life, not what was actually happening to me, and then I put it away.

We watched the dark ocean like it was TV.

After a while I caught sight of this lonely little fishing boat way out there and tried to decide who could be on it. Maybe some old dude fishing late night with no family. A grizzled beard and yellow rain boots as he pulled up a net full of tuna or salmon or whatever. Or a group of science people doing research about plankton or the chemicals found in floating seaweed, all these waterproof monitors beeping and flashing next to 'em on deck. Or what if it was a couple kids lost at sea. What if they snuck on the boat when it was tied to a dock somewhere and ducked into the cabin to rifle through drawers looking for money or valuables they could sell. And while they were down there the rope came loose and they drifted out to sea and got stranded with no oars. At first they probably yelled and yelled and got all pissed at each other and maybe even fought a little. But when nobody heard 'em they just went quiet and sat with their backs against the cabin, rocking back and forth, confused as hell. Now they're just floating around out there, lost at sea, stranded. Eating scraps of food and drinking warm beer and not talking. Thinking their own thoughts about what next and how to keep alive, imagining the first thing they'd do if they could wake up and shit was just magically back to normal.

I glanced at Rondell, and he was staring out there too. I looked on the ocean again. Even though I'd never been on a damn boat in my entire life. Still, man. I knew exactly how those two lost-at-sea kids felt.

I stood up and looked inside the lifeguard tower, Rondell watching me. The plastic windows were all scratched up, and it was dark, but I could still sort of see what was inside. A tiny white card table and two broken fold-up chairs. A book turned upside down. Somebody's flip-flop. An open magazine.

I slid back down the wall and reached into Rondell's bag for *The Catcher in the Rye*. Started reading under the dull light. But I couldn't concentrate. My mind kept wandering. I had to read the same paragraph over and over, like six times. And I *still* didn't get what it said. I couldn't stop thinking about what was gonna happen to us. And Mong. And the kids on that boat.

Rondell pulled out his Bible and opened it up. Moved it under the dim light next to my book.

I looked at him.

He looked at me back.

Then we both turned to our books—this time *neither one of us* understanding a word we were reading.

July 25

When I woke up I had to look around a while before I remembered where we were. And what had happened. I fingered Mong's tooth around my neck, and somehow I knew I wouldn't go south today.

Now that it was light I saw we were back in Venice Beach again. Only this time we were at that part where all the freaks hang out, the strip or whatever. We stretched our stiff arms and legs and pissed in the sand and ate the few scraps of food we had left, and then we wandered up to the boardwalk to check it all. We sat there watching as more and more people showed up and old men opened their stands and set out the products and price tags. There were some people with crazy hair and weirdo outfits, like you'd expect—my favorite was this dreadlock guy Rollerblading and playing electric guitar—but mostly it was a lot of fat tourist families with bad sunburns and cameras strapped around their necks.

We walked over to watch the dudes playing ball on that famous beach court, right there between the walkway and the sand. The guys were big and cut up, but they weren't really that good, which surprised me. All they did was argue and talk a bunch of head at each other and strut around the court like they were acting in a movie. I thought about telling Rondell he should go out there and bust their asses, but I didn't really wanna talk to him yet, so I kept quiet. I knew if I said anything he'd bring up Mong and what happened, and I didn't feel like having some big talk about it.

When we got bored of watching fake-ass hoop games we walked over to Muscle Beach and watched these big 'roidheads growling and throwing around weights for everyone to see. There were even a few chicks in there getting their lift on.

I watched this one burly blond woman doing curls and I felt like I was about to throw up.

Yo, man, I gotta say something for the record. I'm not really feeling no buff chicks. Imagine you were making out with some Muscle Beach girl and you felt her big-ass biceps and triceps rubbing all against you. Or she went to hold your hand and her shit was all callused from gripping so many damn barbells. Or even worse, if she went to hold something *else*! Nah, man. I'd probably feel like I was with a damn dude.

It goes the other way too. I don't get a *girl* going for no muscle-head guy either. To me the shit just doesn't look natural.

When we left there we ate a couple dogs each on a bench in the middle of the boardwalk, checking out all the weirdos walking past and the tourists pointing at 'em behind their backs. Then we went down on the sand to watch the beach again.

Out on the water now there were all these white dudes sitting on their boards waiting for waves. A couple even had floppy blond hair like you see in magazine ads about surf clothes or flip-flops. It made me think about my moms, man. How fifty percent of me was the exact same as these guys. I bet if I'd have had a white pop instead of a Mexican one I'd be sitting out there too. On my board, fingers dangling in the water, watching for when another good wave might come. I'm not even playing, if we'd have had a white old man me and Diego's lives would be totally different from how they are now. I probably wouldn't even be here, on the run from a group home, trying to get to Mexico.

Or not trying, I should say. At least not today. 'Cause just like I had a feeling about earlier, me and Rondell hadn't moved south not one damn foot the entire day. I don't even know why.

.I glanced at Rondell and his eyes were closed again, head all leaning back against the wall. I cracked up picturing his big ass trying to sit on a surfboard. Dude would probably sink right to the bottom. Crush a little innocent shrimp that was walking by.

Whenever a wave would finally come all the surfers would drop to their stomachs and start paddling like crazy trying to get in the best spot to catch it. But only one guy would ride it in. The second he popped up on his feet, the rest of them would pull back and start looking for the next one. It seemed like there was some kind of rule about that.

This was the first time I'd really watched people surf. I mean, everybody knows what it is, and sometimes it shows on TV for a quick sec, but it's a totally different thing when you sit there and pay attention. I couldn't believe how many tricks they could do on a wave. Like going up and down it and spraying water and squatting to let it cover them for a few seconds and then popping out again and standing back up. It was amazing, actually, almost like they were doing some kind of dance on water. And anytime one of them came back in to shore they'd shake their hair out, wrap their leash around their board and walk past us with these big-ass smiles on their faces, like they'd just had the damn time of their lives.

It almost made me wanna try it someday. Was there such thing as a Mexican surfer? Not on this beach, I know, but on other ones? Like what about in Mexico? There had to be Mexican surfers in that resort part Mong told us about. I decided maybe that's what I'd do when me and Rondell finally got down there. Become a surfer. Rondell could go get himself a fishing pole and sit out there all day in a boat trying to hook himself a trout. But not me, man. Stockton was the only placed I fished at. Diego was the only dude I shared bait with.

Nah, I was going down there to find me a surfboard and learn how to ride some damn waves.

A few hours later I woke up in the same spot and looked all around. Our bags still under our feet. Rondell still asleep with his mouth hanging open, a nasty string of drool going from his bottom lip to his sweatshirt. The sun was falling into the ocean and the sky was warming up for the colors. All these people with bongos were gathering in the sand straight down the way from us, and this beat started growing, making this hypnotic rhythm. It was the craziest shit I'd ever woken up to.

It wasn't just young hippie kids like you might think either—though there were a lot of those kinds of people too. It was also normal adults in regular clothes. Ones who looked like they just got off work at a bank or some business. And teenage kids. And blacks and Mexicans and Asians. Even a few old people that could only walk stooped over like turtles. They were hitting bongos too. As the sky went into a perfect sunset over the ocean, more and more people started joining in. There must've been over a hundred.

Me and Rondell walked down there with our bags and sat right near the middle so we could totally feel the beat. We both moved our heads with the rhythm and I shut off my brain. After a while this lesbian hippie chick tapped me on the shoulder and held out a little kid drum. "Here, play this," she said with a big smile. She had short spiky hair and a tattoo of the moon on the side of her neck.

I took the drum, and me and Rondell started hitting each side of it with the rhythm. It was actually one of the coolest things that's ever happened to me. We hit that little drum for so long my fingers started losing feeling. They went numb. But I didn't even care. The beat we were all making together was so sick. Not like a rap song but something else. A chant or something bigger. Hundreds of drums getting smacked at the same time. Nobody talking. The ocean right next to us and the sky all orange and pink and purple. And you could feel how happy everybody around you was.

At one point I closed my eyes so I could just *feel* everything. The beat and the crowd and the sand. I pretended like it was a ceremony about Mong. Or my pop. Or something with Diego. It didn't even feel like I was in the real world, man. But somewhere else. An alternate reality where people talked in drumbeats and always made time to look at the ocean—and I mean *really* look at it too, the way Mong did. I can't even explain how it felt like with all those drums. If somebody would've tapped me on the shoulder right then, told me this was God, I'd have signed up for damn church, man. Committed for every single week and even brought a donation.

I wished it could've kept going and going, but after the sun went all the way down, and the colors disappeared, the drumming died out little by little and people started getting up with their bongos. They shook hands with everybody around them and had little smiling conversations as they made their way back toward the road and the so-called real world.

I gave the kid drum back to the hippie lesbian and told her thanks.

"You guys ever drummed in the circle before?" she said.

"Nah," I told her.

"It's pretty amazing, isn't it?"

Me and Rondell nodded.

"You should come back tomorrow," she said. "I'll even bring your drum with me."

I looked at Rondell and then back at her. "Yeah, man. We could do that. For sure."

Rondell looked at me, and I wondered if he was smart enough to know if I was lying or not.

•

"Great," the girl said, holding up her drum.

"Cool, man."

"I'll find you guys, okay?"

"We'll be here," I said.

We all smiled and nodded and then her and this other hippie chick walked off together holding hands, like they were girlfriend-girlfriend.

Everybody else was leaving too, but me and Rondell didn't go anywhere. We sat right back down in the sand and watched the last few people gather up their stuff and go home. Watched them walk away together, talking and laughing and rubbing each other's shoulders. And soon it was just us two left. Me and Rondell. It was dark, too. But the summer air was still warm. I breathed it in deep and tried to think who came up with the idea that everybody should come to the beach and bang drums while the sun went down. It had to be one person who started everything, right? How long ago was that? Maybe if I ever made it back to Stockton me and Diego could try and start it going at the levee. I pictured everybody showing up at our favorite spot. All of us banging drums or buckets or whatever we could find and then shaking hands and smiling and talking. Me and Diego telling new people they should come back and join us the next day.

Then I felt guilty for being happy. I knew the shit wasn't right 'cause of what happened with Mong. So I stopped.

I looked at the fingers I was using to smack that little kid drum. I was kind of bummed the feeling in them was now coming back. I wished they could stay numb like that for the rest of the week. Then I could remember how it felt.

Rondell tapped me on the shoulder.

"What's up?" I said.

He shrugged, told me: "We really comin' back here to-morrow?"

I shook my head. "Can't."

He nodded and set his head down on his bag.

It was our first words to each other in over a day.

I set my head down too. And when I closed my eyes I was happy 'cause I could still feel the hypnotic vibrations going through my body.

July 26

Took most of today to make it to Long Beach. When we were too tired to walk anymore we got slices of pizza and Cokes at a shack near the strip and sat on benches watching everybody walking around, doing their thing.

Rondell asked me was our plan still to go to Mexico, but I just stared back at him without answering. Something bad was happening in my head, man. I couldn't barely even stand Rondell all of a sudden. I couldn't stand me, either. Us two meaningless kids with some meaningless plan, and how if you got right down to it absolutely nothing we did or planned to do even mattered. Nothing I said or did or even thought. It was worse than a cliché. It was nothing. And if it was nothing then why shouldn't I just go swimming too, like Mong?

Worst thing is, I sat there for over an hour thinking about it. And I couldn't think up even one reason why not to. Not *one*. The only explanation for me not dropping my shit right that second and sprinting to the ocean is 'cause I was too much of a pussy to actually do it. Which is even sadder than nothing maybe.

Rondell asked me about Mexico again, but I just stared at him with this crazy-ass smile on my face. Like the one Mong used to get. And I thought how much different it felt to be on the inside of a psycho look instead of on the outside. Or maybe the look isn't psycho at all. Maybe it's just somebody fully understanding how alone we really are, which makes what people say to each other seem like empty sound, no more important than a dog barking or a cat meowing. It's just random noise, not words, because how can two people communicate if they're actually existing in completely different worlds?

Does that make sense? 'Cause I don't even know.

Actually, what I really wanted to do was just go to sleep. Like Rondell always could. Only I'd sleep for as long as humanly possible. For days or weeks even. Months. Then I wouldn't have to think for a while, and thinking is what was making me tired as hell.

The only problem was I didn't feel tired.

I laughed at myself, and Rondell turned away, probably thinking I was turning crazy. But that wasn't it. I was just completely stuck in my breakthrough about nothingness with no idea what to do or think and Mong's psycho smile somehow transferred onto my face.

When it got late and we were bored of watching people we went down by the beach and found this quiet place, hidden from the boardwalk, where we could sleep for the night. We set up our stuff without talking.

After laying there for like an hour, with my eyes wide open, head propped on my bag, I sat up and turned to Rondell, and I couldn't believe it. Dude was actually awake for once in his life.

"Yo, watch our stuff," I told him. "I gotta do somethin'."

He didn't look at me.

When I got up and stood next to him he turned away.

"What's wrong with you?" I said.

"Nothin'."

I booted a rock that was under the toe of my kick and said:

"Look, man, we can talk about shit tomorrow or whatever. Tonight I just don't feel like it."

He shrugged, stayed looking away from me.

"Yo, Rondo," I said.

He didn't answer.

"Rondo!"

Nothing.

I got a frown on my face and said: "Oh, you ain't talkin' to *me* now?" I went around the other side of him, where he was looking, and he turned his head the other way, like a stubborn little kid. I stared down at the guy for a sec, shaking my head. I wasn't some damn counselor, man. How could somebody expect *me* to talk his ass through what happened to Mong?

"Whatever," I said, and started walking off.

I didn't get too far, though, before Rondell called out after me: "Hey, Mexico!"

I stopped, turned around.

He sat up and looked at me but didn't say anything.

I rolled my eyes at him. "Come on, man. Speak. You can do it."

He looked down at the straps of his bag, said: "If you gonna leave me then just say it."

I shot him a confused look. "Yo, you lost me, man. What are you talking about?"

"It ain't right if you don't tell me," Rondell said. "That's my word."

"Who says I'm leavin' you?"

He stared at his straps, shaking his head. "If you do, though."

I marched back over to the guy and dropped my bag. "Look at me, man," I said.

He looked up at me.

"I ain't leavin' *nobody,* all right?"

He scratched his big head and nodded, said: "It just seems like maybe you is."

I stared at him for a sec, thinking. "Okay, what do I gotta do, Rondo? I gotta say it for the record?"

He shrugged.

"All right, man, listen up, then. I, Miguel Castañeda, ain't leavin' Rondell Law under no circumstances. All right? That good enough for you?"

A small smile came over his face. He looked down at his sweatshirt, started messing with the zipper.

It wasn't until I said it that second time, and saw his smile, that I knew it was true.

"Check it out," I said, "I'll even leave the petty cash in your bag. I wouldn't go nowhere without any money, right?"

"Wha'chu mean?" he said, looking up at me again.

"I need money to survive, right? I'm not out here tryin' to starve to death."

Rondell looked crazy confused. "Nah, if you don't come back is what I was sayin'."

"Say what?"

"Wha'chu mean?"

I stood staring at the guy, completely baffled. Sometimes you honestly couldn't communicate with Rondell. I'm not even saying that shit to be funny. It was like we were speaking two totally different languages.

He lowered his eyes, said: "I'm sorry, Mexico."

"For *what?*"

"If I did anything wrong to Mong—"

"Nah, nah, nah," I interrupted, shaking my hand at him. "You don't gotta be sorry for nothin', man." I kicked him in his shoe. "Mong was sick, all right? You even know about that? He had a screwed-up kidney. Why do you think he kept throwing up all the damn time? Why you think he was always getting tired?"

Rondell was looking at me with total concentration.

"You know what else?" I told him. "I think he planned on doing that shit the whole time. For real, since the day he came in and asked us did we wanna leave too. I think he only brought us along so he wouldn't be alone on his last couple days."

"He did?" Rondell said.

I nodded. "I doubt he even has a boy in Mexico like he said."

Rondell shook his head, said: "Still, though, Mexico. I'm just so sorry about it. I liked him a whole lot."

"Stop sayin' you're sorry, man," I said. "You don't got no reason to be sorry. It had nothing to do with me or you. It was totally separate. And besides, he told me that last night how you were his best friend in the world."

Rondell pulled his zipper down an inch or two, pulled it back up. Pulled it down, back up. He looked up at me and said: "He did?"

I nodded.

He got a little smile on his face.

"Look, I'll be right back, okay? I promise. If I don't show up you got the money anyways. You can go buy yourself all the hot dogs and beer in the world."

He nodded and laid back down, closed his eyes.

I stared at him for a few seconds longer, shaking my head, and then started back toward the street.

My Phone Call:

I got two dollars' worth of change from this tiny liquor store that had bars on every window, walked over to a pay phone outside a bar playing old-school rock songs. I picked up the phone, dropped in two quarters and dialed my moms at the house.

She picked up on the second ring, said: "Hello?"

Just hearing her voice, man. I had this stupid-ass lump come into my throat and my stomach got mad butterflies.

"Hello?" she said again.

I tried to think quick what I could say. Like "Hello" right back or "Yo, Ma, it's Miguel." But everything sounded all fake-like in my head. And I knew my first words to her in so long had to be real.

"Hello?" she said a third time, and when I didn't say anything back she hung up.

I pulled the phone from my ear and looked at it. Then I hung up too, stared at the number pad. I didn't even know why I was calling her in the first place. She especially wouldn't wanna talk to me now that I was on the run. But it felt like there was something I had to tell her. I tried to think what it was but nothing was coming. I pulled the phone off the hook and slammed it against the change part as hard as I could. Then I slammed it again and hung up.

This old drunk dude who was stumbling out of the bar turned to me and said: "Hey, hey, hey, young fella. Whatever it is, it ain't the phone's fault."

"You don't know shit about it, old man," I shot back. "Best keep your old ass walkin'!" I took a step his way in case he had something else to say.

The guy waved a hand through the air and staggered off, whistling. I watched him round a corner. But soon as he was out of sight I felt ashamed 'cause my old man always taught me and Diego to respect people older than us. And I definitely hadn't respected his old ass.

I looked at the phone again and tried to think some more about what I wanted to say. But still nothing was coming, so

I started back to where Rondell was with our stuff. I only made it halfway down the block, though, before I spun around and went right back to the pay phone.

I dropped in more change and dialed my mom's number again.

"Hello?" she said off the first ring.

I didn't say anything back.

"Hello?" she said again.

I got another lump in my throat just hearing her voice again. But I couldn't talk. I had no words to say.

"Miguel?" she said.

My eyes went wide.

My stomach dropped out.

I hung the phone up quick as I could and backed off a few steps, staring at it. My legs went to Jell-O right there, like I was about to fall over, but I didn't.

I hadn't heard my moms say my name in forever. But at the same time it felt normal, too. Like nothing ever happened and she was just asking me a question about something back home. Or saying if I could help do the dishes. The lump in my throat grew so big it felt like it was gonna choke my ass to death. But when I tried to spit it out on the sidewalk, nothing came out. It was just stuck there.

I looked at the pay phone again, gave myself a little shot in the ribs. One in the temple. I grabbed my left arm with my right hand and squeezed as hard as I could. I spit again, then smacked the shit out of the cut on my lip, where the guy hit me. It started bleeding down my chin and neck. I touched two fingers to it and looked at 'em and for some reason seeing my own blood like that made me calm down some.

I sat down on the curb and leaned my chin in my hands, stared at the bar across the street. The bouncer was in a chair in front of the open door, looking down at a newspaper. I listened to the music, ignoring my stinging lip and the blood running down my chin, into my hands, down my arms. I wanted to see if they'd play one of the songs Moms used to make me listen to back in the day. Like maybe that "Don't Think Twice" song by Bob Dylan. Or something by Simon and Garfunkel or Cat Stevens. I thought maybe it could be like a sign or whatever. Like me and her were talking even though I'd just hung up the phone.

I sat there listening for a long-ass time.

Concentrating my ears. Waiting.

But one never came on.

July 27

This morning I woke up feeling much different about Rondell. It was just me and him now. I woke him up by piling both our bags on his legs and laughing my ass off when he popped his head up all scared. When he saw it was just me he laughed too.

We pulled out the leather petty-cash envelope and counted the money we had left. It came to $482.

We decided we should still go to Mexico, and I said we'd just pay for a bus to take us down to the border. Then we could cross over and live off what was left until we got jobs at some resort place like the one Mong told us about.

We looked in a phone book for where a major bus station was and found a Greyhound on Long Beach Boulevard. We went in a gas station and got directions and started walking east like the guy told us, along the busy street.

It's pretty trippy, by the way, being on city streets again after you've spent so much time walking on the beach. It's mad stressful actually. The constant sound of traffic going and people blowing their car horns and sirens blaring. I decided it's a better life when you're away from all that stuff. When you're hearing waves instead of cars. Smelling the salty ocean and seaweed instead of bus exhaust. When you're sleeping on the sand.

When we went past this one section where a guy was digging up the street with a jackhammer I started thinking how Mexico was *exactly* where me and Rondell should go. Mong had it right all along—even if it was just something he was making up to get us out of the Lighthouse with him. A resort place on the beach where we could live simple. Cook fish Rondell caught and meet pretty girls. Never again worrying about cop cars coming up over the hill or policemen walking into the store you're at.

I actually got so hyped thinking about it I yelled out to Rondell: "Yo, let's get our asses to Mexico, boy!"

It took him three times to hear me over the jackhammer, but when he finally did he yelled back: "I'm gonna be a fisherman!"

Me and him slapped hands, and I could tell by the look on his face he wasn't worried about me leaving him anymore.

When we finally got to the bus station we bought tickets to San Ysidro, the last city in America before you're in Mexico. We had a little time to kill before our bus left, so I dragged Rondell with me to another pay phone, pulled out the leather petty-cash envelope and dialed the phone number on the front.

"Hello?" Jaden said.

"We aren't dead."

There was a short pause. "Miguel?"

"Yeah. And Rondell. Mong isn't with us no more."

"Bro," Jaden said. "You don't know how happy I am to talk to you. Everything okay? You guys all right?"

I switched the phone from one ear to the other. "I know it's pretty messed up how we took the money."

"Look, I'll say it outright, bro. I'm really disappointed. I really am. But right now I just wanna make sure you guys are safe and sound."

"We're good. But Mong isn't with us no more. He went somewhere else."

"Okay, okay. But you two—"

"To be honest, I don't even know why we left in the first place. We just did it."

"I think a lot of decisions are made that way, Miguel. People act on impulse. But, bro, sometimes spur-of-the-moment decisions don't turn out to be so good."

There was a gap of silence. I looked at Rondell and he mouthed: *What're you doin', Mexico?*

Don't trip, I mouthed back. It wasn't like I was gonna talk to Jaden forever. I just wanted to reach out real quick to see what he said.

"Miguel," Jaden said. "I want to ask you something—"

"Do you surf?" I said.

"Wait, what?" He paused for a sec and then said: "Yeah, I surf. Or at least I used to when I was a kid. Why, bro?"

"Me and Rondell were watching these guys surf yesterday. Do you think Mexican people surf?"

"Absolutely, bro. I knew a guy growing up. Jesse Avila. He was probably the best in our group, actually."

I pictured myself out there at Venice. On a board. Dropping to my stomach when a wave was coming. "Only one guy takes a wave at a time," I said into the phone.

"Look, Miguel," Jaden said. "What's your plan from here? What's past is past, okay? But what you guys do *now* . . ."

"Anyways, I just wanted to tell you we're still alive."

"Good. I'm happy, bro. But listen—"

I hung up the phone and turned to Rondell.

"Why you callin' there, Mexico?"

I shrugged. "I don't even know."

Rondell didn't say anything else, and neither did I.

We walked back to the bus station waiting room and sat in a couple plastic chairs, slipped our bags underneath us. I looked around at all the other people sitting with us, wondered if any of them were going to Mexico too. If any of them were going to resorts there, not to work but to vacation. But it didn't seem like any of them were.

Then I looked up at the board, waited for information to come up about our bus to San Ysidro, the last vehicle we'd ever be on in America.

July 27—more

Soon as the bus let us off, we hurried through the crowded station, cruised right up to the border of America and Mexico and stood with our faces pressed against the towering fence looking into Tijuana. Me and Rondell, side by side, holding our group-home bags and gripping the chain-link with our free hands, staring in. Here we were, the two remaining escaped Lighthouse kids, tired as hell from another long bus trip, from sleeping outside in the cold, from eating as little as possible and always having to look over our shoulders.

But we made it.

Nobody caught us.

We were as far south as two people could get without leaving America. All we had to do now was join the line to our right, walk across the border with everybody else, and we'd be free. It was that simple.

I peered through the fence. Somewhere on the other side

were me and Rondell's brand-new lives, and I wanted to catch a glimpse before we walked into it.

What Mexico Looks Like:

It was mad weird seeing across the border for the first time in my entire life, taking in the country where my grandparents were born. Where my pop used to go to visit his aunties and uncles and cousins every month before he got married, moved to Stockton and had kids. The day I was born he hung a huge map of Mexico on me and Diego's wall, and it's still there, but I've never actually looked at it. Not really. Once I remember pulling up the bottom corner and tripping out on how much whiter the white paint underneath was. But mostly it just hangs there in the background, hardly visible, hardly registering in my mind. Mostly it just blends with the rest of how our room's always been since I can remember.

And now here I was, standing just outside the actual country. Only inches away. Studying all the little plywood shops along the roadside where people who looked like my grandparents sold oversized stuffed animals and colorful straw chairs and rolled-up Mexican rugs and ponchos and churros and street tacos and blown-up smiling Disney characters and every size, shape and color piñata you could even think of. Little Mexican kids darted in and out of all the cars stuck idling in traffic, selling packs of gum and cigarettes and shaved ice and batteries. And they were all brown like me. Everybody was. A hundred different shades of brown hair and brown faces and brown eyes and brown arms and legs. But not just the people—all of TJ seemed brown. The ghetto-looking boards that held up fruit stands. The dirty streets and sidewalks. The mangy dogs laying along the sides of stock-looking buildings, sleeping. The street signs written in both English and Spanish. But at the same time it was colorful, too. What they were selling. The rugs and chairs and ponchos and piñatas. It was like they were brown people living brown lives in a brown place who made bright colors to sell to America.

"Hey, Mexico," Rondell said, tapping me on the shoulder. He set down his bag and stared at me.

"Mexico," he said again.

White people sat in cars facing us, waiting. The traffic lined up as far as you could see. Everybody inching along, trying to get back home. Get back to America. Back to where it was clean and safe and their houses waited for them on quiet streets with locked doors. Sometimes they'd buy a souvenir. Or a drink with a straw. Or a pack of gum. Sometimes they'd roll down their window, pull in something colorful, place crisp American bills into brown hands and then roll their window back up. But mostly they just waited. Eyes focused straight ahead.

Border-patrol cops leaned into every car, talked to every driver, scanned tires, backseats, popped open trunks, checked under hoods. Sometimes they'd wave a car over to the side for further inspection.

"Mexico," Rondell said, holding his hands out. "Hey, Mexico. I'm tryin' to tell you somethin'."

I locked eyes with this one Mexican kid, about me and Rondell's age, and I felt like I was lifting off my feet, floating into the air. He was leaning against a big wooden stand full of clay suns. The kind Mexican people like my gramps hang on the front of their houses to bring good luck and welcome guests. And he had every kind of sun you could think of: big ones, little ones, smiling ones, laughing ones, mean ones. All of 'em made of orangish-brown clay and hung on a warped wall so you could get a good view as you sat in traffic waiting to get back to America.

But nobody stopped at his stand.

No American people wanted his suns.

As me and this kid were staring at each other, thinking our own thoughts, something clicked in my head. For the first time. I was Mexican. Like him. Like my pop and my gramps and all the people me and Diego picked berries with that day in the fields of Fresno. Me. Miguel Casteñeda. I was the same as this kid selling suns. We were both tall and young and skinny. We both had short brown hair and bony elbows and the ability to stare without blinking.

But at the same time I felt like a damn poser. 'Cause why was he on the Mexico side of the fence, and I was on the American side? How'd it happen like this? If our country's really so much better than Mexico, like everybody says— 'cause we got more money and better schools and better hospitals and less people get sick just by drinking the water—then why should I be here and not him? Why was I on the better side of this big-ass fence? Just 'cause my moms is white? 'Cause of the story my pop always told me, how gramps snuck through a sewage drain, crawled in everybody's piss and shit, just to make it to America? But that's nothing to do with me.

What did *I* do?

And what did this kid selling clay suns *not* do?

I stared into the Mexican kid's eyes. And he stared right back. Neither of us looking away. Or even blinking. But really I was floating into the air. All the way up past the birds, past the clouds. We were the same, me and this kid, but we weren't the same at all. Exact opposites, even. He was real, and I was fake. It all had to do with what side of a fence you were born on. And the fact that I was on the better side made me feel sick to my stomach.

Rondell waved a big-ass black hand in front of my face and shouted: "Yo! Mexico!"

I turned to face him.

He shook his head and turned his palms up at me. "We goin' in there or what?"

I looked back at the kid selling clay suns, but he was looking somewhere else now. He was concentrating on the people passing him in cars.

"Are we?" Rondell said. He grabbed my face and turned it so I had to look him in the eyes again. "What's wrong with you, Mexico?"

I shook out of his grip, said something I didn't expect: "I can't, man."

"Wha'chu talkin' 'bout?"

"I can't go to Mexico."

He frowned. "Wha'chu mean by that?"

"I don't deserve it."

Rondell looked at his shoes. He picked up his bag and hung it on his shoulder, then looked at me again. "Why not? You *from* there, ain't you?"

"No, I'm not," I said, looking back to the kid selling clay suns. He was sitting down now.

I looked all around TJ, at the ghetto buildings and the narrow bridges and the run-down shops and beat-up roads. I felt something strange happening inside me. Like when you watch your favorite team play a basketball game on TV and you want their asses to win so damn bad. Almost to the point that you can't even watch. 'Cause if you watch you might jinx 'em, might make 'em lose. And if that happened you'd never forgive yourself.

I turned back to Rondell. "I can't explain it, man. I just know it ain't right for me to go there yet."

Rondell stood there for a sec, staring at me while I stared at Mexico. "But we was all three of us supposed to be fishermans."

I picked up my bag and looked at him. "I'm sorry about this, Rondell. But I really can't do it."

Rondell started playing with the zipper on his sweatshirt again. He looked at Mexico and then back at me. "I could still go, though, right, Mexico?"

"Hell yeah, Rondo. You can go."

" 'Cause I wanna go be a fisherman."

"I know. And you'll be the best damn one, man. I guarantee it."

A little smile came on his face. "Why do you think I'll be so good?"

I shifted my bag to my other shoulder and told him: " 'Cause for one thing, man, you're patient as hell. You can just sit in one spot for hours. And second of all, I saw you play ball, yo. You got natural talent for shit like that. Just trust me, man. You could be whatever you want."

He nodded his head and then laughed a little. He put his hand on the fence and watched the people filing through the border on foot a few yards away. "Hey, Mexico," he said, turning back to me. "Maybe I could just go there tomorrow, though. I don't wanna leave just yet. Is that okay?"

"You ain't gotta ask my permission, man." And then this thought came in my head and I smacked Rondell on the shoulder with the back of my fist. "Yo, I got an idea. What if we go get us a fat meal somewhere. A place with waitresses and cloth napkins and all that gourmet kind of shit. You feel like some steak, man?"

"I'm hungry as hell, Mexico."

"Bet you ain't never had no filet mignon, though."

"Nah," Rondell said, shaking his head. "What is it?"

"Yo," I said, "I hear that kind of steak is sick, Rondo. It's supposedly like *this* thick." I held up my thumb and finger, as far apart as I could get 'em.

"And it taste good?"

"What I just tell you, man? It's the best steak you could buy. It's what all the rich people eat."

Rondell nodded and scratched his head. A huge smile came on his face. "I bet I could eat like three of them mignons, Mexico."

"You a straight lie, Rondo!"

"Watch. Let's go right now."

I smacked him on the shoulder again, said: "Yo, check this plan. We go track down the best filet mignon in San Diego, right? And then we crash on the beach tonight, like we been doing. And then first thing tomorrow morning we'll buy you a map of the streets in Mexico, and then we'll come back here. And you can go across and be a fisherman, and I'll stay here until I figure some shit out. That cool with you?"

Rondell nodded, excited as hell, and we both looked back toward America, for where all the fanciest-ass restaurants in all of San Ysidro might be.

July 27—more

After the most amazing meal we've ever had—we both got filet mignon and these huge baked potatoes and dinner rolls and asparagus shoots and then cheesecake for dessert—me and Rondell walked along the border until we made it back down to the beach. It's crazy how they do the fence when it gets to the water, by the way. Thick rusty posts, curling toward TJ, going all the way into the ocean. The waves break right around 'em. And you can see them perfect 'cause they got these border-patrol vans parked right there on the sand, shining their headlights over the border part of the water.

One thing you figure out quick is America doesn't play when it comes to letting Mexicans sneak in their country.

Me and Rondell leaned against a couple posts in the sand, outside of the vans' line of vision, and rested our hands on our full stomachs.

I took out the leather petty-cash envelope from my bag and counted the cash we had left: $386. Then I counted out half of it and held the cash out for Rondell.

"What this is for?" he said.

"Tomorrow, man. When you go to Mexico."

He stared at it for a few more seconds and then a look of understanding went onto his face, like he just remembered what he was doing tomorrow. "Oh," he said, smiling. "Thanks, Mexico."

The guy was just holding the money in his hand, like he didn't know what to do with it next so I told him: "Go on and put that shit away, man. You better not lose it either."

"I won't, Mexico."

"Or waste it on no hookers."

"I won't."

"Or on one of them donkey shows."

He looked up at me, confused. "Wha'chu mean a donkey show?"

I cracked up a little and waved him off. "Nah, man. You don't even wanna know. I'm just sayin', you gotta make that last until you find a way to get more."

"I could make it last," he said. He folded the bills in half, pushed them into his bag. Then he thought better of it, pulled them back out and slipped them in his jeans pocket. "Wha'chu gonna do with yours?" he said.

"I was just thinkin' about that at the restaurant," I said. "How much we start with? Like seven hundred fifty, right?"

Rondell shrugged.

"I think it was seven fifty. Anyways, I'm gonna find a way to pay it all back, man. I don't know how yet, or if it'll take me forever, but that's what I'm gonna do. And then I'm gonna mail it back to the Lighthouse."

Rondell started smiling like maybe I was messing with him. "I get it, Mexico. You playin' with me. You ain't really sendin' back no money."

"I put it on everything," I said. "I don't like how we stole Jaden's cash, you know? Leavin' is one thing, 'cause it's on us, but takin' a group home's money isn't cool."

"Why you think so?"

"It just doesn't feel right."

Rondell stared at his shoes for a little and then he looked up at me and said: "I don't think it's right neither."

I watched him pull the money halfway out of his pocket and look at it, then shove it back in.

We were both quiet for a little while. I looked at the border-patrol vans just sitting there, shining their lights on the water. For some reason I didn't worry about 'em that much. I knew they weren't like real cops. They only cared about finding illegal aliens trying to come into America. They didn't give a shit about me and Rondell.

I picked up a rock and thought how weird it was that people call 'em aliens. Like they're from outer space and look like damn Martians. All green with big-ass Rondell heads. And not just aliens but illegal ones too. I wondered who made up that term. And how weird is it they put cops all along the border so no Mexicans could sneak in? But on the other side it was straight crickets. Nobody was there making sure American people like me and Rondell didn't sneak into *Mexico*. Shit like that is weird if you really stop and think about it.

How a Normal Conversation Usually Goes When You're Talking to Rondell:

"Know what, Mexico?" Rondell said, smelling his hands. "I could eat that mignon food every single day."

I laughed a little, said: "Yeah, man, but your ass would go broke in a week." I reached into Rondell's bag for *The Catcher in the Rye*, pulled it out and flipped to the page I was on.

"When I get rich, I mean," Rondell said, pulling out his Bible.

"Oh, I see," I told him, looking up from my book. "And how you plan on getting rich, Mr. Trump? You think you could catch that many fish?"

He shrugged as he opened the front cover. "Maybe I might win the lottery," he said. "You ever think about that one, Mexico?"

"Where, in Tijuana?" I pictured Rondell in some taco hut in deep Mexico, ghetto fishing pole laying across his lap as he sat there scratching off Mexican lotto tickets. I shook my head, cracking up. "How many pesos you think they gonna give you if you win, man?"

He shrugged and then gave me a confused look. "What's 'pesos' mean?"

"That's the money they use."

"Why?"

I closed up my book and looked at him a sec. I knew I'd be going down a pointless road if I answered his question. But at the same time, man. What else was there to talk about, you know? And since this was our last night together I thought I should maybe talk with Rondell as much as he wanted to talk.

"Okay, look," I said. "You know the money you got in your pocket right now?"

He nodded.

"Those are dollars, right? Dollars are American money. But every country has their own kind. In Mexico it's pesos."

A frown came over his face. He looked down at his hands, shaking his head. "But that don't make no *sense*, Mexico."

"What doesn't?"

He looked up again. "They should just use dollars and cents like everybody else."

"I just told you, though," I said. "Every place has its own kind of money."

"But how come?"

" 'Cause they're a different *country*, man."

Rondell thought about that for a sec, then he told me: "Wouldn't it be more easier if everybody used the same kind?"

"Probably."

"So why don't they do it, then?"

I set my book in the sand next to me. "Check it out, though, some places are a far-ass ways away. Like New Zealand or Iceland. Of course they're gonna do their own thing over there."

He pointed over his shoulder. "But Mexico's right there behind us."

I looked at him, shaking my head. I could tell I was about to get mad frustrated. I took a deep breath, said: "America wasn't even the first country, Rondo. Most countries are way older than us."

Rondell nodded his head, thinking that one over. You could tell the guy thought it was some kind of deep-ass, important conversation we were having by how he was stroking his chin and squinting up his eyes. "Okay, then what was the first one?" he said.

I pulled my hood up over my head. "I'm pretty sure it was Rome or some shit."

"Where's Rome?"

"In Italy."

"And what kind of money does Italy use?"

"I think Euros."

Rondell held out his hands. "Then everybody should just use *that* kind of money. Since it was the first kind."

I shook my head. "Nah, man, it *wasn't* the first kind, though. The first kind of money wasn't even money. People traded shit, like ten chickens for a pig or a sack of coffee for a crate of corn. Shit like that."

"So, what if you didn't have no chickens, though?" he said. "Them people couldn't never get themselves a pig? That don't seem right."

"Maybe they could trade somethin' else," I said. "Like a goat or a bunch of clothes. It wasn't like there was a set thing you had to trade to get a pig, man. That's ignorant."

"I ain't eat pork anyway," Rondell said. He shook his head. "My aunt told me pigs is the dirtiest animal. She said we ain't supposed to eat 'em 'cause it'll make humans dirty too."

I rolled my eyes at Rondell. I had to shut this meaningless conversation down or else who knows what we'd start talking about. "Anyways," I said. "Mexico's lottery is in pesos, man. That's all I was sayin'. Now if you'll excuse me, dawg, I got a damn book to read."

I reached in Rondell's bag again, pulled out the three books I'd yet to get to and stashed them in my own bag.

Rondell watched me do this and a look of sadness went into his eyes. Like him not carrying my books no more made it official we were splitting up. He lowered his face, flipped the page in his Bible, scanned a finger across a couple lines.

Then Rondell Takes Shit to a Whole Other Level:

We both read for about a half hour and then I heard Rondell giggling a little so I looked up. He was staring at where we'd walked down to the beach from with this big-ass grin on his face.

I knew it wasn't the smartest idea, but I couldn't even help myself. "Yo, Rondo," I said, "what's going on over there?"

He turned to look at me, said: "Nothin'."

"Nah, come on, man. What's so funny?"

He shook his head. "I was just laughin' 'bout somethin'."

"No shit, Rondo," I said, closing my book. "I'm saying, what the hell was it?"

Rondell giggled again. "I was just readin' my Bible and thinkin' 'bout how I was gonna be all alone when I go to Mexico. But then my mom and dad told me it wasn't true. They said they was gonna be right there with me, especially if I won all them pesos. But I told 'em it ain't the same thing 'cause they ain't real people, and my dad got all pissed off and said, 'I see we ain't good enough for you now, Rondell. After everything we done. Go on then, leave us be.' He always sayin' things like that to me, Mexico. Like he don't care none. But I know he care. That's my word."

I stared back at Rondell with my mouth hanging open.

I honestly couldn't believe what I was hearing. I'd known all along his ass was special ed, even before I read his file, but now the dude was on some next-level shit. He was seeing ghosts and hearing voices.

Rondell laughed again, said: "I know it sound weird to say it, Mexico. That's why I didn't wanna tell you nothin'."

I wanted to see just how schizo he really was. "Go 'head, Rondo. Tell me what they're sayin' now."

"They fightin' 'bout me."

I nodded. "Okay, they're fightin' about you. What else? I sure wish I could see 'em or hear 'em like you can."

"They just right there," Rondell said, pointing at the line of boulders that separated the sand from where the houses started. "See them two big ones? That's my mom and dad, Mexico."

"The rocks?" I said, turning back to him.

He nodded. To him it seemed simple.

I looked at the rocks again. The two biggest ones were right next to each other, facing us.

"I know it sound weird," he said again.

"Well, it don't sound normal, Rondell."

"It's what I say in my head, though. Especially when I feel lonely. See my mom's the littler one who's smilin'. And look how my dad be lookin' all mad. He always that way. Like he don't really care 'bout nothin' to do with me. But I know he love me, Mexico."

"How do you know?" I said.

" 'Cause he's always followin' me. Sometimes he's on a rock like that one, and sometimes he's in the clouds or on a store window or a stain on a building. But he's always there with me, every single place I go."

I stared at the two big rocks. I looked at Rondell again, then went back at the rocks. If you looked hard enough, it really did seem like there were little faces there. Maybe Rondell was crazy. Or maybe he wasn't. Maybe everybody *else* was crazy. Maybe he was just doing what he had to do to get through a hard life. The guy had either lived in foster care or prison ever since his grandma died. Who was I to say how somebody was supposed to deal with that kind of shit?

"Know what I think?" I told him, nodding my head a little. I looked at him, right in the eyes.

"What?" he said, looking back at me.

"I think maybe that's one of the smartest things I've ever heard somebody say, man." I nodded a little more. "I'm for real about that, Rondo."

"What is?" he said back, a little frown going on his face.

"About your mom and dad."

He didn't say anything.

"How you see 'em in different places," I said. "Like they're always keeping an eye on you."

"Who you mean?"

I stared back at Rondell for a few long seconds, said: "Are you serious?"

He looked at me even more confused. "Wha'chu mean?" he said.

"You know what?" I shot back. And then I paused to spit in front of me and shake my head. I could feel myself getting pissed off. "Just forget it, dawg. Forget everything I just told you. I take it all back. Goddamn."

"Wha'chu mean, though, Mexico? I ain't get it."

"No shit, Rondell. You never do. That's the problem. You haven't understood one word I've said since the day I met you. It's a waste of my damn breath."

"If you just tell me—"

"Nah, man," I cut him off. "We done talkin'."

He shrugged, and I shook my head.

We were both quiet for a while. I went back to reading my book, and Rondell went back to looking at his Bible. But I couldn't concentrate. I looked all around us again, at the rusted border poles coming out of the water, the headlights shining across the waves. I even looked over at Rondell's imaginary parents.

Being down here was such a trip. At the very end of America. The start of Mexico. Isn't that weird, when you think about it? That people back in the day actually decided the split should be right here. Not a few feet this way or that way but right here, at these poles we were leaning against. I pictured all these old-time people in suits from both countries pointing down at the sand, speaking in their different languages. And I wondered which side actually built the fence. And who had to pay for it.

I looked up at the border-patrol vans just sitting there in the sand, facing Mexico. Waiting for some Mexican guy's head to peek up out of the water as he swam around the boundary. What would they do if they saw it? Come running toward the water with a big-ass net? Like a cartoon dog-catcher? Or would they actually pull their guns?

I was busy picturing how it would go down when Rondell leaned over and tapped me on the shoulder. "Hey, Mexico," he said.

"Hey, what?"

"Thanks."

I turned to him. "For what?"

"For sayin' I was smart."

I shook my head at him. "I was just fuckin' with you, Rondo. Don't get too hyped on that shit."

He nodded, dead serious. "Nobody ever said nothin' like that 'bout me before."

He went back to looking at his Bible.

I stared at the guy for a minute or two. Schizo as his big ass was, I thought how I was probably gonna miss him. All his questions and his made-up parents and the way he dunked on fools playing ball and called me Mexico and never complained about anything. But this was what I was gonna remember more than anything. Watching Rondell pretend to read the Bible. If I lived to be a hundred ten and got the worst case of Alzheimer's possible and they shipped me out to some old-fogey home in the boonies where all I could do was look at trees and drool all over myself. Still, man, I'm pretty sure I'd remember Rondell leaning over his damn Bible like this, scanning a finger across words he couldn't read.

"Yo, I meant that shit, Rondo," I said. "You're smarter than you realize."

Before he could look up at me I went back to reading my book. Hoping like hell he didn't say something to mess it all up.

July 28

Early this morning me and Rondell were back at the San Ysidro border. But this time we weren't looking into Mexico, we were looking at each other to say goodbye.

"Mexico," Rondell said, holding out his hand for me.

"Rondell," I said, slapping it. He pulled me in for a little dude hug, and then we both pulled away. He looked down at his shoes all shy and then peeked up at me. His eyes were glassy.

I nodded at him, thinking how for a guy I first met in Juvi he turned out to be a pretty solid dude. But it's not like I was gonna get all choked up or whatever. He wasn't the first person I'd had to say bye to.

"You got the map, right?" I said.

He held it up.

"And you got the money?"

He slipped the wad of bills halfway out of his pocket for me to see.

"All right, then," I said. "I guess you just go stand with those people." I nodded my head toward the small line of people waiting to get into Mexico.

He looked at the line and then looked back at me.

I punched his big ass in the arm and then walked away, telling him over my shoulder: "Good luck, big Rondo. Don't get nobody pregnant."

"Good luck, Mexico," he called after me. "I'm gonna miss you!"

I didn't even turn around once as I walked away. I learned the best system for saying bye to people is to just keep walking and not think about it that much. You can't stress about every single person you say bye to, right? That'd be like half your life spent worrying about people you're no longer gonna see.

Nah, man, you gotta look forwards, not backwards.

Rondell would figure his shit out over there. Or he wouldn't. Same as me. But there was no use stressing about it. I couldn't sit there and wonder if he'd be okay on his own or not, if people might take advantage of him. It's not like I could do anything when we were in two different countries.

That's just how life is, man.

I walked back to the main road and headed north this time, back into San Ysidro. Into America. I didn't even know where I was going yet or how I was gonna get there or how I could make back all the $750 to send to the Lighthouse. If you think about it, I didn't know nothin' about nothin' anymore. All I knew is I had to stay in America until I got my shit straight.

About a mile down the busy road I cut into a minimall and hit the first pay phone I found, this one right at the edge of the huge parking lot. I set down my bag on the thin bed of grass and tossed some change in the coin thing and dialed my moms.

It rang five times and then the answering machine picked up. I wasn't surprised she still had the same message as when I called from the Lighthouse. Diego's voice saying: "Peoples, we're not home right now. Leave a message at the . . ." My moms laughing in the background and then the beep sounding. I remember 'cause I was sitting right next to him when he said it. I remember looking over at Moms, watching her crack up a little.

That's something you should know about Diego, by the way. He can pretty much make Moms laugh any time, any place. No matter what mood she's in.

I hung up.

I sat down and looked at the parking lot for a while. Watched some people pulling in and others pulling out. I tried hard to think what I should do next, but I honestly had no idea. My mind was completely blank. I looked up at the clouds and tried to make out shapes. For a sec I thought I saw Diego's face laughing at me, but when I looked closer I knew I was full of shit. There wasn't no face there. More like a big-ass white bowling ball, one with the finger holes and everything.

I pulled out this journal and read through a bunch of my entries. It was crazy to look back over my last couple months. So much shit had happened. It almost seemed like I had to be making half the shit up, or at least exaggerating. But I wasn't, man. Every single thing in here is completely true.

I still had a bunch of pages left, too, and I wondered if by the time I ran out of pages I'd be done with my story. And how would it end? It's weird when you're writing a book about your own life and you got no clue what's gonna happen next or if it'll even be good or bad.

One thing I can say for sure, though, I was happy as hell my journal didn't have a bunch of that emotional crap most people's journals have. I know that's probably what the judge wanted me to put or whatever, but I like it so much better that I just tell what happens. It seems like more of a real book that way. Like the ones you see in bookstores or school libraries.

I stood and picked up the phone again, dialed the number on the leather petty-cash envelope.

Jaden answered right off and said hello.

"It's me again," I said.

"Miguel, bro. Great to hear from you, man. I was actually just thinking about you."

I rolled my eyes, thought: *Right, money.* "I'm payin' the petty cash back. It might take me a while to raise it up, but I'll mail it soon as I do."

"Yeah?" he said. "Bro, I think that's solid. It makes me really happy to hear that."

"I should just send it to the address on the envelope thing? That's the right one?"

"Read it to me."

I read it to him.

"That's it, bro. That's where I am right this second, in my office. The guys are just cleaning up after breakfast. We had frozen waffles. You remember our frozen-waffle mornings?"

I switched the phone from one ear to the other.

"You liked the blueberry ones, right, bro? Kind of burned on the sides. See, Miguel, I was paying attention."

"Yeah, they're all right."

For some reason just thinking about the Lighthouse made butterflies go into my stomach.

"Anyway," Jaden said. "I'm watching the guys right now and thinking how much this place has changed. We got three new residents. Nice kids. One of them is an amazing dancer, bro. Last night we put on some hip-hop and cleared the living room floor and all the guys broke it down. It was unreal. They took turns in the middle and even made a couple routines. By the end, though, we were all watching Miya. He can do things you've never even seen before. Like he's double-jointed in every part of his body."

"Yeah?" I said, trying to think why he'd be telling me all this.

"It was good for the guys, bro."

As he kept talking I looked over my shoulder to watch this young mom wheel a cart from the grocery store to her car singing to her kid: "Old MacDonald had a farm / EE-I-EE-I-O / And on that farm he had a cow . . ." I watched her pop the trunk and start loading in the plastic bags. Her little kid stood up in the cart, clapping.

". . . and we got a new batch of books, too," Jaden was saying. "I ordered them myself with you in mind. Never know when you're gonna get a resident who reads, right? It's hella rare, bro. But you proved to me it can happen."

I remembered going up to the Lighthouse bookshelf, feeling all the spines and then picking the one I wanted to take in my room. I said: "I'm almost finished with *The Catcher in the Rye*."

"Miguel, my man, that's in my all-time top five. Holden's a trip, right? He says some pretty funny stuff about the people in his life. Ha ha! But at the same time, he's really just a vulnerable, lost kid."

I switched the phone again. "I liked *Of Mice and Men* better. And *The Color Purple*. Mostly *The Color Purple*."

"Yeah, those books are great too. But you gotta understand, Miguel. *Catcher* was way ahead of its time. Nobody'd ever written a character like Holden. He was a true original."

"No, I like it a lot," I said, reaching into my bag and pulling my copy out. "I'm just sayin'."

Jaden said some more about the book, and I stared at the cover thinking how far away I was from my life back at the

Lighthouse. And even farther away from my life in Stockton. From my moms and Diego and our apartment and the levee. I shook my head thinking where I was now. On a pay phone in San Diego with some surfer group-home counselor telling me about his favorite books and how his parents once invited this old English teacher to dinner who had supposedly met the guy who wrote *Of Mice and Men.*

"Bro, listen," he said after a short pause. "From now on I want you to call here collect. You know how to make a collect call, right? You just dial—"

"I know how," I said.

"Good. From now on, bro. I love hearing from you. I mean it."

"Does Lester know I call?"

"He does. I'm not gonna pull any punches with you, Miguel. I told him first thing. He's confused, just like I am. We think we've created a pretty chilled-out environment where guys can get better and move on with their lives. So it was a surprise—"

"Did he call my mom?"

"He did, yeah. She's worried. I called her too. Right after you last called. I told her you were okay and that you were a good kid. We had a nice long talk, bro—"

"Anyways," I said, interrupting him. I didn't want to hear anything else about my moms for some reason. Just in case it was bad. "I'm paying the money back," I said. "That's all I called for. I just don't know how long it'll take."

As I was hanging up the phone I heard him saying something about me coming back and how he and Lester would work things out with the judge, but I didn't really hear the details.

I knew I should start walking again. Go find a train or bus station and buy a ticket somewhere. Or I should at least figure out some sort of plan—even if it was just for the rest of today. But I didn't do *anything*, man. I just sat my ass down on the little strip of grass, next to my bag, and watched that young mother finally pull her car out of her parking space. Watched her loop around to the exit and cautiously merge back into traffic. Then she was gone.

And there was this one memory that kept coming into my head. I don't even know why. It was the time when me and Diego and my moms all went to some ice cream place about two months after we found out my pop wasn't coming home from the war.

Moms, who'd been so depressed she barely got out of bed, came marching into me and Diego's room and said: "You guys be ready in ten minutes, okay?"

"Why?" Diego said.

"Yeah, what's going on?" I said.

"I'm taking you guys out for ice cream sundaes."

Diego looked at her like she was crazy. "Ice cream, Ma? I don't know if you checked a calendar lately, but it's the damn middle of winter."

Moms put her hands on her hips and said: "And your point is?"

"It's rainin' outside, Ma."

"That's what umbrellas are for," she said. "Now come on, I feel like a chocolate sundae."

I automatically started pulling my umbrella from under the bed, but when I looked up and saw Diego watching me I paused.

Moms turned to me and said: "See, Miguel agrees with his mom. A sundae sounds good, doesn't it?"

I looked back at her and said: "I guess so."

Diego shook his head. "Come on, Ma. You know Guelly's gonna just go along with any single thing you say."

"That's 'cause he likes being around his mom," she said.

Diego held his hands out, said: "And I don't?"

"Hurry up and get ready, then. We're going out for sundaes together."

"Okay, okay, okay," Diego said, a smile slowly coming over his face. He pulled his umbrella from under the bed too. "You know I'm just bustin' your balls anyways, Ma."

We all piled in the car and went to Baskin-Robbins and ordered huge ice cream sundaes and sat together in a booth way in the back. And after Moms had a couple bites she flicked a spoonful of ice cream onto Diego's black sweatshirt. Diego looked down at the ice cream, and then looked up at Moms with this shocked-ass look on his face. I remember I couldn't believe she did that. I maybe even thought she was going crazy.

"What?" she said, shrugging and going back to her sundae.

"You just flicked ice cream on me," Diego said.

Moms acted all confused, though, said: "I most certainly did not, Diego. You ever think maybe it was your little brother over there?"

Diego looked at me, and I shook my head. Then he scooped up some ice cream and flicked it on my mom's jacket.

She casually picked up a couple napkins, wiped the ice cream off and told Diego: "That was extremely rude, honey. Flicking ice cream on your own mom. What kind of son would do such a thing?"

Diego was about to say something back, but right then Moms scooped up some chocolate sauce in her right hand and wiped it all over Diego's face. Then she pulled out a long chunk of banana from her sundae and threw it in my lap.

Before you knew it we were all three of us flinging ice

cream and bananas and chocolate sauce all over each other and laughing our asses off.

· The manager stormed over to us and told us to leave immediately. Moms picked up her spoon and flicked ice cream right onto his damn cheek and forehead. Me and Diego laughed so hard we could barely breathe. The manager guy wiped off his face with a rag and got this crazy look on his face. He spun his head to the girl working the register, shouted: "Jenny! Call the goddamn cops! Hurry up! I want these people arrested!"

But me and Moms and Diego were already racing out of the store together, laughing and telling each other to hurry and get in the car. We cracked up the whole way home, sticky-ass melted ice cream all over our clothes and faces and hands. And then, as we pulled into our apartment complex parking lot, Mom's laughing died out and she got this different look on her face as she stared straight ahead. And then she started sobbing. She gripped the wheel and cried harder than anybody I'd ever seen before.

Me and Diego put a hand each on her shoulders and told her, "It's okay, Ma. It's okay. Don't cry, Ma. It's okay." But secretly I think we both knew it was a good thing. It was the first time she'd cried since the army guy came to our house that day and said our pop was involved in a freak training accident and wasn't able to make it through.

I was laying in the grass by the pay phone picturing all of us in the ice cream place, the look on the manager's face, us coming home in the car, when I heard this deep voice behind me saying: "It's the cops. We arrestin' all guys named Mexico."

I spun my ass around to look, and I couldn't believe it. There was Rondell's big dumb ass, bag slung over his right shoulder and this huge grin on his face.

The Return of Rondell (with Two Ls) Law:

"Yo, man," I said, and then I just shook my head cracking up at him. I had to admit, I was kind of happy as hell to see the guy again. Even though I played it like I didn't care that much.

"Yo," I said, standing up. "You're supposed to be in damn TJ right now."

"I know," he said. He put a fist up to his mouth and giggled his ass off for a few seconds. Then he wiped a laughter tear off his cheek and said: "You know what I thought about, though?"

I shook my head. "Go 'head, this oughta be interesting."

"I thought about maybe I don't gotta go all the way to Mexico to be a fisherman. Not just yet, at least. I could probably be one right here in this country first. And then go to Mexico later on."

"I see."

"And while I'm here I could help you raise up the money to pay back them Lighthouse people. 'Cause I don't think we shoulda took it neither." He held his wad of cash out to me, and I grabbed it.

He slipped his hands in his pockets. "Is it okay if I didn't go, Mexico?"

"It's a free damn country, Rondo. You could do whatever you want."

"But is it okay if I go with you instead?"

I made a big show like I was thinking about it for a few seconds, and then I looked up at him, reaching into my bag. "Long as you hold these books for me," I said, holding out the ones I'd took back just last night.

He took 'em and stashed 'em in his bag. "Thanks, Mexico." He sat all the way down in the grass, and I did too.

We were both quiet for a sec and then he looked at me and said: "So, what we gonna do now?"

A big smile went on my face. "That's the million-dollar question, isn't it, Rondo? I was just sittin' here tryin' to figure that one out."

"You'll come up with somethin'."

"You think so?"

He nodded. " 'Cause you smart too, Mexico."

I patted him on his big-ass back and said: "Well, I'm glad you feel that way."

He smiled big and said: "Ain't as smart as me, but you all right."

We both cracked up a little and then I looked out onto the road. Watched the cars drive by. I tried to think what we were gonna do. There were two people to consider about now. I snuck another little look at the side of Rondell's head. Big Rondo. Dude was back. I laughed a little inside 'cause I knew if I had a damn chocolate sundae I'd flick some ice cream right in his baby Afro.

When he turned his head to look at me, though, I went right back to watching cars on the road like I was in deep brainstorm mode.

July 31

What's the last thing you'd think could happen to a group-home kid on the run? Him meeting a girl, right? Think about it, the guy hasn't showered in days, no place to stay, chased by the cops, pretty much wears the same gear 24/7. Shit's basically impossible, right?

Think again, partner, 'cause that's exactly what happened

two nights ago, at some ghetto-ass baseball park in National City: I met a girl. A fine-ass Mexican one named Flaca. And we both fell in damn love, man, almost from the second we met.

Here's How It Went Down:

Earlier me and Rondell were wandering around Imperial Beach for the third day in a row trying to brainstorm our next move. But nothing was coming to either of us. Again. When we were going to Mexico at least we had a goal. Now we didn't have shit. We knew we couldn't go home (Rondell didn't even *have* a home). We knew we couldn't go back to the Lighthouse. We were just two wandering-ass kids now, cruising any which way on random sidewalks in San Diego with bags full of everything we owned hanging from our shoulders. We caught a local bus going north and only got off 'cause the driver called last stop. We bought tacos and ate 'em on a curb between two parked cars, watching these construction guys tear apart an old liquor store and carry pieces of wall to an old dinged-up dump truck. When the sun started going down we just randomly wandered into this run-down park.

As we got down into the baseball field part, though, we spotted a group of like five girls already there, sitting in a circle drinking cans of beer.

We stopped.

They looked up at us.

At first I was gonna have us roll back out, find some other place to chill, but instead we walked way on the other end of the field from them.

They went back to what they were doing.

Me and Rondell sat with our backs against this rusted chain-link fence in right field and watched the sky. I told him we'd probably have to steal from a store to get back the money. It was the only way I could think of. I told him if we tried to do regular jobs they'd look up our names and we'd be screwed. Plus I don't think places will even hire you if you don't have an address to write down—which sort of makes me think about all the times I've walked past a homeless dude begging for change and thought: Yo, money, you need to get up off your ass, find yourself a job.

People reading this journal will probably be thinking that exact same thing about me and Rondell. That we should just get jobs like everybody else. And I wish we could. But it ain't that easy, man. Trust me.

And I know it don't sound right, us robbing one place to pay back another, but like I told Rondell, we'd just steal from a place that makes so much damn money they won't know the difference. Like a McDonald's or Starbucks or Wal-Mart. We both got mad quiet after I told him that, probably 'cause the shit was easier said than done and what if we got caught. Everything, including us paying back the petty cash, would be ruined.

I thought for the first time how basically we might be fucked no matter *what* we did. 'Cause how many more nights could we sleep on a beach? Or in a park? Just so you know, you can't even really sleep, man. You always got one eye open, looking out for somebody who might come try to roll your ass.

Just having a place to crash at night is a bigger deal than most people realize.

Anyways, I started picturing the store we'd have to rob, how we'd have the cash person count out exactly how much we needed to make $750, not a dollar extra, when two girls from the group started walking over to us sipping their cans of beer.

A Mexican Girl Even Diego Would Say Is Fine:

"Who are *you* guys?" the bigger girl said. She had on a black Dickies jacket and these tight-ass white pants. Her bangs stuck all up in the air like ol' girl had on a damn visor.

"We're nobody," I said.

"You gotta be somebody," the prettier one said. "Everybody's somebody." She had on a short jean skirt and a tank top that said HERE COMES TROUBLE. Her legs were long and brown and perfectly shaped.

I told her: "Well, we ain't nobody from around here, man. That's for sure."

The pretty one looked at her friend and rolled her eyes and then looked back at us. "So where you from, then?" she said.

I picked up a rock like Diego would've done and tossed it up in the air, caught it. Real mellow style. Like I wasn't even thinking about them. "Portugal," I said, 'cause it's what popped in my head.

"*Portugal?*" she said, looking all shocked. She took a sip of beer and thought about that for a sec. "Nah, I don't think so. People from Portugal speak Portuguese."

"I promise."

"Then lemme hear you say somethin' in Portuguese."

I made some crazy-ass random sounds and then turned to Rondell, said: "Ain't that right, dawg?"

Rondell looked at me all confused.

"That wasn't no Portuguese," the bigger one said.

"How do *you* know?" I said.

"Okay, what'd you say, then?" the pretty one said. She had a tiny hoop ring in her nose. Silver.

"I said: 'Man, it sure is nice of these girls to come offer us a beer. Especially since we were just sayin' how thirsty we are.'"

She walked up close to me, so close so I could smell her lotion, and my heart started going all quick. She grinned a little and said: "Oh, you're one of those comedian guys." She turned to the bigger one and said: "Yo, Jules, he's one of them comedian guys."

"Great," Jules said, and she took a long swig of beer.

"Yo, we just got your girl Jules's name," I said to the pretty one. "What's up with yours?"

She looked at me for a sec and then held out her can of beer. I took it and pulled a long swig, then rested it on my knee.

"I'm Flaca," she said.

"Nice to meet you, Flaca," I said back. "I'm Miguel, and this is Rondell."

Rondell gave her a what's up with his head.

Flaca snatched her beer out of my hand, told us: "Anyways."

She kneeled down, balanced her can of beer in the grass, and retied her shoelace. Then she stood up and motioned for Jules to follow her over to the other girls. After she got a few steps away she turned around, backpedaling, and said: "You guys can come if you want to. Long as you don't try to rape us or some shit. But I wouldn't 'cause Jules got Mace, right, Jules?"

"Got *two* cans," Jules said. "One for each of them fools."

They laughed and kept walking, and me and Rondell looked at each other. It seemed like we were both sort of curious, or at least I know I was. For the simple fact that I'd never flirted with a girl so fine as Flaca. And my game seemed like it was flowing too. I was saying shit straight out of Diego's playbook without even thinking about it.

I nodded to Rondell.

We got up and followed after them.

We joined in the group and got two warm beers out of

somebody's duffel bag and the girls started talking nonstop. There were five of them and they said stuff about kids in their neighborhood mostly. Or in their school. Or at some fair they'd just gone to the night before. But the whole time I could tell Flaca was kind of looking at me on the slick. Not like how regular people look at each other either. More like how girls look at Diego. After we'd all been talking a while she even made an excuse to come sit closer to me.

She crossed through the circle and got all up in my face, said: "Yo, hold up."

All her girls went dead quiet and turned to look at us.

Flaca pointed at me and Rondell, said: "We're sittin' here tellin' these fools our entire life story, and they haven't said shit."

"Not a peep from either of 'em," this skinny girl with a birthmark on her cheek said.

"Yo, should I get my Mace?" Jules said.

Flaca smiled a little at her girl and then turned back to me on the serious. "I'm for real this time," she said. "Who *are* you guys?"

"And don't give us no shit about Portugal," Jules said.

Everybody got real quiet, waiting to see what I was gonna say back. Even Rondell. I took a long sip of beer and shuffled through shit in my head. "Nah, man," I said all calm, "it's just that me and Rondell ain't nothin' that special. We're visiting from Idaho with his parents, who are both zoologists. They went to Tijuana for a couple days to do some study about these wild rabbits they got down there. We said we'd just stay here and wait. That's it."

Rondell was looking at me with no clue what I was talking about.

Flaca made a face at her girls.

"Boring as hell, right?" I said.

246

" 'Bout as boring as it gets," Flaca said, laughing. She punched me in the arm.

The rest of the girls seemed to think it was boring enough too, and they went right back to talking about themselves. Flaca didn't move back to where she was, though. She stayed right next to me. And before they all left to go home, she told me and Rondell about some house party they were all going to the next night and said we should come with 'em.

"That's cool," I said, and I shrugged how Diego always shrugs when girls ask him to do something.

"It's gonna be huge," Jules said, slipping on her backpack. "The guys throwin' it all go to college. They're in a fraternity."

"You can come with us if you want," Flaca said.

"That's cool," I said again.

"Where you want us to pick you up?"

Me and Rondell looked at each other, and then I turned back to Flaca sipping my beer. I wiped my mouth with the back of my hand, said: "How 'bout you just come get us right here?"

August 1

Yo, some of the freakiest shit you could ever think of just happened. Got everybody mad spooked when they saw it, including me. But lemme take it from the top.

The party was a crazy-ass mix of people. White frat dudes in plaid button-downs and mesh trucker hats. High school kids from the neighborhood in black Dickies or baggy jeans, white wife-beaters, chains hanging off belt loops. Blond college girls in sundresses or short skirts and low-cut tops. Mexican hoochies, like our crew, with huge hoop earrings and too much makeup (except Flaca, who didn't even *need* no makeup).

And then there was us. Me and Rondell. A couple group-home kids from San Jose dressed in sweatshirts and jeans. Runaways who hadn't showered in a *grip* and probably smelled like week-old sweat and seaweed and sand from the beach. Who had their entire lives zipped up in bags stashed back at the baseball field.

When we first walked in I couldn't stop thinking how other people saw us. Or if they even saw us at all. Neither of us had ever been to a college party before. Rondell said he'd never been to *any* kind of party. We were straight outsiders, crashers, and neither of us knew how we were supposed to act.

But after I downed my first cup of this jungle juice they had—me and Rondell and the girls all posted in the kitchen for the first hour, talking just with each other—I automatically switched to having fun, like everybody else.

There were two kegs in the huge backyard—which was where most people were kicking it. There was jungle juice and hard alcohol and mixers in the kitchen. There were five bedrooms in the house, and two were "special rooms," where you could go do bong hits or score an E tab. In the living room guys were spinning records and freestyling over the beat.

After we finally left the kitchen, me, Rondell and the five girls watched dudes rap in the living room for a while, and then Flaca took my hand and pulled me into one of the empty bedrooms to talk by ourselves.

Me and Flaca Alone in a Room:
Flaca opened a random door, peeped the vacant room and pulled me in. Locked the door behind us. As we walked across the room she pointed at my face and said: "I meant to ask you, how'd you get that cut on your lip?"

"What cut?" I said.

We sat in the far corner against the wall, right next to each other so our arms were touching.

"This one right here," she said, touching her finger just over my lip—my skin still tingling there even after she took back her finger.

"I don't even know," I said, looking into my cup of jungle juice. I tried to think if I could still be mellow now that we were alone in a room. 'Cause my heart was sort of going now.

She tilted her head to the side, said: "Come on, Miguel, you remember."

I shrugged. "Me and my big bro were probably messin' around."

"You got a brother back in Idaho?"

I nodded, told her: "Diego."

"Ooh, I like that name."

"You're not the only one."

"I got *two* older brothers. Guillermo and Rene."

I looked in her pretty brown eyes and felt something flipping around in my stomach. I pushed it out of my head and told her: "Yeah? You guys cool?"

I watched her face get all concentrated as she thought about that question. And I gotta say, man, the stomach-flipping thing wasn't letting up. Flaca just looked so damn good. Long brown hair all wavy going down her back, like she'd done it up especially for the party. Or maybe me. A little cutoff jean skirt that covered only half her smooth-ass brown thighs. I tried to think what Diego would say if he saw me like this. Sitting at a college house party in San Diego, drinking jungle juice, a girl as fine as Flaca sitting right next to me. He'd probably be proud as shit. Or jealous even.

"I'm cool with *one* of 'em," she said. "Rene. Guillermo's kind of an asshole sometimes. All he cares about is racing cars. He thinks the entire world revolves around his stupid souped-up Civic. It's not even that sick."

She told me a couple more things about her brother and his car, and then we both went silent for a while. We drank and looked across the bare room. Flaca fixed one of the silver clips in her hair.

I don't know if it was the juice or whatever, but I was starting to feel more chill sitting next to her. Just us. I wasn't even that worried about what I should do next. At least, not as much as I thought I'd be. Plus I figured I should go check on Rondell before figuring out about me and Flaca.

I set down my cup of jungle juice and stood up, said: "Yo, you could wait right here for a sec?"

She looked up at me frowning. "Why? Where you goin'?"

"I gotta go check on my boy."

She rolled her eyes and said: "What, are you like his dad or somethin'?"

"Don't let nobody take my seat," I said.

"Whatever."

I cruised out of the room and through the hall, past a couple girls waiting for the bathroom, and ducked my head into the living room, where they were still banging hip-hop. Rondell was on the couch next to a few college dudes, just where I'd left him. Some neighborhood kids were behind them drinking.

Rondell looked up at me.

"You good?" I said.

He nodded. "We listenin' to records now. Look how many they gots, Mexico." He pointed to a bookshelf stacked to the top.

"People call you Mexico?" some black dude called out from behind the couch. A couple of people laughed.

"Not really," I said. I pointed at Rondell. "He does."

"Yo, man," this big white kid said, looking all around at his boys, "ain't that shit kinda gay?" Everybody cracked up. "A dude havin' a pet name for another dude?"

Rondell turned slowly to look at him.

"Come on, man," I said. "People could have nicknames, right? Why's it gotta be gay?"

"He's just fuckin' with you," this other black dude said. "My boy Jimmy don't got no manners. Don't take it personal. Right, Jimmy?"

Jimmy laughed and took a long swig off his forty bottle. Right then the record ended, and everybody turned their attention to picking a new one.

I looked at Rondell, who was still staring at the guy. "Hey!" I said to get his attention back.

He looked at me and sipped his juice.

"Where the other girls?"

He nodded his head toward the kitchen. He looked back at the white guy, then turned back to me.

"All right," I told him. "Make sure you keep an eye out."

He took another sip of juice.

"You need me I'm right around the corner, man. Second door on the left."

He didn't say anything.

I could see in his eyes he wasn't paying attention to anything I said. Either that or he was just drunk. But all I knew was I had to get back to Flaca.

"I'll be out in a sec," I said, and then I turned and left.

On my walk back to the bedroom I thought about the one time Diego tried to tell me about being with girls. We were cruising home from this movie we got dragged to about relationships. A romantic comedy or whatever they call it. We both thought it was mad stupid and ducked out before it even finished, ditched everybody we were with.

As we were walking he must've still been thinking about the movie, though, 'cause he started telling me how the key to being with girls is to be a hundred percent chill and think about other shit like playing hoop or kicking it at the levee.

"That's how most guys drop the ball," he said as we crossed March Ave, walked past the burrito spot with the huge sombrero on the roof. "They think too much. Girls got mad radar for that shit, Guelly. They got this little alarm system that goes off in their heads like: bleep, bleep, bleep. They hear that shit sound off and think: 'Hold on a minute. Why's this guy sweatin' *me*? There must be somethin' wrong with him.'"

I remember right then Diego got me in a little headlock for no reason and then let me go. I tried to punch his ass in the arm, but he blocked it.

"Don't ask me why," he said, shaking his head, "but almost every girl I know is the exact same way: they only want guys who don't want their asses back. Doesn't make no kinda sense when I say it, right?"

I shrugged.

He pulled his phone to check a text, said: "But it's true, man. You'll see." He flipped closed and looked at me. "Once a girl feels a sweaty palm, yo—and I don't care how fucking *nice* you are, Guelly—she'll never look at your sensitive ass the same."

I nodded but didn't say anything.

Diego laughed and shook his head. "Just don't follow how that movie was. Your big bro'll tell you how shit *really* is."

Me and Flaca Alone in a Room, Part 2:
I walked back in the room all chill, thinking about Diego's talk, and sat against the wall next to Flaca. I looked at her without smiling.

252

"Jeez," she said. "You were gone long enough."

"It's all good," I said, picking up my cup. I took a long sip of juice and stared at the far wall. Being buzzed made it way easier to fake like I wasn't nervous.

She leaned her knee against mine, said: "Did you at least miss me?"

I shrugged, feeling Flaca's knee heat transferring into my leg.

"How much?"

I looked at the ceiling for a sec, said: " 'Bout a six out of ten."

"A *six*?" she said. "That's it?"

"Maybe a six point five."

"Asshole." She shook her head at me and took a baby sip out of her cup. "Anyways, I just told you all about my brothers. Now I get to ask you questions."

"That's cool," I said.

"What's it like living in Idaho? I've never known anybody from there."

I cracked up a little, I don't even know why. I think I pretty much forgot about saying I was from Idaho. "It's pretty regular," I told her, picturing Stockton instead. "Just less people have all their teeth."

She smiled, shifted her knee away from mine. "You got all yours," she said.

"I'm sayin', though. It's rare."

She put her hand on my knee for a sec and then took it off and drank. I peeped my tingling knee and drank too.

The room didn't have any furniture except an old dresser with no handles. And the wood floor was all scuffed up and broken down in places, especially by the door. I was pretty sure she wanted us to kiss, but I didn't know how I should do it. I mean, I'd kissed girls before. Like four or five of 'em. I'd

253

even had sex with this one girl named Cecilia. But they were all Diego's friends. He probably *told* 'em to hook up with me. Either that or it was part of some game we were all playing like Truth or Dare. It's not like I ever had to *do* anything.

"What are you thinkin' about?" Flaca said.

I shrugged.

"Come on, I wanna know."

"You, I guess."

She set down her cup and faced me with this big grin. "Yeah? Like what *about* me?"

I looked at the wood floor for a little while, took another sip. Felt the warm buzz going in my fingers and toes and chest. "I like bein' in here," I said. "In this empty room, against the wall, drinkin'. How you can hear the music in the next room and people talkin', but you're still away from 'em. Two days ago I never even knew this place existed."

She frowned. "That doesn't have nothin' to do with me."

I looked at her without even thinking and said: "It has *everything* to do with you."

Flaca smiled big and touched my face. "All my friends think you're really cute."

"Yeah?" I said. "You gonna hook me up with one of 'em?"

"Which one you want?"

I played like I was thinking about it for a sec, rubbing on my chin and all that. "The one with the nose ring," I said, touching the small hoop in her nose.

"Yeah?"

I nodded.

"I could probably make that happen."

"Is she mellow, though? I only like girls who can chill out and be mellow."

"She's all right," Flaca said. "Why don't you see for yourself."

"Maybe I will."

She leaned in and kissed me.

On the outside I tried to make like everything was super smooth and calm and my palms were dry as hell, but inside my mind was thinking all kinds of crazy thoughts like: How long do I keep my mouth open? And when do I turn my face? And how much tongue do I use? And where do I put my hands? And how are we supposed to breathe?

She ran her fingers through my hair and then rested 'em on my shoulders and then touched my cheeks and then slowly pulled away and just looked at me grinning. "Hey, Miguel," she said.

"Hey, Flaca," I said back, my heart beating all fast like I'd just run a damn lap around some track.

She kissed me again, a real short one this time, but soft as hell, like she made her lips go completely limp or something. "I think I sort of like you," she said. "And you can even ask my girls, I usually don't like *nobody*."

"I sort of like you too," I said.

She touched my cut again, and then kissed it. "How much do you like me?" she said.

I looked at her for a sec, said: "Like an eight point three."

She laughed and play-punched me in the arm again. Then she reached down for my jeans, all calm-like, never taking her eyes off mine, said: "You nervous for what I'm about to do?"

"Nah, I'm cool," I said, even though my heart was thumping its ass off. I swallowed hard and watched her take hold of my zipper and start pulling it down all slow with this big grin on her face.

But right then we heard this loud crashing sound somewhere in the house. It made the wall behind us shake. We both spun our heads toward the door, and Flaca pulled her hand back.

"What was that?" she said.

I shot to my feet. "I don't even know," I said, though I was pretty sure I knew. I pulled up my zipper and started for the door.

"Wait, where you going?" she said, standing up too.

"I gotta check Rondell," I said.

"Okay." She sat back down.

The Fight:

I sprint out of the room and down the hall, my heart climbing in my throat. I already know what I'm gonna find. I get to the living room and there it is: five guys holding back a crazed Rondell. His face contorted and neck veins bulging, arms and legs driving the pile forward like a running back. I follow his eyes to the big white guy now laying on the ground crooked and bloody and motionless.

Everything in my head blurs and speeds up and I shout: "What happened?"

"Your boy!" one of the black guys shouts back. "He just beat the shit out of Jimmy, man. Real bad."

"Kept hitting him even after he got knocked out," another kid says.

"Psycho," somebody says.

"Gotta get him outta here."

"Call the cops!"

"Hurry!"

"Get him out!"

Everybody is talking over each other as I study the guy Jimmy. His face so mangled and bloody I can barely make out features. I look up at Rondell. The devil in his eyes. Every muscle flexed as he fights to get more of a guy he's already beaten down. He's after more than just winning in a fight. He wants to take his life.

But why?

"Rondell!" I yell.

He doesn't look at me.

"Hey, man!"

Nothing.

Flaca comes rushing into the living room. She stops right behind me and stares down at Jimmy. Covers her mouth with her right hand and turns away. Her girls hurry to her side.

A fat Mexican gangster runs in from the backyard with his fists clenched, a smaller one trailing behind.

White wife-beaters. Chains hanging from pockets.

First guy shouts: "Yo, Jimmy! Jimmy!" He looks down at the body on the floor and his face goes wild. Looks up at Rondell, still fighting to get loose. Big Mexican guy charges, throws a wild punch that glances off the side of Rondell's face.

Rondell stumbles trying to get away from the guys holding him back. Goes down on one knee but pops back up. Everybody talking over each other and the music still playing and crowds of people rushing in from the backyard to see.

Rondell throws the four guys off him like rag dolls. Bodies flying over the couch back, into the dining room table. The Mexican guy swinging another wild right, but Rondell deflects it, grabbing the Mexican by his hair and head-butting him right in the face. The loud shattering of the guy's nose like dishes heaved against a concrete wall. A little girl's scream comes out of the Mexican's mouth as he covers his face and crumples to the rug on Jimmy's limp body. Eyes rolling to the back of his head.

Still, Rondell pounces on him, delivers three lightning-quick jabs to his face. Blood spewing out of the guy's nose and mouth and right eye, the back of his head banging the floor.

People grabbing Rondell's sweatshirt, pulling him off. Rondell spinning and swinging fists at anybody, everybody.

Including me. The speed and agility he had on the basketball court. But the look in his eyes a look I've never seen before. Different from Mong's. More desperate.

Everything happening so fast.

The black guy behind Rondell grabbing an empty forty bottle off the table, rearing back to smash Rondell's head in. Me not thinking anything but diving at the guy, knocking the bottle from his hand. Wrestling to the ground, grabbing at each other in the scuffle, and somehow I'm smacking him in the chin with an uppercut and his head is snapping back. His face cringing and eyes closing, then opening. Him rolling onto me, pinning my arms, and I'm turning my head as his fist comes down hard on my ear and my cheek and my neck and the side of my head and everything is turning black and lost.

When I wake up Rondell is wrapping his two huge hands around the black guy's neck and pulling him up. Rondell's staring into his puffy face and squeezing, squeezing, squeezing. Gritting his teeth, shouting: "Nobody touch Mexico!"

Squeezing harder.

Eyes wild and spit flying from his mouth as he repeats this line over and over: "Nobody touch Mexico! Nobody touch Mexico! Nobody touch Mexico!"

Every person in the living room, guy or girl, spooked and backing away, silent. No talking. The music shut off. And I'm getting up and falling against the couch and getting up the rest of the way. Knowing Rondell will kill this kid. That he will stop his breath forever and that tomorrow he will not remember. The black dude's face changing colors, turning bright red and purple, eyes bugging out of his head, looking back at Rondell, scared for his life.

"Let go!" I'm yelling at Rondell, but he's not letting go.

I slap him on the back of his head and shout again: "Let fucking go, Rondell!"

258

Him looking at me.

Him letting go.

The black guy falling to the floor, clutching his own neck and coughing and choking to get back his breath. Flaca behind us crying now. Her girls screaming. Dudes shouting and jostling. My right eye blurred by my own blood falling into it. The Mexican guy moving just his fingers, making weak fists, rolling off the guy Jimmy, who doesn't move at all. Blood all over everywhere on the rug and the couch and the records and everybody's clothes and my own blood running into my eye, stinging, and the sound of the girls behind me and the crowd that's just come in from the backyard to see.

And Rondell is staring at me now. He's looking for direction. His face less crazy but his chest still heaving in and out and heaving in and out and heaving in and out.

I grab him by the sweatshirt and pull him with me, out of the living room and through the front door and across the lawn and into the street. Voices of dudes yelling behind us and girls screaming.

I look over my shoulder expecting everybody to be chasing us down with bats or the cops, but it isn't either. It's just Flaca and her four girls, running after us, bags flailing, their eyes wild with fear.

August 1—more

I was still in a fog as we all walked back onto the baseball field where we first met. Everybody out of breath from running and the girls talking over each other about what happened and where they were when it started and sneaking little looks at Rondell. My head was pounding where I got hit and I kept having to dab my sleeve against my cut 'cause it was bleeding again.

We went into one of the dugouts and sat on the bench. Rondell just listening to everybody with a blank look on his face, like he wasn't even at the party and was hearing about this supposed fight for the first time.

At one point Jules turned to Rondell and shouted over the commotion: "Why didn't you just stop when you knew they were knocked out?"

Rondell made a confused face. He looked to me.

"He could've killed that one black guy," a girl named Rosanna said, refusing to look at Rondell.

"What about the guy on the ground?" Flaca said. "He didn't move since I came in."

The girl with the birthmark on her face was wiping tears from her eyes and shaking her head.

"Look," I said. "We don't even know how it started. They were probably messing with him."

"Jesus, though," Jules said. "I can't get that Mexican guy's bloody face out of my head. His nose was pointing all to the side."

Rondell looked at the ground. He pulled his bag out from under the dugout bench where we'd stashed 'em, but when he saw the look I was giving him he pushed it back under.

"What's that?" Flaca said.

I thought quick and said: "We stashed some stuff here so we didn't have to go back to the hotel."

Flaca looked down at where the bags were, and then she looked at Jules.

"Stupid, stupid, stupid," Rosanna said, shaking her head. "Why do guys always gotta fight each other to prove who's the bigger man? We were just having fun."

"It's like they're roosters," Jules said. "I saw this special on TV about cockfighting. It's the exact same thing."

"But we're human beings," Rosanna shot back. "We're supposed to be more involved than that shit, right?"

" 'Evolved,' " Jules said.

"You know what I mean," Rosanna said.

"God," the birthmark girl said. "I thought I was gonna be sick."

"Yo, could everybody just calm down?" I said, feeling all stressed and confused. "We made it back here. Everybody's okay. That's the main thing."

"You see those guys laying on the floor?" Rosanna shot back with attitude. "They look okay to you?"

"I'm talkin' about us, though," I said.

The girls kept looking at Rondell, who was looking back and forth from them to me like he had no idea what we were talking about. For the first time since I met him I thought maybe Rondell was better off locked up. Where he couldn't hurt somebody or even himself. Maybe there's a reason we have jail.

Rosanna stood up and grabbed her bag, said: "I'm outta here. I'm going home."

"We're *all* going home," Jules said. "Flaca, you too. Say goodbye to Miguel and let's go."

I turned to Flaca, who was giving Jules a look, like they were saying something with their eyes. Then she turned to me. "Miguel," she said, "let's walk your friend to the other dugout so my girls can wait here without worrying while you and me say bye."

I shrugged, told Rondell to come on.

He sat up and reached under the bench for both our bags, but Flaca said: "You could just leave your stuff. We won't be that long."

Jules looked at Flaca and said: "We'll wait here."

I led Rondell into the other dugout and told him to wait for me on the bench.

"How come, Mexico?" he said.

" 'Cause you freaked everybody out, man. They think you ruined the entire party."

"Wha'chu mean?" he said.

"Just trust me," I said. "Look, we'll talk about it later. Right now I'm gonna say bye to Flaca."

He looked at the ground and then looked up at me again, said: "I'm scared."

And that confused me more than any single thing he'd ever said since I met him. The guy beats the hell out of three guys and now he's scared? I looked at him all crazy, said: "What are you even talking about?"

He shrugged and lowered his head and then laid down on the bench.

"There you go," I said. "Take a little nap for a sec and I'll be right back."

He closed his eyes and folded his hands together on his stomach and started mumbling under his breath like he was speaking in tongues. I was tripping out watching him, but just then Flaca took me by the arm and pulled me out of the dugout and back over to the one where her girls were sitting. She told them she needed ten minutes with me alone.

They all looked at each other except Jules, who said, "Okay, just go. We'll be right here."

Flaca nodded and pulled me away, told me we were going to this other part of the park.

My Ten Minutes with Flaca:
The two of us walked together without saying a word. We went along the dark bushes that lined the edge of the park, past an old dried-up fountain full of dead wrinkled leaves, a

run-down tennis court with no net and weeds growing through every crack, and all the way into this abandoned playground. There was only a couple tagged-up swings, a rusty slide and some paint-chipped monkey bars. We cut through the hard sand and sat next to each other on the swings, started rocking back and forth a little.

At first neither of us said anything or even looked at each other. I reached down for a rock and held it in my right hand, looking all around us at the playground. She pushed a little of her hair behind her ear and stared at the ground.

Finally I cleared my throat and told her: "Sorry about the party and all that. I don't even know what happened."

"It wasn't you," she said, looking up at me. "But your friend was scary, Miguel. Something isn't right about him."

I shrugged, tossed the rock outside of the playground, into the grass.

"Anyways," Flaca said. And then she started swinging a little faster. She flung her head back and looked in the sky and then she slowed down again and said: "I grew up in this park, you know."

"Yeah?" I said.

She stopped. "My stepdad used to take me when I was little. He'd push me on this exact swing."

I nodded but she didn't see 'cause she was reaching into her pocket for her phone. She flipped it open to check a text and then flipped it closed, slipped it back in her pocket.

It went quiet between us again, but just sitting there with her, after everything that had just happened at the party and my head still all foggy, it made me have a strange feeling. For some reason I actually wanted to tell her everything about me and Rondell. I wanted to tell someone the truth about us. And I already know how people shouldn't go around telling their business to people they don't even know, but at the same time, besides Rondell I didn't know *anybody* anymore. Flaca and me had at least messed around and talked some.

I looked up at her. She was staring at her right palm, some of her long dark hair spilling in front of her pretty brown face. And then the weirdest thing happened, man. I totally started telling her stuff. I just opened my mouth and it all came pouring out. Shit I hadn't even processed yet.

I told her how five months and three days ago I did something that changed my life forever, something so fucked up I promised myself I'd never say it out loud or feel anything for anybody ever again. Not even myself. I told her how because of what I did I got sentenced to a group home for nine months and how the entire first month I didn't talk to nobody, including the counselors, 'cause I didn't think anybody was worth my time. Then they put Rondell in my room, and even though he was straight special ed and a Bible thumper, he at least got me talking some—which was probably why I had his back now. I told her how another resident, Mong, came in my room in the middle of the night and asked if I wanted to break out of the group home and try to make it to Mexico. How I agreed to go not so much 'cause I wanted to but 'cause I couldn't think up any reasons not to. I honestly didn't give a shit about anything anymore. Who cares what happens to you when you don't care if you're alive or dead, you know? I told her about the night we actually left, how I snuck in the office and stole the petty cash and all our files from the desk drawers and hopped out the window into some flower bed. How once we got to the mall Mong said he knew a resort place in Mexico where we could live and get jobs and be free and how that's the first point I actually thought maybe I could start a new life, one where the shit I did back home no longer existed.

I told Flaca how we got picked up by Mong's cousin Mei-li,

who drove us the wrong way, and how we had to run out of the pizza place while she was in the bathroom and figure out how to get down the coast from the middle of San Francisco without a ride. I told her how me and Mong were having mad problems with each other this whole time, but then we had a long talk at a beach in Malibu about life and the earth and true love and other deep shit, and how weird it was when out of nowhere he told me I was his best friend. Then the next morning, I told her, Mong drowned himself right there in front of me and Rondell. And since neither one of us knew what to say we just didn't say anything and grabbed our shit and walked away.

Once I got started telling Flaca stuff, I couldn't stop, man. It was like somebody else took over my body. I just kept talking and talking and talking, and for some reason the shit was making me feel more and more real. Like the past four months actually happened, it wasn't just something I watched on TV or in a movie or read in one of my books. All this stuff, what I did and the judge making my sentence and us sleeping on beaches and building bonfires and getting in fights and running from cops—even tonight, the party, and me and Flaca hooking up in that empty room and Rondell beating the shit out of those guys and now sitting here on these little-kid swings—all this was actually my life.

I explained to Flaca what happened when me and Rondell finally made it down to Mexico, how once I was actually standing there, looking into the country, I couldn't go across. Something made me freeze up. At the time I had no idea what it was, but now I think it was something to do with my gramps and my pops. How one snuck into America and became a citizen, and the other joined the army and died for our country. And someday I'd maybe go down to Mexico for real, I told her, maybe I'd even live there and learn Spanish and visit where my grandparents were from. But I couldn't do it yet. I still had to be in America. Until I made shit right. And that was why I came up with our new plan, how me and Rondell were gonna get money and replace what we took from the petty cash, send it back to the Lighthouse. After that I didn't know what the hell I was gonna do. I hadn't thought that far ahead yet. Maybe I'd talk to my moms. Or maybe I'd go to the place where they buried my old man and I'd actually sit there on his grave this time, like I'd always wanted to. I didn't even know. But I was gonna handle the petty cash situation. That was for sure.

Flaca didn't say a word the whole time I talked. She just sat there on her swing, rocking back and forth, staring at me, nodding sometimes. And when I finished it got mad quiet between us. Only thing making any sound was the crickets chirping away in the bushes. And how weird is that shit, I thought in my head. That there's such a thing as crickets, these little bugs that hide in bushes at night and make crazy sounds together, who knows why. I know it's just a small part of the world, but for some reason it made me wonder about *everything*. Being alive and God and if me and Flaca were maybe even meant to be and would get married someday and I'd introduce her to my moms.

When I couldn't handle Flaca being quiet anymore I turned to her and said: "You ain't gonna call the cops on us now, right?"

She shook her head, staring right back in my eyes. "It's just so weird," she said.

"What?"

"You totally don't seem like that. My whole life I been around kids who get in trouble. And they're all a certain way. You seem so different."

I didn't say anything back, just looked at the bushes thinking what she meant by that.

She pulled her cell halfway out her pocket to check the time, shoved it back in and said: "What'd you do, anyways?"

I picked up a stick off the ground and didn't look at her.

"To get arrested in the first place, I mean," she said.

I looked in front of us at the bushes where the crickets were hiding and thought for a sec. And I swear to God, man, I almost told her the truth right there. I almost said what happened out loud for the first time ever.

But I couldn't.

I opened my mouth to talk and the words just vanished into thin air.

"Well?" she said.

Maybe it was 'cause I'd already told her so much, or because of everything that happened at the party, or 'cause I just didn't want to say anything more about what I did, but right then I leaned in and I kissed her.

And she kissed me back.

And when we separated I thought how maybe we were together now. In the real way. Boyfriend-girlfriend. Like no matter if we got in an argument or disagreed on something she was still gonna be my girl. And I could just kiss her like this, anytime I wanted.

I leaned in and kissed her again, tilted my head, put my hands on her sides and kissed her as good as I knew how.

After a few seconds like that Flaca pulled back. She smiled at me and pulled her cell from her skirt pocket. "Hang on one sec," she said. "I just gotta call Jules."

I wiped my mouth with the back of my hand.

She slid out of her swing and went over near the cricket bushes to make her call. I watched her trying to think what Diego would say about me telling a girl my business like that.

Or leaning in to kiss her. I picked up a stick, broke it in half and tossed both pieces to the ground. Then I felt around my neck for Mong's tooth necklace tucked inside my sweatshirt. His good-luck charm was now *my* good-luck charm. It's probably how come a girl as fine as Flaca seemed like she was feeling me so much.

When Flaca came back she sat right on my lap and we locked into a nice little making-out rhythm, our best so far. I wasn't thinking random things this time either, I was just thinking about what we were doing. How hyped it was getting me.

She pulled away and touched my face with her hand. "I really wanna be with you, Miguel. Like *so* bad. But I gotta make sure my girls get home okay."

"It's cool," I said, trying to think if "be with you" meant us having sex.

'Cause I was pretty sure she was saying sex.

But I didn't know for sure.

But the way she said it . . .

"I got an idea," she said. "Let's make a pact."

"About what?"

"Let's meet here tomorrow night at exactly ten p.m. Just me and you. And this time I won't have to go anywhere. I promise."

"Yeah?"

"Yeah," she said. "We'll stay together the whole night."

"Okay," I said, my heart already beating faster. Now I *knew* she was meaning sex.

She ran her hand up my arm and bit her lip. "You can wait for me, right, baby?"

"I could wait," I said, thinking if Diego would say he could wait or not.

"Okay, come on," she said, hopping off me. "Walk me back to the baseball field."

We left the playground together and walked back to the field. After we all said bye to each other, and Flaca winked at me, I watched them hurry off together. When they got up the hill they even started running, which seemed weird, but then I thought how Flaca's girls were still scared about what happened with Rondell at the party.

I grabbed me and Rondell's bags and carried 'em over to the dugout where Rondell was sleeping. I pushed 'em under the bench, then stood there looking at him for a while. He was sleeping like a damn baby. I wondered what kind of kid could do all the shit he'd done earlier, beating the hell out of three people, and then just go to sleep like nothing. I actually felt worse for him than ever 'cause of what just happened with Flaca. I mean, here I was having an actual relationship with a girl, something that happens to normal people, and Rondell was just laying here asleep after beating people up. Totally alone.

I went to the other end of the dugout and sat on the bench. I balled up one of the shirts in my bag for a pillow, laid down and closed up my eyes. But I couldn't fall asleep right away. I kept thinking about Flaca, and how it would be the next night when she stayed with me. How maybe she could even chill with me and Rondell for a while, until we figured out how to get the money. Or maybe we could stay down here. In National City. It didn't really matter where we were that much.

I tried to think if I'd ever met a girl as pretty as Flaca.

After tossing and turning a bunch of times I gave up on the whole sleep thing and sat up. Sleep just wasn't gonna happen. My mind was going too much. I stared across the dark baseball field and thought about me and Rondell. And the money we needed. What was gonna end up happening to us. I thought about Flaca. Our pact for tomorrow night. And then for some reason I started looking up into the cloudless sky, touching Mong's tooth necklace and listening to the cricket sounds again. Thinking how weird it was to be alive to actually hear it. But not just alive like I was yesterday and the day before. Alive like I *knew* I was alive. Like I could feel the breaths coming into my chest. And I knew I was the person inside my own body.

August 2

Me and Rondell slept half the next day.

When we finally got up both of us had headaches from drinking, so we went straight to a cheap taco stand and ate dollar tacos and took turns sipping warm water from this hose they had outside, next to the curb where we were sitting. The whole time I was thinking how I could have a talk with Rondell about what happened the night before, but I never said anything.

After lunch we went and sat in the park watching these little kids playing with their parents. This one Mexican girl with a bow in her hair and patent-leather shoes was in the exact swing Flaca was in the night before. As I watched her smiling and swinging back and forth, butterflies went into my stomach. It made me think what might happen later on with my new girl.

By the way, just that alone was tripping me out, having a "girl."

Flaca was my girl.

Yo, I'm gonna go chill with my girl.

Nah, I wasn't at the party, dawg, I was layin' low with my girl.

I'm telling you now, that dude better not step to my girl.

Wait, you never seen my girl? Hang on, I got a picture in my wallet.

Finally, after I was daydreaming for like an hour, I turned to Rondell and told him how he should try not to do that anymore, fight random people for barely no reason.

"Wha'chu mean?" he said.

"You scared the shit out of the girls," I told him. "And what if the cops would've come? And who knows how bad them dudes were hurt, right? They probably ended up in the hospital. We got enough problems as it is, right?"

Rondell looked at me, then he turned his eyes to the ground.

"It couldn't have been that bad is all I'm sayin'. You could defend yourself, I'm not sayin' that, but you don't gotta keep going after the person after they're already on the ground. The shit just ain't worth it."

Rondell didn't say anything.

"Not when they could take us back to Juvi, man. Or not even. This time we'd probably go to *real* prison."

He nodded his head some.

"And you got this look in your eyes, man." I smacked him on the arm so he'd look at my impersonation of the psycho look on his face. "It wasn't my boy Rondo anymore, it was someone else. Trust me, man, nothin' is worth losing yourself like that. You gotta keep your shit centered."

Rondell looked down at the ground again.

I felt like I was his counselor all of a sudden. Like I was Jaden and he was me. Plus I really meant it, though. I didn't want him to need to be in prison. He should be able to have a normal life too.

"So you get what I mean, then?" I told him. "You ain't gonna fight no more?"

Rondell looked up at me and shrugged. "I can't let nobody say nothin' 'bout you like that."

271

I looked back at him, trying to think what that meant. "What're you talkin' about," I said.

Rondell shook his head. "The white one, he said you was a punk and he would take your girl. I told for him to better take it back, but he wouldn't, so I knocked him down."

I turned away from Rondell. It hit me right then how he had my back more than anybody besides Diego. Even after all the shit I'd given him, right to his face. Telling him he couldn't read and making fun of him looking at the Bible and how he thought I was gonna leave him after what happened to Mong. Still. Rondell had my back. He wouldn't even let people *say* something about me.

I didn't know what to think or say about that, so I just sat there nodding, went back to watching the kids playing in the park.

After a good ten minutes I cleared my throat and said: "Still, man. You can't just be fighting over that. Maybe you just have to put it out of your mind. Even if they're talking about me."

Rondell didn't say anything back, but when I snuck a peek out of the corner of my eye I saw he was shaking his head, like he couldn't.

Getting Ready for Flaca:

First thing I did when it came close to when I was gonna meet Flaca was set Rondell up in an all-night coffee shop with enough cash to eat twice. I'd pulled two twenties and a ten from the petty cash for the party and both Jacksons were still in my pocket. I gave him one and put his Bible on the table and told him not to roll back to the field until after two in the morning. Told him he had the close dugout, and me and Flaca would take the far one.

He nodded at everything I said, but when I was getting ready to be out he got this big goofy smile on his face.

"What's so funny?" I asked him.

He shook his head and laughed at me.

"Come on, Rondo."

"What?"

"Why you gigglin' like a girl?"

"Nah, I just never seen you like this, Mexico."

"Like what?" I said.

"All happy."

"You're crazy, man." I waved him off and turned to watch some couple get seated in the booth across from us. What the hell did Rondell know about someone being happy? The girl handed the guy a shopping bag and they both picked up their menus. An old guy in the booth next to them was doing a crossword puzzle.

Rondell pulled his Bible toward him, said: "I could tell by people's faces, Mexico. When they're happy. Your face never been like this ever since I met you."

"I'm as happy as I always am," I shot back. "Ain't no different than any other day."

He just shook his head, still smiling ear to ear.

I repeated my rules: "Not till after two, all right, man? The close dugout."

He put a fist to his mouth, cracked up some, and I left the diner.

Second thing I did was hit this community pool me and Rondell stumbled across earlier, on our way back from getting something to eat. The gate was chained like I figured, so I had to scale over the tall fence. I dropped down on the other side, looked all over to make sure I was the only one around, then stripped off all my gear. I unwrapped the bar of soap I'd picked up at a liquor store, and eased into the water on the shallow end, but it was way colder than I expected. When the water got up to my stuff, man, I almost couldn't do it. Everything shriveled up and begged me not to go in even one more inch. I looked down between my legs and said: "Sorry, yo, but we gotta do this. Now, come on, man, on three." I held on to my whole situation, gritted my teeth, counting, and then dove my ass under the water. When I came up I shouted "Goddamn!" Then I soaped my entire body, head to toe, and rinsed off by swimming around for a couple laps.

And I'm not gonna lie, man, when I grabbed onto the side after rinsing off I thought how weird it was to be skinny-dipping solo. What kind of schizo does *that* shit, right? But at the same time, it was mad cool too. I didn't have to think about impressing nobody. Plus how many people get the chance to have an entire pool all to themselves?

The third thing I did was go into this store on my way back to the park to get a $5.99 watch, a thing of wintergreen Tic Tacs and a big red flower for Flaca that was wrapped in newspaper. I picked red 'cause everybody says that's the most romantic kind. When I got back to the baseball field I laid it on the far dugout bench, where we were gonna sleep together.

The flower was a little wilted at the edges, and my ass straight up smelled like chlorine, and I didn't know how me and Flaca were gonna sleep together on such a narrow bench, but still, man, Rondell was right. I guess I *was* a little happier than on regular days. Maybe that's what a pretty girl could do to somebody.

I checked my watch, saw I still had over an hour until ten p.m. and pulled my journal. To kill time I decided to write down everything I thought while I waited.

9:03 p.m.:

For some reason I was just remembering something to do with my old man. When I was a freshman we had this big basketball game: the students versus the teachers and parents. It was something they did every year to welcome people to Stockton High. Anybody who wanted to play could sign up and they were guaranteed at least a quarter of playing time. And when you checked into the game your pop would check in too. If your old man wasn't around or he didn't wanna play or whatever, one of the teachers would fill in.

Anyways, I remember I was stressing the whole time I was on the bench waiting to play 'cause everybody else's dad had on regular gym shorts and high-tops, but not my pop. He had on his damn army fatigues and work boots. There was even this big controversy when me and him were checking in at the start of the second quarter. One of the refs said he couldn't play because he had on black-bottomed shoes and that those kinds of soles were bad for wood courts. All the refs gathered around and the teachers came over and my dad was saying he just wanted to play some ball with his son and how he shouldn't be punished for serving his damn country and was it really something to do with him being Mexican?

The principal had to come all the way down from the stands and tell the refs it was okay to let him play. They shrugged and waved us both in and checked the ball inbounds.

I remember feeling so embarrassed of my pop, man. To the point that I didn't even feel like playing. I was new to the school and the area, so I didn't know anybody. And here was my old man running around the court in a wife-beater, army pants and combat boots, fouling the shit out of anybody who tried to dribble past him. Yelling at the refs every time they made a call on him. I ended up telling some other kid to come in for me so my dad would have to leave the court too.

In the locker room after the game some of the other kids were talking about the crazy-ass Mexican army dude who was hacking everybody, and when this one kid asked was that my dad I told him he didn't know what the hell he was talking about, my dad was dead. And that shut him up. Nobody said another word about it the whole time we were getting dressed.

Fifteen minutes later I was sitting in the bleachers, waiting for him. Almost everybody else had left. But my pop was talking to these two seniors that said they were interested in maybe joining the army. He was telling them all the cool stuff you get to do and the countries you get to visit and how if you're into the whole school thing they had a great program called the GI Bill.

I remember kicking it there solo, listening to my pop preaching about the army, staring at all the black scuff marks his boots left on the court. They were all over the place. His soles really *did* mess up the wood. And I was just staring at 'em, wondering for the first time in my life what it'd be like to have a different dad. One who at least had regular damn gym shorts. High-tops that wouldn't scuff up a wood court. I even thought how it'd be if what I told the kid in the locker room was true, that my pop really *was* dead. My mind, man. It went there. Even when I tried to stop it.

Three months later he was sent to the war.

A month after that a guy in full uniform came to our apartment to tell Moms the bad news.

I remember sometimes after I'd still go to the gym, when nobody else was in there, and stare at the faded black marks his boots made, remembering how I said he was dead even though he was still alive. Most people couldn't even see 'em anymore, the scuff marks, but I could.

9:45 p.m.:

Yo, I just ate my whole thing of wintergreen Tic Tacs. I bought 'em so my breath would be minty fresh for when Flaca got here, but I forgot how good they taste. And how damn addictive they are. My breath better smell good for the whole night, man. Maybe even into tomorrow morning. I keep blowing into my palm and smelling, and I gotta say, yo. Flaca better check herself. I might mess around and make somebody fall in love with this breath.

I wonder did Flaca try on a bunch of different outfits like girls always do? Or did she spend a grip of time doing her makeup in the mirror? Is her hair done up the way she did it for the party? Maybe she even did her own version of the Tic Tac thing.

Anyway, I'm up here at the top of the bleachers now. I wanna watch her get out of whatever car drops her off. See her before she sees me, if you know what I mean.

10:05 p.m.:

I know Flaca told me ten p.m., but I can't remember if she said to meet her at the baseball field or on the playground where we were hanging out on swings. Maybe it was the playground. That's where we were talking about everything.

Problem is that's a completely different part of the park. I don't know should I run up there and check and then come back down to the field if she's not there? But what if she shows up when I'm gone and thinks I played her?

Nah, I gotta run up there and at least check. 'Cause now that I think about it, maybe she said for us to meet at the playground and then spend the night in the dugout.

10:30 p.m.:

I brought *Catcher in the Rye* up in the bleachers so I could finish it. Man, I haven't really read this thing since we got here. I'll probably have to back up a few pages so I remember what's going on. But after that I only got like thirty pages till the end.

By the way, I made a pact with *myself* this time. If Flaca doesn't show by the end of the book, I'm gonna go on a damn solo walk somewhere. You can't sit in a park all night waiting for somebody. Nah, man, if ol' girl doesn't show before I'm done reading, then I'm out. Maybe even for good. I could just leave a little note telling Rondell where to meet me and when. I ain't decided that part yet, but I can't be hanging here all night waiting for fools.

Girl gots thirty pages before our shit is game over.

11:34 p.m.:

Here's what I think about *Catcher in the Rye*. It really is a great book, like Jaden said. My only thing is I still don't get the title. After I finished the last page I went back to the section where he explains it and I read it over and over, but I'm still not sure, man. Is he saying he's like one of those kids who's running through the fields? Like maybe he used to be innocent like that and people just let him go by without catching him? Or is he saying he's older now and pictures himself saving little kids? Or maybe it's just some metaphor I'm not totally getting.

No matter what, though, it's still a great book. It totally won me over at the end. Mostly 'cause of how much Holden cares about his little sis. I got a theory that if a big brother looks out for his little sis he's probably a good person, you know? No matter what bad stuff he might get into. I was thinking the whole time when I was reading it if I'd look out for *my* sis like that if I had one.

278

And it's cool when you find out the whole time Holden's been talking to his therapist—which sort of makes me think about Jaden and how he was always trying to get me to talk about my past.

Nah, man, *Catcher* is definitely one of the best books I've ever read. I might have to keep it with me. Then I could look at different sections when I finish the rest of the books I got stashed in Rondell's bag.

12:15 a.m.:

I just realized I'm the watcher-over person of this park. That's why we stopped here. It was meant to be. Almost like Holden Caulfield and the rye fields. Only I'm not trying to save random innocent kids who're running around. I'm trying to make a place where so-called bad ones could come when they wanna get away from the world or even themselves. And not just group-home kids like me, Mong and Rondell. But regular ones too, like I used to be. Ones who maybe messed up once or twice, and now that's how people think of them. When they get here they can talk to me and Rondell and each other. Or they can just keep quiet. Maybe they only need a rest. It could be up to each individual kid. And whenever they're ready they can go back home.

I'm under the bleachers now, on my stomach, writing in this journal. Probably sounds schizo or whatever. Me kicking it in the weeds like this. The only person in some run-down park in the middle of San Diego. But I don't even give a shit. This is where I realized I gotta be for right now. So I could think about being the watcher-over of this field. And I can see across the baseball diamond in case somebody tries to come in here and mess everything up.

12:30 a.m.:

We're fucked.

I was chilling under the bleachers, writing in my journal, when out of nowhere this thought came in my head. I slid out from under the bleachers and marched over to the far dugout, pulled my bag. Unzipped. Reached in for the leather petty-cash envelope and looked inside.

I sat down.

The money, man. It was gone.

All of it.

The envelope was completely empty except this little Taco Bell receipt with writing on the back.

I flipped it over and read what it said:

No hard feelings, Miguel. You guys did your thing getting this money, and now we're just doing ours by taking it for ourselves. You understand.

Jules

P.S. Flaca wants you to know she really did like you.

I read the words over and over again until my legs went numb. Until my chest got so it was hard to breathe. The money was gone. All we had was the twelve bucks I had left after buying the soap and the watch and the Tic Tacs.

I stood up and looked across the field. And even though I stayed standing like that for a long time it felt like I was tumbling down into a giant hole. The kind my pop said they had to dig during training for the army. I was tumbling into it and there wasn't nothing to even grab onto. Then a big smile came on my face, I don't even know why. I felt my nose and lips and hair with my fingertips. I crumbled up the Taco Bell receipt and put it in my mouth, chewed it up, swallowed. I swear to God, man. I ate that shit. Then I laughed a little about how dumb it was to eat a damn Taco Bell receipt. But at the same time I didn't even give a shit.

The money was gone.

I sat down on the bench again and felt a lump come into my throat. I dropped the empty petty-cash envelope back in my bag, pushed the bag back under the bench.

A thought kept repeating itself in my head, over and over and over, in Diego's voice: *What are you gonna do now, punk?*

You heard me, punk. What are you gonna do now?

Punk bitch!

I stood up again and went out of the park toward the liquor store where I bought the watch and Tic Tacs and hit the pay phone to call Jaden collect.

You know you're a punk bitch, right?

That's what's up.

You heard me.

I wanted to ask Jaden about the title of *Catcher in the Rye*. But when I picked up the receiver I realized I didn't have the number with me, so I hung up the phone and went into the store and just wandered around looking at the candy bars and the canned beans and the gallons of milk and six-packs of beer. I went to the magazine rack and picked up a couple different sports ones and read the headlines. Then I picked up a porn mag, flipped it open and looked at the big glossy pictures inside. It was a magazine with only black women in it. This one had bright red lipstick and these giant hanging boobs that were pretty much the size of my head. And I'm not gonna lie, it started getting me sort of hyped downstairs, in my jeans. But then I thought how in some of the pictures the woman seemed like she was looking right back at me. Her eyes staring into mine. And I felt bad 'cause she could probably tell I was a punk bitch like Diego kept saying—though it's not like I felt bad enough to stop looking at her big ol' titties.

The Mexican guy behind the counter said: "Hey, partner. Hey. How old are you?"

"Twenty-three," I told him, barely even lifting my head.

"Yeah?" he said. "Why don't you come over here and show me some ID."

I looked up and without even thinking said: "Either that or you could go fuck yourself."

"What?" he said, and he started coming around the counter with an aluminum baseball bat in his right hand.

I just stood there staring at him, though, still holding open my porn mag. I wanted to see if the guy would actually hit a kid with an aluminum bat. I was watching his face to see how it would change before he swung.

He slapped the barrel into his other hand, said: "What'd you just say to me?"

"I didn't say shit to you, man. I'm just trying to read my magazine."

"You stupid little smart-ass, I could have the cops down here in thirty seconds. How'd you like to spend the night in jail?"

He pulled his cell out of his pocket, punched in a couple numbers, held it to his ear.

I threw his stupid mag on the floor and walked out of the store.

I went right back to the park and ducked under the bleachers again with *Catcher in the Rye* and my journal. I tried to read the section where the title comes again, but I couldn't concentrate on the words, so I got up and went back to the dugout and laid on my back with my eyes wide open, trying not to think about anything except what the graffiti on the roof said. I could barely make out some in the dull light that shines over the field 24/7. It was mostly initials and cursewords and weird designs, but my eyes kept going to this one line in the corner that said in small block letters: EVERYBODY IS NOBODY.

I stared at that line for the longest time, thinking who could have written it, and when, and why, and how strange is it that here I was, however many years later, staring up at it in the middle of the night.

EVERYBODY IS NOBODY.

It was almost like me and whoever wrote it were connected with each other. Put here for each other. Even though we'd never even met or ever would.

After a while I started laughing again 'cause I realized I could sort of smell the red flower a few feet away from my head. But I didn't move it or anything. Just kept laying there, staring at that one line of graffiti, EVERYBODY IS NOBODY, smelling the stupid-ass flower, telling myself I deserved every single thing that had ever happened to me.

1:30 a.m.:

I'm sitting up on my bench now, watching Rondell come back onto the baseball field. Good ol' Rondell. Big as hell. Like a damn bull or some shit. He's cutting across the infield holding his Bible in his right hand, heading for the other dugout. He's not even glancing at the one I'm in. If he'd just peek over, man, just for a sec, he'd see my dumb ass sitting here completely solo. No Flaca. He'd see I got played like a punk bitch. I know if I was him I'd at least get a quick look, man. Check if my boy was getting loose with his girl.

But not Rondell, man. He's doing exactly like I said. And for some reason that shit is making me all choked up, like I'm gonna cry, man. Like a little girl. I don't even get why. I grit my teeth and swallow down as hard as I can, but I'm not gonna lie, a couple tears are coming out anyway, rolling down my punk bitch face and into my sweatshirt. I grab my cheeks in my hands and squeeze as hard as I can. And then let go.

Rondell's ducking into the other dugout now. He's taking off his shoes and putting his bag on the bench for a pillow. He's laying down on his back.

And that's it, there's no more movement from his side of the field. Guy's probably already out cold already.

But not me, man.

I'm wide awake as hell.

Like it's damn noon.

And I just realized something. Mong left some shit out when he said only trivial things don't matter. It's so much more than that, yo. _Nothing_ matters. Not when you break it all down like I been doing in my head all tonight. Trust me. Nothing. Not me. Not you. Not the guy in the liquor store with the bat. Not the Bible. Not the pretty girls. Not being the watcher-over of this park. Not _The Catcher in the Rye._ Not this damn book I'm writing.

Nothing, man.

It's all meaningless.

Everybody.

Is.

Nobody.

August 6

It's been three days and I still haven't told Rondell I lost our money.

That first morning, we just hung out around the baseball field and walked the streets, me secretly looking for Flaca and her friends, wondering what I'd do even if I found 'em. But we never saw them. They probably went on a damn vacation to Hawaii or some shit. For food we just ate cheap at random taco shops with the money I had leftover in my pocket and the change Rondell gave back to me from when he was at the diner. We barely talked.

The next day we made our way toward the beach, every once in a while stopping at a gas station or store to make sure we were on the right track. I kept waiting for Rondell to turn and ask me a question about my night with Flaca, or about why we were leaving without me saying bye, but he never did. He just walked beside me, carrying his group-home bag slung on his shoulder, baby Afro bobbing up and down with each long stride he took.

Once we came to this footpath near the beach we started heading north, who even knows why. We walked at a steady pace, and just like the day before neither of us said much. All I cared about now was putting miles between me and National City and getting played like how I did. Didn't even matter where we were going or when we got there or anything else. It just seemed like the farther we got from that baseball field the less I'd remember.

It wasn't until the sun started going down yesterday that Rondell finally asked me anything. And all he wanted to know was when we were gonna eat. I realized we hadn't had any food the whole day.

I felt in my almost empty pockets and looked up at him.

"We gonna get some more tacos?" he said.

It's one thing to mess up shit for yourself, but when it affects somebody else, too . . . Yo, that's when you wanna jump off a damn bridge.

I know from more than just this time.

"Wait here," I told him, and I ducked into this big supermarket. I checked where all the mirrors were and the checkers and the other store workers and then started shoving random things in my bag on the slick: a loaf of bread and jelly and peanuts and a few oranges and cans of Coke. Then I just walked out like there wasn't nothing in there I wanted. Nobody even looked up as I went through the automatic glass doors and cruised through the parking lot back to where Rondell was sitting on the curb. That's the thing about stealing shit. If you act like you know what you're doing most people don't even look twice.

"Come on," I told him, and he got up and followed me.

We ended up on this bus-stop bench a few blocks down and Rondell wolfed down anything and everything I pulled from my bag. I don't even think he looked at what it was first, he just shoved it in his mouth.

I ate a couple things too, but something wasn't right with my stomach.

A group of dirty-ass pigeons gathered under our feet waiting for scraps. Every time I kicked at 'em they'd back off for a few minutes, then slowly start waddling under our feet again. When a bus pulled alongside the curb, Rondell hopped up like we were gonna get on it, but I tugged the back of his sweatshirt, told him: "We gotta walk it this time, Rondo."

He sat back down not even asking why.

As we kept eating, I thought how crazy it was to have

somebody trust me so much. I could pretty much tell the guy anything and he'd go along with it. Hey, Rondo, I could say, we're going to Australia to hunt us a couple damn kangaroos, man. Dude wouldn't even think twice about it. He'd just nod and tell me: How we gonna catch 'em, Mexico? With nets?

I pulled a slice of bread out of the bag thinking how come Rondell trusted me so much. But then when I took a bite my stomach started feeling even sicker. I actually had to lean over like I was gonna heave even though nothing came up.

Rondell stopped his chewing and looked at me funny. "You okay, Mexico?"

"I'm fine," I said.

I looked at the piece of bread I was holding and tossed it to the pigeons. They all attacked at the same time, their crazy little beaks pecking at the bread and each other, darting in and then backing away and then darting in again.

"You sick or somethin'?" Rondell said.

I shrugged and told him: "Nah, man, I just ain't really that hungry."

I watched the pigeons devour my bread, trying to think why my stomach felt so bad. It wasn't nothing to do about Rondell trusting me. And the food wasn't spoiled. Everything else about me felt fine. It's weird, man, sometimes figuring out about the title of a book ain't nothing compared to figuring out about your own damn body.

After we finished eating, we walked a little farther up the beach, and then we crashed for the night in this big patch of ice plant that was sort of hidden by a boarded-up public restroom.

I looked at Rondell at one point, when we were laying there. I almost told him about the money, but I just couldn't do it. It seriously killed me how bad I'd let the guy down.

August 7

Today we made it all the way to this beach area called Cardiff-by-the-Sea before Rondell asked about food. I looked in my bag and there was barely anything left of the bread and oranges. My stomach still felt sick as hell, so I handed it all to him, and we wandered into this campsite area that was on a cliff overlooking the ocean. There was a little paved road going down the middle and on both sides there were these marked-off spaces where people had tents or RVs and picnic tables full of food and drinks and board games. It was getting dark and almost everybody was hanging around their barbecue pits where they'd built little fires and were roasting hot dogs or burgers or marshmallows. Me and Rondell sat down on a big wood stake that was overturned at the end of one of the few empty campsites and put down our bags.

"You still hungry?" I asked him.

He nodded, and we both watched this brand-new RV pull into a campsite down the way.

"Okay, lemme think for a sec," I said, peeping our beat-up shoes. You could tell how much walking we'd done since leaving the Lighthouse just by looking at 'em. Both pairs were dirty as hell. One of my shoes had a rip in the heel and every time I took a step it looked like my shoe was opening its mouth to say something. Both of Rondell's had big holes at the toes and you could see his dirty-ass socks poking out. The bottoms of our jeans were caked with mud too. We looked like we were damn homeless or something—which I guess we were.

I thought about that for a sec.

And then the shit really hit me.

We were homeless.

I was a homeless person.

I'd never considered it that way before. I always just said we were on the run to Mexico. But that wasn't true anymore. Me and Rondell were homeless. To make things even worse, while we were walking I'd realized why I got sick the last time I tried to eat. It's 'cause the food was stolen from that grocery store. After all the shit that happened with Flaca and Jules and the petty cash I decided I'd rather starve to death than steal from a person or even a store. And I know how stubborn I get when I decide something. I really won't do it. Ever. So not only did we not have money, we also didn't have the option of stealing anymore. Or at least I didn't.

I stood up and told Rondell: "Wait here with the bags, man. I'll be right back."

I cruised out of the campsite area and jogged across the busy Highway 101. A little ways down the street I found this cheap taco stand and set all the money left in my pocket on the counter (mostly change and a couple crumpled dollar bills). I told the little Mexican guy: "Lemme get as much food as this buys me, man. Doesn't matter what it is. I don't need no drinks."

He gave me a weird look, then scooped up my money, counted it and put it in the register. He disappeared for a minute. When he came back he handed me a big bag with a bean and cheese burrito, two chicken tacos and an empanada. I thanked him and went back across the street to the campsites.

I took a taco for myself and handed the rest of the bag to Rondell.

He tore through the bean and cheese and empanada like a damn wild animal. Dude was swallowing shit whole. As he unwrapped his final taco he looked over at me and said: "That's all you eatin', Mexico? Just one little taco?"

"I'm not that hungry," I said.

"That's why you so skinny," he said, smiling.

"I could still whup your big ass," I said back. But I didn't say it with much energy 'cause I wasn't really in the mood to mess around.

He took a huge bite and looked at me, smiling and chewing at the same time.

The Part Where I Finally Tell Rondell the Truth:

Later we were just chilling in our empty campsite, under a full moon. I was supposedly writing in my journal and Rondell was supposedly looking at his Bible, but really we were both watching these white kids in the campsite across from us drinking soda and eating pizza and pretty much having the damn times of their lives. The guys all had on surf trunks and flip-flops. The girls were wearing skimpy sundresses over their bikinis. Ugg boots or sandals. A boom box played mellow indie rock as they all sat around their campfire eating and talking and laughing.

I turned to Rondell, said: "Hey, man."

He turned to look at me.

"I been meanin' to tell you somethin'."

He closed his Bible.

"I got some bad news, I guess."

"Wha'chu mean?" he said.

"You know all our petty cash?"

"What we gonna pay back, you mean?"

"Yeah." I shook my head a little. I couldn't even look Rondell in the eye. "Shit's gone," I told him, and right that second my stomach dropped out, like I'd just jumped off a cliff. My ass was totally off balance even though I was just sitting there.

A confused look came onto his face.

I made myself look in his eyes. "I messed up, Rondo. Let somebody take it."

His eyes went big and then he looked down at his bag of trash, like he was thinking about what that meant. He looked up at me again and said: "That's why you wasn't hungry earlier?"

"Not really," I said. "I guess a little."

He paused a sec and then said: "What we gonna do, Mexico?"

I shrugged, said: "I don't even know anymore."

He looked back at the campsite across from us 'cause one of the guys (long blond hair with green tips) was chasing a blond girl around one of the tents. She was laughing her ass off and shouting: "I was just kidding, Jackson! I swear to God! Jackson!"

He was laughing too, shouting back: "Dude, that's so messed up!"

Eventually the guy caught the girl and they fake-wrestled around a sec, cracking up, and then went back to the circle around the fire and sat down.

I cleared my throat, told Rondell: "I just wanted to tell you, man. You know. I'm sorry or whatever."

He looked down at his closed Bible, said: "It wasn't nothin' you did, Mexico."

"Actually, it was—"

"Nah, Mexico," he said, cutting me off. "It ain't nobody's fault."

"No, really," I said. "I let that girl Fl—"

"It ain't nobody's fault," he interrupted again, and this time he slapped a big black hand on my shoulder and smiled at me.

I looked back at him without saying anything.

"You'll just figure somethin' out new. I know how you is, Mexico."

"You don't understand, Rondo," I said, pushing his hand off my shoulder. "We don't have money to eat, man. We're gonna starve."

"It's okay, Mexico." He shook his head at me and tapped the cover of his Bible. "God won't let nothin' bad happen, watch. He'll make you think up somethin' smarter than you ever thought of in your whole life, Mexico. Watch."

I looked back at the surfer kids talking around their barbecue pit. Skateboards turned upside down beside their tent. A couple beach cruisers leaning on kickstands. And for some reason I felt like my chest was gonna straight up explode on me. Like I was gonna start bawling like a little bitch. I swear to God, man. It was all just sitting right there at the top of my throat, just behind my eyes, all the sadness and guilt that's built up inside me like a pile of trash at the dump. But the main thing wasn't that we didn't have money or food or a place to sleep or any idea what we were gonna do next. It was 'cause stupid-ass Rondell actually believed I was gonna save us.

Me!

The same guy who just lost all our money in the first damn place. Got punked by a girl.

I took a couple deep breaths to push the trash pile back down and said: "I just wish your boy would hurry his ass up."

"Who?" Rondell said.

"Jesus or whatever," I said.

And then I just laid my head back on my bag and closed my eyes.

Rondell started saying something else, about God or Jesus or the damn Immaculate Conception, but I didn't hear a word. All my mind could concentrate on laying there was the sounds of them surfer kids across the way talking in their low voices and laughing and being all happy. And me and Rondell laying on the dirt like bums, no money and no place to go and our stomachs full on the last food we'd be able to pay for. I knew soon as we woke up the next morning things would be getting worse.

August 18

I haven't written in here in forever, I know. *Eleven days!* Haven't even cracked the damn cover the past week. But that's 'cause I never knew what it meant to be truly hungry until now.

Back home, me, my moms and Diego may not have much money—and, yeah, we don't go to restaurants or out to movies or anything like that—but we always got enough food to eat. Moms hooks up these huge pots of pasta with meat sauce, or she'll scramble eggs with potatoes and chorizo, like my grams showed her, roll everything in flour tortillas. We always have homemade bread in the bread drawer. And milk. Moms pretty much thinks milk is what could make me and Diego grow up to be big and strong like our old man. She's always asking us at the end of dinner: "You guys finish your cup of milk?" Or when she comes home from work and sees me rummaging through the cupboards: "Why don't you just pour yourself a cup of milk?"

Moms, man.

The woman's straight up obsessed with milk.

Anyways, we may be poor back home or whatever, but we always got food. That's why the past couple weeks have been so damn hard. I'm not even used to it. Me and Rondell wake up on the beach and the first thing I think about is food.

There's this hollow pain that comes riding up into my stomach and chest. My head gets all fuzzy like I'm buzzing on beer, but I'm not even drinking. And then the worst part is when the pain goes away, 'cause then you're on some next-level hunger.

Lately I've been getting mad dizzy too. Me and Rondell will be walking around looking for something to eat and I'll have to double over for a sec 'cause I'm so damn weak or I feel like I'm about to pass out. It's gotten to the point that I actually know when a bad hunger cramp is coming, and I'll dig my fingernails in my shoulder so I could feel something different than hunger.

Rondell's just as hungry, man—and he's twice as big as me—but he hasn't even asked once how come we're not just stealing from stores. And he never complains. Part of it's 'cause he's also willing to scarf down sketchier shit than me. He'll pull damn near anything out of these trash Dumpsters we always hit behind the row of restaurants by the beach. Moldy-ass bread. Slimy half-eaten Chinese noodles in an old Styrofoam take-out container. Dude doesn't even care. And he never gets sick either.

Me, I'm way more picky. It can't be too nasty or else I'll gag while I'm trying to chew it.

Being so hungry is why we haven't walked north in so long. We're both too tired and weak. We spend all our time every day looking for something we could put in our stomachs. Then the minute we find some bread or whatever and scarf it down, we immediately start thinking about the *next* thing we're gonna put in our stomachs. It's a cycle like that. There's no time to think about anything else—unless it's raining and we gotta find another place to sleep than just the beach, like the public restroom.

And then if I haven't eaten in more than one day my

stomach sometimes gets sick on the next thing I eat. You'd think it'd be happy just to have something coming in, right? But nah, man. A couple times I ate something and threw it right back up. I tried to eat more and threw that up too. It's so mad frustrating I can't even tell you. I looked down at my damn stomach this one time and said: "Yo, man! If you so damn hungry why don't you keep that shit down and do the digestion thing!"

My stomach didn't say nothing back, though, just had me lean my ass over to throw up again, Rondell watching me.

And being hungry makes us talk about the most random things, man.

A Random Example of One of Our Talks:

Two nights ago, on the beach, we argued all the way past midnight about our favorite Looney Tunes characters from those old cartoons that always play as reruns. You should've heard us, man. You'd think we were debating the death penalty or some heated war topic.

Rondell tried to tell me his favorite was Wile E. Coyote, and I went off about how retarded that made him sound.

"How could somebody's favorite cartoon character be one that always messes up?" I told him.

"He ain't always mess up," Rondell said.

"Hell yeah, he does."

"Nah, Mexico. You thinkin' 'bout some other one."

"Every single episode it's the exact same thing, Rondo. Trust me. I've seen 'em all. The coyote makes up some stupid plan to get the Road Runner, the shit backfires, and his ass ends up in a damn body cast. That's the script, yo."

"I don't know if you been watchin' the right one," Rondell said, waving me off.

"I have. Trust me."

Rondell shook his head. "I just still like him, though. He make me laugh."

"Okay, maybe Coyote makes you laugh sometimes," I told him. "I'll give you that shit. But that's enough to say he's your *favorite*?"

Rondell got a big smile on his face and said: "And he fast, Mexico. I like when they both speed down the street and then they stop and look at each other and the Road Runner goes: 'meep, meep.' It's so funny whenever that happens."

I pulled my hood off, said: "Nah, but the best character is my boy Speedy Gonzales."

Rondell hit his head like he couldn't believe I would even say that—though I wasn't sure he really knew which one I was talking about.

"Wha'chu know about Speedy," I told him. "He's faster than the Road Runner and Coyote put together. Plus he gets all them little women mice. I don't even care if it's supposedly a racist cartoon or whatever, 'cause he gots on a damn sombrero and plays in a mariachi band. That shit is still funny as hell. And besides, Speedy's mad smart, yo."

When Rondell finally admitted he didn't even remember Speedy, I explained every single scene from all my favorite episodes.

Anyways, we sat there and talked about Looney Tunes for hours and hours. Like it was the most important thing in the entire world. And I could tell you right now it wasn't 'cause we were bored or 'cause we love cartoons so much. It was 'cause our brains were going mad loopy from being so damn hungry. And sometimes when you're that hungry you just get on these stupid topics and talk about 'em for days and days. Or at least that's how it is with me and Rondell.

Other Times How We Don't Even Say a Word to Each Other:

But then the next day we'll just lounge around the sand on the beach not talking, just watching the waves or checking out the people who roll by. Especially girls in bikinis laying on their towels. I don't know what's wrong with me, man, but lately I've been consumed with how fine some girls are. I know I'm not in a good spot to talk to nobody, but it's always in my head.

I play out these little scenarios where I go up to a girl on the beach and start talking to her. And we go swimming together and then have lunch somewhere and then she wants us to promise we'll meet at the same spot the next day. But I tell her I ain't doing that shit, I'll just see her if I see her. And then the next day she comes and finds me and we go swimming again and talk on her towel.

After a couple times of hanging out like that I ask her would she wanna be my girl and she says she totally would, so then we're officially together. And later on it trips me out how many times she wants to be with me. And you know what I'm saying about "being" with me, right? *Being* with me. Like for real. She's always wanting to make out and take each other's clothes off and hook up like the crazy kind, yo. Right there on the beach. At night. On some towel she's brought. Or we'll hook up in the public restroom. Or she'll take me to her house when her parents are out to dinner and we'll do it in her bed next to all her stuffed animals even though it's mad creepy 'cause they're just sitting there staring at me. Or she'll take me to her friend's place. But it's amazing how many times we do it. Just over and over and over, without barely any rest in between.

I never said it wasn't schizo, man. But that's what I do

every once in a while to kill time. I make up scenarios in my head and then play 'em out for mad hours, like they're really happening.

Bad News About Books I'm Reading and This One I'm Supposedly Writing:

Probably the worst thing about being so hungry is I don't even have enough energy to read my new book: *The Stranger* by Albert Camus. I've opened it a few times and tried to read the first couple sentences, but my mind keeps going right back to how hungry I am.

And why do you think this is the first time I've written in here in so long? I seriously can't do it, man. My mind isn't working right. One time I tried to write a page about how Diego looks so much like my old man and how it used to make me jealous, but I ended up ripping the page out and crumpling it up. This other time I tried to write about this dream I had where my moms suddenly shows up to the campsite across from us with some new boyfriend and we run into each other, but I ripped that one out too.

I just can't think right. Which pisses me off, man. 'Cause if you think about it, this stupid little book I'm making is all I have left in my whole life.

Pretty damn sad, right?

Only reason I have energy to write today is 'cause I finally came up with a new plan. Me and Rondell talked to some kid on the beach earlier who works at Kinko's, and he said he'd let us make copies for free. Of whatever we wanted.

After he took off I thought and thought and thought about what we could copy. And then it hit me.

About an imaginary basketball team.

August 21

Today was our trial run, and it came through way better than I ever thought it would. Me and Rondell went around to all the campsites with this signup sheet I made at Kinko's about people giving money to help our basketball team. The guy even gave me a clipboard to put it on so it'd look all official. And after only a couple hours we actually had enough money to eat a real dinner at McDonald's.

We sat down at a booth in the back and just killed a Quarter Pounder each. We were eating so damn fast the people all around us started watching.

"Yo, you ever had a burger taste that good?" I said to Rondell as he ripped open his second Quarter Pounder.

"It's the best one in the world," he said, and he took a huge bite.

"And how 'bout them fries?" I said.

He shook his head, chewing, grabbed a few fries and held them up. After he swallowed he said: "They so crispy, Mexico. You the smartest person I ever met."

I shrugged and sipped my soda. I had to admit, it wasn't the worst plan somebody could make up.

I got the idea 'cause kids used to do it at my school back in Stockton. And yeah, okay, those dudes were really on a team, but I guarantee they kept half that money they raised for themselves. Me and Diego always used to talk about that.

And I already know what you're thinking. It's pretty much stealing if we're not really using the money for a basketball team, right? But I don't think so. It's not like we're taking anything people don't wanna give up in the first place. We're not reaching into fools' pockets and jacking their wallets. Nah, man, they're pulling that shit out on their own. And they get something out of the transaction too. They get to tell all their friends how they helped these two scrubby-looking minority kids with their basketball team.

Trust me, yo, people love it when they get to feel all warm and fuzzy about shit they do.

Plus, if you could actually see my boy Rondell sitting here looking all happy as hell eating his third Quarter Pounder.

How you gonna call this a crime?

For real, man. *You* gonna be the one to take this burger out my boy's hand?

I didn't think so.

August 27

You wouldn't believe how many people wanna help out your basketball team. Me and Rondell have stood outside a grip of different spots over the past week and we've already made back more than fifty bucks. We're eating real food every day now. And we've worked up enough strength so that we're even back to walking north again, along the coast. Every time we get to a new town we cruise into whatever shopping center there is and ask random people to make a small donation to help our hoop squad.

It's a trip, man. People actually pull out their wallets. Everywhere we go.

I told Rondell just last night: "Yo, I feel like we've played on every high school team in California."

He laughed and said: "And plus my grades won't even make me ineligible or nothin'."

I didn't know what the hell he was talking about, but we both laughed and laughed and laughed after he said that.

We have two clipboards now instead of one so we can

split up and talk to twice as many people. Each clipboard says our names and has a picture of a basketball and places where people can sign their names and put down how much they're donating. Rondell goes to one end of the shopping center and I hit the other side.

But you're not gonna believe this part, man. Since the first day we spread out, Rondell's been pulling in twice as much scratch as me. I was so shocked the first couple days he came back with a pocket full of cash that this morning I decided to hide behind a row of shopping carts to hear how he does it.

I watched dude go right up to this older lady coming out of Payless Shoes with her little granddaughter in a stroller.

Rondell got this big goofy smile on his face and said: "Excuse me, ma'am. But could I maybe tell you somethin' 'bout my basketball team real quick? How we collectin' money to go in some tournament in San Jose?"

The woman stopped, said: "Why, it seems you just did, young man." Then she gave him a big old-lady smile.

"Wha'chu mean by that, ma'am?" Rondell said.

She shook her head and told him: "I'm sorry, honey. Please, go on and tell me about your team."

Rondell tapped his clipboard and said: "Nah, it's just we tryin' to get money so we could go in this tournament, ma'am. In San Jose. So we could maybe take a plane up there and stay at a hotel. We're real good at basketball, ma'am."

"I'm sure you are," the woman said. "How tall are you, anyway?"

Rondell shrugged, said: "Taller than most people I walk past."

The woman laughed and reached for her purse. "Well, I'd

certainly love to help out your team, son. I think I have a few dollars in here. Yes, here we go." She handed the cash over to Rondell and signed his clipboard.

"Thank you, ma'am," Rondell said, showing all his teeth.

"Just go beat those guys in San Jose," the woman said, shaking her fist and wheeling her stroller down into the parking lot, toward her car.

I popped out from behind the row of carts and said: "You're a damn natural, Rondo."

He jumped back, said: "Where you come from, Mexico? You scared me."

"The way you talked to her, man. That was perfect."

"You think I done good?" he said.

"You're ten times better than me," I told him. "I put that on everything."

He got this huge proud grin on his face and handed me the money. I slipped it in the leather petty-cash envelope and patted him on the back. "I'll come back in like an hour so we could go eat," I said.

He nodded.

Then I went back over to my side of the shopping center trying to practice smiling all big and goofy like Rondell.

August 31

We've been making our way back up the coast this whole time. Going on foot, stopping off at whatever beach town we're at before the sun goes down, collecting money for our fake basketball team, eating real food, then going back to the beach to sleep. We're easily pulling in enough money to survive now. The only problem is we're not really making enough to pay back the petty-cash envelope that fast. Some days we only pull in like ten bucks and we gotta use most of that just to eat.

But it's all good, 'cause this afternoon I came up with a new and improved plan. I thought it up after this old Mexican man in a sombrero handed me a dollar bill, and I thanked him so damn respectfully I actually bowed. I promise, man, I *bowed.* Dude didn't look like he had much, yet he found a dollar he could give me. But what it was is he reminded me of my gramps.

Here's the New Plan:
Soon as we got back down to the beach with a big bag of Mexican food I told Rondell: "In a couple more days, man, me and you are takin' a bus up to Fresno."

He nodded and took another big-ass bite of his taco.

I thought the guy would at least ask me why, but he didn't seem to care one way or the other. "No more beaches," I told him. "We 'bout to hit the fields."

Didn't even look up at me.

"Yo," I told him. "Aren't you even curious about what we're gonna do?"

He stopped chewing and turned to me. We locked eyes for a few long seconds. Then he swallowed and said: "What we gonna do?"

I shook my head, told him: "You know what? I ain't even tellin' you."

"How come?"

" 'Cause you don't even care, man."

"I *do* care, Mexico."

"You don't care *enough.* Now you'll just have to see when we get there."

"Okay," he said, and he unwrapped another taco, took a huge bite.

I stared at him, shaking my head. "I just hope you're good at leaning over all day," I said.

"Wha'chu mean?" he said.

"Nothin', man. Forget it."

He shrugged and took another supersized bite of taco.

That's what seriously kills me about Rondell. You could tell him the greatest master plan anybody's ever invented and he'd just nod at you and keep eating his taco. The guy totally lives for what's happening right that second. That's it. Bring up something a year from now, a month from now, a week from now, even a damn day from now, and it won't even register in his big-ass head.

I used to think that had to do with his learning disabilities or whatever, but now I'm not so sure. Maybe it's *better* if you live in the moment. Rondell's easily one of the happiest people I've ever met, even with all the bad shit he's had to deal with in his childhood. Me, on the other hand, I get stuck on the past. Especially on my life in Stockton. I don't know if I could ever move past what happened. Mong even said so himself when we were in that cave by Santa Cruz. He said it's like I wanna punish myself. If that's true, man, no wonder I'm not as happy as Rondell. We're both dealing with the same shit on the day-to-day, but it's like only one of us is actually here experiencing it. Him. Sometimes I feel like I'm only *halfway* alive.

But at the same time, man. You gotta look far enough ahead so you could make a plan, right? Or else you'll never even move off your damn spot on the beach.

I thought about that for a while and then said to Rondell: "Hey, man, you know what I bet?"

He finished dribbling salsa onto his fourth taco and looked up at me.

"I bet if some scientist took half of my outlook and half of your outlook they'd come up with a perfect balance of how people should see the world."

He tossed his salsa container into the paper bag and stared at me, trying to figure out what I meant.

"Go 'head, Rondo. Say it."

"Say what?" he said.

" 'Wha'chu mean by that, Mexico?' "

"Wha'chu mean— Hey, why you call me Mexico, Mexico?"

"I was just sayin' what *you* were gonna say."

Rondell got a concerned look on his face. "That don't make no sense. And why you bringin' up science for?"

I shrugged my shoulders and ate the last bite of my taco. "Doesn't even matter, Rondo," I said. "I was just talkin' 'bout the different ways people think."

After a full minute of silence he nodded and patted me on the shoulder, said: "Nah, you ain't gotta worry 'bout nothin' like that, Mexico. You just gotta believe in God."

"Yeah?" I said. "It's that easy?"

"That's how my auntie always said it."

I shook my head, shot back: "You're always talkin' 'bout what other people think. God or your auntie or your parents. I wanna know what *you* think."

He just sat there, staring at the sand. After half a minute or so he turned his head to me like he was gonna say something, but nothing came out of his mouth.

I laughed at the confused look on his face, said: "Don't worry, Ro—"

"You know how I didn't go to Mexico?" he interrupted.

"Yeah."

I could tell by his eyes that he'd flipped his brain into a

high-ass gear. His shit was working its ass off trying to come up with something to say. You could damn near see steam coming out his ears.

He nodded and said: "Do you even know why I didn't go be a fisherman? Why I found you instead?"

"Why?"

"I had to make sure you was okay, Mexico."

We looked at each other, and then I looked down at my wrapper and crumpled it up, threw it in the bag with the rest of our trash.

"Wasn't God who told me I had to do it neither," he said. "It was me. Rondell."

I didn't answer him. I just laughed for some reason, got his big ass in a tight headlock and squeezed as hard as I could. "Say mercy!" I shouted in his ear. "Say mercy and I'll let your sorry ass go, dawg!"

"Nah!" he said back between his laughing.

"Say mercy, dawg."

"Nah, Mexico."

"Say mercy."

We both laughed and laughed and finally he said: "All right, all right. Mercy."

I let him go.

We were both still laughing when I got up and gathered all our trash together, walked it over to the trash can and dropped it in.

When I got back Rondell was already laying with his head on his bag, eyes closed. I just stood there for a while, shaking my head. And then I saw him crack a smile and we both laughed some more.

September 2

We finally made it back up to Santa Monica Beach. The first thing I did was find a pay phone and call the Lighthouse collect. Jaden picked up, told the operator he'd accept the charges.

"Hey," I said.

"Miguel, hey, bro. Been a while. I was starting to think we lost you."

"Somebody stole the money," I said.

There was a short pause between us.

"Oh, no, that's awful, Miguel. You guys okay, I hope?"

"It was some girl. She stole it when I wasn't payin' attention. I'm just callin' to tell you we're still gonna pay it all back."

"Look, bro, Lester and I talked a couple weeks back—"

"Don't worry, it's gonna be legal," I said, cutting him off. "I don't even steal no more. Not from grocery stores or nothin'."

"Bro, that's great to hear. You're taking responsibility. I'm really proud of you."

I switched the phone to my other ear.

"What I was gonna say," Jaden said, "is that I talked to Les and he told me you guys could pay restitution by doing odd jobs here. He'd put you to work, basically. Long as you turn yourselves in, bro. Why don't you just come on back and—"

"I'll probably be able to send the money in two or three weeks, I think," I said. And I thought how it was his job to tell us to do something as stupid as going back to the Lighthouse. They'd probably arrest us and take us to real jail.

"Okay, bro. Look, I'm just saying. There are other ways."

After a short pause, I said: "Are people still dancin' up there?"

"What do you mean, bro? Oh, our dance-off? Ha ha! No, that was a one-time deal. But we did start a garden in the back. Les had some guys come in and dig up some of the cement, and we went to Home Depot and bought really good soil and different packets of seeds and gardening tools. Me and the guys are gonna try and grow our own tomatoes. I know it doesn't sound like the manliest of hobbies, but you should see the guys, Miguel. They love it. Who knew I had a house full of green thumbs. Ha ha!"

"That's cool," I said. I don't even know why, but I was sort of curious about what people were doing there. Even if it was something as boring as gardening.

"Bro, can you imagine these so-called tough guys clipping dead leaves, packing in fertilizer? I wish you were here to see it. I'd even let you be in charge of the watering can. Believe it or not, that's what everybody fights over."

"Yeah, but you can't water plants too much or it'll kill 'em," I said.

"No, bro. You're exactly right about that."

"My moms had plants on the balcony. One time she watered 'em too much and they got all brown and died."

"See, you already *know*. I'd definitely put you in charge of the entire operation. But don't worry, bro, until you get back here I'll keep an eye on these guys and the amount of watering they do. Ha ha!"

I turned around, saw Rondell standing outside the store across the street, holding his clipboard, waiting for people to walk past so he could give them his magical pitch.

"Oh, and we went on a pretty sweet outing two nights ago," Jaden said. "One I know you would've liked, Miguel. We went to an NBA summer league game. Actually, three of them. We got there in the afternoon and stayed through all three games. The guys had an amazing time, bro. Even got a few autographs after the last game. I wish I could remember the players' names—I'm not a huge basketball fan like you are."

I pictured Rondell playing in one of those games. Schooling fools. Jaden didn't even know how good Rondell was. Barely anybody did.

"Anyways," I said. "I just wanted to tell you we're still sending the money. It's just gonna be a little later than I said."

"Hey, okay, bro. All right. But I want you to keep in mind what Lester proposed. If you want, you can come back here and we'll put you guys to work—"

"I'll just send it to the address on the envelope," I said.

"Okay, bro. If you say so."

There was a short pause between us.

"They didn't take the envelope," I said. "Just the money."

"What are they trying to say about my petty-cash pouch? Huh, bro? I had that thing engraved myself."

"Be lookin' for it in the mail."

"Of course—"

I hung up the phone and crossed the street to where Rondell was. I waited for him to finish asking these three guys in suits to help our basketball team. After they waved him off, I told Rondell we could be done for the night.

"What we gonna eat?" he said.

I looked at him, shaking my head, said: "I don't even know, man."

After standing there a few seconds, staring at his clipboard, I realized I wasn't even sure what he'd just asked. I was too busy thinking about what Jaden said about Lester putting us to work, how that was probably bullshit, something to get us back there and send us to real jail.

"I don't know" was pretty much gonna be my answer to anything Rondell asked.

September 4

This morning we were walking north up the beach, like every other day, when all of a sudden we came up on a blue beach house that looked exactly like Mong's. I stopped cold and stared at it. No way it could be the same one, I thought. But then this weird feeling came into my stomach. And my hand automatically reached up to touch his tooth necklace, and I thought how it totally could be. I forgot how Malibu was right next to Santa Monica.

Rondell stopped too. He looked at me.

I scanned all around us to see if anything looked familiar and it did, especially across the street where all the stores were. Then I looked down at the sand and actually found what was left of the little makeshift barbecue Mong had made. I couldn't believe it was still kind of there. I walked over to it and squatted. Rondell followed me.

We both set down our bags, and I picked up one of the few rocks still in the circle we'd made weeks ago and held it up for Rondell, said: "You know where we are, right?"

He nodded.

I tossed it back in the sand, picturing Mong sitting there with his shaved head, drinking his bottle of whiskey, talking all crazy about true love. Then I looked up, checked the line of big rocks between the sand and his blue beach house. I could still see him kneeling there, carving something into one of 'em with a smaller rock. I realized I never checked to see what it was.

"This where Mong was, right, Mexico?" Rondell said.

I nodded.

"And we made a barbecue and ate hot dogs?" he said.

I nodded and walked over to the big rocks, started scanning the surfaces of them all, looking for what Mong could've put.

Rondell caught up with me, said: "We got food in that store right across there, right?"

"That's right," I said.

He leaned against one of the bigger rocks and looked out toward the ocean, said: "And that's where he went out in the water."

I looked all around on every rock but couldn't find anything. I checked again. I totally wanted to see what he put, 'cause it was the last thing he did, but it wasn't anywhere. I touched his tooth necklace again, thinking. Maybe the weather wore it away. Or maybe the rock he used didn't scrape that deep. Or maybe I was just looking in the wrong spot or this wasn't even where we were. Other people probably made barbecue pits like that.

But when I looked back up at the blue house I knew this had to be the spot.

Rondell picked up a smaller rock and stared at it.

"Yo, lemme get that," I said, taking it out of his hand. I spun it around and studied it. The tip was all worn down. I looked all over the surfaces of the rocks again but there was still nothing.

I thought for a sec.

And then it hit me. I told Rondell to get up, and when he did there was Mong's message, written in big block letters:

MONG WAS HERE

I kneeled in front of it. Touched the letters with my fingers. I thought how weird it was that this Chinese kid I knew, who said I was his best friend, sat in this exact spot with this

313

exact rock in his hand and made this exact message. And now he was gone. Forever. I'd never see him again.

But his words. They were still on the rock.

MONG WAS HERE.

I looked up at Rondell, said: "You know what that says?"

He stared at me for a long time, looking all confused. Then he nodded and said: "I could read it."

But I knew he was lying, so I read it out loud anyways. "Says 'Mong was here.' "

"I know that," he said.

"I'm just sayin'," I told him.

He looked at the message, then back at me, then at the message again. "Mong put it?" he said.

I nodded.

He stared at the words on the rock and then a fat tear came down his cheek and he quickly turned so I couldn't see.

We both stood there for a while, me looking at Mong's last words and Rondell looking at the ocean. Straight down from the blue house Mong's dad used to take him to every summer, just the two of them. I tried to picture little Mong running around on this sand. Before what happened with his parents and the cheek scars and him getting sent to a group home and breaking a kid's arm and all his health problems. A little-kid Mong. Just innocent and smiling and playing with his dad.

Rondell turned back to the rock and he kneeled too, put his hand on the words. He didn't have any tears now, but his eyes were mad glassy.

I patted his shoulder, and he looked at me.

And then this crazy thought came in my head. I stood up and yanked off my sweatshirt and shirt. I ripped off both my beat-up shoes and peeled off my filthy-ass socks.

Rondell stood up too, said: "Wha'chu doin', Mexico?"

314

"Goin' swimmin'," I told him.

I pulled off my jeans, wadded up all my clothes and set 'em on one of the rocks and then I just stood there a sec, completely naked except my boxers. And Mong's necklace around my neck. My chest going in and out and in and out.

Rondell's face got mad concerned and he said: "Nah, Mexico. Don't do it."

But I took off running toward the water.

Right before I reached it, though, I got hit from behind so hard it felt like I was run over by a car. I ended up with my face buried halfway in the sand. When I looked up Rondell was sitting on top of me and full-on crying.

"I can't let you, Mexico!" he screamed. "You can't!"

I spit sand from my mouth and yelled back: "What the hell you talkin' about, Rondell! I'm just going swimmin'!"

"I can't let you, Mexico," he said again, this time in a slightly quieter voice. He wiped his face and said: "I's supposed to make sure you okay."

I was about to yell at him again, but then I realized he thought me going swimming meant I wasn't coming back. Like with Mong.

"Nah, Rondell," I said, spitting out more sand. "I'm just gonna go in there for a little bit. Then I'm coming right back out and we can keep walkin'."

He wiped his face again and looked at me. "You comin' back?"

"I promise." I tried to push him off me but he was too damn heavy to even budge.

"You promise, Mexico?"

"I promise," I told him again. "Why don't you just come with me?"

He wiped his face again and looked at me for a couple seconds. Then he said: "I ain't know how to swim."

"Just go in a little. You don't gotta go in that deep."

He looked out at the water and then back at me. "You promise you comin' back?"

"I promise," I said. "Now get the hell off me, man."

He got off me, and I stood up, brushing sand off my boxers and spitting.

"Why you goin' in there?" he said.

"I don't even know," I said.

The Best Swim of My Entire Life:

I turned away from Rondell and jogged the rest of the way to the beach. I hopped through the cold ankle-deep water, then leaped over the small knee-high whitewash, splashing everywhere with my hands and breathing in the salty air. I didn't have to have no talk with my stuff this time 'cause instead of easing in I dove my ass under the first swell I saw. Under the water I kept my eyes shut and touched the sandy bottom with my hands and feet and felt a couple slimy seaweed limbs brush over my back and legs. I stayed down as long as I possibly could in that other ocean world, until my lungs started burning, and then I shot back into the air and took the biggest breath my lungs could do. I never felt so awake, man. Or alive. I don't even know why, but it felt like I could run a damn marathon without even getting tired.

I looked back to the shore and there was Rondell's big ass inching into the ocean too, in just a pair of bun-huggers. He was huge, bigger than most grown men, even though he was only sixteen. He stopped when he was knee-deep and wrapped his big arms around his black body like he was freezing cold.

"Come on!" I called out.

He unwrapped his arms from his body and started stepping in a little deeper.

I put my head down and swam all the way out there with the bigger swells, where I couldn't touch anymore. I was a little scared but I didn't even care. The waves weren't that big or strong, and when they rolled toward me I'd dive under as far as I could, wouldn't come back up until everything quit jostling around like the inside of a washing machine. Then I treaded water and looked all around the ocean and out at some boats and back at Rondell. There wasn't another person in sight, just us. The sun was hidden behind a giant puffy white cloud. Seagulls were flying over the ocean's surface together crying out their seagull cries and flapping their wings every few seconds. And my heart got so it was racing so hard you'd have thought it was hyperventilating. But it wasn't 'cause I was scared about being so deep or nothing. It was 'cause at that exact moment I felt so damn happy to be alive and breathing and free. Like I was the luckiest kid in the whole damn world, man. Including rich people and famous people. Just being able to swim around in Mong's ocean. Getting moved around every once in a while by a thick swell rolling past. Rondell doggy-paddling out to where I was. I was so happy and alive that every time I took a breath it felt like I was gonna breathe in the entire world.

When Rondell finally made it out to where I was, he shouted: "I ain't know how to swim!"

"Me neither!" I shouted back.

Both of us stayed out there anyway, dog-paddling and diving under swells and splashing water at each other and laughing. And then after a while the ocean got calm and both of us went quiet and Rondell drifted back to where he could touch and I just floated around in the deep part, staring out over the water, past where the waves started, where I'd last seen Mong's shaved head bobbing up and down and up and down over the surface of the ocean and then disappearing.

I just looked out there for a long time. Not thinking anything anymore. Just floating and breathing. Living in the moment.

After we finally came back in we dried off with our sweatshirts and got dressed and made our way up to Mong's rocks again. I took the smaller rock and scraped in a message of my own, right under Mong's. I scraped and scraped to make sure it would last.

When I was done I handed the rock to Rondell, and he looked at me, confused.

"Go on, man," I said. "It's your turn."

"I ain't know what to put," he said.

"Put anything you want," I told him. "It doesn't matter."

He stared at me for a while and then he stared at the rock. After a few minutes he squatted and started carving into the rock, under what I just put.

As he scraped away, I looked all around Mong's beach, trying to think if I was taking advantage of my life. I thought how even though I didn't barely have any money or a place to live or a family that wanted me anymore—and even though I could get picked up by a cop at any time and sent back to jail—still, man. This was probably the best day I'd had since my moms dropped me off at Juvi in the first place and they led me down the hall, away from her, and I thought it might be the last time I'd ever see her.

I don't even know why it was that way, but it was.

And I really think for the first time in forever I was looking forward to the next day instead of feeling depressed about the past. Standing there next to Rondell, my mind didn't go to anything else, just what we were doing and where we were.

When Rondell was finally done he stood up and handed

back the smaller rock and we both turned to what the three of us had carved into the big boulder. As we stood there staring at it a lump came in my throat:

MONG WAS HERE
MIGUEL WAS HERE

RONDELL

September 8

It's late and I'm sitting on a hill of old hay and dirt and a cou-ple worn blankets in an abandoned horse shed outside Fresno. Rondell's on the other end of the shed, head propped up on his bag, snoring in a mixed-up rhythm that could only come out of a dude as big as Rondell. There's a dull lightbulb buzzing over my head, hanging on a skinny wire from the ceiling. It gives off just enough light so I can write my book.

And, man, my shoulders and back and hands are so sore I can barely even sit up. Plus my legs ache like they never ached before. The work we did all day was the hardest thing I've ever done. Even the back part of my knees and between my fingers is sore as hell. Spots where you never even knew you had muscles, man. And I can't really even write that much 'cause we gotta be back up and on the truck in like six hours.

My gramps and his crew don't pick fruit out in the fields anymore. They work for a private landscaper on these huge mansions being built on old Fresno farmland. I used to think picking fruit was hard, but that wasn't nothing compared to doing landscaping, man. Rondell doesn't seem to mind it, but I don't even know how much more of this I could take. I'm not even gonna lie. Soon as we make back all the money I'm gonna be ready as hell to move on.

But here's the thing: it's not just the work that's gonna run me off. It's also the fact that my grandparents don't really seem like they want me here. Especially my gramps. Me and Rondell showed up outside their door early this morning and gramps didn't even look surprised or happy to see me.

Soon as he opened the door I went right up to him and shook his hand and smiled big and said: "Hey, Grandpa, nice to see you."

He didn't say anything back, just looked at my grandma, who was drying her hands behind him on a dish towel. And then he looked back to me.

I moved back a step and started stuttering my ass off: "Anyways, Grandpa, I was just— Me and Rondell here—this is my friend Rondell, by the way—we were wondering could me and him get work with you. Not for that long or anything. And for just whatever money you regularly give to people."

He looked at me for a sec and looked at his watch.

Then he led us out to this other old Mexican dude wearing a sombrero, said something in Spanish, and they both nodded. His friend threw our bags in the shed we're in now and handed me and Rondell a bunch of work tools. Then he pointed us to the back of an old run-down pickup and drove us down a bunch of dirt roads toward their work site.

As we pulled up the driveway of this guy Mr. Easton's house, Rondell nudged me with his arm and said: "Hey, Mexico."

"Hey what," I said, but my mind was still trying to figure out why I ever thought my grandparents would want me here after everything that happened in our family. First of all their son (my pop) dying in the war, and second of all the terrible thing that happened in Stockton and how Diego has always been their favorite, not me.

"I was just thinkin' somethin'," Rondell said.

"I ain't really in the mood, to be honest," I told him. "Nothin' personal."

He stared at the side of my face for a minute and then said: "All right. I was just thinkin' if you's all right, 'cause it seem like somethin' be botherin' you. But I ain't gonna ask it."

I shook my head, picturing my gramps's face again when

we shook hands. I told Rondell: "Maybe I messed up bringin' us here, man."

He looked at me like he didn't understand what I was saying, but I didn't feel like going into shit.

The Rest of the Workday:

It was even worse with my gramps once we started actually working. He barely acknowledged my existence. After the lunch break we even got matched up together, just the two of us, digging main line—eight inches wide, eighteen deep—where they were gonna install a fancy sprinkler system. Gramps didn't say a word the whole time, just kept slamming his pick in the ground, breaking open the earth, then raising it up and slamming his pick in the ground again. My job was to follow in his tracks, take shovelfuls of loose dirt and rocks and clumps of old crabgrass, toss everything into piles on my right.

The whole time I tried not to think how much it was killing my back and shoulders and hands, the streaks of dirty sweat running into my eyes and stinging. I tried to not even look up, just put my head down and pretended to be in a machine trance—which really I wasn't.

Even when I did accidentally look up all I'd see was my grandpa's ass.

Whenever I got behind a little he'd shake his head and sigh, toss down his pick and grab a second shovel. He'd start shoveling from where he left off with the pick. When we met in the middle, the metal from our tools clinking as we tried to pick up the last bits of loose dirt, he'd toss the shovel to the side again and grab his pick.

He didn't even look at me the whole time.

* * *

When they drove us back here at the end of today my gramps's friend told us when to be on the truck tomorrow and then some young girl brought us a big plate of egg and chorizo and tortillas.

The best part of the whole day, though, was when my gramps's friend came back to the shed twenty minutes later and handed us seventy-five bucks each, cash. It felt pretty damn sick shoving all that scratch in the petty-cash envelope.

But overall I don't know, man.

My gramps seriously doesn't seem too happy to have me here. And even my grandma ducked right back in the kitchen when she saw me at the front door this morning. I knew the work would be hard as hell, but I don't even care about that. I just feel weird that my grandparents are acting so bummed out to be seeing me. They're seeming just like my moms.

You know what I think? I think no matter how long I live or where I go or what I accomplish—even if I became the damn President of the United States or a famous actor or businessman—I think none of us will ever get past what happened with me and Diego. Including me.

Everywhere I go there's gonna be someone who knows me, and it'll be right there in their eyes. What I did. And I'll always see it. 'Cause I'll be looking.

Even if I went on some remote island where there wasn't any other people besides me. Still, man. There'd be a mirror somewhere. And I'd see it in my own self.

September 9

Me and Rondell got put at a different site today. Our job was to dig out this tree, roots and everything, in front of a huge house that's still under construction. It didn't seem like much when we first went up to it. The tree was scrawny as hell and barely had any leaves. But we spent all damn day digging around the base and couldn't even budge it. The minute I'd think we had it surrounded, I'd bang my shovel into another fat root and Rondell would have to swing on it with his pick again.

At one point I stood up straight, balanced my tool against the damn tree and wiped the sweat out of my eyes. I looked around at all the other workers on site busting their asses. Some were young, some old, but they were all Mexicans. And not one of 'em was struggling as much as me. Not even Rondell, man. They just kept going and going like it wasn't nothing.

I almost threw my shovel down and quit my ass right there, man. I thought how maybe I wasn't cut out to be no good worker or whatever. Maybe that's what my gramps still sees every time he looks in my face, like when I showed up to his front door yesterday morning. Just some blond boy from Beverly Hills with no heart.

But I didn't quit, though, man. Nah, I just grabbed my damn shovel and dug my ass back into the fat root again. No way I was gonna let everybody think I was a punk. I smacked down with the sharp edge over and over until I finally broke through. Then I stood looking at the two separate pieces for a sec, and I dropped the shovel and flexed my biceps, told Rondell: "Yo, Rondo! You see these guns, boy? This tree can't fuck with nobody this jacked!"

I know I was acting like a damn schizo, but I didn't even care.

Rondell looked up at me and giggled a little in his cupped fist. Then he went right back to digging.

I looked back at the roots and thought how I had to show my gramps I had heart. I didn't like him thinkin' of me havin' no heart.

Soon as we came home tonight we got paid again, and the same little girl brought us a plate of egg and chorizo and tortillas. I tried to talk to her this time, asked her what her name was and how she knew my grams or whatever, but she just handed us the plate and then ran out of the shed all embarrassed. Me and Rondell laughed and then reached for the food and ate like two of the starvingest dudes you ever met. It's pretty crazy how hungry you could get after trying to dig up a damn tree all day.

After a few minutes there was a little knock on the outside of the shed and my grandma came walking in. She stood a few feet away from us and got this sad look on her face. "Miguel, *mijo.*"

Me and Rondell both stood up and I said: "Hey, Grandma."

"*Mijo,* are you okay, honey?"

My eyes started getting all this pressure on 'em after I heard her say if I was okay.

"I'm okay, Grandma," I said. "What about you?"

"Okay, *mijo.*" She ran her hands down her cheeks and sighed. "Me and your grandpa, we're getting by."

Then she just stood there for a while, staring at me. For the last twenty years my grandma's been teaching English to all the kids that work with my gramps—which makes it crazy he's never learned it himself. She's pretty short and thin with big dark eyes. I don't know if you've ever seen an old Mexican grandma, but she basically looks just like that. Only her skin is a little darker than most grandmas, like she's got mostly Indian in her. And her gray hair is almost always tied back in a ponytail, but for some reason tonight she had it just regular. I was shocked about how long it seemed that way.

I looked at her for a while and she looked back at me, and it started feeling mad awkward 'cause nobody was talking, so I pointed at Rondell and said: "Grandma, this is my friend."

She turned and said hello to him.

"He's Rondell," I said.

They both nodded some more and then my grams went right back to looking at me. And this time her eyes got all glassy and a couple tears came running down her cheeks, which made the pressure on the back of my eyes get way worse. But I clenched up my whole body so nothing would come out.

She wiped her face with her sleeve and said: "*Mijo*, I can't believe I'm looking at you. It's been long."

I felt all awkward and my eyes were acting up and I didn't know what I was supposed to say back, so I spun around and went to my bag, unzipped the zipper and acted like I was looking for something. "Anyways, Grandma," I said, over my shoulder. "Me and Rondell came up here to say hi to you guys and do some work. Just for a week or whatever. We owe somebody money and we gotta pay 'em back, so it's nice of Grandpa to let us work for him."

I pretended like I was digging for a few more seconds. When I turned around, though, she was wiping more tears. "Oh, *mijo*," she said in this incredibly sad voice.

I thought how this was the first time I'd seen her since what happened. My moms didn't say for anybody to come up and visit me before I got put in Juvi. Actually, I'd only seen my grandma like two times since my pop died and we all went to his military funeral together. Plus maybe she even knew from my moms how I was AWOL from the Lighthouse too. I guess when you think about it, there was a lot to be sad about when it came to me. Especially if you were my grandma.

I didn't know what else to do or say, so I just stayed there at my bag, digging my hand around my extra shirt and other pair of jeans, acting like there was something I couldn't find.

Rondell stood there too, looking back and forth between us, not saying a word.

I said over my shoulder: "You wanna sit with us for a minute, Grandma?"

"Oh, no, *mijo*," she said. "I just wanted to say hi while your grandfather was out. Maybe I can heat up some soup or leftover tamales?"

I looked at Rondell and then back at my grandma. "Nah, that's okay," I told her. "Those egg tortillas were perfect, right Rondell?"

He nodded.

"Thanks, though," I said.

All of a sudden she started sobbing and she rushed up and hugged me mad tight. Laid her old grandma head on my shoulder. And I'm not gonna lie, man, I went stiff as a board in her arms. And it wasn't nothing to do with *her*. I love the hell out of my grandma. I just knew her hug was trying to tell me I was still her grandson, even after everything I did, and it made me sick about myself. 'Cause we both knew I didn't deserve it.

She squeezed and sniffled and tried to get her breathing regular. After a couple minutes like that she said: "I'm so sorry, *mijo*."

"I know, Grandma," I said, but I only said it 'cause I didn't know what else to say.

She pulled her head back and looked in my eyes. "I'm just so sorry for you."

I pulled out of her arms.

She took my face in her strong hands and made it so I had to look her in the eyes. "I'm so sorry for you, Miguel. I pray about you every night. I know you didn't mean it."

I nodded, looked down at the dirt floor.

"I pray about you, *mijo*."

She hugged me again and then kissed me on the cheek and said: "I'm so glad you came. Your grandfather is too."

I stayed staring at the ground.

My grandma turned to Rondell and said: "You too, honey. I'm happy you're here. Look out for my grandson, okay?"

"I already been doin' it, ma'am," Rondell said. "You ain't even gotta worry. That's my word. It's how come I didn't go fishin' in Mexico."

"I know you'll watch him for me, honey," my grandma said, and then she turned back to me.

She stared for a while longer, wiping a few more tears, and then she left the shed.

Soon as she was gone Rondell said: "What's she talkin' about, Mexico?"

I wanted to answer the guy. Wanted to tell him everything. I was so tired of keeping shit to myself.

But I just couldn't.

All I could do was shake my head.

I kneeled down, pulled my journal out of my bag and opened it up. Pulled out my pen and started writing.

Rondell looked down at me for a few minutes, but he didn't ask me again. Eventually he reached into his bag too. Pulled out his Bible.

And that's how we both are now.

I'm writing all this down in my book, and he's looking at his Bible.

September 10

We worked on the tree all day again today. And for the first couple hours I was struggling just as bad as yesterday. Maybe even worse. While I shoveled I tried to think what everybody else working had that I didn't have. Why their backs didn't seem to be aching as much. And why their hands didn't seem as blistered and rubbed raw. And why their faces weren't all frowned up like mine.

But then after lunch something weird happened.

I decided to try as hard as I possibly could and locked into this unexplainable work rhythm. I'd stab my shovel in, pull up on the dirt, and toss my shovelful over my shoulder. Then I'd stab my shovel back in, pull up on the dirt and toss my shovelful over my shoulder again. Kept doing it that same way, over and over and over, to the point that I wasn't even aware of time passing.

I matched my breathing with my shovel stabs. And it was strange, man. I actually stopped thinking about the pain in my back and shoulders and hands. After a while of doing it like this, I looked up and saw myself as part of the whole work site. Everybody's head down, working and breathing and thinking their thoughts and helping the people around 'em. Looking everywhere, I could actually see us changing the yard. Little by little. With every shovelful and pick swing.

And me too. I was part of it. We were all our own people but we were one. Even though we weren't talking to each other.

For some reason it made me think about that drum circle we did at Venice beach. Everybody pounding their bongos at the same pace, the sounds we were all making together, how it was so hypnotizing and spiritual. The sun going down over the ocean. It was just like that only in a different way. 'Cause in Venice everybody went there to be a part of something. But here, we were just working. We were just doing our job, making money to survive.

In that way it was almost better. You had to actually look up to realize you were part of something bigger than just the hole you were digging.

I don't know why, man, but I got so hyped I started working harder than I'd ever worked in my entire life. At anything, including playing ball with Diego at the park or even writing this book. I kept digging and digging alongside Rondell. And when the boss whistled and said it was quitting time I couldn't believe it. It seemed like we'd just barely had our lunch.

We carried all the tools back to the truck and it felt like I was supposed to be there. All the Mexican guys were joking around with each other in Spanish and a couple of them even joked with me and Rondell. Who cares if I couldn't understand. I laughed my ass off anyway.

Me and Rondell hopped in the back of the truck and my gramps handed me an empty bucket and nodded at me, and I nodded back.

As we drove home my entire body felt tired as hell, but it was a good tired. Like I was gonna deserve to eat the food the girl brought us later. And I was gonna deserve my sleep on the hay.

I punched big Rondell in the shoulder and we both laughed and I showed him how I could make centipede movements in the wind with my hand.

Rondell looked at me and nodded his big head up and down and up and down. And then he did it too. On his side of the truck. We kept doing that stupid shit the whole drive home. And after we got out, put all the tools away, my gramps's friend came and gave us more money. And the little girl brought us a big plate of tamales. And I felt mad happy. The happiest since we went in Mong's ocean.

As we ate I thought how even though we still didn't get that damn tree out, for the first time since me and Rondell had been working on it we got it to budge. And we were both sweaty and dirty and tired as hell from a hard day of work. And I felt proud.

Like I earned something.

Like I had heart.

September 11

Today work went the same exact way. I struggled in the morning, and then after lunch I locked into the same strange rhythm. By the end of the day me and Rondell got it so the tree was almost ready to go. We could move it back and forth with our hands and lean it way to the side when we jimmied it from underneath with a pick. But we still couldn't get it all the way out.

A couple other guys came over and yanked on it too, jimmied with their picks, but nobody could totally pull it out.

"Is a stubborn one," my gramps's friend said as we were loading up the truck. "Roots are deep, huh?"

Me and Rondell both nodded.

"Sometimes roots are like that. Very deep. Much deeper than people can see."

We nodded some more.

"Like life," he said.

"I know," I told him back, even though I wasn't sure exactly what he meant.

He patted me and Rondell each on the shoulder, and then he got in the cab of the truck with my gramps and they drove us back.

We got paid and ate a big plate of chicken tacos and then my grandma came back over and sat with us at the little table in our shed for a while. We went through the same things as we did the night before, about how she was happy we'd come and could she fix us any leftover tamales or empanadas. But then all of a sudden she had mad tears running down her face.

"Your brother," she said, grabbing my hand. "He was such a good boy."

I looked back at her, my stomach flipping over inside my body, my head getting woozy like I was drunk even though I didn't have a sip of alcohol in forever. And I couldn't stop swallowing. I don't even know why, but I kept swallowing like every two seconds.

She wiped her face, and I stood up and went to my bag again.

I could feel my grandma and Rondell following me with their eyes.

"Such a good boy," my grandma said again.

"Who is?" Rondell said.

"Miguel's brother," my grandma said. "His name was Diego."

"What happened to him?" Rondell said.

My grandma didn't say anything, just cried even harder and touched Rondell on the arm. Then she put her face in her hands and said through her fingers: "But it's gonna be okay, *mijo*. I pray about you."

She said it again before I spun around, shaking my head. "It's not okay," I told her.

She looked up at me with a surprised look on her face. "It *is, mijo*. It was an accident. I know because I prayed about it."

"It's not okay," I said again. And I kept shaking my head back and forth and back and forth. "It's not okay, Grandma."

"Your brother would want you to go on living your life. He loved you more than anyone."

Just hearing her say that made a small tear push out of my right eye. I wiped it real quick, told her: "I loved him too."

"We all did, *mijo*."

I stared back at my grandma, wiping my face.

Rondell kept his eyes on me, his mouth hung open.

Then my grandma broke down even more, started sobbing. She ran her hands down her face and said in this crazy crying grandma voice: "I'm just so sorry for you, Miguel."

I stared at the ground.

She stood up. "It's too much," she said. "For a boy to take. I pray every night for you to be okay. But I don't know."

She backed up toward the shed door, crying, and then she sort of waved at us and said: "I'll come talk to you tomorrow. I can't right now."

She left.

It was just me and Rondell now. And he was staring at me. And I already knew his question so I told him: "What, Rondell? You wanna know what happened to my brother, right?"

"What was your grandma tellin' us, Mexico?" he said.

I tried to smile at him, but some tears came trickling out of my burning eyes. I just let 'em too, and nodded my head for a while.

I looked Rondell right in his eyes and said: "You wanna know what happened, Rondell?"

He nodded at me.

"I killed him, man. Killed my own brother."

He stared back at me like he didn't understand.

"That's what you wanted to hear about, right?"

"Your brother you told me about?"

"Yeah, man. I killed him." I said it at him again and again, and Rondell just sat there, looking back at me, stunned. His eyes bugged and his mouth hanging open.

"But I thought you and him was gonna meet up–"

"I lied, Rondell!" I shouted. "I been lying to you this whole time. I can't never see my brother again for the rest of my life 'cause I killed him!"

I realized I was crying now for real. Tears streaming down my cheeks and in my mouth and I didn't even try to stop 'em. Everything was coming out of me at once, climbing up through my throat and into my mouth and shooting out from behind my eyes. Somehow it was a relief to just say it, over and over. "I killed my own brother, Rondell. My own brother. Dead, man. 'Cause of me."

It was the first time I'd ever said it out loud.

"My brother's dead," I told him again, " 'cause I killed him."

Rondell sat there quiet for a few minutes, just looking at me. Bugging. Then he cleared his throat and raised his head up and asked me how, and I stared right back at him, crying and smiling at the same time.

He didn't look away. Asked me again even.

I wiped my eyes and nose on my sweatshirt and thought about that for a while. What he wanted to know.

Then I decided to say it to him.

The Truth:

I'm back in Stockton, at our apartment after school.

Six months and fourteen days ago.

I'm sitting in the living room eating a piece of Moms's homemade bread with butter and sugar when Diego comes strutting through the front door. The TV's on to some show I used to like. Diego tosses his backpack on the couch, points at me and goes in the kitchen to make his own pieces of bread.

I watch him go through the door.

He comes out a minute later with three pieces on a paper towel and sits in Pop's old chair. "Yo, Guelly," he says, picking up his first bread. "Lemme get the remote."

"Nah, man, I'm tryin' to watch this," I tell him.

He pauses his bread before it gets to his mouth. "Guelly," he says.

I look up at him, almost smiling but not yet. "What, man?"

"Lemme get the remote."

"Can't do it," I say.

He nods and sets down his bread, stands up. "Guelly," he says.

"What?"

"I gotta *make* you give it up?"

I start laughing and toss the remote at him. It bangs off his chest and falls to the floor. When it hits one of the batteries flies out and we both watch it roll under the couch.

Diego looks up at me, laughing a little too, now.

And the reason we're laughing is 'cause we *always* mess around like this after school. It's like our ritual.

It's how we have fun sometimes.

He charges, jumps on me, gets me in a tight headlock. My sugar bread goes flying on the rug, butter side down. And Diego shouts through his laughter: "You gonna disrespect your big bro like that? Huh, Guelly? That's what's up?"

"Come on, D," I say. "Lemme go, man."

"Say mercy, bitch!"

I laugh without sound, shout: "Hell nah!"

I reach up, trying to pry his hands away from my head one finger at a time.

"Say mercy!"

"Hell nah!"

"Say mercy!"

"Hell nah!"

I use all my strength and for the first time ever I actually pry his hands off me and get myself free.

I stand up and look at him.

He looks back at me.

I feel stronger all of a sudden, almost as strong as Diego. It's the first time I've ever felt as strong as Diego in my whole life.

We both look at each other, smiling.

I feel incredible.

"Oh, I see what's up, Guelly," he says. "You think you some kind of badass now."

"Better watch it, D," I tell him. "One day I'm gonna mess around and make *you* say mercy."

We both crack up a little and he says: "Too bad one day ain't today, little bro."

He charges again, dives toward the sofa at me but I side-step him, hop over the cushions and land on the other side on my back with a thud. We both get up and look at each other.

Him on one side of the couch, me on the other.

Still just playing.

Still just having fun like every other day.

And I'll never forget the look on his face. Not for the rest of my life. It's the look I've dreamed about every night since, and will dream about every tomorrow after. My big bro, laughing, happy, his hair cut short and mad cool, sideburns long and thin and perfectly trimmed, his face the face all the girls at our school die over, his clothes the clothes all the dudes at our school try to copy on the DL.

My big bro.

Diego.

Him staring at me, breathing a little hard from us messing around. Alive. About to chase after me one last time.

Every dream I think back to this moment I try to make it so I just give myself up, let him tackle me, tell him mercy, tell him he's right how one day ain't today.

But I don't give myself up.

'Cause at the time I feel so strong. I'd just pried him off me with my bare hands. And anyways we're just messing around like any other day.

He races around the couch and I dart in the kitchen, scoop the steak knife off the table he's just used to butter his bread.

I turn around and try and tell him: "Back off, yo!" But I can't quite get the whole thing out 'cause I trip going backwards and fall on my back against the sink, my head smacking on the door of the cupboard.

Diego flips the kitchen table the rest of the way over laughing and dives on me. Tackles me. Like any other day. But this time he doesn't get me in a headlock. And this time he doesn't tell me to say mercy. And this time he just has his eyes on mine and a smile that's fading off his face, draining like water from a bathtub, like sand through your fingers at the beach. This time his eyes get mad big and wide and scared and then they drift to the side, emptying out.

This time our messing around isn't just messing around because I trip and fall with the knife and my head bangs the cupboard door and when he goes to tackle me there's the knife and he falls on it and it goes in him.

The knife.

It goes in him.

I feel this happen.

I look in his face and know something forever has happened and try and push him off but he's stuck on me and I have to shove him with all my new strength and finally he rolls over onto his back and I stare at him, breathing hard.

The knife is sticking out of his chest. Out of his heart, the Indian doctor will later tell my moms in the waiting room of the hospital, and after she hears those words she will go down on her knees holding on to the doctor's arm and screaming and everybody looking at her.

At first my head is a blur 'cause I can't catch my breath, but then it gets clear. The knife I was holding. It pierced Diego's heart and killed him dead. I stabbed my big brother in the heart.

My Diego.

My family.

My entire life.

I scream like a little girl. His blood pouring out of him like a water fountain and onto the kitchen tile and I'm scooping it up and trying to push it back in him but I can't, and I'm looking down at my shirt at all his blood on me, too, and on my arms and my face and my pants, in my hands.

I lean over him and scream and scream and scream.

And then my face goes normal for a sec and it seems like I'm thinking but I'm just trying to realize this is real and my brother has a knife in him and then I scream and pick up his face in my hands and look in his eyes big and empty and drained.

I lay his head back down soft even though he's dead.

I stand up, make Diego's head go straight and stare at the

knife in his chest and scream again, but this time no sound comes out, like I'm mute, but then when I scream a second time there's sound again.

I run in the living room and look at the couch and the TV and the bread on the rug. I grab the remote and think how to put it back together. Grab the battery from under the couch, push it back in, snap on the cover. I set the remote on the table by the couch and run back in the kitchen and kneel next to my brother who still has a knife in his heart and spit bubbling from his mouth and eyes that are drained.

I grab his face again and yell at him I don't even know what words but he doesn't hear me.

I yell and yell and yell not even real words and then start telling him his name: "Diego! Diego! Diego!"

Right in his ear.

But he doesn't hear me.

And then the sirens are outside.

And then the cops and firemen are coming in the kitchen and saying things I can't understand and spreading out and kneeling by Diego.

And then I'm with one of them in the living room next to the overturned bread and he's holding up my chin so I'll look him in the eye and tell him my name and say what happened but I can't understand him.

He's saying his questions over and over and over.

And I'm crying.

And then I'm in the front of the squad car. I'm looking in the back. It's empty. I'm looking at the cop who's shaking his head, talking in his radio. And I'm wishing he would put me in the back, 'cause I know it's where I'm supposed to be, not the front, in the back, how it always is on TV and in movies and on the show I used to watch after school.

And then I'm at the police station and my moms is rushing

in and I'm standing up and shouting her name, Mom! And we're making eye contact, and then she's looking away. And her face is scrunching up and she's looking at the cop and then turning away from him too and leaving me at the station, in the cell, and one of the cops is running after her, yelling for her to hold on, Mrs. Casteñeda!

Mrs. Casteñeda!

Mrs. Casteñeda!

And then I'm in front of the judge, who's telling me my sentence.

And then I'm in here.

In this horse shed in Fresno, where my whole body is sore and trembling and everything smells like hay and my chest is going in and out and in and out faster than is even possible.

And I'm crying tears and telling Rondell about killing my own brother.

And he's staring back at me with his mouth open.

September 11—more

I let my face fall in my hands. Just like my grandma. Only I pretended my hands made up a dark cave like the one me, Mong and Rondell went in by the beach.

I started calming down by taking deep breaths and concentrating on the smell of dirt on my palms.

Rondell came over and put his hand on my shoulder and said: "It's okay, Mexico."

"It ain't," I mumbled at him. "I can never change it back."

"Nah, it's okay, Mexico," he said, nodding at me. " 'Cause it ain't really your fault."

I lowered my hands and looked at him. "What are you talkin' about, Rondell? I did it."

"Nuh-uh, Mexico."

I stared back at him without blinking. Somehow I already knew what he was gonna say, but I wanted to wait until it came out of his mouth.

"It's the devil," Rondell said, nodding his head and squeezing my shoulder. "The devil done came up in your head like he does mine sometimes. He *made* you do it."

I stared at him for a few long seconds, the anger rising in me like a boiling thermometer. I told him: "What'd you just say?"

He nodded some more, like it was simple. "The devil, Mexico. He came up in your head, like he do with me sometimes. He who made you kill your brother."

No thoughts, and I was reaching out and cracking Rondell in his face with a closed fist and his head was snapping back and blood was trickling out his nose.

He looked at me without really reacting.

"It was me, you fucking retard!" I yelled. "I did it!"

I kept waiting for him to grab me, hit me back, throw me out my chair, stomp my neck, but he just sat there looking at me, still nodding.

"It's the devil," he said. "He twist people's thoughts like that."

I stood up and punched Rondell again. This time right on the side of the head. I shouted: "Shut up about the devil, Rondell! It was *me*! I killed my brother!"

He touched his face where I smacked him but he still didn't do anything back. "It's okay, Mexico," he said. "The devil came in your head like he doin' right now. It ain't even you tryin' to hit me. It's the devil, Mexico."

I lost it. Marched around the table and started swinging on Rondell. He covered his face to mute the blows but didn't fight back. And that shit made me even more crazy and angry and I punched and punched and kicked and spit and yelled in his ear how it was me and not no devil, I killed my brother, how he'd even know there was such a thing as a devil or God or heaven or hell, maybe it was just people like me and him and Mong and if we did something it was us and nobody else. I yelled at him and threw haymakers from every direction and blood started coming out his mouth, too, and his ear got all red.

For the longest he just took it, telling me about the devil, and saying I was okay, and he'll watch over me, until finally he got tired of getting hit and stood up and wrapped me in a bear hug and threw me to the ground.

"Stop it, Mexico!" he yelled, wiping blood from his nose and mouth on his sweatshirt.

I yelled: "Fuck you, Rondell!"

And finally he stepped his broken-ass shoe down on my face, slid it down to my neck, just like he did the first day I met him in Juvi, and started pressing down hard, still telling me it was okay. My face was mashed down so hard my teeth were partly in the dirt and I could taste it and feel my lip about to split and I couldn't hardly breathe, and I tried to tell him: "Do it, Rondell! You fuckin' illiterate! Push down all the way! Do it!"

He pressed down harder and started talking in tongues or something and then he told me about God and the devil and cleansing both our souls so it would never happen again and then suddenly he went quiet.

"Do it, Rondell!" I shouted, 'cause all I wanted was to be punished or to disappear or go to sleep forever, get erased, go in space, where I could tell Diego I'm still his brother and he's still stronger than me and mercy!

But Rondell lifted his foot off my face.

I looked up, still crying, watched Rondell walk off and lay on his part of hay on his back by his bag and look up at the roof.

"What're you doin'?" I said. "I want you to push your foot all the way to the ground. Don't you understand I deserve it?"

But he just shook his head and wiped the trickle of blood coming from his nose and mouth. "You don't deserve to get hurt, Mexico."

He touched his red ear and said: "You my only friend I ever had."

Then I woke up.

And tears were running down my face and I stared at poor Rondell lying there. Who was trying to help me. I let myself cry and cry and cry, for what I'd just done to Rondell.

I wiped my face on my sweatshirt and told Rondell in this weak-ass voice, "I'm so sorry, man."

I said it a few more times, in a quiet voice, one that I don't even know if he could hear, 'cause he just stayed there on his section of hay, staring at the roof, wiping blood from his face every couple seconds. And I thought how I was saying sorry to him, but I was also saying sorry to Diego and to my moms and to my grandma and grandpa. And even to me. I was saying it to everybody all at the same time.

After a while Rondell told me to go in my bed, but I just stayed where I was. In the dirt. I couldn't even move.

And I slept there the entire night.

September 12

When we woke up today and went to work, me and Rondell acted like nothing ever happened with us. We just got up and ate the fruit the little girl brought us and grabbed our tools and climbed in the back of the truck and sat there with the wind blowing on our faces going to work.

I looked at the dried blood on Rondell's face and I felt so bad my stomach hurt, but I didn't say anything.

When we were walking to the tree I tried to tell Rondell I was sorry again, but he just got this big goofy smile on his face and said: "It's okay, Mexico."

I patted him on the shoulder, and he did the same to me, and it seemed like we were cool, but I knew I still had to make it up to him somehow.

We tossed all our tools down by the tree and got set to start working, and you wouldn't believe what happened.

I just barely put my pick under the tree and the thing fell over on its side. Me and Rondell looked at each other, and we both started laughing.

Some of the Mexican guys saw and started whistling and clapping and everybody set down their tools and came walking up to us and patted us on the back. And these two big dudes moved the tree away from the hole we'd dug. They shouted stuff to each other and us in Spanish. And then my gramps and his friend came over and put their hands on the tree and laughed to each other and my gramps's friend said: "Told you about these roots. Look at 'em." He pointed at how long and thick and deep they were, and me and Rondell nodded and laughed with everybody else.

And eventually a guy in a small tractor came driving up the hill to drag away the tree and they put me and Rondell on another job in the backyard.

When we got home, after we got paid again and ate eggs and tortillas, I counted up our money and we had more than enough to pay back the Lighthouse. I looked up at Rondell and said: "Just so you know, man. Tomorrow I'm going back to do my time. I already told my grandma and grandpa."

I thought he'd be surprised, but he wasn't. He just nodded, said: "Okay, Mexico."

"What about you?" I said.

"I'm gonna go back to Oakland and find my auntie. Or else my cousins. Maybe one of 'em got a room I could be in."

I looked at him, nodding, said: "You can have all the left-over money, man. I think there's like a hundred something."

"Thanks, Mexico," he said.

And then I don't even know what came over me but I hugged his big ass. It was a real quick one, barely lasted a second, but he knew it was a hug too. Because when we got on our separate piles of hay for the night he had this huge smile on his face, and he said: "You like me again, Mexico."

I told him: "I always liked you, Rondo. You my boy, ain't you?"

"Yeah," he said.

"I just lost it last night."

"It's okay, Mexico."

"Nah, it's not," I told him. "I'm really sorry. I realized I need to go back and do my time and figure out my shit."

We both got quiet for a sec and it seemed like maybe we were going to sleep, but then Rondell said: "Hey, Mexico."

"Hey what?" I told him.

"You think we could still be friends even after we go different places?"

"Hell yeah," I said. "People don't gotta be in the same place to be friends, man. Some people have friends that live in whole different countries. But they're still friends."

"I thought so," Rondell said.

I considered something for a sec and then said: "You know why I know we'll still be friends?"

"Why?"

"Because we been through shit together. When people go through shit together, like walking miles and miles and what happened with Mong and them taking our money, it makes 'em mad tight."

"That's how I thought it too, Mexico."

It was quiet for a couple minutes and then Rondell said: "Hey, Mexico."

"Hey what?" I told him again.

"You know what I just been thinkin' 'bout?"

"What?"

"I maybe could still go to Mexico."

"Yeah?"

"Yeah," he said. "But it ain't just to be a fisherman, even though I still wanna do that, too."

"What do you wanna do, then?"

"The person who gave us a ride from the gym, you remember what he said? He said people play ball for money in Mexico just like they do in the NBA, too. I been thinkin' I could maybe be on one of them Mexican squads and it'd pay enough for me to live somewhere nice. That's my word."

I smiled in the dark, said: "I think you should, man. Shit, when I'm done with my time maybe I'll go down there too. I could be the scoreboard operator or whatever."

"You really would, Mexico?"

"Hell yeah. I still think it'd be cool to go to Mexico. My grandparents are from there. I just know I gotta make shit right here first."

"Maybe they could give me enough money so I could get a big ol' house. And you could have one of the rooms, Mexico."

"That'd be sweet, Rondell," I told him. "I'm gonna remember this conversation, you know."

"Yeah."

"I'm gonna hold you to that."

"I want you to," he said.

It was quiet between us for a bit and then Rondell said: "You'd really go there, Mexico?"

"Yeah, man," I said. "Maybe I could marry a Mexican girl who'd teach me Spanish and then when I came back to visit here I could actually talk to my gramps. He'd trip out, man."

"Yeah," Rondell said, and then he laughed a little, who even knows why.

I could hear him rolling over on his pile of hay, so I told him good night. He told me good night back.

And then I sat up and pulled out this book. And that's how I am now, sitting here writing. Trying to get down every single thing that's happened the past two days. Even the parts that are hard to talk about or even think about. The stuff with Diego. But I'm just writing it anyway 'cause I know that's how those authors I've been reading would do it, like in *The Color Purple*. They'd just tell the whole story, no matter how hard it was to say, because people need to read it.

That's why I'm telling everything too.

September 13

And then it was the big goodbye scene for me and Rondell.

We were back in San Jose again, at the bus station, standing next to the Coke machine talking about what we were gonna do. Soon as he boarded his bus I was gonna walk all the way across the city to the Lighthouse. Rondell was taking the bus to Oakland, where he was gonna look for his auntie and his cousins.

I know what I said earlier about goodbye scenes and how it's best if you can just walk away and move on. And I still believe that. But me and Rondell had entered a different category. We'd turned into almost family if you think about it. So it was different. I stood there with him until his bus came and then we shook hands like we were two grownups.

"I ain't never gonna forget you, Mexico," he said as the driver swung open the doors and people started filing in and finding seats.

"Same here," I said.

"And if you really wanna go to Mexico and be in my big house you can."

"I'll track you down, Rondo," I said. "Especially if you got a big house.

"You promise?"

"I promise." I swung my bag from one shoulder to the other, said: "You got the money I gave you in your pocket?"

He reached his hand into his pocket, pulled his wad of bills out far enough for me to see and then shoved it back in.

"All right, then, man," I said. "Take care of yourself."

"You too, Mexico."

We were quiet for a few seconds, neither one of us knowing what else we were supposed to say.

"All aboard," the bus driver called out.

"You better get on," I told Rondell.

And then, out of nowhere, he stepped forward and gave me the tightest hug you could possibly give another person without breaking their damn spinal cord. Wrapped his big arms around me, lifted me off the ground and squeezed to the point that I couldn't hardly even breathe. My head pinned to his damn chest like I was a little kid.

I thought what a crazy sight it probably was for everybody

on the bus: this big black dude with a baby Afro hugging some skinny half-Mexican kid with holes in his shoes and sweatshirt.

I finally wrestled myself out of his grip and told him: "All right, all right, let's not get crazy, man."

He wiped a tear that was falling down his cheek, said: "You the first person who never left me."

I shrugged and told him: "Yeah, well, it ain't nothin' to cry about, man. Pull your shit together."

The driver yelled out to Rondell: "Bus is leaving right now, sir."

Rondell looked at him and then turned back to me.

"You better get on," I said. I reached out my hand and we shook again. "You gonna be all right, Rondo."

"You too, Mexico. I know it."

"Maybe I'll see you in Mexico."

"You better come there like you said. You promised." He wiped his face again with his sweatshirt sleeve and then spun around and climbed on the bus.

He waved at me through the window as his bus pulled away.

The Walk Back to the Lighthouse:

On the long walk back to the Lighthouse I thought about all the shit I'd been through since we went on the run. Mei-li and the cave and getting chased by the cops and Mong saying I was his best friend and then going swimming and me staring through the Mexican border at the kid selling clay suns. But soon I was thinking about my brother Diego again. I thought about that look on his face, the one in the living room when we were both just happy kids still, playing around.

I kept thinking about it so hard that at one point I actually stopped cold and went down on one knee in the middle of the damn street. I let it really hit me how he was gone. Before, I knew it was true, and I knew he was never coming back and it was because of me, but I never let it go deep in me. My whole body went numb and I almost couldn't breathe, like I was drowning, and then I felt like I was gonna faint but I didn't.

It was so overwhelming.

My brother was gone.

The person I loved more than anything in the entire world.

I stayed kneeling on the asphalt like that for a long-ass time, even when a couple cars came. They had to drive all around me honking their horns and saying stuff out their windows. But it was like I was paralyzed. I just couldn't get up. Because what I did is real. I can never change it back. It's forever. And for the first time since what happened I admitted that to myself.

And then when I reached up and touched Mong's tooth necklace I just stood up.

My good-luck charm. I stayed holding on to it.

I thought how I couldn't just stay kneeling in the street for the rest of my life. I had to get up at some point. So I did. It wasn't like I was sick or anything. And it wasn't like if I stayed kneeling in the street Diego would come back. Nothing will bring him back. So I told myself I might as well keep walking. Might as well go back to the Lighthouse and finish my time. Might as well pay my restitution and not owe anybody anything. Might as well finish this book I been writing and give it to the counselors so they could see how I think. And know about me, Mong and Rondell. Might as well try to make good with the rest of my life (even though I'd still trade mine for Diego's any day of the week). Might as well call my moms next Sunday when it's phone day and actually talk to her. Tell her I'm so sorry about what happened and I love her even if she doesn't feel the same way right now.

Might as well keep moving forward.

And before I knew it I was all the way back to the Lighthouse, standing in front of the door.

I was knocking.

Some big white dude opened it and then stood there staring at me for a while.

"Who are you?" he finally said.

"Don't worry about it," I said back. "Just go get Jaden."

"Miguel?" Jaden shouted, pushing past the white dude. "Miguel! I can't believe it. You made it back, bro. You have no idea how good it is to see you."

He shook my hand and I held out the petty-cash envelope. He took it.

"I wanna do my time," I said.

Jaden looked at the envelope in his hand and then looked back up at me. "That's all anybody can ever ask of anybody else, Miguel."

I shrugged.

"You know we aren't here to make life hard. We're here to help you build coping skills so you can get back out there and attack life again."

He held up the envelope. "This is the first step, bro. I'm really proud of you."

I switched my bag from one shoulder to the other.

"Look at my manners, bro. Come on in." He took my bag and led me into the house. "Take a seat on the couch. Guys, this is Miguel Casteñeda. He was in here at the start of the summer. Move over, Dimitrius. Let the man have some room, bro. He's come a long way."

Nobody said hi or anything, but this time I didn't call

anybody a bitch. I just smiled to myself and told everybody "Hey."

Some of them said hey back.

Jaden smiled at me and set my bag on the floor by my feet. He was about to go into the office to call Lester when there was another knock on the door.

"That's probably him right now," Jaden said. "Wait until he sees who came back."

The same white kid went to the door again and pulled it open. He stood there a sec, and then he said: "Who are you?"

Then we all heard the voice on the other side of the door, and it wasn't Lester's.

"Rondell Law," the voice said. "Got two *L*s at the end of that first part."

He pushed past the white dude and stood huge in the living room, looking all around until he turned and found me sitting on the couch.

"Mexico," he said, smiling big and goofy.

"Rondell," I said back.

He turned to Jaden, said: "I come back to do my time, however much they gave me."

Jaden said: "Rondell Law! Come on over here, bro. Grab a seat next to Miguel. It's like a reunion in here."

Rondell looked at him funny and said: "Wha'chu mean?"

"I mean you guys coming back," Jaden said.

"Oh," Rondell said, turning to me.

Jaden held out the cordless and said: "You guys sit tight while I call Lester, all right? We're doing everything by the book, bro. You guys made the right decision, I promise. Just sit tight and we'll handle all the technicalities involved."

Rondell sat next to me and looked at me with that simple-ass look he always gets. The thing that makes him Rondell.

I gave him a little shot to the arm, said: "Thought you were on that bus, man."

"I told him to stop a little ways down, Mexico. We was goin' and then I thought of somethin'. Maybe I could make good here too. Before goin' to Mexico. And plus then I could do like your grandma told me and look out for you." He shrugged and said: "So that's how come I got off."

"You're crazy," I told him.

He tapped my arm and said: "And you know what, Mexico?"

"What, Rondell?"

"Wasn't God who told me to do it neither. It was me."

I nodded at him as Jaden stood a few feet away with the cordless up to his ear, saying: "Les! Yeah, listen, bro. You're gonna wanna come over to the Lighthouse on the double. I got two kids here who are ready to make good on their time."

ACKNOWLEDGMENTS

I'd like to thank the following folks: Steve Malk, amazing agent, friend and sounding board; Krista Marino, for believing and pushing and always being such a pleasure to work with; all the awesome people at Random House, especially Beverly Horowitz, Angela Carlino, Dominique Cimina and the entire publicity department; Matt Van Buren, great friend, reader and writer; Albert de la Peña, the most authentic dude I know, *pari passu;* Roni de la Peña, the reason I try hard at life; Brin Hill; Rob Jones; Nora Jones; Gretchen Wolf, Amy and Emily, the de la Peñas; Rachel Sherman; Sandra Newman; David Andrews; Kuros Charney; Lindsey Davis; Ciro Parascandola; the painter downstairs (punk!); and Caroline Sun, my girl and my best friend and the star of all those three minutes.

Caroline Sun

We Were Here is Matt de la Peña's third novel for young readers. His first novel, *Ball Don't Lie,* was an ALA-YALSA Best Book for Young Adults and an ALA-YALSA Quick Pick and was made into a major motion picture. *Mexican WhiteBoy,* his second novel, was an ALA-YALSA Top Ten Best Book for Young Adults, an IRA Notable Book for a Global Society, and a Junior Library Guild selection. He attended the University of the Pacific on a basketball scholarship and went on to earn a master of fine arts in creative writing at San Diego State University. De la Peña currently lives in Brooklyn, New York, where he teaches creative writing.